# Bound

# Bound

## A Faery Story, Book 1

**Lexi Blake
writing as
Sophie Oak**

Bound
A Faery Story, Book 1

Published by DLZ Entertainment LLC

Copyright 2019 DLZ Entertainment LLC
Edited by Chloe Vale
ISBN: 978-1-942297-26-0

This is a work of fiction. Names, places, characters and incidents are the product of the author's imagination and are fictitious. Any resemblance to actual persons, living or dead, events or establishments is solely coincidental.

Sign up for Lexi Blake's newsletter
and be entered to win a $25 gift certificate
to the bookseller of your choice.

Join us for news, fun, and exclusive content
including free short stories.

There's a new contest every month!

Go to www.LexiBlake.net to subscribe.

# Dedication

For my girls. Every time I write a heroine, I think of you, my daughters. You girls are everything I could want in a heroine – smart and honest, loyal and brave. May you both find your happy ever afters, my loves.

Now put the book down. Until you're at least thirty. Forty. Just put the book down…

# Dedication 2019

Still for my girls who are really young women – one of you is far closer to thirty than I would have imagined. I still pray for your happily ever afters and know that they might not look the way I thought they would. Your happily ever afters can be anything, my loves. Life does not have to end in a white picket fence and two point five kids. Your happily ever after could include a man you love or a woman. There is no one way to love. You might find it in being happy with yourself. No matter what, know that I am your champion. I am always behind you. I might not always be able to catch you, but I will be there to help lift you back up. I'm something better than a fairy godmother. I'm your mom. Forever.

# Chapter One

*O*nce upon a time, in a land closer than you would think...

She was having the weirdest dream. Megan Starke stared at the scene around her. She called it a scene in her head because it wasn't real. She was in some sort of luxurious tent. There was lush carpet on the floor, but on the outer edges of the space she could see grass and patches of loamy earth. The tent was lit by odd lanterns. Odd because there didn't seem to be a flame. The light was strong, but it was almost like it was moving inside the opaque glass.

Like fireflies flickering.

"Are you okay?"

She glanced up from the cage she found herself in. Cage. Yep, she was in a cage. When she thought about it, the cage totally made sense. The gorgeous, slender blonde chick in the cage across from her did not.

"I get the cage," she explained to the blonde, who also happened to be naked, but then everyone in the cages were naked, including herself. "I even get the nudity. I've got a meeting with my regional manager next week and I'm not ready for it. Nudity is a sure sign of anxiety. The cage is because I hate my job and my life and I can't seem to find a way out. Hence the luxury of the cage, though I think my subconscious is wrong about that. I mean my paycheck is good enough to keep a roof over my head, but nothing like this."

The bed she'd "woken" on was the most comfortable she'd ever been on. She found her naked body covered with soft silken sheets. She'd been brought delicious foods. It was only when she'd asked for coffee and the small serving lady had asked her what coffee was that she'd realized she was dreaming.

And it might be a nightmare.

The blonde's head turned as though seeing her from a different angle might help her understand. "You speak too fast. I understand some of your plane's words, but not all. I am fresh from the old plane."

Yeah, a gorgeous blonde who didn't speak her language and flew on old planes. She didn't know how to interpret that one.

*A withered hand reached out to her and when that hand touched her arm, the world had gone cold.*

*What a find you are, my dear. I think I know just where to take you.*

She shook her head, forcing the vision back. The last thing she wanted was for this weird dream to take a turn. It was natural that she was anxious. In a few days she would take a step that could change her life forever.

"I'm going to a munch," she said to the only woman in the tent who seemed interested in her. "That's a safe way to meet people in the lifestyle. I'm going to see if this is for me, and no anxiety dream is going to make me change my mind. Ah, that's why you're here. You're the inner symbol of my insecurity. I'm fairly certain I'll be the worst-looking potential sub at that munch. Yeah, that's what this is about."

The woman merely shook her head and turned to the equally stunning woman in the cage next to hers. They began a conversation in a language she didn't understand, and Meg sat back.

She would forget all of this when she woke up in her own bed. It would be a blur in the early morning light, an echo of some dream life she'd had. She should really put a notebook beside her bed so she could write down these crazy dreams she sometimes had.

Maybe one day she could turn them into a story.

"Miss Meg, I need you to come with me. I know our ways seem strange to you, but one day you'll see what a great honor all of this is." The small woman who'd greeted her with pastries and hadn't known what coffee was stood at the door of her cage. She was dressed like she was participating in a Renaissance fair. And she was seriously tiny.

Meg stood up, pulling the sheet around her. Just because it was a dream didn't mean she shouldn't be modest. "I'm sure being put in a cage is a great honor."

Cara—she'd called herself Cara—held a circle of keys in her small hand. "You'll be saving a life and maybe a whole kingdom if you are what we think you are. Please come with me. Miss, if you try to run, you should understand that there is nowhere to go."

She said every word carefully, as though she had to think about each one.

"Well, naturally there's nowhere to go. I think that's what this whole dream thing is about." She moved to the door of the cage as Cara opened it.

She didn't even think about running because all that would do was morph the dream into something terrible. All her anxieties would chase after her.

Wasn't this what she was supposed to do? When she realized she was dreaming, she should take control and then she would be in charge.

She stepped out, ready to tell Cara that she wanted coffee and a TV brought to her room because she was going to clear off her DVR in this dream.

Instead, two large men stepped from the shadows, and before she could pull away, each had a wrist in his grasp. Men? She wasn't sure they were men at all. They were humanoid, but their skin wasn't a color that came from human DNA.

Fear snaked along her spine as they dragged her hands up over her head and the sheet dropped away. Cold metal pressed against her palms and suddenly she was tethered to something above her head.

This was the part where the dream went bad.

She cursed her freaking subconscious for punishing her even while she slept.

A bright light swept through the tent, a tidal wave to her senses. Someone was coming. She couldn't see them, but she thought Cara and the others were moving away from her.

Were they running? Leaving her to whatever her fucked-up brain had decided to send after her?

A massive shadow blocked the sun and she shrank back in fear. Well, she shrank back as far as the chains she was in allowed her to.

That shadow was a man. It became clear as he stepped inside, though he was backlit by the sun. Strong shoulders that seemed to go on for days, big arms. He was muscular and masculine, and she was naked in front of him.

A deep voice said something in a lilting language she didn't

11

understand, and suddenly, the curtain to the tent dropped. She could see again. Yes, the shadow was a man, a beautiful, terrifying man, but at least he seemed human.

"She does not speak Gaelic, Your Highness," the small man who served as her jailer said softly.

The man with the pitch-black hair grimaced, his sensual lips curving down as he switched to English. "I have no title here, Reeve. Speak to me as you would any other customer."

He looked at her straight in the eyes for the first time. She felt a thrill of excitement. Not excitement. Fear. The racing of her heart had to be fear, right? She couldn't figure it out, but she knew the huge man in front of her made her do the one thing she was worried she might never do again—feel.

And wasn't that the cruelest dream of all?

She needed to wake up and now. She didn't want to know where this dream went.

"What's your name then?" His voice rolled over her skin, even from across the tent.

It was obvious where this dream was going, and she would play along. She wanted it over with. She always woke up before the truly bad stuff began. When she had dreams about being killed, she always woke up right before the first blow. So all she had to do was push this and it could be over.

*He'd hit her, that thing that had taken her. He'd reached out with his emaciated arm and struck her into darkness. She hadn't imagined he would be so strong, but then he hadn't been a man at all. He'd been a shadow stalking her on her way home, following her into the alley, and then she'd woken up somewhere else.*

"Are you all right then?" The man in front of her drew her from those dark, confused thoughts. "Come on. Don't be afraid. Tell me your name."

Was it two dreams sliding against each other? Maybe she was sick and this was some kind of fever dream. She had been stuffy the last couple of days.

"My name is Twenty to Life because that's the time you'll do for kidnapping me, you son of a bitch."

She waited for the broad man to strike her, then she would wake up and she could go about her dull life.

Then she could forget those red eyes and how cold his hands had felt. She would forget how those eyes had burned into her as he'd chuckled, and right before she'd lost consciousness, she'd been certain he was taking her to Hell.

She'd gotten out of that nightmare. She could get out of this one.

She should have known it wasn't a pleasant dream and that these weirdos with their soft beds and good-smelling food would eventually turn into monsters. It was how her damn brain worked since the divorce. Sure enough, someone was going to smack her, rape her, and then potentially gut her. It looked like it was the big, hot guy's job. She waited to feel the terrible blow that would likely signal the end of this dream, but the man with the long black hair simply smiled, showing even, white teeth.

Her breath caught in her chest. When he smiled, he was devastating.

"All right then, Twenty," the man allowed in his lilting accent. "My name is Beckett, but you can call me Beck. And my mother was actually quite nice. I would prefer you didn't curse her. Yell at me all you like, but let's leave my mother out of it. Tell me, why should I purchase you instead of these other lovely women?"

She hated being naked in front of him. Where the hell was this thing going? "I'm being sold? Someone is selling me like a piece of fucking meat?"

Beck shook his head. "Language there, darlin'. You're in a market, trussed up like a pretty, plump pigeon. Did you think you were just hanging on the chains for show?"

"Your...I apologize, sir. The girl is rather ignorant," said the small man named Reeve. He barely came to Beck's waist. Compared to Beck, he looked like a boy. A boy with a bushy beard and a pointy red cap. All the jailers wore them.

"I am not ignorant." She also hated feeling small, and that was where she was now. Trapped. She was trapped and she couldn't find her way out. Anger started to flare through her. She was always trapped, wasn't she?

"I did not mean it that way." Reeve's fists clenched in obvious frustration. She'd noticed that he always tried to maintain a soft tone when speaking to her. He was polite, even when she cursed him. "The lady is obviously intelligent, though lacking in any kind of manners.

13

She is from the Earth plane."

Beck turned from the smaller man and back to her, his mouth hanging slightly open. He stared at her, as though he couldn't quite process the words. It gave her a chance to study him.

He was tall. He had to be at least six foot four. He would tower over her. She was only five foot five, and a rather round one at that. The god in front of her didn't have an ounce of fat on him. He was broad-shouldered, his arms thick with muscle, though he didn't look like some steroid-crazy gym guy. He'd earned his muscles. She would bet he hadn't earned them pumping iron. He worked, and at hard, most likely physical, labor. His skin was bronzed from the sun.

If his body was heavenly, then she didn't know how to describe his face. It was all sharp planes and harsh angles that came together to form something truly beautiful. His jaw looked like it was carved out of granite. But his eyes were like soft, gray stones in his face. He was, without a doubt, the loveliest man she had ever seen.

It was too bad he was a dream, and not one she would have thought to have. She'd never gone for his type before. Beck looked like an escapee from a Renaissance fair, with his open-necked, linen shirt under a leather vest. His trousers were made from some sort of animal skin, as were the boots that came to his knees. A sword peeked from behind his shoulder, held by a scabbard across his back.

"Is she truly from the Earth plane?" Beck asked.

"Yes, sir. You can see why I called you." They both stared at her like she was some rare, exotic creature at a zoo.

Suspicion tickled at Meg's consciousness. Why exactly was she here? She'd read articles about human trafficking. Had they led to this particular nightmare? Maybe there was another way out. She bit her lower lip and looked at the five other girls in the tent with her. They were caged in the same fashion, though these women kept their heads lowered and complied with their jailers' requests. "You shouldn't buy me. I'm not very pretty. The other women are prettier. They're thinner, too."

The other women were all blondes. They looked like something out of a Swedish high-fashion magazine. She did not fit with them. She carried around an extra five or ten pounds that never seemed to go away. She was an overblown hourglass in a world where svelte was worshipped.

14

Beck frowned. It did nothing to mar the perfection of his face. "Are you cruel then, love? Funny, I wouldn't have thought that of you. It's mean to point out their flaws. They can't help that they don't get enough to eat. Why do you think they're here selling themselves?"

"You don't want her, Your Highness," a soft voice said. Meg looked over to see the blonde nearest her staring at Beck through the bars of her cell. "She doesn't understand a thing about our world. She yelled at Cara for not having all the foods she wanted. I believe she is cruel. I would be thrilled to belong to you."

Way to throw a sister under a bus. "Yeah, fuck you, too."

Beck shook his head and looked slightly disappointed in her. The spark of shame that went through her was unexpected.

He walked over to the young, waifish blonde. "She is not from this plane. She is frightened. Allowances must be made. I hope you all find kind mates today. I hope your masters value you all for the precious gift you give them, but I must find a bondmate."

Beck gave Reeve a hand gesture that sent the smaller man into action. Within seconds, drapes were drawn, and she found herself in a private room with only Beck inside. Sunlight poured in through a hole in the top of the elaborate tent that seemed to function as some sort of skylight. Now that they were alone, it felt like a spotlight. She was painfully aware of her unclothed state. She could feel her nipples puckering under his steely gaze.

"It is not kind to flaunt your beauty to less fortunate women." Beck's voice was deep and allowed no room for disrespect.

She wasn't sure why, but she needed to know where this went. She was here and he moved her. Maybe there was more to this than she'd thought.

If this was some kind of bondage fantasy her libido was playing out, she would go with it. "I don't understand. I wasn't trying to be mean. I wanted you to buy one of the others. I've decided you might be difficult to get away from. I thought you would do it because they're prettier than me."

Beck's handsome face bunched up as he seemed to mull her words. "On what plane are they prettier than you?" He laughed. "Sorry, love. I do remember hearing stories of where you come from. Food there is plentiful, yet the women starve because the men won't take care of them."

She relaxed. He was the gorgeous god of a man who happened to adore fluffy women. Yep, she'd been reading too many romance novels. "It's not like that. That woman you talked to, she would be considered a great beauty on my plane."

"But I would have to feed her for a month before I'd even consider bedding her," Beck muttered. "I don't understand humans. Do human males not like breasts?"

He asked that last bit with a distinct huskiness to his voice. His hand came out, and he palmed one breast, his thumb rasping over the nipple.

That caress shot from her breast to her pussy like lightning. "Oh, please, don't."

That was what she was supposed to say, right?

Beck moved in, his big body crowding her as his other hand reached up. The sunlight hit his face. His gray eyes were heating up, and he ran his tongue over his lips to wet them. He seemed to be a man about to enjoy a good meal. He caressed both breasts with a languid sigh.

He breathed deeply, his nose at the top of her head. "And why not? How will I know if we're compatible if I don't touch you? If I'm going to pay this much for a female, then I want to be sure I'm getting what we need."

She didn't even think about the "we" part of that sentence because Beck's warm hands were trailing a path across her skin as he looked her over. His fingertips brushed her nipples before closing over them. He rolled them between his fingers, pinching down on just the right side of pain. Her nipples peaked, sensitized to his touch. This was the part where she should protest, but it had been so long since anyone had touched her.

She'd been so lonely.

When he was satisfied with her breasts, he moved around to her exposed back. He traced the length of her spine with a single finger. She shuddered with desire under his touch as his finger lightly delved into the valley of her cheeks.

His mouth was mere centimeters from her ear. "You're gorgeous. Do you have any idea how long it's been since I saw a woman as fuckable as you? And as to your earlier statement about being worried I might be hard to get away from, I promise you, you won't get away from me. Not ever."

"Please," she begged as her entire body went hot with wanting. This was a fantasy she didn't want to wake from. Meg gave herself over to the dream, letting her good sense go and playing along. She couldn't let this man seduce her. She had a life back home. It wasn't much, but it was hers. She couldn't let herself be sold at some marketplace to the highest bidder. "I want to go home."

She struggled to get enough oxygen. She could feel the hard ridge of his erection gently brushing her backside. She forced down the impulse to beg him to use it on her. She'd never wanted a man's touch so much in her life.

Then he was gone, and she wanted to cry at the absence of his warmth. He circled around her and seemed satisfied he had seen what he needed. Beck's gray eyes were kind as he looked down on her. His sensual lips were close, so close she could feel the heat coming off his body. His face was barely an inch from hers. He kissed her forehead gently.

"Sorry. I'm your home now." He leaned over, and his mouth covered hers.

All thoughts fled. She could do nothing but concentrate on his lips and the feel of his hands. When his tongue brushed her lips, she found herself softening under his dominance and letting him inside her mouth. His hands tightened and wound around her waist. She felt delicate against him, a sensation she'd never had before. With previous lovers, she'd always felt ungainly and awkward. She never knew what to do to please them. She was far too shy to ask them for what she wanted. The result had been a short series of disappointing encounters. Her own husband had left her, telling her she didn't know how to please a man.

But she could feel Beck's desire. He wasn't playing a game. He took what he wanted, and it did something for her. She'd read about Dominance and submission and the fine art of BDSM, but putting the theory to the test was something different. The chains suddenly felt sensual rather than menacing. They held her for his pleasure.

"You're so beautiful." Beck sighed in her ear when he broke the kiss, moving to press his lips to her neck. His hands traced a path from her waist to the cheeks of her ass. He pressed his body against her. "I have to know for sure, though. Please understand, I have to know…"

His fingers found her clitoris and began rubbing sweet, firm circles.

This was insane. Her pussy was wet and pulsing for him. She pushed against his hand. Oh, she wanted this. "Don't stop."

"Oh, I won't stop." Beck groaned between his clenched teeth. "Come for me, *a stóirín*."

She had no idea what he'd said, but she felt the intent behind the endearment. His hands felt perfect on her body. Never before had anyone played her like a finely tuned instrument, but Beck was her musician.

He gently forced two fingers high into her, keeping the pressure on her clit with his thumb. An amazing sensation swept through her as he fucked her with his fingers. In and out. In and out. It was better than any previous cock she'd had. Something was happening. Some odd and yet familiar connection seemed to open between them, but before she could process it, she fell over the precipice, and she couldn't think any more. She came, sobbing against his shoulder. The orgasm strummed neatly through her body, making her languid and submissive.

At the instant of her orgasm, she would have sworn she could feel herself as though she was Beck. She'd felt his fingers pressed high into her heat as though for the slightest moment she could feel what he was feeling, warmth, sweet wetness, and a rigid hardness begging to be set loose. It had been odd. It was almost as if she'd been inside Beck. She'd shared what his body experienced as he brought her to orgasm. A connection had opened between them. It was an intimacy like nothing she'd felt before.

She floated down, suddenly aware that Beck had pulled his fingers from her pussy and wrapped both arms around her. He hugged her to his hard body. This had to be the best wet dream ever. She let her head rest against his shoulder. She'd never come so fast and so hard.

It was a sweet dream, and she should hold on to it. Any minute the alarm would go off, and she would have to face another day at the Software 4 U store. Being Beck's love slave was much more interesting.

Beck kissed her one last time, his mouth playing sweetly against hers. He seemed as satisfied as she was, though he couldn't possibly be. His hands played with her breasts for a moment, and she could feel her own juice on her skin. He brought his right hand up to his mouth and sucked his fingers in, licking her cream. He finally placed an almost chaste kiss on the tip of her nose and stepped back.

"Aye, love, you'll do." With that, he started out the door.

That was a perfectly unimpressive bit of wooing. Her subconscious needed to work harder. She'd been utterly overwhelmed by what they had shared, and that was all she got from him? Damn it, even the men in her dreams were unromantic.

"Seriously, that's what I get? I'll do? Send in the next guy. We'll see if he can do better." The next guy might be even hotter. He would be French or maybe Italian.

Beck turned around, and she found herself shrinking back again. His gray eyes were as hard as stones, and his demeanor had changed from lazy to menacing in a heartbeat. "What did you say?"

The question was a challenge. The chill in his voice almost made her shiver.

"Nothing." She had a healthy sense of self-preservation that kicked into full throttle now as Beck stalked back toward her.

"Excellent. Best you say nothing right now if you can't say something sweet." Beck's entire body was rigid, every muscle screaming his frustration. "I'm exhausted. I rode all night to get here before the tournament. I've eaten very little, and now I'm horny as hell. I am not in a good mood. You have no idea the trouble you're going to cause me."

Though she was tired, she held her head up. The last thing she needed was to be told how much trouble she was. She knew. She'd been told her whole life by a mother and father who hadn't really wanted her and a husband who felt the same. She might be in chains, but she held on to her pride. "I wouldn't want to cause you any trouble. Please feel free to not purchase me."

Beck sighed and she could sense the weariness in him. That connection she'd felt during the sex seemed like it was still open. His emotions were almost palpable to her. His tiredness went far past the physical. That weariness invaded his soul. His shoulders slumped slightly forward. She had the sudden desire to wrap her arms around him, to lend him her strength.

"I've waited years for this day," he explained in an emotionless voice. "You cannot understand the joy I should feel at finding you. If there was any other choice, I would walk away. I can offer you nothing. I'm going to spend the last of my gold entering the tournament. I won't even have the money to feed you. If I had an ounce of pride left, I would let you go, but my brother is dying. I can't allow that to happen. You're the only one who can save him. I swear on everything I am that I will find a way to take care of you."

He started to turn to leave. Tears welled in her eyes. She didn't understand everything he'd said, but she knew he'd meant every word of it. Even in chains and terrified for her life, she felt safe with this man. Somehow, she'd formed a strange connection with him in those moments his hands had been on her body. "Stop."

Beck turned to her, his stance wary. She knew he was waiting for her to yell at him again. She couldn't blame him. She'd been a bit difficult.

"My name is Meg," she said softly.

She was rewarded with a slight curling of his lips. His pitch-black hair was gathered in a ponytail at the nape of his neck. She wondered how it would feel flowing all around her. "I like that, Meg. I'll call you my own sweet Meggie."

"If I help you with your brother, will you let me go home?"

The smile died, and Meg wished she hadn't asked the question. "I told you, I'm your home now, me and Cian. There's no way back. Even if there was, I wouldn't let you take it."

So this dream was going to continue. She had to admit, she was intrigued. Somewhere in the middle of their intimacy, she'd even forgotten she was dreaming. "Are you going to buy me now?"

Beck shook his head. "It's not like that. This is a tourney. The gnomes make more money this way. Every male who wants to purchase you buys into the tourney. We then fight until there's only one left standing. That man will be your master."

"But what if you don't win?" She was now horrified at the thought. There were other men? How bad would they be? At least Beck had proven he could be somewhat kind.

A slow, intensely confident smile split his gorgeous face. "Don't go worrying. I always win."

He strode out of the tent, letting the heavy curtain fall back into place, and she was alone again.

What was happening and why did it seem so damn real? What if this wasn't a weird dream. What if that creature she caught glimpses of had taken her to some strange place? The people seemed to speak

English, but there had been that strange lilting language as well. Gaelic, Reeve had said.

Maybe she was in Ireland or Scotland. She'd hit her head when she'd been kidnapped.

Her stomach churned. Had she been kidnapped?

Her head came up as a squat woman entered the room with a pitcher and washcloths. Meg sighed. She was getting used to being bathed. The little woman would be professional and gentle. In truth, Meg realized she should be happy that the woman was here, humming as she went about her work. Beck had left her with the evidence of her orgasm all over her thighs and pussy. It would be rather embarrassing for someone else to come in and find her covered in her own juices.

The short, blonde woman smiled up as she washed away Meg's reaction to Beck. "Don't worry, miss. His Highness will be kind to you."

"His Highness?" Meg asked, but the woman finished her work. With a mysterious smile, she walked out. "And what the hell did he mean by gnomes?"

# Chapter Two

Beckett Finn, the former heir to the Seelie Fae throne, sank into the too-small chair in the gnome's tiny but well-appointed office. Everything seemed too small right now. His trousers certainly were. Touching Meg had him hard enough to pound nails with his cock.

She was the one. He knew it deep in his soul. He had been able to feel what was happening to her at the moment of her orgasm. It had taken everything he had not to form the bond with her that moment, but now was not the time, and certainly not the place. Forming a bond with his soul's mate was a sacred thing, and he wouldn't do it here. He was going to have to put her through too much to force that on her as well.

Reeve of the Gentle Hills walked in and placed a large platter of food on the desk between them. "I thought Your Highness might join me in the noon meal."

Beck's stomach rumbled at the sight and smell of so much good food. Gnomes knew how to cook. He nodded, trying not to betray his excitement at the thought of being full for once. "I would be honored. I thank you for your hospitality, but you have to get out of the habit of calling me by titles that no longer have any meaning."

He picked up two slices of dark bread and made a huge sandwich of venison and a pleasant-smelling cheese.

Reeve poured water into two mugs. "You're giving up, then? You are content to allow your Uncle Torin to remain on your father's throne? The very throne he slew your father on?"

The food turned to sawdust in his mouth. He took a long drink and forced himself to continue eating. He would need the energy for the battle to come. He needed to maintain control at all times.

"There is nothing of contentment in my life. There hasn't been for the past thirteen years." Beck's mind started to go back to the terrible night when he lost both his parents and his sister. He had only been able to save his twin, Cian. He chose, as he had since that day when he was seventeen, to look to the future. "It is not that I don't dream of taking back what rightfully belongs to me. It is simply a matter of practicality. My loyalists are gone."

Reeve shook his bearded head vigorously. "That is untrue, Your Highness. There are many here, and many more on the home plane. Tír na nÒg is full of Fae longing for Your Highness."

Beck sighed because he would have to put this to the gnome in blunt words. It would likely ruin the man's illusions of him, but then, Beck no longer had use for illusions. "Peasants. You're talking about peasants. While I am thrilled to have the love of the people, money is needed to wage war, and I have none. I am barely able to buy my way into this tourney. I have no idea how I'm going to clothe my mate after I've won her. She'll be roaming the forests in one of my beat-up old shirts. If I can't even take care of my mate, I've got no idea how I should go about fighting a war."

Reeve leaned forward. His small, ruddy face was fervent. "The loyalists heard that Cian was fading. They know that if Cian dies, you will be half a man. Symbiotic twins are very powerful, my liege, but everyone knows that if your intellectual half fades, you will not be fit to rule."

"Hence my long ride through that bloody forest to get here," Beck admitted. "Cian is fading because we have no female. We are long past the age when a suitable bondmate would have been found and our triad formed. He has lost hope. He's dying. Your summons could not have come at a better time, old friend. We're desperate."

Beck polished off his second sandwich and thought about a third. It seemed rude to eat the majority of the meal.

Reeve pushed the plate toward him. "Please, Your Highness. I'm not the richest man but allow me to aid you. Our food is plentiful. My wife will make sure your mate has suitable clothing. My son has ensured that your steed is stabled and well-fed. You will find your saddle bags filled with everything you need for the journey. I'm pleased to serve my king."

A deep sense of gratitude filled him. Reeve's family had once served the King of the Seelie Fae, and Reeve and his family had preferred exile to serving Torin, the Pretender. "I don't know how to thank you, old friend. If you ever have need of a sword, I trust you will call on me."

The gnome grinned. "I know who to call, but no one bothers us. The deal we made with the Planeswalker clan protects us."

Beck knew the deal well. The Planeswalkers came from a plane many called Hell. They were a demonic clan and quite mercenary, but easily controlled with an ironclad contract. Demons could access all planes and were great believers in contracts. Reeve and his tribe of ex-patriots served as salesmen for the demons' wares. The demon tribe would gather items of interest. Reeve would sell them and take a cut. It had worked well for both sides.

Beck finished the last of the food and took a deep breath. It felt good to be full. Now he needed to take a nap. He had several hours before he would fight. He just had to be sure of a couple of things before he found a corner to curl up in. "I want my mate covered."

He couldn't stand the thought of her beautiful body on display. She was his. He should be the only one to enjoy her loveliness.

Reeve frowned. "You know I cannot, Your Highness. The female must be properly displayed. If the Planeswalker discovered I was treating you differently, he would accuse me of breaking our contract."

He didn't like the answer, but he had to accept it. He'd had to accept many unsavory truths since the day his world fell apart. "Do the vamps know she's here?"

"Yes," came the quiet reply. "I had to inform the Vampire Governments as well. I gave them short notice, but fifteen have already shown up. You know they can move very quickly when they want to. You were the first to see her. I have to open her to public view soon. I must have at least ten warriors in the tourney to see a profit."

"Well, you'll have that if fifteen vampires are here. They'll all fight for her." It was a sad coincidence of fate that bondmates were so alluring to vampires. Since his uncle had closed the Seelie homelands to all outsiders, it had become difficult to find a bondmate, and the practice of vampires wooing faery bondmates had disappeared. Luckily

24

it wasn't all vampires, just the ones of royal blood, who required a woman like Meg as a mate. He'd asked a vampire once why they needed Fae bondmates to procreate. Beck had been told that there was something about their blood that strengthened the vampire. They called the women "consorts." A vampire of royal blood could form a psychic bond with the female, much as Beck intended to form with Meg. "The vampires will all fight and they will all lose."

Reeve nodded his head. "Yes, sire, they will. I'll make you a deal. I will personally ensure that no one else is allowed physical access to the bondmate. The other suitors will only be allowed to view her. I will tell the other Fae that we've had an expert prove her ability to bond. You are certain she can form the bond? The demon seemed sure. He said she glows to him, and that is how he knew."

"I'm certain." He'd felt her response to his every touch. She'd been open and vulnerable to him. "The vampires say our bondmates glow, as well. I can't see it, but I feel her. She's perfect."

"Perfect enough to form a true triad?" Reeve asked speculatively. "You know what the legends say."

He laughed long and hard. Legends. They were ridiculous. They were stories to tell children at bedtime. The legend Reeve was referring to claimed that one day, a pair of symbiotic twins would be born of royal blood. They would form a triad with a mysterious bondmate, and she would allow their true powers to flow. The intellectual half, who the people called the philosopher king, would become a Green Man, bringing prosperity to the tribes. The warrior king would gain the strength of a Storm Lord. The threesome would usher in a time of great joy for the Fae. It was a nice story, but Beck had stopped believing in legends a long time before.

"Don't pin your hopes on that, my friend. Meggie is a bondmate. Nothing more. Nothing less. She's beautiful and suits my purposes. She will save my brother and balance us. I'm not immune to the effects of not bonding at a proper age. I feel it, too. Meg can reverse those." He hoped everyone wasn't as prone to believing old stories as the gnome. "You mentioned a deal? What is my end of this bargain?"

Reeve was every bit the savvy businessman. "Please stay out of sight of the others until the tourney. If they realize you are fighting for the female…"

"They'll turn tail and walk off."

"But, if they pay their money first, we have a strict no refund policy, Your Highness," Reeve explained.

"Fine," Beck said, covering a yawn. "I'll stay out of sight. I need a nap, anyway."

Reeve stood and gestured to the room at the back of his office. "I had a pallet made out for just such an occasion." Beck stood as the gnome frowned. "Your Highness, would you like for me to find a female for you? To take care of your needs?"

Beck growled, but it was at himself. He was still hard as a rock. "No. I can't now. I've seen her, touched her. She's mine, and that makes me hers. I'll be fine."

He pushed through the curtains and gratefully sank into the down mattress on the floor. The curtains closed and Beck was alone. He heard Reeve exit the main section of the tent. Beck pulled his boots off, thinking of what his mother had told him about the bonding. Meg was his, and the thought of another female was now repugnant to him. Beck laid back and loosened his trousers. He smiled up at the canvas roof of the tent. But the thought of her...

His hand closed around his swollen cock. He slowly pumped up and down, thinking of her luscious tits and that pretty mouth of hers. She could spew some shrewish waste out of that mouth, but she could also kiss like a goddess. Whenever she said something he didn't like, he would simply have to kiss her until she forgot she was angry with him.

His cock lengthened further. He brushed his thumb across the swollen head. The small slit in the head of his dick was weeping. He used the cream to facilitate his masturbation. He stroked from the base to the head and back, taking his time. He wasn't in a hurry. While his hand worked his cock, Meg played through his brain. He couldn't wait to get her breasts in his hands again. He would palm them and gently pinch her nipples until they were ready for his mouth. He would suck those ripe berries until she begged him to move his mouth lower. He would, but in his own sweet time. He would learn her body. Once he had her gorgeous body between him and Cian, she would know the true meaning of pleasure.

He would make sure he was always in control. She was small, and he didn't want to hurt her. She wouldn't be able to handle his demanding nature, but he could please her all the same. Cian was going to love her. It had been almost a year since they'd shared a woman. Beck had been fucking a local woman from their village. She was lovely, but Cian couldn't stand her. He refused to have anything to do with Liadan. Beck could admit that Liadan was a bit cold. She was a demure and perfect Fae lady. That had never done it for Cian. Cian liked a woman who gave him a bit of hell. There was no way he would refuse their own sweet Meg. Cian was going to lose his mind when he saw her.

Beck felt his balls squeeze, and he picked up the pace. His breath labored in and out of his chest. He squeezed his cock as it started to swell. She was going to taste so good. That little snack he'd had would be nothing compared to making a full meal of her. He would love eating that sweet pussy. He would get his mouth on her, and he wouldn't let up until she begged and pleaded that she couldn't take another orgasm. Beck's entire body flushed. He pounded away at his cock. She would taste him, too, he promised himself, and sooner than she could imagine. But he had to remember to treat her with the gentle care a bondmate required.

He came, envisioning himself shoved halfway down her throat. He came in hot spurts, covering his belly. It didn't matter. For the first time in a long time, he found it easy to sleep.

* * * *

Meg was shaking slightly as the gnome, and now she was pretty damn sure it really was a gnome, removed the collar from around her neck.

"Was that…?" Meg found it difficult to form the words. It was ridiculous. It was stupid. It just might be real. "Holy shit, were those men vampires?"

Cara laughed gently. Her light blonde hair shook. She looked at her husband, the gnome named Reeve, and said something in that other language they spoke before turning back to Meg. "Aye, mistress, they are vampires, but don't worry none. We won't let them bite you. They only want to see what they will be fighting for."

She put a hand on her hip and said something to her husband.

Reeve rolled his eyes. "Fine then, woman. Meg, my wife wants to unchain you. We're taking you to the arena where the tournament will occur. You can watch one of two ways. I can keep you bound and naked like that, or I can give you a robe and let you sit with us in the stands."

"I think I'll take the robe." She wasn't going to let this chance get by her. The gnomes were small. One well-placed kick and she would be on her way.

Reeve's eyes narrowed on her. "If you run, you should know that one of them vampires will be on you before you can think to shout. They'll play by the rules as long as you do, but the minute you run, they'll chase you down. It'll be a free for all."

Meg thought about the fangs and the look of hunger in the vampires' eyes. She shivered. "I'll stay close."

At least she would be out of the chains and clothed. She wondered where Beck was and if he'd changed his mind. He hadn't been back to see her, and it had been hours. No one else had been allowed to touch her. When they tried, the gnomes explained that if they did not follow protocol, they wouldn't be allowed to fight. Meg hadn't asked why Beck had been special.

According to the other women, Beck was a king.

Reeve allowed his wife to unchain her.

"Where am I?" Meg asked. It was becoming very plain that if this was a dream, she wasn't waking up anytime soon.

She was in denial. Something had taken her and her brain hadn't been able to deal with it. It was time to start dealing.

"You truly don't know?" Cara asked with a look of sympathy on her face.

Meg shook her head. For the first time, she tried to look at these people as something other than her captors. If she was going to save herself, she needed them. If this was really happening to her, she would have to get away. She couldn't run if she didn't know where she was.

She was beginning to understand that strange creature who'd kidnapped her had brought her somewhere…else.

Cara brought over a gossamer robe and handed it to her. Meg pulled it over her head, the soft fabric caressing her skin. Though it was practically sheer, it warmed her.

The dress-like robe cut a deep V at the neck, showing off her breasts. She tried to tug it closed, but it didn't work. Cara moved in behind her and expertly tied it in the back. The garment molded to her curves. It was utterly unlike the shapeless clothes she preferred at home. Her ex-husband, Michael, had always said she needed to lose twenty pounds and bleach her hair blonde. She'd never been willing to go blonde. Her auburn hair was the only thing she truly liked about her looks, but she'd tried to lose the weight. It hadn't worked.

Beck hadn't seemed to mind her weight.

"Bloody hell. You're gorgeous, sweetheart. Seriously, you are one fucking beautiful consort. Look at that glow." The words came from behind her, peppered out in quick order. "Are those tits real? No one has real tits where I come from. Fucking plastic surgeons screw up everything. Pretty soon we'll all have plastic dicks, and what fun will that be? Let me tell you something, babe, the day they come for my cock and fangs is the day I leave my home plane forever."

The man was one slick-looking vampire. Perfectly white fangs peeked from behind sensual lips, so there was no denying what he was. He was a vampire. And she wasn't home anymore.

She was going to be forced to be some kind of bondmate or consort to a man she didn't even know.

So why did she want to see him again? Why wasn't she fighting her way out?

"Oh, no, Mr. Dellacourt," Reeve was saying with a shake of his red cap. "The tourney is about to begin. Her viewing is over. If you wish to buy an entry, there is still time. However, her viewing is done."

The vampire named Dellacourt shook his head. Strangely, the vampires were the closest thing to a normal human she had seen, if one forgave the fangs. This particular vampire's skin was light, almost alabaster, and his green eyes were like emeralds. He was dressed, as his fellow vamps had been, in an elegant approximation of a business suit. They wore somber, deeply colored jackets. The blacks and grays and navys seemed almost luminous. Dellacourt was wearing black from head to toe. He had on a sleekly cut jacket that reached his knees and a matching vest. The only color he had on was a ruby red shirt that peeked out from under the vest. His trousers and loafers were midnight-colored as well. Unlike Beck, the gnomes, and the other men who had come to "view" her, the vampires seemed to have left the feudal era behind.

"Yes," Dellacourt said slowly. "We need to talk about that. What would you say if I told you I could triple your business on this sweet

29

thing?"

Reeve sighed, and she decided that he and Dellacourt probably had a long history, and not a lot of it was good. "I would say that the day I start listening to a slick vampire salesman is the day my wife should carve me up with a piece of wrought iron."

Cara nodded somberly. "I have it all ready, too. The minute he goes soft, I'm taking him out."

Cara held out her small hand, and Meg placed hers there. The little gnome started to lead her out into the sunlight. Dellacourt didn't miss a beat.

"Seriously, I can make this a very profitable venture for you, Reeve." Dellacourt followed them into the sunshine. There was a small whirring sound. She gasped as sunglasses formed around the vampire's eyes. Dellacourt grinned down at her. "Nanites, babe. Those are tiny computers, to the less technologically advanced. All of our clothes and accessories have nanite tech in them. They are intensely useful little fuckers. Of course, every now and then they band together and try to take over the world. Hey, what's progress without the occasional apocalypse?" He turned back to Reeve. "Back to my point. I only need a few hours. I'll give you a half million in gold, and all you have to do is delay this tournament until, say, eight o'clock."

"That ain't happening." Reeve turned from the vampire and continued walking.

Meg studied her surroundings as Cara led her into what looked like a small marketplace. There were stalls with vendors hawking their wares in odd languages. She had calmed down from her initial rage and terror. Now she could concentrate on her surroundings.

The gnome had mentioned that she didn't speak Gaelic. This was the language that was spoken all around her now. It made sense in a weird way. The creatures around her appeared to be straight out of Irish lore. Gaelic was the ancient language of Ireland. While she was bound in the tent, she had decided to use some of her old literature training to figure out what Beck was. It was obvious he didn't think of himself as human. From the way the gnomes treated him, she'd come to the conclusion that he was a faery of some kind. From the looks of him, he was more than likely a *sidhe*. They were the human-looking faeries and the ruling class. She wondered which tribe he came from. Human myths broke the Fae into two tribes, the Seelie and the Unseelie. The

Seelie were the blessed, shining ones while the Unseelie held all the monsters the Fae had to offer. She rather thought him a Seelie. She hadn't gotten a look at his ears. According to some lore, they should be slightly pointed. Of course, not all myths were proving true in this strange place. The vampire was proof of that since he was walking around in the daylight.

"Hey, vampire guy, shouldn't you be all crispy and fried by now?" Meg asked bluntly because he seemed like a blunt kind of man.

Dellacourt stopped in his tracks and laughed. "Damn, she really is from the Earth plane. Darling, the vampires there are idiots who got lost and couldn't find their way back. I read all the DLs on the subject. Horrifying stuff, really. You see, your sun is different. It has a bad effect on my kind. It puts us into a weird fugue state during the daylight hours, and if we get caught in it, we sort of explode."

Reeve pressed on. "Don't go filling her head with nonsense. Don't believe a word he says. Vampires like to make themselves seem more important than they really are. The Earth plane is one of the inner planes. It's why it's protected the way it is. Everyone knows we all came from there originally. There was a heavenly plane and the place where the demons come from, and there was Earth."

Dante shook his head. "We'll have to agree to disagree but I for one am thrilled I'm not an earthbound vamp." He shuddered. "Apparently, the animals there aren't fit for consumption, so they end up eating a diet made up entirely of human blood. Though I've heard your kind tastes spectacular, sweetheart. I've often thought that if I could get a trade route onto the human plane, I could make a ton of money selling human blood."

Reeve frowned at the vampire. "Don't go scaring the poor girl."

"Mr. Dellacourt doesn't scare me exactly, though I find him slightly repugnant," she admitted, eliciting a snort of agreement from Cara. Reeve was right.

The vampire didn't miss a beat. "Oh, no, that won't do. The name's Dante, sweetheart. Please, all the beautiful women call me Dante. And I'll have you know I am considered extremely good-looking."

Meg shrugged as she walked on. She supposed he was. He was tall and lanky but seemed strong. His hair was a thick reddish gold and cut in a stylish fashion. It was long and spiky and probably required a lot of upkeep to look that messy. She'd noted his eyes were green before they were covered by his sunglasses. "You sound like a used car salesman."

"His sister runs one of the biggest corporations on the vamp plane, but Dellacourt here is only allowed to oversee the family's computer chain. They rebuild old machines," Reeve piped up, seemingly eager to pile on to Dante.

"Yep," she said with a satisfied smile. "Used car salesman."

They were getting close to what appeared to be a massive arena. It was circular and constructed from a combination of wood and stone. There were several arches that appeared to be entryways. Meg could hear a crowd roaring their approval.

Dante pulled on Reeve's arm, getting down to one knee. All previous sarcasm had fled, and in its place was an earnest desperation. "I am begging you. Give me half an hour. You can delay half an hour. Look, Beckett Finn is in the woods somewhere hunting. I'll pay his fee to enter the tournament. His brother is dying. He needs her. Don't you owe your king something?"

"Reeve of the Gentle Hills is forever loyal, Dante," a soft voice said.

Meg turned and saw Beck standing mere feet from her. He had removed his vest and changed into dark pants and a different shirt. He held that long, ornate sword in one fist as he moved toward the arena.

"Excellent." Sarcasm poured out of the vampire. "I just spent the better part of the day running around a freaking forest searching for you, and here you are, looking fresh as a daisy. Cian said you had gone hunting. I went to your *brugh* when I heard about the tournament."

"I told Cian I was hunting because I didn't want to get his hopes up." Beck spoke to the vampire, but his eyes didn't leave Meg.

He was gazing at her like a predator preparing to pounce. His gray eyes blazed through her, and she knew exactly what he wanted. He wanted to take her away from here. He wanted to go somewhere private where he could lay her down and spread her thighs.

And she might let him. Might. Probably.

"Are you going to make big puppy eyes at the woman for the rest of the day, or are you going to go kick some ass?" Dante asked.

Beck shook his head and walked straight up to Meg. "You'll have to forgive my cousin. He's a bit of a pain. You'll get used to him. He can't help it. He's a vampire." He leaned over and brushed his lips against hers. He set his forehead on hers and seemed to breathe her in for a long moment. Her hands had moved to his waist and she wasn't sure why, but it felt right to be with him. "I know you're scared but remember my promise. We're in this together now. I won't let you down. And, love, please remember anything I do, I do to protect you."

This was when she should pull away from him, the moment she demanded he never touch her again. She simply stood there, letting the moment lengthen between them until he sighed, kissed her forehead, and stepped back.

And she watched him.

As he walked toward the gates of the arena, he shouted back to Reeve. "What did he promise you to try to get you to put off the tournament?"

"Half a million in gold, Your Highness."

Beck stopped in his tracks and turned to look at his cousin. He had an expression of shocked awe on his face. "You broke bastard. You didn't have half a million even before your sister cut you off."

Dante Dellacourt shrugged elegantly. "If I'm going to lie, I'm going big. There's no use in doing something halfway."

Beck shook his head and turned back. "Take care of her, cos."

The vampire smiled down at her and gallantly offered his arm. "Well, we have our orders, my lady. Come along. Let's find a good seat and pray Beck doesn't get himself killed."

Meg let the vampire—the flipping, freaking vampire—escort her into the arena. Her heart was pounding, but she put one foot in front of the other. She knew that whatever happened in here would change her life forever.

# Chapter Three

Meg found herself watched by every eye in the arena. Only Fae like Beck and vampires like Dante had come to view her in the tent, but now all manner of creatures stared at her as she forced herself to climb the stone steps to the chaise Reeve and Cara had motioned her toward. She found herself staring openly at what had to be an enormous troll. It was six feet tall, and that was its sitting height. She couldn't imagine what it would be like standing up. It was also extremely hairy. Behind the troll looked to be a group of what she could only term goblins. They were small and muscular, with leathery skin and wild tufts of hair sticking out in odd places.

Somewhere in the back of her head, she could hear the cantina music from *Star Wars* playing.

"Never been off the Earth plane, huh?" Dante had a dumbass smile on his face.

"Do those fangs ever go away?"

The vampire seemed to take it all in stride. "Certainly not when I am in the company of a half-naked female with a heart-shaped ass. Sorry, they pop out when I'm hungry or horny. Can't help it. And as I recently dined on a first-grade meal pill, courtesy of Dellacorp, I think we have to assume it's your fault. What do you say we ditch His Highness, go somewhere private, and make some baby fangs?"

"Pay him no heed, miss." Cara looked at the vampire, shaking her head. The chaise was plush and covered with a tent of ornate fabric that kept the fierce late-afternoon sun off her skin. "Vampires are not known for their manners."

"Is that blood?" There were pockets of red dotting the arena floor. Groups of gnomes were hurriedly shoveling out the offending sand.

"Damn." Dante sank down beside her. "They already got rid of the chopped-off limbs. That's my favorite part."

"They're really going to fight?" It was ridiculous, but she felt such a strong connection to Beck that she couldn't stand the thought of him getting hurt, much less dying. It must be Stockholm syndrome. Or maybe it was because he had given her the first honest-to-goodness, real live, no-double-A-batteries-involved orgasm she'd ever had. Whether she turned out to be Patty Hearst or just some desperate girl, she didn't want Beck's blood staining the arena.

"Yes, miss," Reeve answered, taking a seat next to his wife. "Your tournament is the last of the day. It is also the largest. The rest of these females are simple mates. You are very rare."

She let out a sigh of frustration. The whole thing was terribly confusing to her. She looked to the vampire. He didn't seem to have a problem telling her the painful truth. "Why? Why do all these men want me?"

His sunglasses receded, and he looked her in the eyes. His green eyes sparkled in the shade. "The vamps or the Fae?"

"Both."

His manner took on a distinctly academic tone. "The Fae are interested in you as a bondmate. Certain Fae have psychic abilities that are greatly enhanced in the presence of a female whose brain is tuned to theirs. In Beck's case, it's more urgent. Beck was born with a symbiotic twin, Cian. Think of them as halves of a whole. Beck is the practical half. He's the warrior. Cian is the intellectual half. When symbiotic twins turn twenty-five years old, a bondmate is found for them, if they aren't already contracted. The female forms a triad with the males. She bridges their minds through hers, and they're able to function together. It makes all three stronger. When Beck's uncle took over Tír na nÒg, he closed the plane. He did this for several reasons, but no doubt one was to keep his nephews from finding a bondmate. They've been forced to look elsewhere."

"So Beck is twenty-five." He seemed older, but perhaps it was his regal authority that made him seem that way.

"My cousin turned thirty nearly three months ago," Dante replied, all teasing gone from his attitude. "Cian is fading. The intellectual half is in desperate need of the bond. It is killing him to go without. If Cian fades, all that will be left is the warrior with nothing to balance him. Beck will likely go mad. If that happens, he'll have to be put down."

She didn't understand completely but she hated the idea of someone putting Beck down like he was a dog. "That's horrible. But how can he be sure I'm this bond thingy?"

Now a slow smile curled the vampire's lips. "There's only one way to know for sure. Tell me, sister, was it good for you?"

Embarrassment flashed through her. The scene in the tent had been Beck's way of telling if she was compatible. He'd even told her that was what he was doing, but the thought of everyone knowing what he'd done made her skin turn red. The vampire threw back his head and laughed.

"You are so rude." How long would this take? When would they start?

Dante shrugged, but the grin didn't leave his face. "I don't see what's rude about it. It's a simple fact of life. We all like to get fucked, sweetheart, and from what I've heard, old Beck there knows how to do it right. Of course, it would be slightly different with a bondmate. Even without the full bond, during sex, you would have a connection with him."

"I would feel what he felt." She remembered that odd, erotic moment when she could feel his hard-on, feel her own pussy gripping his fingers as she came.

"Congratulations," Dante said almost sweetly. "You're a bondmate. I've heard it's the most intimate connection a being can have."

She wasn't here to fall in love. She shouldn't be here at all. She would suffer through this. When she had the chance, she was going to get away, and no intimate bond was going to stop her. "Okay, that explains the Fae. How about the vampires?"

Dante leaned in, his fangs showing beneath his wide smirk. "Darling, the vampires are here because you taste really fucking good."

Cara leaned over Meg's lap and slapped the vampire. Dante took it with good grace, merely leaning back as though he was slapped by females on a regular basis. "Stop teasing the girl. Miss, the vampires are looking for what they call a consort. You have to understand there are two types of vampires, the peasant and those of royal blood."

"Don't call them peasants." Dante whistled under his breath. "Them's fighting words. One day you call them peasants, and the next day they unionize."

Cara ignored him. "The royals are the vampires with ancient blood. They are pure vampire. If they can find a proper consort, their lives are greatly elongated by taking his or her blood. The consort also receives a much longer life by taking the vampire's blood into his or her body. The consort's blood makes the vampire stronger than he or she would normally be. I heard your sister recently married her consort, Mr. Dellacourt."

Dante's nose wrinkled in distaste. "Yes, now our house is filled with love and roses every day. I'm not having any of it. What's the point in an extra couple of hundred years if you can't party? Susie and Colin. They walk around like lovestruck teens. It's disgusting. See, the bad part about finding a superhot piece of tail like you is the inevitable, long decline into idiocy."

"He's trying to say that vampires fall deeply in love with their consorts," Cara said primly.

"You say potato, I say potahto," Dante sang.

"You, miss, could serve as either a bondmate or a consort," Reeve interjected over the increasingly impatient crowd. "The psychic connection goes hand in hand with the differences in the blood. Normally, there would be plenty of suitable men and women. It is a common thing in Fae creatures. It's why our poor king is related to that one. Mr. Dellacourt's father took the king's aunt as his consort. The Fae and Vampire planes are closely linked."

"Well, they were until that bastard Torin took over," Dante said.

"Why does everyone speak English?" She was still trying to understand, still not quite sure whether this was a dream. "I don't get it. Dante sounds like every half-assed player prowling the bars on a Saturday night."

Dante touched his chest and looked horribly offended. "Now who's rude? For your information, I speak English because my people created it a long time ago. You can't possibly think your ancestors were intelligent enough to come up with such a convoluted and ridiculous language. At some point in time, my people found the door to your plane and taught you a thing or two. It probably happened around the time your people started standing upright. By the way, fire? Also a vampire discovery. You have us to thank for that, I'm sure. As to my speech patterns reminding you of your home plane, I can only say, ick. I don't mean to sound like some human. It's an unfortunate truth that our planes are closely connected. If our research on the subject is correct, there are a lot of similarities between the two. Think of it like this—our planes started out on the same track, but humans took over your plane, and vampires were the evolutionary winners on mine. There are bound to be many, many similarities."

"Like the potato song," Meg mused.

"You have that, too? Funny how that happens sometimes. I've heard you can run into yourself on planes like that. The Vampire plane and the human plane are parallel. I wonder if there's another me on the human plane. I bet I'm getting an enormous amount of tail there."

"Hush," Reeve said. "It's starting."

Meg's heart threatened to stop as a line of men walked out from the far side of the arena. A masculine voice boomed loudly, announcing each as they walked through. It was easy to tell the Fae males from the vampires. The Fae wore only pants and boots. Their chests were bare, and their long hair was pulled back and knotted behind their heads. The vampires had on long sleeves and gloves on their hands. They wore sunglasses like Dante's, and their shirts came with a hood covering their heads.

"We burn easily," Dante said when he noticed her staring. "Our skin is delicate. The sun on our plane isn't as strong as the others. We don't have a lot of ultraviolet light. Dellacorp is currently working on a cream that will protect the skin."

"Yes, it's called sunscreen. It blocks UV rays." Finally something her plane did better. "We piddling humans came up with it long ago."

"Seriously? You don't happen to have any of that on you? I could make a killing with that." Dante's business sense was quickly shelved as a vampire walked into the arena. He stood up and went to the railing, his sunglasses flowing as he moved into the light. "Well, if it isn't Kinsey Palgrave, you stupid ass. You suck, Palgrave! And your profits were down ten percent last quarter! Yeah, everyone saw it, you pathetic chump. Your stock's going to take a nosedive."

The other vampire shot Dante the bird and bared his fangs. "Why don't you get down here, Dellacourt? Or do you need your sister's permission?"

"My sister would never allow me to fight in this tournament," Dante shot back.

The big vampire, who looked like he might be taking steroids, laughed. So did all his friends. They seemed to be having a laugh at Dante's expense. "Big sister doesn't want baby brother to get a boo-boo?"

"Big sister knows it's stupid to fight the warrior half of symbiotic twins." Dante's face twisted into a smirk. "Besides, I would never fight my cousin."

It seemed to Meg like the entire arena suddenly fell silent. The vampire named Palgrave went even paler than before as he stared up at his rival.

"Beckett Finn is here?"

Dante pointed at the back of the arena, and there was Beck, striding in. There was confidence in his easy gait as he strode into the arena. The rest of the males had sunk into the sand, but Beck seemed to almost glide above it. He was graceful. He was a shark, and suddenly everyone else looked a little like guppies.

"They're scared of him," Meg breathed, sensing the anticipation in the crowd. The minute Beck stepped out, the crowd fell silent and the whispering began. Every eye in the arena was on the big, dark-haired man with the stormy gray eyes.

"He's the greatest warrior of his generation." Dante sat back down. He opened his jacket and pulled out what looked like a tablet computer. He pushed the screen a few times and then touched his ear. Meg hadn't noticed it before, but there was a small device there. "Yeah, give me my sister. Hey, Susie, you gotta dump all the stock we have with the Palgrave funds. No, I am not out drinking. Listen to me. Kinsey Palgrave is about to fight Beck. Yes, that's what I said. Even if Beck lets him live, he'll be out of commission for weeks. His even dumber brother will be acting CEO. Dump it now before the price goes down. You're welcome." He smiled smugly at Meg. "That will teach them to call me a screwup."

"How many does he have to fight?" This was really happening. These men would fight. The one who was left standing would expect her to go home with him.

"Stop panicking," Dante said, leaning back negligently. "It's all going to be fine. You'll love Beck, and you'll be crazy about Cian. No woman can resist Cian when he's on his game. They'll treat you like a princess. This is going to be a piece of cake for him. There's only twenty-five, no, there they go…fifteen to fight. Wow, they must be desperate. I was sure we'd get it down under ten."

A group of men shook their heads in disgust or fear and walked out of the arena.

"They don't want to fight the great Beckett Finn," Reeve explained. "He's a legend across the planes. The vampires will stay because of pride. If the word got out that they paid for an entry and then wasted the money by walking away, they would bring their families shame."

Dante nodded, agreeing with the gnome. "Vamps are damn serious about corporate funds. The Fae can walk away because there's no shame in surrendering to the king."

"King?" She'd heard Beck referred to that way, but now it seemed serious.

Dante's arrogance was gone, and in its place was an earnestness that made him almost angelically attractive. "Yes, Beckett Finn is the rightful King of the Seelie Fae. A pretender sits on his throne and has since Beck was seventeen years old. Beck lost his mother, father, sister, home, and kingdom all in one day. He's been on the run ever since. He's been forced to live as a peasant, barely getting by. He sells his sword to put food on the table. All he has in the world is his brother." Dante sat forward. He placed his hand on hers. It was slightly cool to the touch. "You can change that for him. You can make his life worth living. I love my cousin. He's more like a brother to me. If Cian makes a comeback, it is entirely possible I can get my sister to back them financially. Once the money starts flowing, Beck's loyalists will come back."

Meg sighed. She knew there had been more to this than simple lust-at-first-sight. He had ambitions, and she figured into them. "He wants to take back his throne?"

"Yes," Dante replied, as though it should have been blatantly obvious. "He wants to overthrow his murdering uncle. I know that you intend to run at the first opportunity. Don't try to deny it. I would do the same thing in your place, but I'm asking you to give him a chance.

Is there anything you could do on your home plane as important as freeing an entire population from tyranny?"

Well, put like that, getting home so her DVR didn't fill up seemed self-absorbed. What did she have to go back to? When she didn't show up at work, the district manager would fire her and put another in her place. She'd been told on more than one occasion that she was a dime a dozen. There were overeducated morons everywhere who needed a job. Her parents had divorced years before and started new families. It would be months before they even realized she was gone.

This was not her problem.

She hadn't asked to be brought here. Just because her life was dull didn't mean it was inconsequential. She had friends. Well, she'd had Michael's friends, and they had all taken his side in the divorce, but she intended to make friends one day. She couldn't do that if she didn't get home. Cara's small hand patting her in a comforting way didn't count as friendship. The little gnome was her jailer.

No, no matter what that vampire said, she was leaving as soon as she could.

A loud horn sounded, and the crowd leaned forward expectantly. The battle was beginning. Her breath caught as she saw Beck scan the crowd. Somehow she knew who he was looking for. Their eyes met, and he bowed formally to her.

She could feel his pull as though they'd already connected on some intimate level she couldn't deny.

Yes, she would leave. Even though he made her heart pound, she couldn't stay. Could she?

# Chapter Four

Beck had to force himself to look away from her. It was as if he was already caught by the thread of psychological bonding that would tether him to his own sweet Meg forever.

That bond was the thing that would save he and his brother, but right now it was a distraction. The fact that she was out there made him…antsy. He couldn't protect her yet and that anxiety sat in his gut.

He had to tamp that down. He couldn't afford to get emotional now. Cian wasn't the only one feeling the lack of a bondmate. He was simply far more dramatic about it. Beck had felt his hold on his temper slowly dissolving over the last few years. His rage seemed to build after a fight rather than dissipate.

He'd become brutal when he didn't need to be.

Just weeks ago, he had been hired to clean out a group of bandits plaguing the road to the marketplace. When he'd been surrounded by them, he'd gone a little crazy. He killed all thirty, and only barely managed to hold off killing the females traveling with them. His rages were getting worse.

Cian might fade from existence like a candle being slowly snuffed out, but Beck feared he would go out in a blaze of blood and death. Dante was under strict instructions to use vampire technology to kill him if necessary, but he doubted his cousin would be able to do it.

Meg was the answer to all his problems. He bowed formally to the woman he intended to wed. At least she wasn't trying to run. Yet. He would have to deal with that eventually. He'd felt a small piece of her soul when he'd touched her before. She was a stubborn young woman. She was also a lonely woman. He didn't need to see into her soul for that. She was lonely and scared.

What had she left behind on the Earth plane? Had she left behind a husband, or worse, children? She was of an age to have children. His conscience hurt at the thought of leaving a baby without a mother, but there was nothing he could do about it. She would learn that there was no way back to her plane. Only a Planeswalker could take her, and she wouldn't like the cost of the trip.

He shook off the thoughts of her and tried to concentrate on the battle ahead. He took a deep breath and felt the sand beneath his feet. He'd trained in an arena like this one back when he'd had loyalists who thought they could get him on the throne. Fighting in a place like this was second nature to him. The vampires would struggle in the beginning because they trained in far more modern settings. It wouldn't take them long to adjust. He never underestimated the vampires. They might seem soft because their true passion was business, but they were fierce predators. When the fight began, they would be in touch with their primal natures.

"Your Highness," a young Fae said, not quite meeting his eyes as he walked toward the exit.

He was the first of ten men who walked past him. Their disappointment hung around him like an albatross. They'd paid their money and laid their hopes on the line, too. He couldn't afford the guilt he felt. He had to do whatever it took to save his brother.

"Bastard," one of the vampires spit as he walked up to Beck. His fangs were out, a sure sign of his rage. "Don't even try to pull that shit on me, Finn. You aren't a late entrant. Those fucking gnomes kept you out of sight until it was too late. None of us would even have tried, knowing you were going to be here."

Beck went still, though his eyes watched every move the vampire made. He looked vaguely familiar, but he couldn't place the name. "I paid my money like the rest of you. I wasn't responsible for the list of competitors."

The vampire sneered, and now he had others backing him up. The *sidhe* had all left, but the vampires were standing against him. "Right. You don't have any sway with the gnomes." His voice was filled with sarcasm. "They still see you as their king. Are you taking a cut?"

Anger thrummed through him. A few of the smarter vampires took a step back. "I only want the woman. I'm not getting anything out of this except her."

Meg was watching. He should have forbidden it, but he didn't have the right yet. He couldn't lose control or she would be terrified of him. She probably still would be.

"We'll see about that." The vampire's fangs were already long in his mouth as the referee entered.

The vamps retreated. They talked amongst themselves as the gnome needlessly explained the rules.

Everyone knew them. No technology was allowed. Ancient weapons were the only ones permitted. The vampires were able to use their fangs and claws. If Cian had been here, Beck would have been allowed to use their psychic connection. Other than that, there were very few rules. Mercy must be given if asked for. If a combatant requested quarter, the warrior fighting him must give it. The fallen fighter would leave, and the battle would resume. If no quarter was asked, then death was an acceptable outcome.

Beck focused on the weapon in his hand. It was his sword, once his father's. It had been one of the few things he'd managed to save as he fled Tír na nÒg. It had been said that his uncle mourned its loss. The sword in his hand was the traditional weapon of the Seelie King. No amount of money or power could replace what it meant to their culture. Some claimed that as long as Beckett Finn still carried the sword, there was hope. He wasn't sure about that. A large part of him simply wanted to live out his life in some form of comfort. The idea of being king was nothing more than a vague dream. He only wanted to save his brother and find a stable life. Winning Meggie was the first step.

A roar went through the crowd as the referee held up a small black flag. A battle horn sounded, and the tournament began.

There wasn't a burst of fighting. The vampires had used their time well, plotting and planning how to take him out. The vampires stalked him, attempting to distract him while some of their brethren worked their way around to his back. They intended to surround him. They would work together to take him out, and then they would fight each other.

They didn't understand a thing. He very much preferred it this way. Chaos was his enemy. If he knew they were all coming after him, he knew exactly who to kill—every blasted one of them. Adrenaline began to course through his body like an old familiar drug in his system. He held his sword calmly at his side, patiently waiting for them to get into position.

"Fucking idiots! He loves the pack rotation," his cousin was shouting. It shouldn't have surprised him that even in a crowd of peasants watching a fight, Dante stood out as obnoxious.

It was a technical term for this type of fight. The vampires were circling him like a pack of wolves. He happened to be particularly talented when it came to defending against a pack rotation, but Dante didn't need to point that out.

Beck made the mistake of glancing his cousin's way. Dante had left his seat and stood at the edge of the railing. The problem was he wasn't alone. Meg was right beside him, her face sheet-white as she watched the men surrounding him.

She felt the connection. A surge of hope spilled over his rage. He'd expected the connection. He'd opened himself to it slightly, but if Meg had felt it, too, it must be strong. It was the only explanation for why she was standing there, looking like her world was about to fall apart. She knew they belonged together. She might not be willing to admit it, even to herself, but the bond was already being formed.

This could work. If he treated her gently, she might be happy with him.

And then all thought fled and instinct took over. Beck sensed something coming at him, fast. He had a bare second before the vampire was on him. He leaned over, trying to time it perfectly and get the right angle. The vampire hit his back. Beck shoved up with everything he had. It sent the vamp flying through the air, knocking down a rival on the other side of the circle. Beck was immediately back on his feet, anticipating the attack from the other side.

Vampires were fast. They talked fast and moved even faster when they needed to. When battling a vampire, it was more important to rely on his instincts than his eyes. Sometimes a vamp could move faster than the eye could track. It came down to anticipating the next move. Vampires were immensely logical creatures. They trained and tended to do everything by the book. It was why Dante had trouble fitting in. Dante thought more creatively.

In this case, the vampires' slavish devotion to the method came in handy.

In his mind, Beck numbered them one through fifteen. Eight had tumbled straight into Two across the ring the vampires had formed. Both were struggling to get back to their feet. It gave Beck a chance to concentrate on the next assault. It would come from Twelve and Five.

He thrust out with his sword, catching Twelve in the belly as he kicked out in perfect precision, shoving Five back. He twisted his body slightly to take out Ten and Three in the same fashion.

Instinct took over as his sword bloodied. He no longer thought about Meg or Dante or even Cian. He and the sword moved in perfect harmony. The blade became an extension of his being. He relaxed, letting his hearing confirm the order in which his brain told him they would attack. He danced as they played out the scenario, his sword finding purchase in their strong bodies.

Every time he sank the sword into another body, his hunger grew. He wanted to kill. The horn blared, calling an end to this round of fighting. It was an intrusive sound. An unwelcome sound.

Beck breathed deeply, fighting the instinct to attack the gnomes as they ran onto the field to pull off the injured competitors who called for quarter. He wanted to skewer the little ones. They would look good on his blade, the dark voice in his head whispered. *It was their fault.* They had walked onto his killing field. They should expect death. They were dragging off his prey before he even had a chance to finish them. It was his right. He turned to raise his sword and take care of the interlopers when the sight of Meg's face stopped him.

She stood, her fingers gripping the railing and her face pale. He could feel her worry. She was worried for him. She shouldn't be worried for him. She should be scared of him.

It was enough to pull him out of his impending rage. Meg would never come to him if she saw what an animal he could be. He couldn't allow that to happen. He swallowed as the horn blared, and the battle began anew.

The remaining vampires didn't wait this time. All eight rushed him immediately. He was knocked back by the unexpected charge. Though his back hit the sand, a fierce joy took over. He did love a good fight. Up until now, the battle had been rote. Now, he was thrown a bit off balance and it set him free.

A big vamp, with fangs and claws out, leapt on top of him. Sharp claws sank into his left shoulder, pain flaring. The blood start to flow and it would make the vamps a little crazy. He'd feared chaos, and now he was going to get it. Shoving his foot upward, Beck launched the vamp up and over as he swung his sword in time to skewer the next vampire who jumped on him.

Gravity pulled the vamp down, and Beck noticed his aim had been perfect. As the vampire sunk onto the sword, the iron of the ancient weapon tore through his heart, one of two sure ways to kill a vampire. The race was tough as nails but vulnerable when it came to their hearts. Even a minor injury to the heart usually killed a vampire. The only other sure way was decapitation. Beck rolled away as fast as he could, knowing what would come next. Vampires didn't die quietly. They sort of exploded.

The rest of the vamps took a quick step back as their fallen compatriot came apart. Beck narrowly managed to avoid being covered in gore, but his senses filled with the smell and scent of blood. It did nothing to calm his inner beast. The warrior soul inside him gloried in the death of his opponent.

They deserved death. The female was his. They were attempting to take what was rightfully his.

He moved out of the way of the next assault. Two vampires threw themselves down, one catching Beck while he was still blinded by the bits of dead vamp covering his eyes. Beck roared as he felt the vampire sink his fangs into the vulnerable flesh between his neck and shoulder. Luckily, he'd squirmed enough so the bastard hadn't gotten his jugular.

He heard, no, felt, Meggie's scream. It spurred him to action. He took a single, strong punch to his face from a second attacking vamp. Several more were stepping forward to take a shot, too. The vamp on his neck pushed at him, trying to get a better angle. Beck reached up and pulled him off his back, tossing him into the vampires attacking his front. The place where the vamp's fangs had sunken in ached. The fucker had gotten away with a hunk of his flesh.

It didn't matter. He healed quickly.

He moved even faster. He skewered the vamp who had taken a chunk out of him, and his aim was perfect. The vamp exploded, even as he pulled his sword out and moved on to the next.

The blood and gore was having an effect on the vamps as well.

47

Two of the vampires had turned on each other. Out of the corner of Beck's eye, he caught sight as they screamed, fangs and claws out. The pair attacked each other viciously. They sunk their claws into each other's bellies, and the high-pitched sound of their pain riled him up even faster. The two quickly dropped to the ground. They rolled in the sand, each desperate to gut the other. Vampires, for all their claims to civilization, were as brutal as the rest of the planes.

There were only six left, and two were doing their damnedest to kill each other. A fierce joy raced through him as he brought the hilt of his sword down on a vamp he had tripped as he attempted to run away. *Silly creature.* There was nowhere to run. He raised his sword to bring it down on the vamp's throat. He was swinging it in an arc toward the unconscious rival's body when he was tackled from the side.

Beck roared as he toppled over.

"Quarter!" the vampire yelled as he scrambled to get his knife properly in his hand. "He's out, Beck. You can't kill a man who's already gone down."

It was the same vampire who had drawn Dante's ire before the battle. He was covered in sweat and blood. His hood had fallen back, and his pale skin was already burning. "Give it a rest, Beck. It's over. The female is yours. We surrender."

Beck's brain was too far gone to properly process the words the vampire spoke. All he knew was he was on his back in a submissive position, and that was never acceptable. With a single hand, he tossed the vampire away like he was a child's toy. Somewhere in the back of his rage-addled head, he recognized that the gnomes had taken to the floor. They were trying to help out the injured combatants.

It no longer mattered. His rage required blood.

"He's gone insane!" Palgrave shouted, trying to get the referee's attention. "You have to put him down." The vampire backed up as Beck growled low in his throat and began to stalk him. He tossed down his knife and showed Beck his empty hands. He had retracted his claws, but the fangs remained. "I concede, Beck. We all concede."

A horn blared. It seemed a distant, meaningless thing. There were still twitching bodies, so his work couldn't possibly be finished. His senses opened. Everywhere he smelled glorious death. The vamp was forced against the arena wall. He tried to shrink back as though he could force the stone walls to pull him in.

"I am asking for mercy, Your Highness." There was a hitch in the vampire's voice. He pulled away as though trying to disappear into himself.

Beck could smell the fear on him. It was good. He raised his sword as the crowd began to scream, but it was a single voice that stayed his hand.

"He asked for mercy, Beck," a soft feminine voice said. "There is no reason to kill him."

Meggie. She was here. The vamp took the opportunity to run. Beck was too shocked by Meg's presence to do anything about it. Dante stood at her side.

Beck chose to turn his rage on his cousin. Dante had been tasked with protecting her. "Get her out of here. How dare you allow her on the battlefield!"

Dante had the good sense to back up. "The battle is done, cos. It's time for you to come down now."

"Not until I'm finished," Beck promised, his voice rough with dark emotion. His jealousy threatened to take over. What had his cousin been doing all this time he was sitting beside his woman? Had Dante been courting her? Dante had no consort. Did he think he could steal Meggie? "You should never have walked out here. Are you challenging me?"

Dante's eyes got wide, but Meg moved between them. "Beck, Dante is not challenging you. No one is challenging you anymore. They're all running away. You scared the crap out of them."

Beck bared his teeth as he realized she was correct. They were running. He took a step and made to follow when her soft hand found the middle of his chest. She didn't seem to notice he was covered in blood.

"Meg, he's too far gone," Dante said. "You'll have to…"

"I heard you in the stands." Meg placed her other hand on his chest and stood very close. Her delicate scent washed over him. She smelled sweet, nothing like death. Meg smelled of flowers and some womanly scent he couldn't name. She smelled of life. "Beck, I'm yours. Are you going to leave me alone to chase after the others? Shouldn't you take care of me?"

"Not going to work." Dante continued to back up. "Meg, if you can't handle it, then I need for you to run. Run to the stands. I'll distract

49

him."

"Shut up," Beck yelled at the vampire. His jealousy was a roiling pain in his gut. "You don't talk to my mate."

Meg huffed at the vampire. "Fine, but you better be right. If I find out this was a stupid joke, I'll stake you myself." Beck was trying to move her out of the way. She threw her arms around him and went on her tiptoes to press her mouth against his. "Please, Your Highness, I am yours. You have to take care of me."

Beck's sword fell to the side as another type of need blazed through his body.

* * * *

Terror sparked through Meg as the second horn blew and the vampires charged Beck. "They didn't get in a circle."

She hated the fact that he was out there and so completely outnumbered.

"No, they seemed to have figured out that won't go well for them." Dante's sunglasses covered his eyes, but there was concern in his tone that hadn't been there moments before.

"Is he in trouble?" It was a stupid question. He was one man versus a whole bunch of vampires. She was on the verge of panic and it didn't make a lick of sense. She barely knew the man.

*And if he dies, you'll get sent off with one of those vampires. Wouldn't it be better to end up with the man you feel something for?*

"No, not from the vampires," Dante said, not taking his eyes off the fight.

Beck seemed buried under the group of vamps.

"It looks like he's in trouble to me." The thought made her physically ill. Would she have to watch the gnomes take his big, gorgeous body away? Would they drag him across the sand and declare one of the vampires the winner?

Dante finally turned her way. "Yes, he's in trouble, but not in the way you think. You remember I explained about the symbiotic twins thing?"

She nodded. "Yes, he needs a bondmate because his brother is dying."

"It's beyond that. Beck is the warrior half of unbonded symbiotic twins. He needs Cian to balance him," Dante explained, leaning in so she could hear. "Cian gets lost in his thoughts. He's the intellectual half of the man. Beck gets lost in something else."

Her stomach turned as there was suddenly blood all over the sand. Not Beck's. He was knee deep in bodies and blood, but he seemed to simply keep going. Almost as though he was enjoying it.

"He can't control his rage." He'd been so controlled with her only hours before. He'd taken what he needed and nothing for himself. She would have let him have her in that moment, but he'd walked away.

Now there was no mercy or kindness in the man who might be king.

She watched as one of the vampires tossed down his weapon and seemed to be trying to talk to Beck. "Isn't this the part where he backs down?"

It was easy to see the vampire was trying to surrender, but Beck wasn't listening.

"Shit." Dante looked down at the railing and seemed to be judging the distance to the floor of the arena. He looked back at Meg and took her shoulders in his hands. "Okay, sweetheart, I've got two choices here. I can pray that Beck gets his shit under control or I can ask you to take one for the team. Actually, there are three but I can't accept choice number three."

The crowd was roaring around her. Beck had started to prowl toward the vampire who kept pleading. The gnomes had started to creep out and they seemed to have weapons in their hands.

"They're going to go after Beck, aren't they?" She asked the question despite the fact that she knew the answer.

"They will try to contain him, but they'll fail," Dante said, his mouth turned down. "They'll die, too, and I'll have to put Beck down. It's stupid but I actually carry around something that will do the trick. That's how serious this is. If he starts, he won't stop until he's dead, and then all is lost. Look, I owe my cousin everything. I'm going to beg you to help him."

"Me? I can't fight..." The connection. She was the bridge. "How can it work if his brother isn't here?"

"He is nothing but instinct right now," Dante said. "His instinct is to kill, but there are other instincts. You are very important to him. I need you to get him to see you, to need you. He'll want to protect you but beyond that he's going to want to claim you."

"I thought that was what this whole thing is about. He has to win and then he gets to…" Did he mean what she thought he meant? "Are you talking claiming in a biblical sense?"

"I don't know what that means," Dante admitted. "I'm talking about sex. There's a ritual. Beck has to prove he can physically claim a mate or he can't take you with him. Women and men who can form the bond are highly prized. If he doesn't have at least a shot at making babies with you, you'll be given to someone who does."

"I'm a human being, you know." She felt like she had to point out a few of this plane's inequities.

"Yes," Dante agreed. "It wouldn't work if you weren't. What's it going to be? Because we're minutes away from me having to take out my cousin. I'm begging you. You're the only one who can save him."

She looked down and Beck had backed the vampire against the arena wall. He was going to do it. He was going to kill that vampire who was begging for his life.

But he didn't want to. He didn't want to be this man, this rolling ball of pain rage that would someday suck everyone into his hell.

She wasn't sure how she knew it, but this wasn't Beck. He wasn't a killing machine. He was a man trying to save his brother and she was the key.

Again, she felt his pull and realized she had to follow the call. Dante went first, gracefully jumping over the wall and then turning to offer her assistance. She wasn't so graceful, but it appeared there wasn't time for it. The vampire Beck was about to kill had nowhere else to run and was seconds away from being skewered.

Beck wouldn't forgive himself. Not if he killed someone like this.

"He asked for mercy, Beck. There is no reason to kill him." Strangely it felt right to be here. She knew she should be scared, but suddenly she also knew she could handle him. Dante was right. She was the only one who could handle him.

She was not without some power.

Beck stared at her long enough for the vampire to get away.

He turned to Dante, his mouth a flat line. He was splattered with blood and pointed back toward the seats. "Get her out of here. How dare you allow her on the battlefield!"

Dante put both his hands up as though trying to show Beck he didn't have any weapons. He also moved back a good five feet. "The battle is done, cos. It's time for you to come down now."

"Not until I'm finished." Beck's voice was rough and his eyes narrowed on Dante. "You should never have walked out here. Are you challenging me?"

She was really going to have to save them all. "Beck, Dante is not challenging you. No one is challenging you anymore. They're all running away. You scared the crap out of them."

Beck looked around and she could plainly see that he was angry they were getting away. It was time to step up her game. She moved in and placed her hand on his chest, his skin under her palm.

Dante stayed where he was, but he held a hand out as if to ask her to come to him. "Meg, he's too far gone. You'll have to…"

"I heard you in the stands." It would be a terrible mistake to try to walk away now. She wasn't afraid for herself. If Beck thought for a second Dante was trying to take her away from him, things could take a bad turn. She softened her voice, trying to sound vulnerable even as she weirdly felt empowered. "Beck, I'm yours. Are you going to leave me alone to chase after the others? Shouldn't you take care of me?"

Dante shook his head. "Not going to work. Meg, if you can't handle it, then I need for you to run. Run to the stands. I'll distract him."

"Shut up," Beck barked in a deep voice. "You don't talk to my mate."

Oh, he was going to be such fun. If he weren't so hot and she couldn't feel how emotional he was, she would walk away. But something compelled her to stay even though she knew she was about to join the exhibitionism club. "Fine, but you better be right. If I find out this was a stupid joke, I'll stake you myself." She threw her arms around his neck and molded her body to his. The minute she touched him her whole body came to life. It was suddenly easy to go up on her toes and brush her lips over his. "Please, Your Highness, I am yours. You have to take care of me."

She took a deep breath and prayed that damn vampire was right. She pressed her body against Beck's. Finally, she had his full attention.

He towered over her. His gray eyes had been filled with rage before, but now they gleamed down on her, a mixture of the rage he was fighting, and something else entirely.

"You shouldn't have come out here." He growled as he took her face between his hands. He shifted them slightly until they tangled in her long hair. He looked righteously masculine, and she felt her heart speed up.

It took her a moment to form the words. "I had to come."

He was so close. His neck and shoulder were injured, the wounds seeping blood. There was a part of her that wanted to shrink back, but seeing this piece of him was important. He was a warrior, and not the kind who dropped a bomb from above or pushed a button from miles away. He fought in close quarters. His life was always on the line. He was a knight, and she suddenly felt like his lady. He'd been intent on destruction, but she'd stayed his hand.

It was a heady feeling.

A deep growl came from him and then his mouth was on hers. The world fell away. Somewhere in the back of her mind, she knew that others watched them. She could even hear the announcer call the battle in favor of Beck. The crowd cheered, and then she heard something about a public display of sexual compatibility, but his tongue was sweeping inside her mouth. He held her head where he wanted it, and she was deliciously powerless against his assault. Her skin tingled everywhere it met his. He hauled her tightly against his frame, allowing her to feel his desire. His erection pressed long and thick against her belly. His body moved against hers, and she found herself rubbing helplessly against him.

Even as his body prodded hers, she felt his mind playing at the edges of her consciousness. It was almost as if there were gates to her mind, and like the marauder he was, Beck wanted in. This was the connection she'd felt, the one that could be addictive. She relaxed and let go of any thought of keeping him out.

She was completely overwhelmed.

Insanity. It threatened to take over Beck. So much rage and it suddenly had a place to go. It poured into her brain. For a second, she was suffused with it, but instinct took over. It was odd. She could push it out of her own mind. It was almost as though she was a filter for him. The rage swept over her, but she could hold her soul apart from it. There was so much anger inside him, a volcano that had almost overflowed. This was what Dante had been afraid of. This was why he'd been worried they would be forced to put him down.

He kissed her as his rage moved from his mind into hers, and then like a faucet that had been turned from cold to hot, it was replaced with desire. It raced through her body like a wildfire, and this time, she didn't try to filter it. She wanted this feeling. It was completely different than anything she had experienced before. This wasn't the sweet, slow arousal she normally experienced that typically led to nowhere. This was a blazing aggression that she knew would end with a dominant, overwhelming pleasure.

This need would not be denied, and it was something she could share with him. Something deep and intimate. Something she'd never felt before.

She sighed and gave over to Beck when she realized that what she was feeling was his arousal. He wanted her, needed her. It was a desperate thing. He was starving for her, and everything female in her needed to feed him.

She tightened her arms around him, reveling in the hard feel of his muscles. His hand slipped inside the gossamer bodice of her robe and closed over her breast. His thumb brushed the nipple and she cried out against his mouth. He was hot to the touch.

"You feel so good." Beck's voice was a low growl, and there was an almost drugged quality to it.

Her hands went to the front of her robe. She felt how much it would please him to see her. He wanted to look at her breasts and see her pussy. He wanted to lay her bare and fuck her until she couldn't remember a time he wasn't inside her. She couldn't hear his words, but she filled in the intent. She started to pull off her robe, but his hand came out and stopped her. His face was filled with a savage possessiveness. The fine edge of his madness was still present, still trying to take over.

"No," he bit out, the word grinding between his teeth. "That is mine. It is not for their eyes. On your knees, bondmate. They need a show before I can claim you, but they will not see you."

He pushed her down by her shoulders. Her knees hit the sand, sinking in slightly. The entire episode felt like a hazy, utterly erotic dream. She knew exactly what he wanted. She could see a picture of it in her mind and knew that Beck was putting it there. She could have told him that she wasn't very good at that. Her ex-husband had told her that she wasn't good at anything when it came to pleasing a man, but it might be different with Beck. If she listened carefully, he could show her what he wanted.

With shaky hands, Beck untied the fastenings on his pants and roughly pushed them down to his knees. His cock sprang forward, erect and enormous. It was thick and long, red at the base but gradually giving way to a gorgeous plum color at the head. It pulsed in his hand as he stroked himself. Meg could see a bead of milky white moisture glistening on the tip.

He moved forward and pressed the head of his dick against her lips. "Take me."

Tentatively, she reached out and brushed the tip of her tongue across him, gathering the arousal on the head. He tasted salty and masculine. As she watched, another drop wept out of the slit, and she swiped her tongue across it again. His cock jumped, and pleasure curled in her womb. She was already getting soft and moist thinking about taking him in her mouth.

His hands curled in her hair. She felt the full force of his will like a drug pulsing through her veins. His voice was dark with need as he pulled her head forward. He left no room to argue or for her to think about what she was doing. She only knew that she wanted him. She wanted this.

"Open."

She obediently opened her lips, groaning at the feel of his cock pressing into her mouth. She only had the head of his dick inside her lips, but she was already struggling. He filled her mouth. She whirled her tongue around the head of his cock, though the fit was tight. She explored the velvety smooth skin. Such soft, silky flesh covered his raging hardness. A wave of warmth infused her, and she knew what Beck was feeling. His head was thrown back as he fed her his dick.

"More." He seemed capable of only one-syllable phrases now.

She looked up and saw his eyes were dark and filled with unmistakable satisfaction as he watched his flesh disappear into her mouth. His hands tugged at her hair, urging her on. He pressed forward. He was so big, she wasn't sure she could take more, but she had to. It felt so good. Beck's pleasure coated her in need. She whirled her tongue around his thickness as much as she could. It was almost more than she could take. She could feel what he was feeling. She felt the softness of her tongue and the heat of her mouth. She felt how much he wanted her hands on him, so she lifted one hand to gently caress his balls.

"Yes." Beck groaned as he thrust his hips forward, forcing in another inch.

She relaxed and tried to ignore her gag reflex. She swallowed around his cock. It seemed to break something in the big Fae warrior. He growled, and Meg was almost overcome with his need to dominate her. She gave herself up to the experience.

She knew somewhere in the back of her mind that she should be gagging. She should be fighting him off, but the sensation of sharing the experience with him was far more powerful than any physical reaction. His fierce bliss as he fucked her mouth was beyond anything she had ever felt. He was ruthless. He shoved himself inside, all caution gone. Her pussy was soaking wet, and she was sure if she touched her clit she would go off like a rocket. She was giving him such pleasure, and it aroused her. She could see herself through his eyes. She was sexy and hot. She was a goddess, and he was going to tame her. He was going to fuck her until she promised never to leave him. Because he couldn't lose her now that he'd found her. She was perfect for him. She was going to be everything to him.

Beck fucked his way to the back of her throat. He shoved his cock in, even as he pulled her head forward. The twin sensations called to her submissive nature. He was so deep, she could feel his balls hit her chin with each thrust. He was close. She felt as though she was in his body. An almost painful anticipation was coursing through him. His balls squeezed. A warning prickle tickled at the base of her spine. It was coming from him. He was so close. Instinctively she swallowed around him. Beck threw his head back and roared as he came.

She was suddenly full. Her mouth was filled with his essence, and she was suffused with his orgasm. It rolled across her like a powerful wave, bashing against her senses. Only Beck's strong hands kept her from falling over. The entire experience had been exquisite and completely draining.

"Lick me clean," he ordered, keeping his hands tangled in her hair.

She obediently licked his softening cock, running her tongue along his skin. She tried not to miss a drop. It felt so good. The orgasm itself had been massive. It was like a high-powered locomotive barreling into her. This pleasure was softer, sweeter. It felt like tenderness and caring.

And then it was gone. The connection was cut abruptly, and she felt cold at its loss.

"What am I doing?" Beck asked in a rough voice. He let go of her.

She fell to the sand, completely exhausted.

She watched through languid eyes as he tucked himself back in and refastened his trousers. A peaceful lethargy had overtaken her. Now he would tell her how pleased he was with her. He would kiss her and hold her. He would see to her pleasure. It would feel so good to make love with him.

He didn't look pleased as he reached down and hauled her up into his arms.

"Cover yourself," he ordered harshly.

Her robe had come open. Her breasts were bare, the nipples puckered and wanting.

That hard command forced her to come out of her pleasure-induced haze. Seconds before, she wouldn't have cared if she had been completely naked to the world. She'd only cared about pleasing Beck, but now a flush of shame suffused her. What had seemed so loving before now seemed perverse without his kindness.

What had she done? She'd been connected to him. She'd known how pleased he'd been, but the moment that door had slammed shut, all her insecurities crawled back into place.

She pulled the sides of her robe together so she didn't offend him with her nudity. As he carried her out of the arena, she kept her hands at her sides, sensing that he wouldn't welcome her touch.

She was alone again.

# Chapter Five

She wouldn't touch him.

Beck kept his face painfully passive as he marched back to the tent Reeve had put together for the compatibility ritual. If everything had gone as it should have gone, he would have taken Meg back to this tent and very gently, respectfully made love to her in front of two witnesses. Reeve would have been one, and the vampires would have selected one. It was a simple ritual to prove he could take care of her sexually.

Instead, he'd proven that he was an animal.

Now she wouldn't look at him, and he didn't blame her. He had to hold her tight because she refused to put her arms around his neck.

Cara was at the door to the tent and held it open as she eyed him. She looked at the pale female in his arms. She was looking with pity on the woman he had just married. He'd treated her like a whore. Beck sighed inwardly, avoiding Cara's eyes. He'd never treated a whore that way.

Beck laid her down as gently as he could on the bed that had been prepared for them. It was covered with thick, soft blankets and pillows. Flowers had been strewn—marigolds, St. John's Wort, and shamrocks. It was a lovely setting and would have made a beautiful bridal bed. Instead, he'd shoved her to her knees in the middle of a bloody arena and throat-fucked her in front of a crowd.

He tried not to think about how soft and sweet she looked lying on the bed. There was nothing he wanted more than to climb into bed beside her and attempt in some fashion to make up for the way he had treated her. He wanted to kiss her and hold her. He wanted to tell her how much she was already coming to mean to him. He wanted to beg her forgiveness and promise to never, ever treat her that way again.

She wouldn't believe him. He was obviously a man of no honor. He'd proven it in the arena today. If he had a shred of honor, he would walk away from her now. He could provide her with nothing but a dying brother and a ramshackle *brugh* on a meaningless plane of existence. He should allow Dante to take her to his plane. At least there she would be fed, clothed, and taken care of.

"Clean up." His words were harsh to his own ears. "We leave in an hour."

"Sire," Cara blurted, a startled expression on her face. "Surely you cannot expect your bondmate to travel this evening."

He stared down at the gnome. He'd been raised to be a king, and though he was no longer that man, he still expected to be obeyed without question. It had been bred into his character. A king never explained his actions, even when they were wrong. He was sure Cian would have knelt and explained himself to the small woman, but then Cian would never have been in this mess in the first place. Cian would never have screwed up so badly with a woman that she couldn't stand to look at him.

"If you have a problem with it, I'll take her now," he said softly.

The gnome held her ground, but he could see it cost her. "No, Sire. I will make sure she is ready for the long and arduous journey."

Beck strode to the door. He needed a bath, but he wouldn't disturb Meg's. If things had gone as planned, he would have cleaned her up himself. He would have shown her how tender he could be. He would have eased into the hot tub with her, kissed her, and washed her hair. He would have bonded with her.

"If she runs, I'll hold you and yours personally responsible," he growled. He was somewhat satisfied by her nervous nod.

The waning sunlight was still hot on his skin. That would change. By nightfall the forest would be cold. If he took her out there, she would have no choice. She would have to cling to him for warmth and protection.

Perhaps out in the forest she would begin to learn to trust him.

He strode through the market, ignoring those who called out

greetings to him. He didn't want to hear about his soon-to-be-legendary victory. The damn bards would be singing about it soon enough. They had no idea how close that victory had come to being a bloodbath. Only Meg's sweet hand had stayed him, and she'd paid for her interference. He left orders with the stable boy to get his horse ready then made his way to the river that ran near the marketplace. He tossed his shirt, boots, and trousers on the grass and dove in where he knew the water was deep and cold.

The chill hit his system like a bloody winter blast. He gritted his teeth against the bite of pain along his skin. He dove deep, refusing to come up for air or warmth. His lungs could handle it. He wrapped his hands around the strong reeds, anchoring himself to the bottom. It was quiet here. There was no incessant chatter. There was no one to constantly remind him of duties that were no longer his. They didn't understand. He had been the deposed King of the Seelie for almost half his life now. Couldn't they leave him be?

Beck watched a small school of fish swim by. The river was remarkably clear and lovely. It reminded him of the river that ran by the white palace in Tír na nÒg. His mother would take him, Cian, and their sister Bronwyn down, and she would sit with her ladies while they swam. Cian would splash their sister and tease her mercilessly, but Beck wasn't able to join their fun. He was expected to act the king always.

*"Eyes are always on you, son,"* his father would say. *"They expect Cian to act the fool, but you must be the warrior king every minute of your life."*

What would his father have thought of his actions this day? Would his father understand that life had dealt him a horrible set of cards and he'd played them the only way that made sense? Or would he turn away in shame? Beck rather thought it might be the latter.

All of his life he had been trained to ruthlessly hide the beast that lived inside him. His own mother had always told him that symbiotic twins were considered powerful, but everyone knew they were difficult to raise. The warrior half required balance to stop his violent nature from running wild. The intellectual half needed grounding or he spent his life in daydreams. It was only through bonding with a proper mate that the two halves could truly live balanced lives.

The bonding was a sacred act. It was a gift from the bondmate to her husbands. It was to be treasured and revered.

He'd forced it on her when she didn't even understand what she was accepting.

Finally his lungs burned, and he allowed himself to float toward the light. He broke the surface, taking a deep breath.

"I was wondering if you were going to put in an appearance or if you would allow the kelpies to take you." Dante sat against a large tree, his long legs spread out in front of him. He had his tablet out. Like many vampires, Dante was almost constantly attached to his computer. He was always looking for downloads, better known as DLs. DLs consisted of everything from entertainment to education.

"There aren't any kelpies here." Beck smoothed his long black hair from his face. "There are some in the forest, but none this close to a village."

The forest where he was about to take his Meg was considered a bit dangerous. It was full of all sorts of nasty creatures.

Dante tossed him a bar of soap. It was pink. The vampire had probably stolen it from the females' tent. Still, it would take the stink of battle off him. He soaped up, grateful for the cold. It was the first time since meeting Meg that he wasn't uncomfortably hard.

Not true. There had been that moment after Meg had swallowed him down. Her throat had closed around him, and she'd taken every drop of him. Even after he was done, she had been sweet and submissive. He'd wanted nothing more than to praise her for her gift to him. He'd wanted to haul her into his arms and fuck that sweet pussy of hers. She wouldn't have said no. She would have spread her legs and welcomed him.

But she'd been under the influence of their connection.

If she'd been in her right mind, she would have been terribly insulted. She was a lady, a bondmate. She deserved respect. His wants and needs were perverse. She would help him overcome them. Once he and Cian had properly bonded, the overwhelming need he felt to dominate his lovers during sex would go away.

It had to.

"I don't understand you, cos," Dante admitted. The light was fading now. The vampire didn't need the hood of his shirt. He sat negligently in the shade, but then everything Dante Dellacourt did had an air of privileged negligence about it.

"I don't expect you to." Beck soaped his long hair. It should have been Meg's job. Washing her husband's hair was the responsibility of a Fae woman. He'd given up the right when he treated her like a piece of trash.

"You're tearing yourself apart over what happened out there, and I'm not sure which part is killing you. You aren't responsible for the fact that you're losing control. You should have been bonded five years ago. If I recall, your parents had already betrothed the two of you to a nice royal girl."

Beck snorted. He remembered Maris. How could he forget? He'd known since he was very young that she was his future bondmate. She had been a cool blonde and aware of her position, even as a young teen. If she had been with him in the arena, she would have slapped him silly. "I don't think my uncle intended to allow that contract to be fulfilled."

The vampire sighed impatiently. "That's my point, asshole. You did everything right. It's not your fault that it all went wrong. Meg saved you."

"Don't you think I know that?" Beck asked irritably.

"Then why did you treat her like crap?"

"It's your fault," he snarled, lying through his teeth. Maybe if he pissed his cousin off enough, Dante would go away and leave him alone. "You were the one who was stupid enough to bring her into the arena."

Dante stood. He walked to the water's edge, proving he did, indeed, have a death wish. "It was the only way I could think of to salvage the situation."

"I can think of another," Beck replied, narrowing his eyes in challenge.

Dante threw his head back and groaned. "I am not going to inject you with cold iron, asshole. Get over it. If you want to commit suicide, I'll give you the needle, but I won't push the plunger. I wouldn't just be killing you. I would be killing Cian, too, and I happen to like him. I like him a hell of a lot more than I like you right now. You had no right to treat her like that."

"I know." His anger deflated and he was left with the hollowness of guilt.

"She gave you everything she had and you tell her to cover up,"

Dante complained. "No, 'wow, baby, that was one hell of a blow job. You've got the sweetest mouth known to man.' Just 'cover up so no one sees my bitch.'"

Beck's anger was on the rise once more. "Hey, don't you talk about her like that. She's my wife."

"Then why is she crying alone? I checked in on her, and she was crying."

His gut clenched at the thought. She was crying, and he was the bastard who had caused her pain. "I won't ever hurt her like that again. I can't take it back. I can only promise to treat her with respect from this point on."

Dante rolled his eyes. "You are such an idiot. You honestly think that she's upset because you fucked her? She's heartbroken because you fucked her, bonded with her, and then dumped her ass. Seriously, you need to take lessons in how to woo a woman because they don't like it when you use them and walk away. Even I know that."

Beck marched out of the river, shaking the water off his skin. Dante had brought along a towel, and he tossed it toward Beck. Beck wrapped it around his waist. "I didn't dump her. I lost my fucking head. I treated her like a piece of meat. Can you blame her for not wanting to be near me?"

"Oh, cos, that wasn't the problem," the vampire said, bringing the attitude down a notch. "I was watching. Hell, I couldn't take my eyes off it. I think she's more perfect for you than you could have hoped. She enjoyed it."

Beck twisted his hair, trying to get the water out. "That was the bond. I flooded her with it. I pushed myself at her."

"That is your nature," Dante said quietly. "But I think you are underestimating *her* nature. She was happy afterward. She wasn't ashamed. You made her feel that."

Beck pointed an accusatory finger at his cousin. "You don't understand. Maybe vampires treat consorts with such blatant disrespect, but we do not dishonor our bondmates in such a fashion."

"We vampires make damn sure that our lovers are satisfied, and after they're satisfied, we thank them and cuddle them. We find out what they need and give it to them. If what my lover needs runs counter to what society or my father taught me was acceptable, then fuck society." Dante had to talk around his fangs. It let Beck know how

64

irritated his cousin was.

"Don't you talk about my father." His father was always a touchy subject.

"Of course, it all comes back to your father. He was a good man, but he wasn't perfect. He wasn't a perfect king, and he damn sure wasn't a perfect father. He pushed you too hard, and he completely ignored Cian. Cian was supposed to be king, too. He didn't value Cian's input, so he focused all his time on you. No one could live up to his standards. Gods, Beck, when are you going to be who you are and not who he thought you should be?"

"Get out." He would not listen to anyone talk about his father that way. He hadn't been able to save his father, but he could damn sure preserve his memory. "Get the fuck out of here. Go back to your cushy little plane and make all the scandalous news you possibly can. Don't come back. You won't be welcome."

Dante dropped his hands in defeat. "Fine. I'll go, but I'm only going as far as your village. I'll head out and make sure Cian doesn't fade before you can get to him, but you would do well to listen to me. You'll make yourself and that woman you married miserable if you deny who you are."

Dante stalked off, his lanky body disappearing in the tall, thin trees that quaked in the wind.

Beck sank to the ground. It was a long time before he rose, and the whole time he sat wondering if the vampire wasn't right.

* * * *

Meg tried not to feel anything. Cara's small hands smoothed the soft fabric over her shoulders. The gnome had to stand on a chair to reach her. Meg knew she should be helping, but she felt so empty that she allowed the gnome to dress her as she would a doll. She had merely answered the female's softly spoken commands. *Lift your right leg. Lift your left leg. Bow your head so I can get the shirt on.* Cara sang quietly while she worked. Everything the gnome did was soothing, but Meg still felt dead inside.

She was supposed to go with him. How could she do that?

In the mirror, she could see that she was wearing what looked like suede pants, though god only knew what kind of animal had actually given up its skin for them. Her shirt was a bit tight in the chest, so she immediately buttoned the collar up to her throat. It wasn't flattering. It looked much better unbuttoned. Unbuttoned, it showed off a creamy expanse of skin and a faint hint of round breast. It looked rather sexy. But Beck hadn't found the sight of her naked body sexy at all. Cara had wrapped a leather belt around her waist then helped her into a pair of knee-length boots. Her hair was braided and marigolds were woven into it.

All Meg could think about was how she was going to get away.

"Well, look at you," a low voice said. "Fae Barbie."

She shook her head. As upset as she was, the vampire made her smile. He might be the only thing she halfway understood in this strange world. "You have Barbies, too?"

"Oh, yes," Dante confirmed. "My sister filled the house with them. I used to have my soldiers take them hostage. She had to pay me to get them back. It was my first business. The consort Barbies come with bite marks on their necks. I bet yours don't have that."

"No," Meg said and sort of wished Dante had been the one she was tied to. She was bouncing all over the place emotionally, but she couldn't help it. At least he had a sense of humor, and apparently, his plane had things she was used to like running water and indoor toilets.

"Hey." Dante brushed a tear off her cheek. "None of that. It's going to be all right. You'll see."

"I'm sure it will be fine." It would be perfectly fine once she got the hell out of here. Someone would be willing to help her. She didn't buy that no-going-back crap. If she got here, she could get back.

Dante's perceptive eyes narrowed. "Don't run. It won't go well for you. There are things in that forest you can't imagine. Promise me you won't run until you meet Cian. Please, give him a chance to be less of an asshole than Beck has been this afternoon."

"If he's anything like his brother, there's no point." She couldn't help the bitterness in her words.

"But he isn't, sweetheart. That is the point. Cian is the intellectual half. He's also the more romantic half," Dante mused. "It's odd how they split. Beck is all the hard and pragmatic bits. He's all about responsibility and honor, while Cian is playful and instinctive. Sometimes I think Beck got the short end of the stick. Of course, Beck is not the one who lies down from time to time and decides to fade because the world is too much for him. It's all very dramatic, trust me."

Meg huffed and began to pace. "You are seriously telling me that this Cian person isn't really Beck's brother, but the other half of him."

Dante looked thrilled. "Her human brain works! Yes, that is what I'm telling you. Two bodies, one soul." Dante gently touched a finger to her forehead. "You bridge the two right here. They balance through you. You complete them."

"And if I don't want to complete them?"

The vampire smiled sympathetically. "Just meet Cian. You can't begin to understand Beckett until you meet all of him. And he wasn't disappointed in you, sweetheart. He was upset with himself."

"Sure he was." She'd heard that one before. *It's not you, Meg. It's me.*

"He was," Dante said seriously. "He has odd ideas about how a bondmate should be treated. On his plane, a bondmate, especially one of royal blood, expects to be treated like a princess. It took my mom years to relax and learn to take my father in stride. Right now, Beck sees you as a perfect little possession, and he wants to take good care of you. Watch him. You'll see. He won't let you do anything. He'll wait on you hand and foot."

She'd worked since the day she turned fifteen. No one had ever accused her of slacking off. Of course, she hadn't had much of a choice. "I'm not asking him to do that. I'm not a princess."

"I know that. You know that. Teach him. You'll all be happier if you're a fully functioning member of the team rather than a porcelain doll they take down and very gently make love to, but only after asking politely." Dante shuddered as though the thought made him ill. "You are the best thing that could have happened to him. Work on Cian first. He's the openly passionate one. He's the one who never wanted that polite bargain where he loved you from afar because he was worried his passion would be too much for you."

"Beck doesn't love me," Meg said. "He just met me."

"He won't be able to help himself, and neither will you." The vampire picked up a small satchel Cara had filled. He settled it over her shoulder, giving her a sharp slap on the back. It moved her forward a little. "Be careful out there and remember what I told you."

"And just what did you tell my mate, vampire?" Beck's eyes were a glacial gray as he stood in the doorway.

Meg froze, but Dante merely rolled his eyes. "It's always *Dante* or *my cos*, when he wants something. And when he's pissed off he calls me vampire. He says it like it's a bad thing. I'll have you know that vampires are the most advanced of all the races. Come to my plane sometime, sweetheart, and I'll show you. We're launching a mission to test a deep space shuttle. Vamps in space. It's going to be awesome." Dante jauntily slapped his cousin on the back. "See you at the village. I'll give Cian your greeting, but I'll keep my mouth shut about her. It's better if she's a surprise."

The vampire left, and she was alone with Beck. He'd had a shower, or whatever they took here, and now he was clean and so gorgeous it hurt to look at him. His linen shirt was open at the throat. It showed off his rock-hard chest to spectacular advantage. How had she even thought for a second he could want her? She wasn't even in his league.

"Are you ready?" The question was quiet, but as with everything the man said, there was an order in there. He stood looking at her, and Meg heated up, even after everything he'd done.

If he had shown her an ounce of kindness in the arena, she would have been an eager puppy following him without question. She would have written off her previous existence and done everything he asked of her. She was truly pathetic. He'd done her a favor. "Does it matter if I am or not?"

"No. We need to leave now if we're going to make it to the lake before midnight. I want to spend the night there." He held the flap to the tent open and gestured for her to exit.

Meg stepped out and quickly took a step back. "What the hell is that?"

It was monstrous. It looked like a horse, but someone had put it on steroids and dyed it a dark blue. It was so dark that one could mistake it for black, but when the late-afternoon sun hit the thing's coat, there was an unmistakable midnight blue shining there.

Beck ran a strong hand along the beast's back. It was obvious he had a fondness for the enormous animal. Even Beck, as big as he was, would have to haul himself into the saddle. "This is Sweeney. He's a good boy, aren't you? He won't hurt you, love."

Meg forced herself not to soften. He sounded like he had before the events of the arena. She remembered how gentle he had been with her when he'd rubbed her to orgasm. She'd liked that almost as much as what happened later.

But she knew the truth now and was having none of it. Nor was she getting on that horse. "I'll walk, thank you."

She turned on her heels and started down the road. There was no way she was getting on the back of that thing. She might have been born in Texas, but she'd never really left the city. She'd never been on a horse, much less an elephant, and that's what that thing reminded her of. She ignored the odd looks she received as she walked down the lane.

In the distance, she could see the forest ahead. The trees were unbearably thick. Only the road seemed to be clear, as though the forest around it was a living thing, waiting to pounce on anyone who walked into it. That forest would swallow her. She was just about to turn back into town to protest when she felt a strong hand lifting her into the air by the back of her shirt.

"Hey!" Meg screamed in shock as she found herself across Beck's lap. Without thinking about it, she threw her arms around his chest and clung to him, afraid to fall off the beast. It was an awfully long way down, and there wasn't a handy ER around to set whatever would break.

Sweeney huffed and pranced, getting used to the new weight on his back. After a few seconds, Beck made a clicking sound. The horse took off.

"Hold on tight, love," was all he said as he kicked the horse into high gear.

Meg did as he asked, holding on with all her might. The forest loomed large, getting closer every second. Like it or not, she was going into the woods.

# Chapter Six

$M$eg shivered, even though the fire was crackling nicely. Beck had spent the better part of an hour building it. He stoked it until the orange and red flames flared and gave a warm glow to their camp. She was all alone with a complete stranger. Oh, sure, they'd had a couple of sexual encounters, but she didn't know him. She sat back against the trunk of a huge tree and watched the man who had claimed her.

True to what Dante had told her to expect, Beck had let her do absolutely none of the work. He'd helped her off the horse and settled her carefully on her feet. His first task was to make a comfortable place for her to sit. He'd taken two blankets out of his saddle bags to make a nest for her while he gathered wood for the fire.

She removed her boots and pants before wrapping up in the blankets. He was never out of sight. After he started the fire, he'd pulled out bread, some cheese, and what looked like beef jerky. Her stomach rumbled. She decided not to honor her New Year's Resolution to avoid meat and dairy.

Beck hadn't touched a thing until she declared herself full, and then he'd eaten everything she hadn't.

He was such a puzzle to her, sweet one minute and completely shut down the next.

"I need to know something," he said quietly as he sat down across from her.

She nodded, not trusting herself to speak. He was heartbreakingly beautiful by firelight. The glow of the fire delineated the lines of his face. His jaw was carved from granite, but his eyes were soft. He was a real, actual faery prince, and according to him, he was hers. Even after the way he treated her this afternoon, she wanted nothing more than to throw herself into his arms.

She never, ever learned.

"Did you leave a husband behind?" Beck asked. "Do you have babies who will wonder where their mama is?"

All she had to do was say yes. If she said yes, cried prettily, and talked about her sweet babies, he might try to get her home. She could say she had two, a boy and a girl. She could also tell him about the husband she loved more than life itself.

"No," she admitted quietly. "I'm alone."

He seemed confused by the statement and moved to sit beside her. He pulled the blanket up around her. Beck carefully placed his arm around her shoulder. "Did your parents die before they could find a husband for you?"

Meg laughed at the thought. Her parents couldn't be in a room together for more than two minutes before a war broke out. They hadn't attended her wedding, much less tried to advise her on who to marry. "No. My parents divorced when I was twelve. Mom remarried roughly six months later. She married the guy she had been having an affair with. Dad married his secretary, excuse me, administrative assistant, two months after that. Neither one of them wanted to deal with a teenage girl, so I got shuffled around. I'd stay with Mom until she got tired of me, and then I'd get shoved off on Dad. Casey, his ten-years-older-than-me wife, didn't like me very much. They both had new children with their new spouses. Needless to say, everyone was happy when I left for college. So, to answer your question, no, they didn't bother to find me a husband. That's not something parents do in my culture."

Beck's eyes were dark in the firelight. "What is divorce?"

She studied him for a moment to try to figure out if he was pulling her leg. "You don't know?"

He shook his head. "I don't understand your story, love. Your parents did not die? They left each other and formed bonds with other people? They had children with people who were not their mate?"

"You don't have a way to dissolve a marriage?"

71

"No. Why would we have that?" Beck asked, his face showing no signs of teasing. "Marriage is sacred."

"Okay, how about if the husband abuses the wife? Is she supposed to stay in the marriage?" Again, he looked blankly at her. "What if her husband smacks her around? What if he cheats on her with the local floozy? What if he calls her names and is generally unpleasant to be around?"

Beck nodded, finally getting her point. "If this happened in a Fae marriage, then the female would beat the male into submission. If she is too small to beat him properly, one of the larger women of her family would perform the task for her."

"And the man stands there for the beating?" Meg asked incredulously.

"If he has any honor at all," Beck replied with a frown. "If his abuse of the wife continues, the males of her family would take care of him. As I said before, the only way out of a Fae marriage is death, but that can be arranged."

Meg couldn't help but smile. "I kind of wish those rules had been in play when I got married."

Beck turned her to look at him. His lips were down in a scowl, and his eyes pinned her. "They *were* in play when you got married. I assure you, our marriage was properly witnessed. I signed the paperwork with the gnomes before we left."

He'd done what? "Marriage?"

"Yes, what did you think I was doing with you? I told you I needed a bondmate. You're my wife now, and there is no divorce." He said the word as though he found it distasteful.

"I thought you were buying me," Meg stammered, trying to wrap her head around the fact that she had apparently gotten married, and no one had bothered to tell her. She looked at Beck, a bit panicked at the thought. He was her husband? "You know, like a slave."

"You have strange words, wife. I don't know what a slave is, but we're married, and nothing is going to change that." He took a deep breath. "If you are angry with me for what I did today, you have my permission to hit me. It might make you feel better. I can only promise I won't do it again. I was overwhelmed by the battle."

An alarming thought struck her. She wondered if the whole beating thing went both ways. "So if I step out of line, you'll hit me?"

Beck shook his head. "I would never beat you, Meggie. It's different for a man. We're bigger. We could hurt you. I know after what I did to you earlier you must think me a man of no honor, but I would never, never beat my woman. I might put you over my knee if I thought you were stepping out on me, but I would only use my hand."

"You would spank me?" It was supposed to come out as an outraged question. It was supposed to show that she would never put up with such a thing. Instead, it kind of came out as a breathless, curious query. The thought of being put over his knee, completely naked and open, and having that big hand smack her ass was stimulating. She thought about the one time she'd asked Michael to spank her. She had been curious. He'd rolled his eyes and called her a pervert. Beck might think the same thing.

"If I had no other choice, I would spank you," Beck said grimly.

She nodded, trying not to think about how he would trace the line of her spine while she was across his knee, open and vulnerable to him. She turned back to the fire so he wouldn't see how her cheeks were flushed as she thought about how she would wait, anticipating the blow, her pussy getting wet at the thought.

"You talked about marriage and the Fae rules being in play when you got married. What did you mean if you weren't talking about our marriage?" There was suspicion in his voice, like he already knew the answer.

It was an effective way to shut down her arousal. Thinking of Michael Starke immediately made her think of humiliation. Despite his assertion that she was a pervert, humiliation wasn't her thing. "I was married once. We got a divorce."

"He allowed you to get away from him?"

She laughed, but it was a bitter sound. "He packed my bags and shoved me to the street. He literally did that. He needed me out of the apartment before his new girlfriend showed up. She was a nurse. She made more money than I did, so she could take better care of him than I could."

"What?" Beck was on his feet, his hand rubbing his head as he paced. "He forced you to support him? What kind of a man was he?"

The truth was she was tired of being pissed off about the divorce. Somehow the events of the last twenty-four hours made her rage at a marriage gone bad seem a small thing. Beck's whole life had been destroyed. At least Michael had the good sense to divorce her before they had kids. It had been a mistake, and it was past time to move on. "He was a young man. We were really young when we got married. I was only twenty-two. I was twenty-five when we divorced two years ago. We were stupid kids trying to be grownups. I wanted a family. He wanted to play Xbox and drink beer. It's a typical American story."

Beck's hair was long and flowed around his shoulders and down his back. He'd taken it down after he'd gotten the fire going. It had been an oddly erotic moment. His eyes had been on her, and she'd watched as he brushed it out. Now, it was a silken blanket around his body.

It was also a fire hazard. She held out her hand. "It was a long time ago, Beck, and in a galaxy far, far away. Please come back over here. I don't want to have to put out your hair when it catches on fire."

He looked back and seemed surprised that he hadn't caught that himself. He sat down. When she held open the blanket for him, he moved close and wrapped it around the both of them.

"Sorry, love," he whispered. "I can't imagine anyone letting you get away."

"You must have a very small imagination," she said solemnly.

"I am not known for my creativity." Beck frowned and stared at the fire.

Meg laughed. "I was teasing you. You take things too literally. Don't give my ex another thought. I don't intend to. He was an asshole."

Dark eyebrows drew together. "You sound so much like Dante. Are you sure you're not from the Vampire plane? They are entirely obsessed with anuses, too. I don't understand it."

She giggled and let her head drop to his shoulder. She would have immediately brought it back up, but his hand was there, smoothing her hair back, holding her close. His arms went around her. He was so warm. She gave in and snuggled closer. He was a furnace.

"I would like very much to make love to you, Meggie," Beck said, his voice low and painstakingly gentle. The hand in her hair was gentle, too, unlike the way he'd fisted her hair in the arena. He touched her like she was made of glass.

"How very polite." She thought about what Dante had said. She didn't want a polite bargain. She wanted his passion.

It didn't matter. She would be gone in a day or two. She hadn't changed her mind about that. Even though he promised not to treat her the way he had before, she knew it was inevitable that he would.

Before all of this happened, she'd been giving an enormous amount of thought to her sex life. It had been pointless and futile up until now. The two men she had gone to bed with before marrying Michael had been utterly boring, and she'd just wanted to get it over with. Michael had been the same way. It was why she'd started exploring Dominance and submission in the first place. She hadn't gotten past the Internet, but she'd ordered some books on the subject and she'd planned to meet some people in the lifestyle.

Being out in the arena with Beck had been a revelation. It was the single most erotic experience of her life, and he rejected her afterward. He thought she was just as much a pervert as Michael did, and she refused to be trapped in another marriage where her husband didn't truly want her. But she was stuck for now. Why not enjoy what he could give her? She had just taken her birth control shot before she'd gotten kidnapped. Why not enjoy a little sex? Even if it wasn't as mind-blowing as before, it would be better than anything she'd had on the Earth plane. She would have to make sure she came off as vanilla as possible so he didn't get angry with her again.

She let her hand find his sculpted chest. "All right."

He sighed, and she felt that strange connection between them open slightly. It tingled there on the edges of her consciousness, and she opened eagerly to it. She could feel his arousal. She could feel how much he wanted her. It made her feel special and desirable.

He closed it down immediately.

"Sorry." He eased her onto her back. "I have to get used to the bond. It's particularly strong when we make love. I promise I won't flood you with it again."

"I didn't mind," she said as he touched her lips with his. It was a gentle touch, a light melding of lips. She found it slightly frustrating.

"Of course you did," he murmured as he kissed her, a little harder this time.

He pressed his mouth over hers. His tongue requested access. She allowed herself to soften beneath him, and his tongue lazily plunged in. He explored her mouth, mating his tongue to hers, devouring her softly. His hands gently framed her face as he stroked her hair.

She shuddered with pleasure as he moved from her mouth to her neck. He was so big against her. He tried to keep his weight off her, but she wanted to be crushed under it. She wanted him to hold her down or tie her up. She couldn't ask him to do that. He would probably turn away from her in disgust, but she wanted it so badly. "I'm cold. Won't you cover me? I might be warm if you lay on top of me."

He wasn't able to completely close off the surge of desire her request brought out in him. He wanted to be on top of her. He wanted her helpless underneath him. She felt it briefly before he shut it off. "You don't think I'm too big for you? I don't want you cold. Let me get undressed first."

He got out from under the covers and quickly shucked his clothes. She watched, her mouth watering, as his big, strong body was revealed by firelight. He was all steel and smooth muscles. The wounds he had taken in the arena had closed and were healing. His body, he'd explained earlier, could take a lot of damage and repaired itself quickly. The slight pinkness of the healing flesh didn't detract from his perfection. He was a work of art. Michelangelo would have been proud to sculpt that body. And then there was his cock. She had more time to study it now that he wasn't shoving it at her face. It was big and thick, and pointing straight up, reaching his belly button. His balls were heavy and taut against his body. Even in the firelight, she could tell his cock was so hard it was purple.

How had that ever fit in her mouth? That dark voice from her fantasies reminded her. That monster cock had fit because Beck had made sure it fit. He'd shoved and pushed until she'd accommodated him.

"Let me help you." He knelt down and reached for the hem of her shirt.

The linen shirt was all she was wearing. It was the only protection she had. If he ordered her to take it off, she would throw the damn thing into the fire. He didn't, and she was reluctant. He'd seemed to like her body before, but the arena had changed that.

He pulled the shirt over her head, and she fought not to cover herself. She sought that connection between the two of them. It would tell her what he was feeling. Now that she'd had that connection with him, being without it made her feel alone. She tried to brush her thoughts against his, requesting the contact.

76

"Shhh," he whispered, getting under the covers with her. He pulled her into his arms. "Don't be scared, love. I won't hurt you. I'll be gentle."

She gritted her teeth. He'd gotten the message, but he wasn't very literate yet. He thought she was afraid, not frustrated and nervous.

"Just kiss me." She could lose herself in his kisses. The man knew how to kiss.

He smiled, his generous lips tugging up before he planted them on her. He kissed her as he covered her with his hard body. They met, skin to skin. She loved the way he pressed her into the ground. It wasn't the most comfortable she'd ever been, but something about being held down did it for her. She let her hands drift above her head and imagined he had tied them down.

"You are so beautiful," he whispered as he left her mouth. His hands traveled down her torso, making her skin sing wherever he touched her. "I want to kiss you everywhere. May I?"

"If you like."

He nodded and kissed his way to her breasts. The kisses were gentle, like butterflies landing and taking off again. He took one nipple in his mouth and curled his tongue around it. He drew on the bud, sucking and playing with it. She bit back a moan. Even though it wasn't as rough as she liked it, it still felt good. It felt fantastic. Beck plucked at her other nipple with his fingers. Meg imagined that he had placed her in nipple clamps. He would tighten them to the point of pain, and then his eyes would heat as he looked at her, trussed up and gilded for his pleasure. She would be his plaything.

His hand left her nipple, traveling down toward her pussy. He slid a finger through her labia. His head came up in surprise as he found the folds of her pussy already slick.

"You're wet." His fingers slid all around her pussy, delving deep and then shallow, as though he couldn't quite believe what he was feeling. "You're soaking wet."

She felt her face flush. She tried to pull away. She was sure he would take it as proof of her wantonness. "Sorry."

He put his hand around her throat to stop her from squirming, and she felt a fresh rush of arousal spark through her. His hand was still moist from her pussy as he circled her neck. He couldn't know what his hand collaring her neck did for her. He would be shocked if he did.

"You still want me." It seemed to break something in him, and he kissed her harder than before. He was still careful, but he seemed less tentative.

She could feel his iron-willed control. He was using it to hold himself back. She wanted to beg him to let go, to use that will on her. She would like it. She craved it. But she held her tongue, knowing he wouldn't welcome that part of her.

Then she wasn't thinking at all as his hand trailed back down, and he started to rub circles around her clitoris.

"Tell me you want me," he ordered.

Her body tightened at the masculine will in his voice. "I want you. Please."

"Yes, wife, I will please you," he promised as he disappeared under the blankets. He forced her legs apart, spreading her and placing himself between her thighs.

When his tongue replaced his fingers on her clit, she fought not to scream. His tongue slid all over her pussy, lapping and sucking and nibbling. He ate her like he was enjoying a rich dessert. She held her hands tight over her head and pretended he'd tied her ankles down, too. She imagined she was completely at his mercy, and he had none. He licked from her clit to her pussy then plunged his tongue in. He moaned as though he loved her taste and couldn't get enough of her. He fucked her with his tongue. Meg pressed against him as he firmly stroked her clit with his thumb. She went flying, keeping her mind open so that she knew he felt her orgasm.

He reared up, the blanket he'd pulled over them falling to the side. He got on his knees and purposefully slid his cock over her soaking pussy, moistening it. He pulled down on her hips, slamming her onto his pulsating cock.

Meg nearly screamed. It felt so good to be impaled on him. Nothing in her life felt as good as Beck ramming his cock into her pussy. He looked down at her with stark eyes. His face was savage in the fire's glow, and though she had just come, she felt it build again as he pounded into her.

He was so big inside her, she felt like she might split in two, but it was a good pain. She wrapped her legs around his waist, trying to tempt him deeper. She hadn't taken all of him yet. He stared down at the place where his cock met her pussy.

"It's beautiful," he muttered as he watched himself fuck her. "You're beautiful."

She felt beautiful. She let her hands trail down his strong back to his muscular buttocks and let her nails dig in lightly. She wanted all of him.

"You open up for me." He spread her legs further and shoved that last inch in.

She'd never been so full. This was connection. This was what she'd missed all of her life.

He leaned forward so his pelvic bone ground against her clitoris as he swiveled his hips and panted. His long, dark hair flowed all around her. It tickled her skin, making her feel like he was touching her in a hundred spots. Then only one spot mattered as he pushed himself deep.

This time Meg didn't hold back her moans. She groaned as he stiffened above her. She could feel his cock pulsing deep inside her. The orgasm rolled across her, leaving her trembling as he fell forward against her body.

She wrapped her arms around him. She could feel his heart beating against her breast. He nuzzled her neck. His cock was still inside her, and if she could sleep that way, she would. He was everywhere, all around her. She'd never felt so safe.

He rolled off her, and a wave of disappointment flooded her. It was coming from him.

"I lost my head at the end." He spoke through clenched teeth. "I'm sorry. It won't happen again. I know I keep saying that, but I mean it. Did I hurt you?"

Meg turned her back to him, so he wouldn't see her face.

"I liked it," she said hollowly. She had until he opened his damn mouth again. "I'm not some fragile thing. I won't break. I liked it, especially at the end."

He sighed and put a hand on her hip. "No, you didn't. You're just trying to be a good wife. I'll be more careful next time."

"Sure."

There wasn't going to be a next time. The sex was incredible, but it wasn't worth the way he made her feel afterward. She thought what they shared was beautiful, and he kept making it something to be ashamed of.

He pulled her close, wrapping his thick arms around her body. He threw a leg over hers. She found herself thoroughly trapped in his embrace. She tried to pull away.

"Stay still," he ordered quietly. "It's cold. I'll keep you warm."

"And if I don't want to be warm?" She squirmed against him.

"Then I'll keep you warm anyway," he said, his voice rough with command.

He was so frustrating. He was the essence of the dominant male. It was in everything he did. Why did he deny it? She settled down. There was no way she was getting away from him tonight. He set his face against the nape of her neck. His warmth was so sweet. She found herself pulled in again.

She was leaving in the morning. He'd explained that he would get up and go find them some breakfast. While he was hunting, she would leave. Dante was wrong. It wasn't up to her to train him. It wasn't up to her to teach him that it wasn't wrong to love the way he wanted to. He wouldn't listen, and she would end up hating him and herself.

She would leave, and he would find a more proper bondmate.

"Good night, love," he whispered in her ear.

She was silent because good night was good-bye, and she couldn't say the words.

# Chapter Seven

Meg woke the minute he left the small bed they slept in. She'd felt him disentangle himself and missed the heat of his body. He had draped himself around her all through the night, tangling their limbs together. She'd never slept so well in her life.

She remained still, listening as he dressed, rebuilt their fire, and prepared to hunt for their breakfast. He leaned over and kissed her softly before he stalked off to find food.

She forced herself to count to one hundred before getting up and tossing on her clothes. She pulled on the boots last and then retrieved the saddlebag Dante had given her the day before. There was food and a canteen, and what looked like a first aid kit. He'd also slipped his business card in. It declared him Head of the Green Sales Unit. She shook her head. Used car salesman to the core. There were a few other things she didn't recognize, but she threw the bag over her shoulder and wondered which way to go. She decided on south, since she could make it back to the market. Perhaps there would be someone on the road who would help her.

As she began to walk, she wondered how Beck would take her leaving. Her heart hurt when she thought of him. How could she get so close to someone in so little time? He was a heartbreak waiting to happen. He couldn't accept himself. How was he ever going to accept her? The endless forest seemed to fly by as she walked briskly, unable to get her mind off the faery prince.

He was a victim of his own success. He had proven to her, once and for all, what she wanted in a relationship. Then he'd turned around and told her he wouldn't give it to her. She'd suspected for a while that she preferred to be submissive during sex. She wasn't sure how she felt about submission outside of the bedroom, and that was the reality that gave her pause when she contemplated jumping into the lifestyle. It was probably asking far too much to get what she wanted in the bedroom and still remain autonomous outside of it.

She'd been walking for a good half an hour when she felt the panic attack threatening her. She couldn't find the path. This wasn't the one they'd taken the day before, and it seemed to get narrower and narrower. She squinted, trying to see ahead. Did it stop?

What the hell was she doing? Her blood pressure was rising. She could feel her heart beating a hundred miles a minute. She was lost. She turned, but everywhere she looked was exactly the same. Hadn't she passed that tree before? She was sure she had. It leaned the same way as the other one. Which way was she supposed to go?

Hadn't Dante told her the woods were dangerous? She'd thought he was exaggerating to make her stay close to Beck, but now she felt real fear.

Oh, why had she ever left the comfort of their bed?

It was stupid decisions like this that always got her in trouble. She was impetuous. She got lost at DFW airport, but she thought she could navigate on an entirely different plane of existence? She should have waited until she made it to a village. Maybe there, she could have hired a guide or something. What the hell was she doing walking through the woods alone?

"Can I help you, miss?"

Meg started and spun on her heels. She barely missed clocking the little man with her twirling bag. She ended up on her ass in the dirt, looking up at the strangest thing she had ever seen. Given her recent travails, that was saying something.

He was small, no more than four feet tall, with a stocky body. He was barrel-chested with squat legs. His torso was the longest part of him. His face was dominated by a large, doughy nose, and his skin had splotches of yellow across it. He seriously needed to get his liver checked.

The suit was the most disconcerting thing about him, though. It was a brilliant, vibrant red. From the top hat on his head to the socks and shoes on his small feet, every piece of clothing he wore was red. The man brushed invisible lint off his coat and shook the tails out. They trailed along the dirt. He looked down at her and waited for a response.

"I'm lost," was the only thing she could think to say.

The red man cocked a bushy eyebrow. His accent was even heavier than Beck's. "Are you, now? And here I was thinking you were out for a pleasant walk in the woods."

She shook her head. "I need to get back to the marketplace."

The red man frowned. "And why would you need to do that? See, I was thinking a girl like you would prefer to go home to the Earth plane."

On that announcement, the red man turned and began walking down the path. She scrambled to her feet to chase after him. Could he really get her home?

Did she want to go home?

"How did you know that?" she asked breathlessly.

He winked a dark eye her way. "I know everything, little human. I know you couldn't possibly want to stay here. Your home is waiting for you."

"Yes." Even though he was a good foot and several inches shorter than her, he moved quickly. She had to jog to keep up with the little man. "I was taken from my home, and then they sold me at some tournament thingy and apparently now I'm married, but I didn't say 'I do,' so I don't think I am. I just want to get home."

That was the right answer. Yes, she should hurry. She needed to get home to her fantastic life on the Earth plane. She needed to get back to work, so she could go back to her dreary apartment at the end of a long day and microwave something she didn't want to eat and watch television. She didn't want to stay and explore this strange place. She didn't want to give that gorgeous hunk of a man a chance. She certainly didn't want to meet the other, possibly even hotter, half of him. No, she wanted to go back to a place that probably wouldn't even realize she'd been gone.

She was an idiot.

Meg stopped in the middle of the trail. A vision of Beck swamped her senses, and she was stunned by how much she felt for him. She was walking away from Beck after a day?

Everything crystallized as she stood in the middle of a faery forest. She shook her head. She was in the middle of a freaking faery forest! All of her life, she'd daydreamed and read fantasy novels and done anything she could to escape reality. In her daydreams and the stories she wrote that she never let anyone read, she was a different person. She was a confident, lovable woman who faced challenges head on.

Maybe it was time to be the person she always wanted to be.

She'd waited for this all of her life, and now she was running away?

"Come along, miss." The red man looked at her curiously. "Well, what are you waiting for? I can get you home."

She shook her head. Her decision was made. "I changed my mind. I don't want to go home. Honestly, my life there kind of sucked. Maybe life here will suck, too, but shouldn't I give it a chance? When you think about it, it's kind of cool. I mean, I have seen more weird-ass shit in the last twenty-four hours than most people see in a lifetime. Vampires! How freaking cool is that? They have their own plane and apparently are just as interested in their stock portfolios as they are in blood. And gnomes! Sure, they didn't actually have any travel tips for me, so they weren't like the ones at home, but the ones at home are ceramic. They aren't half as awesome as the ones here. And the *sidhe*." Meg sighed. "I think I care about him. He needs me. I can't walk away."

"So you don't want to go home?"

Meg rolled her eyes. "Screw my home. Somewhere out there is this superhot faery. He paid a lot of money for me. My ex-husband never took me to any place nicer than a Chili's because he was a cheap ass. Beck already spent more on me than any man ever has, and then he had to do the *Fight Club* thing. No one ever fought for me before. Sure, he was kind of a dickhead afterward, but I think I can work on that problem. And I haven't even met his other half. I think they're identical. Twins should be identical, right? Even if they aren't, even if he's unattractive, I'll be okay with it because Cian is a part of Beck. If I care about one, then I have to accept the other. Right?"

The red man took a deep breath. "You're a strange girl. You speak faster than my ears work. Are you saying you no longer wish to return to your own plane?"

"Yes. I'm going to give this marriage thing another shot.

Apparently, if it doesn't work out, murder is always an option. Beck promised me."

"Well, that throws a different light on the thing, then," the red man muttered.

"What?" Meg wasn't sure she'd caught that last part. The small man didn't make sense.

His face was jovial as he looked up, as though all his consternation had floated away. "Nothing, dear, nothing at all. I think it's marvelous that you've decided to give the king another chance. Love is more important than any other consideration. I know how to get you back to your husband, dearie."

He started down the path again. Meg followed eagerly. It would be best if she could get back before Beck realized she was gone. She would get back to camp and throw off her clothes. When Beck showed up, she would tempt him back into bed where she intended to prove to him they were perfect together.

"How do you know all this stuff?" She hadn't mentioned that her husband was the king. She followed the red man off the path and could hear water flowing somewhere close by. Maybe she hadn't gotten so far. They had followed a river last night to get to their campsite by the lake. She must be getting close.

"I know everything, dearie," the man stated plainly. "It's all a part of who I am."

Before she could continue the line of questioning, she was halted by a sight so beautiful it took her breath away.

They had crested a small hill and the river came into view. There was an early morning mist floating off the water giving everything a hazy, soft feel. Standing gracefully in the shallows was the most elegant horse she'd ever seen. It was pure white and gave off a sheen of sweetness and innocence as it leaned down and drank.

Magic. This whole place was magic. How could she have ever thought about leaving?

"It's so beautiful." She spoke in hushed tones, not wanting to scare it off.

"She's magic, dear," the red man explained. "She roams the forest and aids travelers in getting to their destination."

She searched her brain, trying to remember the one class she had taken in lore. It had mostly been about the Greek and Roman gods, but there had been a small section on Irish folklore. She might have skipped that day. Her penchant for urban fantasy and romance novels were the only reason she knew what a *sidhe* was.

"She'll take me to Beck?"

There was an odd light in the red man's eyes. "Yes, dearie. She'll take you to your husband." He noted her hesitation and shrugged. "Or you can walk aimlessly through the woods and never find him. These woods are enchanted. If you don't know your way around them, you could be lost forever. Your husband will wander the woods, seeking you. It happens all the time."

The red man looked like he couldn't care less what she did. Time was running out. She'd decided to take a chance on Beck, so it only followed she could take another. "All right. How do I get back to him?"

The red man was already retreating. "She will tell you." Meg turned and the red man was completely gone. His voice still echoed through the trees. "Just let her lead you home."

A shiver passed through her, but there was nothing else to do but take the chance. She started toward the river anyway. The horse turned her head toward the interloper, and for a moment Meg worried that she would startle it away. Then the gentle eyes looked right through her, and she felt as if the horse could see to her soul. Now that she was close, she could see that there were flowers woven into the mare's mane. The mare had obviously been swimming in the river because the mane was dripping with pure river water.

Feeling more comfortable, she stepped closer. The horse's eyes seemed luminous in the early morning light. It felt like a magical moment when she held her hand out and gently brushed the horse. She was surprised to find the skin cold. There was no warmth in the flesh, but perhaps she was being fanciful. Of course, if the horse had been wading through the river, it followed that her skin would be cold.

The horse snickered, a welcoming sound. She shook her head and gracefully leaned down, as though inviting Meg to mount her.

"Okay, but I gotta warn you, I'm not good at this." The horse shook her mane. Suddenly, Meg knew the horse wanted her to haul herself up this way. "I hope this doesn't hurt."

She wrapped her fingers in the mane, noting the flowers seemed to be attached to weeds in some places. She managed to get her leg over the horse's back and was pleased when she got into an upright position.

"Piece of cake," she muttered to herself. Her hands were shaking as she tried to pull them out of the mane to get a better hold. "Take me back to my husband."

Her hands seemed stuck in the coarse hairs. She pulled, but they didn't budge. She tried to shift her legs. They held fast to the horse's flesh.

The horse snickered. This time it sounded less gentle, more triumphant, and not in a good way. The horse's eyes narrowed and became somewhat cruel.

"Oh, shit." Something had gone very wrong.

The horse reared up and took off at a gallop. Meg flew with her and then screamed as the horse plunged them both into the deepest part of the river. She felt the horse stiffen as something hit it, but it didn't matter.

Meg's scream was cut off as water began to fill her lungs.

\* \* \* \*

Beck panicked when he realized she had run. She'd done it. She'd left him. His heart started to pound. The anger would come later. Now he was overcome with fear. These woods were dangerous. What had he been thinking, bringing her through here without a proper escort? But then, he couldn't afford a proper escort. Damn him, he shouldn't have purchased a wife he couldn't properly take care of. She was going to die here, and then he would lie down beside his brother and allow himself to fade.

Maybe that was what he should have done in the first place.

*Stop it.* This was no time for doubt or pity. If he was going to save his wayward wife, he needed to think clearly. *Find her trail.*

It wasn't hard. His woman didn't have any idea how to hide it. Her boot prints were plain in the dirt path. He tossed his bow and quiver over his shoulder. He was fully armed. He had the sword on his back and some knives placed in various sheaths across his body. He tossed aside the two rabbits he'd killed for breakfast. His appetite was completely gone. All that mattered was finding Meg before something else found her.

As Beck began to jog down the trail, he watched for signs of her, but his mind was caught in a punishing trap.

She'd run because he had been too rough with her. She'd given him a second chance after he'd treated her horribly in the arena, and what had he done? He'd spread her legs painfully wide and shoved into her as hard and long as he could. He'd covered her with his heavy body and forced her to take all of him. She was so small, yet he'd pushed himself in, all the way to his balls. It had probably hurt. She'd said she liked it, but he knew the truth.

He'd known that his compulsions were perverse since he was sixteen years old. He'd had a strong, overwhelming sex drive from the moment he hit manhood. He'd tried to hide it from everyone except his brother, who matched him. Cian didn't seem to need the same things he did, though. Cian could be gentle and sweet with a woman. Beck needed to bend her to his will. It was his obsession. He'd thought he'd found a good match in one of his mother's handmaids. She'd been a few years older than him and hadn't seem to mind when he ordered her to take his cock in her mouth or spread her legs so he could look at her pussy. She seemed to like it. His father had found them just as Beck was discovering the joys of shoving his cock up her tight ass.

His father had beaten him with the flat of his sword. Then he sat Beck down to explain a few things to him.

According to his father, the maid had gone along with him because he was a prince. He had power over her, and she feared him. Women were fragile creatures. They required gentleness. Anything else was monstrous. If they said they liked his rough ways, they were lying to gain his favor. His father had explained that if he treated his bondmate this way, she would leave both him and Cian, and he would bring great shame to his family.

Beck had been solemn and careful around Maris. There had been no sex at all with her, and sexual contact wouldn't be allowed until they bonded. He vowed to treat her with honor and to never let her know about the beast inside him.

Why couldn't he do the same with Meggie? His heart was sick. He cared about her. He'd seen deep to her soul. He knew that he could never have cared for Maris the way he did Meg. No matter what anyone said, bondmates weren't interchangeable.

Meggie was soft and vulnerable, despite that tart tongue of hers. She wanted to please him. He had to be a man and show her that she didn't need to. She hadn't been born into Fae society. She didn't know about the sacred contract between a bondmate and her husband. It would be easy to take what she was offering. She would never know the difference, but it wouldn't be honorable.

She'd left the trail here. He could see that she had almost walked a complete circle. Maybe she was back at camp, having learned that the woods were tricky. Maybe she was waiting for him.

He would be gentle with her. He wouldn't let his rage at her defiance show. He damn sure wouldn't do what he wanted to. He wanted to pull those pants down, spank her bare ass red, and then fuck her until she begged him to stop. He wanted to imprint himself on her so strongly she would never run from him again.

He had almost made it to the hill above the river when he felt her. He felt her terror before he heard the scream. It flooded his body, causing his heart to pound and his soul to ache. She was so scared, and she instinctively reached across the distance to find him. The bow was in his hand as he crested the hill. In one smooth move, he pulled and notched an arrow. He was aiming before he even knew what threatened her.

A kelpie. A fucking kelpie had Meggie. She was on the kelpie's back, and it was already taking off. Her scream echoed through the forest. That sound would haunt him forever. He let the arrow fly, hoping to hit the heart before the horse got away with his wife. Beck heard the thud of the arrow striking flesh, but it didn't slow the damn thing down. The horse plunged into the icy river and Meg disappeared.

Her panic threatened to take over his mind. He did the only thing he could do. He forcefully cut the connection between them. He couldn't do what he needed to do if he was overwhelmed with her fear. Beck rushed out into the river, cursing the cold. He took three deep, long breaths to fill his lungs, pulled out a cold iron knife, and dove after them.

The river was clear and the early morning light illuminated the scene. The kelpie had gone deep. She was sitting patiently at the bottom of the river among the thick reeds that swayed with the current. It would be a peaceful scene except for the woman struggling to survive. She couldn't. The horse would hold her in place until the river took her life. When she was dead, the kelpie would release her and devour her. If Beck hadn't found her, all he would have been left with was her heart. The kelpies never ate the hearts of their victims.

Meg was still struggling, but he could tell she was already failing. Her eyes flared as she saw him swimming. She tried so hard to push her body toward his, as though in her last moments, she needed to get as close to him as possible. He swam straight to her and took her head in his hands. He kissed her, forcing the air he'd held in his mouth down to her lungs. It wasn't much, but he needed every minute if he was going to save her.

He tried to cut through the coarse hairs that held her hands to the kelpie. The horse was having none of that. She kicked out, trying to catch him with her powerful legs. He didn't dare touch the mane with his own hands, lest he get as trapped as his wife.

The horse caught him in the chest. He flew back in the water, all the air blowing from his lungs. He floated helplessly up to the surface. His mouth opened instinctively. He dragged air into his chest. The knife was still in his hands. He'd managed to hold onto it.

*How long had she been under? How long could a human go without breath in her body?*

She wasn't Fae. Her small body was more fragile. Goddess, he was going to lose her. Beck breathed in one last time and dove again.

This time Meg was slumped over. She moved as the current moved, and her beautiful hair swayed with the reeds. Beck refused to give up. He went straight for the monster who was trying to take his woman. Beck avoided the strong, kicking legs of the kelpie and savagely went straight for its throat. He didn't even try to keep his hands clear. He forcefully planted his left hand in the horse's mane. It stuck immediately. He couldn't move it, but it served as an anchor. If he couldn't kill the fucker, he would go down with Meg. He would die as close to his mate as possible.

With a sort of savage glee, Beck shoved the blade he held in his right hand deeply into the horse's throat. The kelpie, unable to kick him at this angle, tried to use her teeth to bite. Beck dodged her mouth. He used every bit of strength he had left to drag the blade through the kelpie's thick flesh. As the water around him clouded with blood, Beck knew he would kill the monster, but realized it was too late. He felt his consciousness begin to fade. They would die down here. Cian would never know what happened. They were too far from each other. Cian would fade, never knowing why his brother hadn't returned.

Then suddenly his hand was free, and he felt himself beginning to float.

He shook his head as his lungs started to burn and forced himself to move. He had to get a hand on Meg. He pulled at her shirt and started to swim for the surface. He kicked his legs, even though weariness threatened to drag him back down. He used every bit of his will to propel himself and Meg toward the light above.

The sun was warm on his skin when he reached the surface and was finally able to breathe in sweet, clean air. Meg was a deadweight in his arms. He had to get her to land before he could try anything. He swam as fast as his legs would take him. Seeing her skin so blue sparked an adrenaline rush that powered him through the water. When he could touch the bottom, he pulled her small frame into his arms and raced to the shore.

"Please come back," he muttered as he laid her down. He filled his lungs and then opened her mouth. He covered her lips with his, sealing them together, and then pushed the air into her lungs.

Nothing.

He tried again, his heart racing. She couldn't be dead. He would have felt it. He was sure he would have known. But then he'd thrown up barriers. He'd felt like he had to. But if she died alone, he would never forgive himself. She would have died reaching out to him, and he'd coldly closed their bond.

He tried a third time. Suddenly her eyes fluttered, and her whole body convulsed. He quickly turned her over as she threw up the water in her lungs. Her body shook as he pulled her close. He freely opened the connection, letting her feel the relief flooding his body. She started to cry and turned over to clutch at him. Her arms wound around him and she sobbed against his chest.

Beck stroked her hair and rocked with her. He closed his eyes and held her close. She was alive. That was all he could ask for.

# Chapter Eight

Meg was still shivering hours later as she sat in Beck's lap atop Sweeney's great back. Beck had spoken very little. It seemed like a good thing to let him stew at the time, but it had been many miles since he said a word. She was getting tired of the silence.

After the incident with the homicidal water horse, Beck had taken her back to camp and warmed her up. He'd carefully laid her wet clothes by the fire to dry. He cleaned and cooked a couple of rabbits and forced her to eat. He'd lain under the blankets with her until he was satisfied she wouldn't die from the cold. Then he'd given her back the dry clothes and packed up their camp. He'd said all of ten words to her, most of them commands. The silence was becoming unbearable.

She'd done the only thing she knew to do. If she was staying with him, then she needed to start training him. Sure, it usually went the other way. The submissive got trained by the Dom, but she'd decided that her Dom was a dumbass and things would work differently with them. She'd never actually gotten those books she ordered off the Internet, so she was on her own. She would have to let her instincts guide her.

Everything she'd said or done had been consciously submissive. She'd given in to her urge and let herself cuddle up against him. Even while riding, she held on to his waist and buried her face in the curve of his neck. He probably didn't notice it, but he relaxed when she clung to him. He preferred to be in physical contact with her.

Meg had watched from her cozy place as the forest gave way to what looked like an endless field. Still, Beck was silent.

"Are we almost home?" Meg asked, looking up at him.

"Almost," he replied stoically.

Another moment passed and she couldn't take anymore, but she had to tread carefully.

"I'm sorry." She nuzzled against his neck. She absolutely loved the smell of him. "Are you ever going to forgive me?"

His eyes were serious as he looked down at her, but he didn't move away.

"It hasn't been very long, love. My bones are still cold from jumping in the river after you. Perhaps you should let me warm up before we start talking about forgiveness." He sighed and rubbed her back soothingly. "I don't blame you. I should have known you would run."

"I wasn't running," she protested. Beck's eyebrows arched skeptically. "Okay, so I was at first. Then I realized that I want to give this thing a chance. We really do have a connection, and I want to explore that. I know you won't believe it, but I was trying to get back to you. I got lost."

"Of course you got lost," Beck said with a frown. "You don't know your way around the forest. You could have been killed. You almost were."

She smiled up at him. "You saved me."

"Barely."

She thought about the strange little man in his red suit. She shivered now as she considered the fact that he'd told her to get on the kelpie and ride. "Are those kelpie things common here?"

Beck shook his head. "No, but they are very famous."

"So anyone who lives here would know not to ride one." She was starting to believe that little red man had it out for her.

"This is what we refer to as a neutral plane. That means there wasn't a civilization here when we found it. Fae creatures have wandered off and on the place for centuries. Some stayed. I suppose there are plenty of beings on the plane that might not understand what a kelpie is."

"So he might not have known." He might have been confused. She had a hard time believing that. He'd seemed to know the forest very well.

"Who might not have known?" Beck's voice had gone positively glacial. "Did you meet someone in the woods?"

She might have been better off keeping her mouth shut. "It was a man, a little man. He seemed old. He said he could take me to my home plane."

Beck stopped the horse and looked down at her, his expression a mask of horror. "You met a Planeswalker? Oh, goddess, Meggie, that was a demon. What did you promise him?"

Meg shook her head vigorously. "Nothing. I told him I wanted to get back to you, and he pointed me to the kelpie. That was a demon? I thought they'd be bigger. I also thought they would have more style. I guess red is kind of their color, though."

Beck let out a long breath of air. "He was a short man, dressed in red from head to toe?" Meg nodded. "It was *Far Darrig*. He's a trickster. It's his mission to trick travelers. He can read your mind, so he knows how to get to you." Clicking his teeth, Beck got the horse moving again. "Don't talk to strangers. I don't want you to be alone until you get used to this place. If you need to go somewhere, you take me or Cian with you."

Beck returned to his silence, his eyes on the road, watching for threats.

"Will you kiss me?" She didn't want to think about all the creatures on this plane that might kill her. She had other things to worry about. She had a husband to train.

"You want me to kiss you?" His voice rose slightly as he asked the question, as though he wasn't sure he'd heard her correctly.

"Yes," she said with as much innocence as she could manage. "I have since the moment I met you. Kiss me, please. It makes me feel safe."

His gray eyes looked slightly mystified, but he bent his head down and softly kissed her lips. Meg held still, letting him control the kiss. It was gentle, tender even, and when he pulled away, he kissed the top of her head as well. He settled his cloak around her shoulders, surrounding her with warmth.

Meg tried pushing her contentment outward. She wasn't sure about how the whole psychic connection worked, but she knew it was there. He needed to know and come to trust that she was happy with him.

When she felt him chuckle deep in his chest, she knew it worked. It was the sound of a man who was satisfied with himself. For some reason, Beck was unsure of his ability to please a woman. His instincts were all screwed up. Something had happened to make him doubt himself and turn his back on his true nature. She had to smash that wall down if they were going to be happy. She would use their connection to do it. She drowsed, happily thinking of all the ways she intended to get past his barriers.

* * * *

"Wake up, love." His voice pulled her from her nap.

Meg tried to sit up and realized that Sweeney had stopped moving.

"Well, finally," a familiar voice said from below her. Meg rubbed her eyes and saw Dante standing with crossed arms, looking up at them. He looked haggard and tired. "It took you forever. I expected you late this morning."

"Meg decided to take a ride on a kelpie," Beck replied sardonically. "It caused me to push back my schedule."

Dante's green eyes were wide and his mouth dropped open. He was utterly fangless now.

"Seriously?" He turned to Meg. "What the hell were you thinking? Kelpies like to eat people."

She stiffened at the thought of what might have happened. "It was going to eat me? You didn't tell me it was planning on eating me."

"Well, it wasn't inviting you to tea," Beck replied as he handed her down to the vampire. Dante set her squarely on her feet. "It was a close thing. The kelpie took her deep. I had to slit its throat before it would let her go. I damn near drowned myself."

"That explains it." Dante rubbed a palm across his forehead. "Early this morning, Cian stopped breathing. It freaked me out. I really thought he was dead this time. He started again after a minute of my frantically shaking him. I was surprised that worked. He's weaker than I thought."

Beck slapped his cousin on the shoulder. "It'll be fine now." He turned to his horse and released the saddle on its back. With an easy strength, he hefted the heavy saddle with one arm and smacked the horse's rump with the other. "Go on now. Go rest." The great beast lumbered off to wherever it went to rest.

"You haven't seen him." Dante rushed after Beck. "He's worse than ever. I don't know if you can bring him back."

She followed the small procession, trying to take in her new home as she hurried to keep up. It looked like a farm out of the shire from *Lord of the Rings,* if the inhabitants had averaged six and a half feet and let everything decay around them.

The front yard was badly in need of attention. There was a small flower garden, but whatever had grown there lost the battle against invading weeds long ago. There was also an odd-looking motorcycle leaning against a fence. The bike proudly boasted a Harley-Davidson logo.

Beck sighed as he looked at the garden, completely ignoring the bike. There was an air of unsurprised disappointment about him. "I suppose the vegetable garden is the same."

"Worse." Dante's boot kicked the dirt where there should have been flowers growing. "Flanna and some girls from the village came and saved what they could. She said she would preserve the vegetables and make jelly from the strawberries, but that was all she could promise."

Beck nodded. "I'll be sure to thank her in the morning. Her family is good to us. We'll need every bit we can salvage if we're going to make it through the winter."

"Damn it, Beck. I can help."

Whatever the vampire was about to say was cut off by Beck's low growl. "I'll provide for my wife."

She slipped her hand into Beck's. It was a good time to continue his training. "I'm sure we'll be fine."

She wasn't. She was slightly terrified. The house, or *brugh* as Beck called it, was small, and though solidly built, it had an air of neglect about it. She had more work to do than she could have imagined. She tried to let none of that slip through. She focused on giving off an air of trust and love.

"I promise you won't go hungry," Beck said, stroking her hair. He did it unconsciously now. He hadn't started reaching for her yet, but when she touched him, he pulled her close and seemed to revel in the contact.

Beck sighed and squeezed her shoulders. "I'm going in, love. You stay out here for a moment with Dante. Let me get Cian ready. He'd kill me if I let you see him at his worst."

The door opened and closed behind him. Meg was left alone with a grinning Dante.

"The human learns," Dante snarked.

She rolled her eyes and punched him on the arm. She'd never had an obnoxious brother, but that was what Dante felt like. "I'll have you know I'm highly educated, asshole. I have two degrees. How many do you have?"

"Only the one," Dante allowed. His chest puffed with pride. "I graduated from the most respected business college in America."

"You mean Vampire America." She really wanted to see what America looked like with vamps in control. "What did you major in? Boozing? Partying? Falling asleep in class?"

Dante looked thrilled with her new attitude. "The real Meggie Finn comes to life, thank the gods. I thought you were a little boring there for a while, but I caught the faintest hint of bitch, so I had hope. I merely minored in boozing, though I was excellent at it, thank you. I have a degree in management systems. How about you?"

"English and history," Meg replied, looking out at the barn. It needed a coat of paint, but it seemed solid. There was a pen with what she hoped was sheep in the far field. She wasn't going to presume. After all, the horses here apparently tried to eat people.

Dante snorted. "You studied English? Seriously? You got a degree in a language you already spoke?"

"There's more to it than that." It wasn't the first time she'd had to defend her choice of degrees. "There are novels, and the study of how to write."

"The schools must be different there. I knew how to write in first grade. I guess you're slower. All I know is my parents would never have paid for me to lounge around for four years studying a language I already knew how to speak and reading DLs. Maybe you should have taken a course in how to avoid getting eaten by deadly forest creatures."

She planted her feet and scowled. "It wasn't like there was a sign saying *watch out for woman-eating horses*. How was I supposed to know?"

"You weren't supposed to run," Dante said with a sad shake of his head. "You were supposed to listen to my advice and stick it out with Beck. They didn't teach common sense at your school, did they?"

"I'm not running anymore. I am done with running away. It only gets me into trouble. For your information, I've decided to take your advice and work on Beck."

Leaning against the side of the house, Dante's smile became slightly lascivious. "Have you got him to top you yet, sweetheart?"

Meg returned the smile without a hint of self-consciousness. She was also through with feeling ashamed of the things she wanted. Nearly dying in an icy-cold river trapped by a horse with Super Glue for skin had cured her of that. "Not yet, but I'm working on the problem. So you know something about the type of relationship I want with Beck?"

The vampire shrugged. "Sure. It's common where I come from. You've got to understand, he has his reasons for being afraid of what he needs. You'll have to pull it out of him."

"That might be hard. I have no idea what I'm doing. It's not like I've had a Dom before. I know what I want, but I'm not sure how to get it."

"I can help you with that." He pulled out that ever-present tablet. It apparently had a home inside his jacket. He typed something on the keyboard and flipped it around. The LCD screen flowed as an enormous list of downloadable material on the subject came up.

"Have a problem? We've got a DL to solve it." He let his lanky body slide down to sit in the dirt by the front door. "Sit with me, Meg. We'll see what we can learn."

Meg took a deep breath and stared at the vampire. She decided it was time to make a deal. "I will, but only on one condition."

"I'll bite," Dante said with an ironic grin.

"Later, you have to take me for a ride on that motorcycle." The bike looked cool.

"You got it, sister," Dante agreed.

Meg was satisfied and sank down beside Dante.

\* \* \* \*

Beck walked into the house and swore silently. How he'd managed to live with that slob brother of his for thirty years without killing him was a mystery to Beck. The small living room and kitchen area was cluttered, and it looked like no one had done a single dish since he'd been gone.

"You were supposed to be fading, Ci," he muttered to himself. "Not wrecking the kitchen."

He quickly went around, straightening up what he could so Meg wouldn't take one look at her new home and walk out. She might think the woods were cleaner.

"Beck?" Cian's voice was weak and barely carried out of the bedroom.

"I'm here." He walked through the door and was grateful because the bedroom was far neater than the kitchen. Someone had cleaned up in here. There were neat piles of papers and books stacked around the room. More than likely it had been Dante. Vampires tended to be a bit fastidious. If his cousin had spent the night and this morning sitting at Cian's bedside, he'd probably felt compelled to straighten up a bit.

The room was dim. All the shutters were closed. Beck walked to the two small windows and tossed them open, letting the afternoon light in. It illuminated his twin's self-proclaimed deathbed.

Cian lay on his side. His hair was lackluster, and he'd lost weight. In the light of day, his skin looked pasty. Though he probably hadn't been out of bed much for the better part of two months, he looked tired and haggard. Beck tried to summon some sympathy and found none.

"Get out of bed, ya bastard." Beck kicked the bed. The frame shook, but Cian stubbornly stayed prone.

"No," Cian replied with far more bite than a dying man should have. He pulled the quilt up to his neck and pointedly closed his eyes. "I'm done. It ain't worth it. I can't think anymore. My mind won't work."

"You think you're the only one having trouble?" Beck was tired of listening to his brother's whining. Sometimes Cian forgot he wasn't the only one hurting. "I wanted to kill everything in my path for a while there. I had to stop myself from going into a rage and killing innocent people. You just can't focus."

Cian's gray eyes opened suddenly and burned with resentment. "You can't understand. I can't even read a book anymore. My mind drifts. Sometimes I don't remember where I am. Do you know what it's like to have everything that made you who you are taken away?"

Beck rolled his eyes. "I bloody well do. You're not the only one who's in trouble here."

Cian shook his head and dramatically turned away. It apparently took all his energy. "I don't want to fight anymore. There's no point to it. I haven't the energy. Can't we just get along? It won't be long before I'm gone. I feel it. I feel death coming for me."

"You sound like a bad play," Beck said with an affectionate laugh. Cian had always been overly dramatic. Goddess, it would be good to have his brother back.

A sad sigh came from the figure on the bed. "And you sound like you couldn't care less. I suppose I understand. I haven't been much use to anyone lately. Well, did you have any luck on your hunting trip? Did you catch anything?"

Cian was turned away, and Beck knew he couldn't see his sly smile. "I didn't catch anything to eat, if that's what you're asking."

Beck didn't mention that he'd actually eaten Meg's sweet pussy quite a bit the night before. He didn't think he'd ever get his fill, either.

"Oh, well," came the ho-hum reply. "I wasn't hungry, anyway."

"I didn't really go hunting. I went to market and got us a wife."

Cian sat straight up in bed.

"Yeah, I thought that might get you moving, you lazy bastard."

Cian appeared more animated than Beck had seen him in months. His hand went back to smooth down his hair. "There's a girl here?"

"Meggie's a woman," Beck corrected. "She's all woman, not a girl."

"Meggie." Cian rolled the name around on his tongue as if he were tasting it. He seemed to like the flavor. "How did she escape from Tír na nÒg ? Do you think Torin is hunting her?"

"No, you don't understand." Beck put a single hand on his twin's shoulder, a silent request to calm down. "She's not Fae."

Cian slumped back down. "Oh, I thought you had found us a bondmate. I guess that was a stupid thing to think. Well, I hope she brings you some pleasure in our last days."

"She's a human from the Earth plane, and she is most definitely a proper bondmate. She's also the most beautiful thing in all of the planes," Beck said with confidence. "I already bonded with her and feel spectacular, but if you're not interested, I'll keep her for myself."

Cian was on his feet before Beck could finish. "I need to change clothes."

Beck sniffed and shook his head. "You need a bath before I'll let you anywhere near my own sweet Meggie."

Cian's face turned stubborn. "Our own sweet Meggie."

"Fine, then." It was good to see his brother up and about. He wasn't worried about sharing Meg with him. He'd expected it all of his life. He'd shared everything with Cian. Now he wanted to share a life, a real life, with Cian and Meg. He walked to the dresser and pulled out a pair of clean clothes and a bar of soap. "But I should warn you, she slept with me last night. She might not want you."

Cian huffed. "Well, if she's only had you for company, she'll need a little intelligent conversation. I don't know if you've noticed, but mostly you grunt."

"She doesn't seem to mind the noises I make, if you know what I mean." She didn't. She seemed to have forgiven him for his brutish behavior before. She'd been a sweet bundle of soft femininity in his arms while they traveled home. He'd found the ride a bit rough since he'd been hard the whole time, but he wouldn't have changed it. He liked holding her. After nearly losing her, he found it calmed him to have her close.

Cian tossed off the pants he'd been wearing. "I can't believe you bonded without me."

It wasn't what they had planned. It hadn't been anything close to the traditional ceremony they would have had—nor had it concluded in a full bonding. The guilt of that weighed heavily on him, but he hadn't been able to open himself fully to her. She wouldn't have been able to handle some of the things he'd done. "You would have done the same, little brother. Trust me. Once you've seen her, you'll understand."

Holding the items in one hand, Cian walked through the bedroom to the rear door of the cottage. He looked back at his brother. There was the slightest hint of uncertainty in his eyes. "She's a proper bondmate, then?"

Beck cocked an eyebrow questioningly. "The bond works. I know. It will work with you, too."

"That's not what I meant, brother," Cian said. "I was asking if she's like the other bondmates. Is she anything like Maris?"

He remembered well how Cian felt about their intended. He could barely stand the sight of her. She'd made her preferences clear. She wanted to be queen. She would have preferred to only be married to the warrior half of the king. "Not in the way you mean. Meg is sweet, and she's got quite the mouth on her. She wasn't raised to be a highborn lady, but she deserves no less respect. She's a little scared, too."

Cian's spine straightened. "We'll make sure she's got nothing to be afraid of, then."

"Go, make yourself presentable for our wife. I'll find us something for dinner." Beck was grinning as he changed the sheets on the bed and straightened up the room. Out of the back window, he could see Cian hurrying down the path to the pond. It had been a long, long while since he'd seen his brother move so quickly.

As happy as he was, getting married also brought about a range of problems. He was going to have to figure out a way to bring in some steady income because he didn't want Meg to feel she had to keep the house. She was a bondmate, not a housewife. He made up his mind to talk to Dante. Susan Dellacourt had told him she was always interested in his services. The vampire companies had long-reaching arms and always had some strange security problem clogging up the roads of trade. He might be able to make decent money that way.

In the back of his mind, he knew once word got out that he and Cian had bonded, the loyalists would come calling. They would offer him a lot to lead the attempt to reclaim Tír na nÒg. They would come, and the pressure would be on. He would have a decision to make, and now it didn't seem like a clear one.

Once he would have done anything to get the chance to avenge his father. Was he willing to risk Meg? For the first time since he was seventeen, it seemed that he might have a future. It would be a very different one than he was raised for, but it was his. He could have a good life with Meg and Cian, and eventually their children. All of that could be lost if he gambled on taking back his crown.

Beck shook off the dark thoughts. That was a worry for another day. Today he needed to feed them, and that was all that mattered. He hoped Cian hadn't managed to kill all their chickens while he was busy fading. Beck walked out the back and down to the chicken coop where he selected a particularly healthy hen and proceeded to efficiently chop her head off.

The hen was fat and would make a good meal. The day might have started rough, but if it ended with a full belly and a warm bed, Beck would call it perfect.

# Chapter Nine

The cold water shook the cobwebs out of Cian Finn's mind with a teeth-jarring shock. He took a deep breath and forced himself to go under. The chill prickled along his skin.

He needed to think clearly. He couldn't give in to the chaos.

It had been almost impossible lately. The thoughts in his head would come and go like butterflies flitting in and out. He couldn't catch them and keep them. They were too fast. A thought would come, and he would get excited. He would start to follow through on it, and then he would be standing somewhere wondering exactly how he'd gotten there.

He couldn't talk about it with his brother. Beck had his own problems. He didn't need to worry about his little brother's failing brain, but it was becoming something he couldn't hide. Even if he tried to conceal his problems, he would have forgotten what he was trying to do. It was easier when Beck was around to ground him. When his brother was in close proximity, Cian was able to focus for longer periods of time.

He broke the surface of the water. Where was he? Why was it so cold? Terror threatened to take over. He didn't know where he was. He wasn't in bed. Slow down. He took a deep breath and banished the fear. Fear wouldn't fix the problem. It would only make him look like a fool, and then his father would be angry with him.

He seemed to be swimming.

Where was his sister? Bron liked to swim, but she wasn't allowed to go alone. Since Beck was always training, always following their father, Cian was the one who took their sister swimming. Where was Bron? He was supposed to look after her.

No. He was bathing, and his father was dead. Bronwyn was dead and so was their mother. They had been gone a long time. Uncle Torin had killed them and taken their father's throne. He and Beck were outcasts. Yes, he remembered that part. He wasn't a child anymore. He was a man. He had to act like one.

Cian looked down at the soap in his hand and decided that as long as he was here, he would clean up. He felt grungy. He had taken to his bed and he'd been there a long time. It had seemed like a smart thing to do. The big bed was a familiar place. He always knew where he was. Even if he got lost in memory, the bed was safe. There was always a voice whispering to him that the bed was a nice place to be. It was better than eating or being up and about. He could drift away.

He managed to soap his hair before his mind shifted again, and he forgot what he was supposed to do. By then his body had become used to the chill of the pond. It was a simple thing to float on his back and gaze up at the sky.

The sky above him was a vibrant blue. The puffy white clouds took on various shapes and forms. Some of the damn things reminded him of equations. The shapes could be described mathematically. He'd always wanted to study math. His father had promised him when he turned nineteen that they could go to live with his aunt for a while on the Vampire plane. Beck was going to learn their fighting techniques and make political contacts. Cian was going to the university. He was going to study. It would be marvelous. He couldn't wait to meet other students and talk to professors. He wasn't going to the same school as his cousin, but they would be close. He would be surrounded by books.

And he could get away from the stuffy old court. Someone was always watching him, waiting for him to screw up and break the rules. He wasn't good at following protocols or behaving in a matter befitting a prince of the realm. His father was constantly on him about how much he was embarrassing his brother and his fiancée.

But Cian would be free on the Vampire plane. He could meet some girls who didn't look at him like he was a fool. They wouldn't compare him to his big brother and find him lacking.

What was his father thinking? Maris was a righteous bitch who was cold to everyone she met. How was he ever going to work up the will to fuck her? He didn't think Beck wanted to fuck her, either. They were always so polite to each other. There wasn't an ounce of passion between them. Shouldn't he want to fuck the woman he was going to be forced to spend the rest of his life with?

Oooo, that cloud looked like a squirrel.

"Beckett Finn," a feminine voice called out. "What are you doing? Get out of there. You must be freezing."

Cian twisted his body and let his feet find the bottom of the pond. He saw a blonde female gracefully rushing toward him. She was tall and lithe, with straight golden hair that hung down her back brushing her hips. Her skirts floated around her long legs, showing the faintest hint of a nicely turned ankle. Her face was lovely. She had a pouty mouth and sky-blue eyes. She looked every inch the perfect Seelie lady.

Cian didn't want to fuck her either, but he suddenly remembered that Beck did and had, and probably would again.

"Liadan." He remembered her name. It was good. Maybe he was having a good day. He concentrated and pulled the relevant information out of his brain.

Liadan O'Neill was a young widow. She'd fled Tír na nÓg before the plane had been closed. Her husband had died a few years back in a hunting accident. Beck had been visiting her bed for roughly a year now. He'd hoped Cian and Liadan would get along. Beck liked to share women with Cian, but Cian couldn't stand the sight of her. She was cold. He had no idea why Beck couldn't see how calculating she was.

Her lovely face fell. There was a wealth of disgusted disappointment in her voice, and he remembered she didn't like him, either. They had a mutual disapproval society going. "Where's Beckett? I heard from the trolls that he was back from his hunting trip. They saw him riding in from the forest."

She had placed her hands on her hips, all attempts at ladylike perfection gone. She wouldn't waste the effort on him. She'd mentioned trolls with great distaste. She was a *sidhe* who thought all other Fae creatures were beneath her.

"I don't know." Cian was able to answer with complete truthfulness. For once, his blank mind was a blessing. It did give him a good reason to be down here, though. Beck had been gone and then

105

returned. Big brother had likely taken one look at him and ordered him to bathe.

It explained everything. He could still understand logic. That was good.

"Well, ain't that surprising?" Liadan's perfect features made for a perfect sneer. "You're completely good for nothing. I don't know how your brother puts up with you."

"And I don't see how he can stand to touch you long enough to get off," Cian shot back as he made his way toward the edge of the pond, his feet dragging in the mud. The soap seemed to have floated away.

Why was he here?

"I take care of him just fine." Liadan stood looking at him with one hand on her hip. She seemed supremely sure of her own attractions. "He loves me, you know."

"No, he doesn't." There was no question in his mind about that. If Beck was in love, then it followed that he would be in love, too. Liadan had never understood the link between symbiotic twins. She treated them like completely separate beings when they weren't. If Beck's heart was engaged, then Cian wouldn't be able to help himself. He would fall in love, too. He shook his head. Why had the name Meggie suddenly shot through his brain? He didn't know a Meggie. There wasn't anyone named that in the village. Or was there?

Liadan tossed the towel his way. "You're too stupid to remember. Beck and I are getting married one of these days."

Cian strode out of the pond, wrapped the towel around his waist, and started back up toward the cottage. He still remembered where he lived, at least. He didn't pick up the clothes he had brought with him. They didn't matter. "No, you're not. He won't marry you. You aren't a bondmate."

Liadan kept pace. "He loves me, and there are no more bondmates to be had. He needs to marry. He needs to have children. You know it's true. He is too important to languish out here in this piss-poor excuse for a plane. He's let you hold him back far too long."

Cian's heart ached at the thought of children. He'd thought he'd have a few by now. He loved children, and they always loved him. He'd started a small school when he and Beck had settled in this village. It hadn't taken long before an entire community of immigrant Fae had built up around the former heirs. They had brought their children with them or adopted the orphans they found along the way. Those children needed to be educated. Cian could remember looking at their little faces. He'd loved teaching them.

Was he supposed to be at school? He should be dressed if he was going to school.

"Where am I?"

Liadan exhaled heavily. "You really are far gone, aren't you? You won't remember a thing I say five minutes from now, you poor excuse for a royal. You should lay down, Cian. You should fade. The world would be better if you faded."

Cian's vision clouded over. He'd heard this before. He heard that voice when he thought about getting up from time to time. He would wonder about something. His curiosity would urge him to get out of bed, but then that voice came back. Beck would be better if he faded. Sometimes he would wake up, and she would be waiting at his bedside, whispering the words over and over until he believed them. There was some sort of smoke that went with the episodes. He always felt so much farther away after he breathed that smoke.

"Get back in your bed, Cian," Liadan said in a commanding voice. "It's time to fade. You'll be happier, and so will Beckett." The voice became soothing. He felt her hands on his shoulders. They were cold. "It will be nice, won't it? You can go someplace warm. You can be with your mother and your sister again. You miss them, don't you?"

"Oh, yes." A picture of his sister formed in his mind. She'd been his playmate. Beck had been too serious for that. He'd always been with their father in some important meeting, even when they had been young children. Bronwyn had been the one to run through the palace halls, screaming with laughter. She'd been the one to explore the river with him and make fun of him when he started to notice girls.

Bronwyn had died in his arms.

There was something wet on his face. He was sick of tears. Yes, it was best to fade. He couldn't help Beck. He was weak. Beck would have a better chance if he was gone.

Woodenly, he turned toward the cottage. He heard Lia's satisfied sigh as he left her, but it didn't truly register. He began to walk past the barn with one thought in his head. He would lie down, and this time he wouldn't get up for anything. He would be stalwart. He would fade, and the world would be a better place. He walked around to the front of the cottage. He would bolt all the doors and no one would be able to stop him.

"Beck?"

It was another feminine voice that pulled him away from his mission, but this one he didn't recognize. He looked down and saw a petite, curvy woman with a mass of wavy brown hair. It wasn't brown. There was red and blonde in it, too. It was a glorious auburn. The lighter strands caught the late-afternoon light and sparkled. It was beautiful and a bit wild. A proper Fae lady would never wear her hair so wild. Her clothes were traveling clothes, and they weren't perfectly proper either. She'd left the top of the neck unbuttoned. Cian was fascinated by her creamy skin and the soft rise of her breasts.

She was beautiful.

"No, sweetheart," a very familiar voice corrected her. Dante. His cousin had shown up last night, riding that flying vehicle of his. Cian used to love to ride on the back of it. Dante had thrown a fit when he tried to take it apart, though. "That's not Beck."

"Leave me alone," Cian said, trying to take his eyes off the lovely woman in front of him. There was nothing cold about that one. Her hazel eyes were looking up at him with great concern. Those eyes pulled at him. Still, he heard himself talking to his cousin. "Go away, Dante. I have to go to bed. I'm tired."

Dante's sigh told of his weariness of the subject. "Not again."

The woman reached out and put her hand to his chest. Her skin was warm after the chill of the pond. "No, Cian. You need to get dry, and I need to brush out your hair. It's a mess. It hasn't been brushed in weeks, it looks like."

Her small hands suddenly fussed in his hair. She played gently with it, and he liked it. Her hands felt like the flutter of pixie wings against his skin. How long had it been since he'd been touched by soft hands?

"What is your name?" Cian looked down on her in wonder. She was so beautiful. She was a lovely siren, calling him away from his duty. He had something to do, but he'd rather stay here with her.

She smiled up, and all the light and warmth in the world was in her face. "I'm Meggie."

A rush of emotion hit him at the sound of the name. Meggie. He pulled her into his arms and hugged her with all the strength he had left.

After a moment, she wound her arms around his chest and held him close. He didn't know why he felt this way, but he knew she had saved him from something. A word to describe her leapt to his addled brain. It was the only clear thing in his head.

"Wife," he whispered in her ear.

It was a prayer.

\* \* \* \*

Meg carefully drew the comb through Cian's long midnight-black hair. There were places where it was tangled and matted. "Tell me if I hurt you."

"It's all right. It's nice to be warm," Cian murmured, a long sigh making his chest move. "It's a cold winter."

It wasn't winter at all.

She glanced back at Dante, who gave her a shrug.

"He doesn't always know where he is or what year it is," Dante said softly.

Dante sat on a sofa that had seen better days. Everything about the small cottage was threadbare and worn. Still, it was warm and cozy. It had far more character than her apartment in Fort Worth.

She was so far from that place now. She couldn't even comprehend how far she was. Apparently she was worlds away from that life she'd led.

How long would it be before that was the life that seemed like a dream?

Cian felt real. His hair was silky smooth and beautiful. Well, it would be silky smooth when she was done.

"This is the calmest I've seen him in a long time." Dante sat back. "Just being near you is already helping."

"I like her, Dante," Cian said. He turned his head slightly and she could see a vibrant smile on his face.

Oh, that smile could light up a room. Her heart did this weird fluttery thing, but she had to remember that he had issues.

It was odd to be in the room with a man who looked exactly like Beck yet he was completely different. Beck was solid and Cian seemed frighteningly fluid. It had taken time to get him into the house. He'd wanted to show her things. First, it had been the garden. Apparently he thought he'd planted strawberries and he wanted to share them with her. Then he'd tried to take her to the palace so she could meet his mother and sister.

He was so lost, and she wasn't sure he could be found again.

"How are you feeling?" Dante asked.

Scared. Hopeful. Scared again. The fact that she hadn't seen Beck in a while was definitely part of the scare factor. "I'm in between fooling myself that this is still some weird dream I'm going to wake up from and feeling like I oddly belong here."

It was nothing more than the truth. After the initial shock, she'd slowed down and carefully studied the place. There was a softness to the light here that called to her. She wasn't sure how to explain it, but there was warmth and peace to be had here if she wanted it, if she opened herself to the experience.

There might be love here if she was brave enough.

She wasn't sure about the whole two men thing, but Cian seemed more childlike than anything. Perhaps she didn't understand the situation fully. Perhaps Cian was merely a family member to take care of. The "marriage" thing was just a label when it came to Cian.

"You do belong here." Cian's hand came up, catching hers. "You belong with us."

Had Beck been the one saying it, his hand would have curled over hers possessively and she would have felt his need. There was nothing dark about Cian. He was being kind to her. He was a lovely, sweet reflection of the man she was coming to know.

"Of course I do." She used her free hand to pat his shoulder and he sighed again, a sound of contentment as he turned back to the fire and let her return to her task.

They were quiet for a moment, the comforting crackle of the fire the only sound between them. Cian seemed perfectly content to let her pull and tug on his hair until it was smooth.

"There," she said, an unaccountable feeling of accomplishment flowing through her. "That's much better."

Cian turned and she had to catch her breath. He was incredibly beautiful, his face a mixture of sharp lines and sensual planes. The firelight softened him, or perhaps that was simply a function of Cian's own personality. "Thank you, lady. You are very generous. If there is any fashion in which I can repay your kindness, you have but to let me know."

The idea that Cian was a child fled in the wake of the look on his face. He reached out and took her hand in his, drawing it up to his mouth. For a second, she thought he would politely kiss the back of her hand, a genteel gesture. Instead, Cian flipped her hand over and kissed her palm, a deeply sensual action she could feel all over her body.

Nope. Not a child.

His lips curved up and his eyes were hotter than the fire. "I can think of a few ways to express my appreciation."

"Uhm, I'm good. I was happy to do it," she replied. She felt caught by his eyes. They shone like emeralds.

"I will be happy to thank you. Why don't we go back to my room? It's not far. I'll have the servants bring wine and we can get to know each other better," Cian said with a heartbreakingly sexy smile.

"That should be interesting." Dante's sarcasm broke the spell and she pulled her hand away. "Can we all agree I will not be playing the role of servant?"

Cian's expression turned confused and he looked at his cousin. "What are you doing here? I thought you were on the Vampire plane. Where's Beck?"

And they were right back to bonkers. "He's getting ready to cook dinner."

Which she thought meant he was actually murdering dinner. She'd been asking to help all day but had been happy he'd turned her down on that particular task.

Cian seemed pleased with the idea. "Good. Then there's time for a nap. I find myself quite tired. I'll just lay down for a while."

He curled his body up and lay down right there on the floor, his head nestled on her lap. He cuddled up like a big, gorgeous cat eager to find warmth, and in seconds his breathing had taken on the steady rhythm of sleep.

"It's his superpower." Dante crossed one leg over the other and relaxed as though he was settling in. "He always could sleep anywhere, anytime. Although now that's pretty much what he does. You'll have to train that out of him. He can be lazy. The good news is he also got all the obedient genes. Not for anyone, of course. Both brothers are stubborn, but Cian can be led by the right person in a way Beck can't. He's far more easygoing."

She wasn't sure anything about this would be easy. "He can be lazy because Beck probably won't let him do anything."

Dante chuckled. "No, sweetheart. That rule only applies to you. I think you'll find Beck expects Ci to work as hard as he does. He'll leave his brother explicit instructions on everything he's supposed to do. Not that he always follows through, hence the garden being in the shape it's in. Ci usually enjoys farming and working with plants. And kids. I hope the school isn't in the same shape as the garden."

"Well, he seems very sick so he probably shouldn't be working." He was far thinner than his brother, though there was still a lean strength to his frame. She found herself stroking his hair. She couldn't quite help herself.

"Being up and about will help him," Dante explained. "I think it will be easier now that you're here. Once you've bonded, it won't be a problem anymore. You'll see."

She still didn't understand the bonding thing, though she knew she had a connection with Beck. Would having a connection to Cian be twice the frustration? "Sure."

Dante sat up, leaning toward her. "That doesn't sound good. What happened to the woman who was excited about taking down her man?"

She shook her head. "She's not gone. I'm just starting to understand that the job might be harder than I thought."

"You're starting to worry about handling two men? Don't. Cian will be a breeze. I know he's a mess right now, but you'll adore him. Everyone does, and that's why Beck will be the hard case. Imagine always being the bad guy. People walk in and are always attracted to Cian because he got all the light."

"And Beck got the darkness." How isolating would that be? She knew how it felt to be the one not chosen, to feel like she wasn't good enough. What would it have been like to grow up with another her, one who was good enough?

Yet Beck seemed to love his brother. That said something about him.

The door came open and Beck was there, a big basket in his hands. He stepped inside the *brugh* and it suddenly seemed so much smaller. "Sorry I took so long. I went into the village to check on a couple of our elderly folk. Is he all right?"

He might have gotten the dark side of the soul he shared with his

112

brother, but there was still kindness there. "I combed out his hair and he fell asleep."

Beck's eyes widened. "You…he…" He seemed to force himself to calm down. "Of course you did, love. That was kind of you. I'll be in the kitchen. We'll eat in a bit."

He strode out of the small room.

She was confused again and looked to the vampire. "What did I do wrong now?"

Dante was biting back a laugh. "The hair thing. It's a very intimate act for the Fae. It's something that's only performed between lovers. Beck was jealous since he hasn't had you brush his hair yet."

"Well, Beck already got to fuck her so he's still ahead," Cian murmured and tightened his arms around her like he wouldn't ever let her go.

He fell silent again and she wondered what kind of trouble she was in.

* * * *

Beck settled back in his chair after suppertime with a sense of peace he hadn't felt in a long time. The fire blazed in front of him, filling the cottage with warmth. Meg rocked in the chair beside him.

Things felt right.

"I didn't know about the hair thing," she said quietly, her gaze on the fire. "I didn't know it was an intimacy."

He hadn't handled that as well as he should. He'd walked in and been struck by how sweet she'd looked with Cian sleeping, his head in her lap. He'd felt a deep sense of gratitude because he knew he was going to get his brother back and he would have Meg to thank for it.

And then he'd realized that bastard had gotten her to comb out his hair. He hadn't been able to help the tiny flare of jealousy. "I was being an ass about it. Don't think we're going to treat you like two dogs fighting over a bone."

She turned her head slightly and a curious smile curved up her lips. "You really think me combing your hair is erotic?"

She was lovely in the firelight. She was lovely at any time, but there was something intimate about sitting here with her. Everything was going to be fine once she bonded with Cian. Once she bridged their soul, perhaps he wouldn't be so deviant. Perhaps he could be the man she needed him to be. "I find it highly erotic and I'll demand it of you, wife."

Maybe he wouldn't need to use the word *demand* so often.

She sat back. "I think I can handle it, husband."

He liked hearing her use that word. He meant to be a good one to her. Better than that pathetic first husband she'd found on the Earth plane. "I think you can, too. You handled Cian well."

She'd seemed perfectly content to sit in the living room while Cian slept. Beck had cooked dinner while Dante had entertained Meg with stories about how the Vampire plane worked. Her laughter had been music, playing through the *brugh* and turning it into a home.

It was everything he wanted. His family, content and happy.

"What's wrong with him?" Meg asked.

"What's wrong with Cian? The same thing that was wrong with me," Beck replied quietly. "He's out of balance. He needed to be bonded five years ago. For me, it came out as rage. For Cian, he's dissolving into chaos. It's worse than I thought. He's better when I'm around, you see. I had no idea he was having episodes where he forgot years of our lives."

Dante had been the one to tell him that bit of news. Right after they'd eaten, he'd pulled Beck aside for a long discussion. He'd explained that Cian had barely remembered where he was when Dante had spoken to him the night before. Cian had been confused and slightly scared when Dante had awakened him. The vampire had to explain the situation to the *sidhe* every time he woke.

"The sooner you bond with him, the better. You need tonight to rest, but tomorrow it should be done," Beck said soberly.

After the events earlier in the day and the arduous travel, Meg needed to rest. The bonding could be intense. He knew what Dante had told him should make him worried. Cian was pretty far gone and that could put Meg in danger, but then he remembered how lovingly Ci had wrapped himself around her before heading off to bed. Cian might not remember where he was but he knew how important Meg was. He wouldn't hurt her. He would shut it down if he couldn't control himself.

And Beck was all right with that. If Ci was too far gone, they would sacrifice themselves to save her. She was the important one.

He was suddenly intensely aware that he was alone with his wife. Cian was sleeping, and Dante had left after their talk, explaining he had someone he needed to see. That was bullshit. Dante was going to the tavern. He wouldn't be back before morning, if then. It didn't matter. Beck had what he needed from Dante. He'd used the communication device to speak with Susan. She'd promised Beck a good salary to clear out the tunnels in Dellacorp's latest mining project. They were full of some form of monstrous bat. It was amusing that the great and mighty vampires with all their tech were deathly afraid of flying rodents. He wasn't going to complain. Their phobias meant gold in his pocket. Gold he could use to fix up the place and make Meg more comfortable.

He hadn't mentioned his impending trip to his wife. He didn't want to disrupt the happy place they'd found tonight. They needed a few hours of peace.

Meg left her own seat and slipped to her knees beside him. She laid her head on his lap, and he felt his cock respond. It lengthened to painful proportions. He would go slowly with her tonight. The need to make love to her was riding him hard, but he forced himself to relax. It felt like forever, but he'd taken her twice the day before. He needed to show her he wasn't an animal who would fall on her at every given opportunity, even if that was what he felt like doing. He was her husband. She'd been gracious and gentle with Cian, and he owed her nothing less.

He let his head fall back against the wood of the rocking chair. It had been a rough day. Between the kelpie in the morning and the painful conversation he'd had with Liadan this afternoon, he was spent. He hadn't wanted to hurt the widow, but he needed to make it plain he wouldn't see her anymore. Liadan had taken the news of his marriage with tears, but she'd been a lady about it. She'd promised to help Meg fit in.

"He seemed better at dinner," Meg murmured.

She practically purred when he stroked her hair. She was so sweet and responsive. Beck wondered if her pussy was purring yet. His cock tightened again. The simple fact that she was so close made him long to shove her down and thrust into her soft, welcoming body.

"Your presence makes a huge difference." Beck let his fingers play with the nape of her neck. "I felt it the minute I met you. Even before we bonded, I was calmer, more centered."

She looked up at him, her pretty eyes wide. "I have to sleep with him to form the bond?"

"No." There had been a wealth of hesitation in her question and it worried him. Growing up on the human plane probably hadn't prepared her for the reality of taking on two husbands. "Cian can form the bond without intercourse. I could have, too. I just lost my head. I pushed you."

"Don't apologize again, please," she said with a sigh. "I have fond memories of the marketplace and arena, even if you don't." Beck wasn't sure what to make of that, but she continued without explaining herself. "I'm just not sure what I think of sleeping with two men, even if they do look a lot alike."

Beck snorted. "We're identical. He's thinner than I am right now, but that will change. He'll start eating again now that he has a reason to. Our own mother had trouble telling us apart until we opened our mouths."

Her cute little nose wrinkled. "I guess you look that way at first, but I can tell." She got up and eased herself onto his lap. Her hands framed his face. "You have a small scar right here." She leaned over and feathered a kiss above his left eye. "And your mouth," she said as she lightly kissed his lips, "is the tiniest bit wider than Cian's."

"Is it now?" Beck asked as his heart started to pound. His blood worked its way from his brain down to his cock. Her lips were petal-soft against his. Everything about his Meggie was soft and sweet. Goddess, how had he come to need her so much in such a short time?

She stroked a hand down his hair. "Cian's hair is slightly longer than yours, and his eyes are a shade darker."

"I don't think anyone has ever noticed that." He tried to stay focused on what she was saying. It was hard because she was wearing one of his old shirts as a nightgown, and he could see the swell of her breasts. If she moved slightly to the right, he might be able to see her nipple. He loved that she was wearing something of his. It marked her as his wife, his lover. His.

Her face bunched up in a distressed frown. "You're different people, Beck. You're brothers. Where I come from, one woman doesn't sleep with two brothers. It's considered cheating, and most men wouldn't put up with it."

It was Beck's turn to frown. How could he make her understand?

116

"But we're not different. There might be minor differences in our appearance, but we're symbiotic twins. We share a soul. He's the other half of me. You need to understand that we're married, and that means you're married to Cian, too. I won't push you into bed with him. He would never force you, but if you can't accept him, it's going to be hard on us. We would never cheat on you. Cian will never take another woman as long as he's married to you."

"I just need some time. I'll do whatever it takes to get Cian healthy." She wiggled in his lap, seemingly trying to find a comfortable position, but every wriggle of her hips went straight to his engorged cock. "I also would like to explore our relationship a little. Where I come from, newly married couples take this vacation together. It's called a honeymoon. The new couple gets away from everything and relaxes and spends a whole lot of time together. They really get to know each other."

His hand closed over her hip. Could he get her to the floor without hurting her? He could take her in front of the fireplace so she would stay warm. He would keep the blankets around her, and this time he would be in control of his baser instincts. He would very gently make love to her.

"Sweetheart," Beck said soothingly, "I think that's a brilliant idea. I would like very much to know what pleases you."

"I like it when you kiss me," she suggested.

That he could do. He pulled Meg close and nudged her face up to his. "Give me your lips, *a chumann*."

She obediently tilted her head up. He would have Cian teach her Gaelic. Though almost everyone now spoke the vampires' language, Beck enjoyed the old ways. He wanted to tell her he loved her in his own tongue. He wanted her to know she was his darling.

She was sweet in his arms. She clung to him and allowed him to take control of the kiss. It should have made it easier, but every time he felt her soften, his need rose like a wildfire. He meant for the kiss to be gentle, a promise of the way their lovemaking would go this evening. She was so soft under him that his dominant instincts shoved their way past his defenses.

*She is mine.*

He'd fought for her, offered his blood to possess her. His hands tightened on her arms. He deepened the kiss, his tongue forcefully showing her what he wanted to do with his cock. He thrust into her mouth, sliding his tongue against and over hers. She didn't fight him. She surrendered and wound her arms around his body. She told him with sighs and moans that she was his and happy to be so.

He would protect her, defend her, make sure she was happy. What was wrong with what he needed? He wound his hands in her hair to hold her in place. He liked holding her down. He wanted to tie her up so she was utterly helpless and at his mercy. He would show her none. He would make her come under his body until she begged, and then he would make her come some more. She would be utterly his when he was done with her. She would never know that she held all the power, that he would do anything to make her happy.

He forced her off his lap and onto her knees. Meg looked up at him, her lips red and swollen from his kisses. Her eyes were trusting and open. He wanted to eat her up right then and there, so he pushed her to the hard floor and was on top of her before she could breathe. He pressed his rock-hard dick against her pussy, but his clothes were in the way. *Stupid clothes*. He wanted to slow down. He wanted to tell her to undress him. She would sweetly remove his clothes and then her own. He could sit back down in the chair and command her to take his cock to that soft place in the back of her throat. He would hold her head and fuck her throat. She would drink him down, not missing a drop.

Yes, that was what he would do. Later. He didn't have the patience now. He had to get inside of her.

Beck pressed his cock against her, and she moaned, a sweet mewl that made him feel ten feet tall. Her arms went around his chest, and she let her head fall back. He fell on her. His lips devoured her soft flesh. She tasted so good. He opened the bond between them and poured his will into her. He wanted her soft and submissive underneath him, willing to fulfill his every dark and nasty desire. His hands found her breasts. He wanted to make a feast of her. She was the only food he needed.

He looked down at her. Her face, her lovely face, was filled with need. She needed him.

*"They need us, son,"* his father had explained that day so long ago. The words came back to haunt him now. *"They are completely dependent on us. You think they don't know it? It's worse for you because you'll be the king someday. Women will do anything to please*

118

*you. It is your sacred duty not to take advantage of them."*

He was doing it again.

He scrambled to get his weight off his wife. He was pinning her down against the cold, hard floor without even a blanket to warm her. His hands shook as he pushed himself up. He got off her and sat back.

"What's wrong, Beck?" She sounded soft and vulnerable.

She didn't simply sound vulnerable. She *was* vulnerable. She'd been torn away from her plane and forced into a marriage she couldn't have wanted. Then he forced himself on her.

"Beck?" He heard the uncertainty in her voice as he shoved his hands through his hair and desperately attempted to get himself under control.

"Everything is fine." He took a deep breath and banished his own needs to the Hell plane. "Why don't you go to bed? You can sleep with Cian."

She got to her knees. The look on her face quickly turned to indignation. Her hands fisted in the fabric of the shirt she was wearing. "I don't want to sleep with Cian. I want to sleep with my husband."

"He is your husband," he pointed out. *And he won't hurt you.*

"This is ridiculous." She huffed as she straightened her clothes and leaned toward him. "I want *you*, Beck. I want all of you. I want the real you. I don't want you to politely ask if you can make love to me. Here's the deal—I'm giving you permission. Take me. Bend me over, turn me around, spank my ass until it's red. As long as you fuck me afterward, I'll be happy. I won't break. I'll love it. I want you to take control during sex. You don't have any trouble taking control the rest of the time. Why can't you do it in the one place where it's bound to please me? And speaking of the word *bound*, let's talk about tying me up."

Beck turned away. He couldn't look at her for fear of her seeing down to his soul. Bound was exactly how he wanted her. He wanted her tied up for his pleasure. It would be a horrible mistake. This was everything his father had warned him about. "Absolutely not."

She would be helpless against him if he tied her down. If her arms and legs were tied to his bed, she would have no way to fight him, to stop him when he lost control. His dick hardened again at the thought of her in the marketplace. She had been so beautiful with her arms chained above her head. He had wanted nothing more than to take her like that. He had wanted to force his dick into her pussy and then tunnel his way into her tight ass. If they started down this path, he wouldn't be able to stop. She had no idea what she was asking for. He had to stop this here and now.

"Meg," he said, turning back to face her. He had to be firm with her or he would lose control, and she would be the one to pay the price. "I expect you to act like a lady. I know you aren't from this plane, and perhaps the men on your world have no honor, but here we treat our women with respect. We also expect them to behave in a proper fashion."

Her chin tilted upward, and she walked straight to him. She had to crane her neck to look at him, but they were toe to toe. "What are you saying, Beck? What am I acting like?"

"You're acting like a..." Some primitive survival instinct took over, and he shut his mouth. Women didn't like that word.

"I think he meant to say whore," Cian said helpfully from the doorway to the bedroom.

*When the hell had he shown up?* Beck quickly answered his own question. Cian would have felt the minute he started to make love to Meg. They felt strong physical reactions in the other when they were in close proximity.

"Yes," Meg said righteously. "That's what I figured."

She brought her knee up. It met his still hard cock with a resounding thud.

All the air whooshed from his lungs as he went to his knees. He looked up at his wife, who didn't seem the slightest bit regretful. She rather looked like she wanted to do it again. "Damn it. I didn't say it."

"Well, everyone keeps telling me you're one soul in two bodies," she reminded him maliciously. "Your other half was happy to speak up for you."

"I'm not happy about it now." Cian's eyes were wide as he cupped himself.

Beck was satisfied that, at the very least, Cian had gotten a bit of that pain. He'd pushed it outward, and his twin had caught the edge. "That's what you get, you nosy bastard. You had to open your damn mouth."

He managed to stand up straight, trying to ignore the pulsing pain in his cock.

Meg rolled her eyes. "I don't see what the problem is. It's not like you were planning on using it, not for anything interesting."

A flush of rage rushed over him, washing the pain away. He took his wife's chin in his hand and forced her to meet his eyes. "You're pushing it, Meggie."

Her gaze was steady and strong. There wasn't a hint of fear in those eyes. "Yes, I am, and I'm going to keep pushing until I get what I want. I am not a child. I'm a woman, and I know what I want."

He had to turn away. It was too tempting to see if she really meant it. He stalked toward the front door. "I'm sleeping in the barn."

The door slammed behind him, and he wondered if he would survive his marriage.

* * * *

"Bastard," Meg swore as her coward of a husband fled the house.

Her hands clenched and unclenched as she tried to deal with the anger she felt. He was treating her like an idiot who didn't know what she wanted. She had felt his need. It rolled off him in waves. He wanted to dominate her, and she wanted it, too. Why couldn't he trust her? Why couldn't he trust himself?

"I don't think you're a whore," Cian said quietly.

She turned and remembered she was alone with her slightly insane second husband. Her brain hurt. She said the only thing she could think to say. "Thanks."

Cian's face was sweet. It was hard to believe people got him confused with Beck. "Beck's always had a stick up his ass when it comes to sex. You'll have to forgive him. Please don't kick him in the balls again. It hurts me, too."

She hadn't realized it would affect Cian, too. She had just been enraged. "I'm sorry."

He shrugged his broad shoulders. "It's all right. He deserved it. We should go to bed. Will you come with me? I was cold in there all alone."

She hesitated. She didn't really know him. Or did she? Was he truly the other side to the man she'd started to fall for?

"I promise I won't tie you up until you ask me," he said with an innocent look that made her laugh.

She took his hand. Cian was right. It was a chilly night. It would serve Beck right if she stayed warm while he slept with the chickens.

Cian looked down at her. "I'm Cian. What's your name?"

Meg walked straight into the bedroom, pulled a pillow to her face, and screamed.

\* \* \* \*

Deep in the night, Liadan watched as Beck strode across the yard and slammed the door to the barn. She smiled. It looked like there was trouble in paradise already. She wasn't surprised. The girl was human. The woman Beck had married might have everything necessary to be a bondmate, but she hadn't been trained.

Liadan thought of all the curses she could put on the redhead. It would give her great pleasure to watch as the king's new bride's hair fell out or her skin withered and died on her body. It wouldn't take much. The human was ill-prepared for life on this plane. She would likely have no defenses in place against a nicely crafted spell. It was tempting, but there were ways to track a spell back to its originator. She had to be careful with her magic. After all, she was supposed to be a simple Fae lady, not a hag of immense power. She would have killed Cian Finn years ago if she'd been able to truly use her skills without fear of retribution.

It was incomprehensible that Beck had chosen that idiot human over her. Liadan was beautiful. She'd made sure of it when she started this mission. She'd chosen the perfect façade. Liadan O'Neill was every inch the elegant Fae lady. She was the perfect bait. Her looks and manners should have been enough to ensure that the twins fell in love with her. It hadn't happened that way. It had taken a long time to get Beck to come to her bed, and Cian avoided her altogether.

She wasn't sure what was between the human and Beck. He wasn't sleeping with his new bride for some reason. He wouldn't be able to resist her for long. He'd already broken off his relationship with Liadan. Beck had wasted no time doing it, either. He'd knocked on her door earlier that afternoon and refused to come in. He'd told her that he'd married and wouldn't be seeing her again. He had tried to be kind, but there had been a dismissiveness to the whole conversation that infuriated her.

Liadan watched the barn thoughtfully and wondered if the king had mentioned her to his bride. She rather thought not. Perhaps tomorrow she would visit the little human and introduce herself. After all, they were neighbors.

Humming, Liadan walked back across the fields to her own house.

# Chapter Ten

Warmth surrounded Meg as she gradually came to her senses the next morning. She snuggled closer to the heat source and sighed as Cian pulled her closer. He was a cuddler. He'd been a perfect gentleman, but he had been very insistent on spooning her and holding her close all night. His hair had gotten tangled around her. It tickled her skin and warmed her.

She'd thought she would be up all night thinking about Beck, but Cian seemed to have a soothing effect on her. The minute he wrapped himself around her, she'd heard a low, soothing hum in the back of her brain. It had taken her a moment to realize it was coming from him. It was like white noise, and it hummed her gently to sleep.

It was another noise entirely that forced her from the warmth of Cian's arms.

The door slammed, and there was the unmistakable sound of an engine coming to life. It didn't sound like any car she could remember, but she knew instantly what it was. It had to be that cool-looking Harley of Dante's. She wanted to see it in action, so she scrambled out of her warm bed, despite Cian's sleepy protests.

There was a robe lying across the end of the bed. She quickly put it on and rushed out of the bedroom. She threw open the door with a smile on her face, ready to demand a ride from Dante.

Her smile quickly dissolved as she realized Dante already had a passenger. Beck was seated on the back of the big bike that now hovered two feet in the air. The wheels of the bike had disappeared, and there was a noticeable cloud of dust under the vehicle.

"Crap." Dante looked up from strapping his gear on the back, his face falling when he saw her. He stood beside the bike. "We have company."

The last was said to Beck, who turned and stared at her with dark, surprised eyes.

"I left you a note," he said almost defensively.

She felt her heart seize. He'd left her a note? Why did he need to leave her a note if he was going joyriding with his cousin? That was all it could be, right? "Where are you going?"

Dante backed off. He seemed determined to stay out of whatever was about to happen.

Beck stayed on the bike, turning to her slightly. "I explained it all in the note. I have to go to work. The best work I can get is on the Vampire plane, working for Dante's company. It's rough work in a dangerous part of that world. You'll be more comfortable here. I'll be back in a few weeks."

"Weeks?" She practically shouted the question. He was leaving her. They'd been married for two days, and he was leaving her. All her old doubts flooded back like a tidal wave. At least Michael had stayed for a couple of years. Beck wasn't even staying for a week. He was leaving her with Cian, a stranger with a bunch of problems. She had no idea how to help him. She was completely lost in this alien land. She didn't even know which horses would try to eat her. Panic seized her. "I'll go with you."

She wouldn't even have to pack. She didn't own anything.

His eyes seemed cold now, and his sensual mouth was a flat line. "No. It's too dangerous. I have to work. I won't have time to do my job and watch after you."

Tears formed in her eyes and she ran to him. She'd stayed here for him. He was infuriating and she still wanted to be with him. It might be pathetic, but she needed Beck. "Please let me go with you. I don't know what to do here. I don't know how to do anything."

It went against everything she was, but she felt like begging. She didn't want to be left behind with an amnesiac and a farm falling down around her. She wanted Beck. He'd been the rock she'd clung to ever since she found herself on this plane.

Beck gently pushed her back. "You'll be fine. Bond with Cian. He'll take care of you."

She didn't think that was happening any time soon. Cian couldn't take care of himself. Cian couldn't remember who she was for more than five minutes. "You promised *you* would take care of me."

Beck shook his head. He looked so arrogant. "That's what I'm doing. When I finish this job, we'll have enough gold to fix up the place. We can hire a housekeeper so you won't have to work."

"I don't mind working." She hated the fact that she was crying, but she couldn't seem to help it. "I've worked all my life, but I don't know what to do here."

"Nor should you," he replied as though it was a foregone conclusion. "You're a bondmate. You shouldn't be doing housework, and you shouldn't live in a cottage that's falling down around you."

Her frustration made her eyes squeeze shut. "Shouldn't I decide what I want or don't want?"

"You don't know enough to decide yet," Beck explained with a dismissive wave. "Back up. We have to leave now."

She backed off as Dante hopped on the cycle in one graceful move.

"I left you my computer." Dante nodded in her direction. "I showed you how to use it, remember? Look up bonding, and it will give you a description of how to get Cian to bond with you. It's connected to the web on the Vampire plane. You should be able to find any information you need."

Meg nodded her head dully. Beck was really leaving, and he hadn't kissed her good-bye. Hell, if she hadn't woken when she did, he would have left without seeing her at all. She took a deep breath and tried to come to terms with the fact that she had, perhaps, been wrong about him. He hadn't truly wanted her. Men could feel lust for women they didn't care about. He'd explained it at the time. His brother was dying. They needed a bondmate, and she was the only one to be found. Was it such a surprise that, having done his duty, he would want to be away from her?

All that other stuff, all the stuff about caring about her and never cheating on her, had been lies. It wouldn't be the first time some guy had told her what she wanted to hear to get her to do something. She had to give Beck a little credit. At least he had done it to save his brother.

"I'll be back in a few weeks." Beck looked slightly concerned for the first time. He slid off the bike and came to stand in front of her. He towered over her, but this time his massive size didn't make her feel secure. "You'll be fine."

He moved to touch her, but she stepped back. He was trying to keep her in line. Being physically affectionate with her had worked so far. It wasn't surprising he would try it again. "Sure."

He reached out and pulled her into his arms. "Meggie, don't cry. It will be fine. We need money. I have to work. I told you I spent the last of our gold on the tournament."

She stood stiffly in his arms, knowing better than to try to break free. She would only make a fool of herself, and she'd done enough of that lately. "Fine."

He sighed and seemed reluctant to let her go. His hands found her hair. "I'm sorry about last night. I hope you won't hold it against me."

She shrugged and wished he'd go ahead and leave. "I won't bother you with it again. I didn't understand."

She knew he'd been fighting something. She'd just been wrong about what he had been fighting. He didn't want to have sex with her. She was convenient, and he was male. He needed sex, but he'd obviously found the experience distasteful. He always shut down the bond. Now she knew why. He didn't want her to know how he felt. It should have been obvious even without the bond. After all, he had chosen to sleep in a barn rather than sleeping with her.

And yet she'd felt his need the night before. It had broken over her like a wave crashing on a beach. She'd seen pieces of his soul. There was a kindness in Beck that didn't mesh with his current cruelty. He loved his brother. He'd risked his life to save her. At times, she'd felt a genuine affection come from him. The confusion had her in knots. But in the end he couldn't possibly want her if he was willing to leave her.

He smiled, a slight uptick of his lips. "You don't understand our ways, yet. It's going to be fine. You'll see."

"Sure," she replied because he seemed to want a response. She couldn't see that anything would be fine.

He reached out and tilted her head up. A lazy, warm look came over his handsome face. "May I kiss you, wife?"

That seemed to Meg to be the cruelest thing he could do. She pushed away from him. "Don't call me *wife*. Call me your bondmate or whatever, but I'm not your wife."

His eyes flared at the challenge. "You damn well are, and you better not forget it." He took a deep breath and got back on the bike. "Don't try leaving, Meg. I'll find you, and I won't be happy when I do."

He patted Dante on the shoulder. The bike levitated roughly ten feet off the ground, and they took off.

"Where the hell would I go?" Meg asked, to no one in particular.

She was alone in a world that was so foreign it was legendary on her home plane. She was a city girl who didn't know how to make dinner that didn't come neatly wrapped in plastic. She was, once again, in love with a man who couldn't love her back.

Meg sank down, put her head between her hands, and cried.

Cian dropped down behind her wordlessly. She wasn't sure when he had come out, but he'd probably heard everything. She didn't fight him when he gathered her into his arms and rocked her while she sobbed.

\* \* \* \*

An hour later, Meg had dried her tears and gotten dressed for the day. Cian sat at the kitchen table watching her as she tried to figure out how to cook the eggs she'd found when she'd ventured into the chicken coop. That had been an adventure. It seemed to her that all the chickens had been looking at her like they knew she'd eaten their sister last night. There was judgment in those little black chicken eyes. If she hadn't been so hungry, she would have run out because their beaks looked dangerous. But her stomach had warred with her fear of being pecked and hunger won.

She'd gathered five eggs when she heard a low sound. She had looked across the yard and seen Cian milking a cow. He still had to be told her name every few minutes, but he seemed happy enough to follow her around and do the odd chore. He hadn't tried to get back into bed. She'd feared she would spend the day coaxing him out. Instead, he shadowed her.

Now he sat patiently, watching and drinking milk from a mug. Meg had tried it, and despite her fear that warm milk would be gross, she found it slightly sweet.

There was a strange little oven that Beck had used last night, but there was no stove top. There was a grill in the hearth, though. After poking her head into all the cabinets, she came up with an iron skillet. She might never have been camping, but she'd read enough books to know how to cook.

At least in theory.

"Are you hungry?" Meg smiled at Cian as she cracked the eggs into the skillet. She used a fork to whisk them. There were only four forks, two knives, and three spoons. None of them matched.

"I am." Cian studied her for a moment, his eyes moving across her face. "Did my brother send you to take care of me?"

"Yes." She gave him a sad nod. It was the truth. Beck had bought her to save his brother. She had a job to do and it was past time to take it seriously.

"You're very pretty," Cian said, almost shyly.

She wondered how old he thought he was. Sometimes he came off as almost childlike. Other times he looked at her with barely controlled lust in his eyes. He hadn't acted on it. She felt perfectly safe with him, but it could be difficult to keep up with the changes. After they ate, she intended to get this bonding thing done, so she could have another fully functional, non-crazy teammate.

After she had broken down, Meg had made a few decisions. She could lie down and cry. She could bemoan her fate and become bitter, or she could get off her ass and make do. She could be dependent on the people around her, or she could learn really damn fast. As she didn't intend to act as Beck's wife again, she decided she'd better be a fast learner.

She needed to earn her keep, and she wouldn't do it on her back. When Beck came home, she would sit down and they would work out a contract. Not the kind she'd hoped for with him. No, this would be an employment contract.

She would need one because according to that vampire computer, she wasn't going home. Ever.

While she'd been in the barn, she'd come across a small room. It had a cot where Beck had slept the night before and a tiny stove to keep it warm. It wasn't much, but she could stay there and be fairly comfortable. From what she'd read on the computer Dante had left behind, she understood that the brothers needed her to remain physically close to at least one of them. Somehow, her brain formed connections with theirs and allowed them to function. There had been a bunch of mind-numbing chemistry and science that she'd skimmed over.

There was nothing in the vampire information that claimed sex was required at all, so it was best she slept apart from them. She doubted Beck would have a problem with it. Once she made it clear to him he didn't have to worry about her sexual advances anymore, he would probably get on board with her plans.

A room of her own would help. It would be far too hard to sleep beside them every night and not be able to touch them. Once Cian was rational again, she had no doubt he would be slightly horrified to find out he was married to someone his brother had such distaste for.

She pulled the pan off the grill using a thick towel. The eggs were a little burnt, but edible. It was a minor triumph. She scooped the largest part out onto a plate for Cian. He was bigger than she was and looked like he could use the calories. She was going to have to figure out how to fatten him up.

"Thanks," he said gratefully as he dug in. "My sister likes eggs, but she likes them fried. When she gets up, will you make some for her, too?"

It was easier to play along than to explain over and over and over. "Of course," she murmured as she picked up her fork.

They ate in silence for a few minutes. Cian then seemed fascinated by the sight of his hand. He held it up in the light and looked very confused. His head whirled around, and he took in the cottage.

"This isn't my home." Cian looked around the room. He sounded the slightest bit panicked. "Where am I?" He looked so lost. He caught her hand and held it tightly. "I don't know where I am."

If Beck had been standing in front of her, she would have clocked him with the iron skillet. Cian needed him, and he'd left. She understood that they needed money, but it could have waited a day or two. She held Cian's hand in both of hers. "You're safe. I promise you."

"Is he having a rough day?" a voice asked from the open window in the kitchen.

She turned, slightly startled to see a lovely blonde woman standing at the window. "I wouldn't know what a normal day is like."

130

"Sometimes he remembers, but that's only when his brother is around," the blonde explained with a tight smile. "With Beck being gone again, he'll probably deteriorate. It's terrible that he had to leave again so soon. He only got back yesterday, and now he's off to the Vampire plane."

She felt her heart drop to her toes. "How did you know he was gone?"

She thought the only people Beck had gone to see the day before had been an elderly couple on the outskirts of the village. He hadn't mentioned anyone else. She supposed word could have gotten out, but that meant he'd told others long before he'd mentioned it to her.

There was no small amount of sympathy in the other woman's eyes. "He told me last night. He asked if I would come up and see if you needed anything. Cian can be difficult."

Cian was staring at the blonde. He came around and put his hands on Meg's shoulders. Every muscle in his body seemed bunched and tight, almost as though he was ready for a fight. "You shouldn't be here. Go away."

"You see. He's difficult. I hope he doesn't get violent with you. I don't know what Beck was thinking, leaving you with him. He can be so insensitive sometimes. You know men." There was now a slight sheen of tears in the woman's eyes. She made a scene of trying to hide them.

The blonde before her was tall and delicately feminine. She had a perfect face, with light blue eyes and cheekbones any model would have killed for. Meg didn't buy the tears, though. Those seemed fake. She'd been around enough mean girls to identify one even on another plane. The woman in front of her had taken special care to let Meg know she'd spent time with her husband. "What can I do for you, Miss?"

"I am Liadan." The introduction came with a slight sniffle. "I live in the house on the other side of the fields. I've known the brothers for several years now."

"Beck likes her, but I don't," Cian said stubbornly.

Meg didn't like her either. There was something very cold about the blonde, though she was putting on a friendly front. "All right, Liadan. What can I do for you?"

She seemed put off by Meg's forwardness. "Like I said, last night when His Highness visited me, he asked me to check in on you. He wanted me to see if there was anything you needed. He was concerned about his brother, you see. He told me he brought you in to save Cian. The king loves his brother very much. He is willing to sacrifice his own happiness for his brother."

"His happiness with you?" Meg asked boldly because she was done playing around with the woman who had obviously come to size up the competition.

Liadan gasped. Her cornflower blue eyes narrowed. "Well, if we're going to be plain, then, yes, he's sacrificing the happiness he's found with me. We've been together for almost a year now."

"I haven't been with her." Cian seemed very intent on making it clear he had nothing to do with his brother's mistress.

"Like I would have you." There was a sneer on Liadan's face as she looked at Cian. It didn't go away when she turned back to Meg. She didn't seem so pretty now. "Look, I've heard you're human, so you don't know how this works. Beck is mine. He has been for a while now. He chose me. Because of his unique nature, he's stuck with you. He hopes you can keep Cian alive, and he's willing to endure this marriage because of it."

Cian's hands twitched. Even though they weren't bonded, Meg could feel his anger rising. It made it easier to ignore her own emotions. She put her hands over his and rubbed. It seemed to help. "You're upsetting him. I'm not going to do some hair-pulling, name-calling thing with you. If you want Beck, feel free to have him. I don't consider myself married to him, anyway. I am well aware of the place I have in his life. If you can make him happy, more power to you."

Now her husband's honey looked seriously confused. "You don't care that he will continue to come to my bed?"

"I have no intentions of sleeping with him, so go for it," Meg said as simply as she could. Meeting Liadan helped a lot. It explained why Beck would be as hesitant as he was. He was in love with someone else. She wished he'd been up-front and honest with her. She would have helped Cian regardless, and she wouldn't have had her heart broken.

The blonde nodded. "As long as we understand each other." She turned to go, but then came back. "He's going to kill me for this, but I can't say nothing. You should think twice before you bond with Cian."

"I want to bond with her." Cian's hands tightened possessively around her. "She is our wife."

Liadan sighed and rolled her eyes impatiently at Cian. She focused on Meg. "He's too far gone. If you bond with him, he'll pull you into his madness. You'll end up just like him. Beck didn't mention that, did he?"

She shook her head. He hadn't mentioned that possibility at all.

"Of course he didn't," the other woman said. "You would be safer walking away. There is the slight possibility that Beck would die, but he's the stronger half. He would most likely live if Cian faded. It would be hard, but he could be stronger for it."

"I won't fade," Cian swore. He seemed to be talking to himself now.

The blonde shrugged. "I thought you should know. Beck is using you to his own ends, and it could cost you. You should give it a lot of thought before you risk your life trying to save a stranger's."

Liadan walked away, and Meg got Cian calm again. She sat down and pulled out the computer Dante had left her. She pulled up the articles she'd found and reread them. Then she went deeper. She found more information on Fae psychic bonding than she could have hoped for. Vampires were very interested in it as it mirrored their own bonds with consorts. Sure enough, there was a possibility that bonding with someone as far gone as Cian could hurt her. It wasn't a big possibility, but it also wasn't recommended.

And despite what Liadan had said, if Cian died, Beck would more than likely go insane.

She looked at Cian as he sat by the fire. He was watching her, waiting for her to do something or go somewhere so he could follow her. He reminded her of a puppy, eager to please.

If she had half a brain, she would take her husband's mistress's advice and flee the scene. She should take a day or two to decide if she wanted to risk this for one man who had dumped her after two days of marriage, and another she barely knew at all.

If he were drowning, would she not try to help him? Every firefighter who ever ran into a burning building had known he or she could die. They did it anyway. Because they were brave. Because they couldn't live with themselves if they didn't take the chance.

It was time to be brave.

"You're a very pretty lady." Cian's voice was all smooth tones. There was a deliciously decadent look on his face. "Can I buy you a drink? My name is Cian Finn, by the way."

Meg set the computer down. She had never been one to slowly peel a Band-Aid off. It was better to just rip it off and get the pain over with. "Oh, we're so doing this now."

Cian stood up, a seductive smile crossing his face. "I was hoping you would say that, gorgeous."

# Chapter Eleven

Meg stared at Cian from across the bed. He sat with his long legs crossed over each other, his big gray eyes watching her intently. He looked so much like Beck that her heart hurt. He looked like Beck, but he was vulnerable, and that pulled her in. She wanted to lean over and kiss him. She wanted to promise him everything would be okay, but she held her ground. She didn't need to fall in love with a second version of him. One was all the heartbreak she could take.

"I need you to concentrate." Meg crossed her legs and tried to relax. She sat in front of him on the big bed they had shared the night before. Taking his hand in hers, she took a deep breath to settle her nerves. "Do you remember why we're here?"

His lips curled into a tempting curve. He was shirtless and wore nothing except a pair of white linen pants. His long black hair fell well past his shoulders. It shone in the afternoon light. "I think I can guess. Do you want to be on top?"

She shook her head and reached inward for her patience. "We're not having sex. We're bonding. I'm the bondmate your brother found. Beck sent me to you. We need to bond so you can think straight."

That seemed to get through to him. His eyes cleared for a moment, and his hands tightened on hers. "You're my wife?"

"So I've been told. It's okay. I won't hold you to it. We need to bond, and then we can be friends."

He shook his head vigorously. "No. Too far gone. I'll hurt you."

"It will be fine." The fact that he wasn't eagerly going into this made her more comfortable. If he would try to stay in control, she had a much better shot at getting out of this with her mind intact.

His gorgeous eyes filled with frustration. He was trying to make her understand and couldn't seem to form the words. "Please, go. Don't want…to hurt you."

Meg moved closer so their legs were touching. "It won't hurt me. I'm strong. It's going to be all right. Do you remember how to do this?"

His face cleared like a cloud had passed over and now the sun was shining. He smiled again. "*Cad è mar atà tu?*"

*Oh, crap.* He'd gone into Gaelic and now she wouldn't even understand his delusions.

She tightened her hands around his. She was going to have to make the connection on her own. She leaned forward, and luckily, Cian seemed game. He leaned forward, meeting her in the middle. She touched her forehead to his.

"*Is tù mo ghrà,*" he said, his accent lilting around the traditional Gaelic that went with the ceremony. Her bonding with Beck had been devoid of any of the ceremonies that went along with a formal marriage, but Cian seemed to remember.

"You are my love," he had said. She'd seen a couple of ceremonies on the DLs. They were just words. They didn't mean anything.

He pulled back and looked down at her as though waiting.

"*Is tù mo ghrà,*" she repeated.

If Cian needed all the trappings, then she would give them to him.

He smiled, satisfied, and put his head to her forehead once more. He rubbed his head lightly against hers as though he loved the connection.

If they'd been on the twins' home plane, there would have been a great deal of pomp and circumstance involved in the ceremony. There would have been witnesses and a decorated altar. The downloads she had read on the subject talked about the beauty of the ceremony. There would have been flowers—marigolds, St. John's wort, and shamrocks. There would have been a length of ornate rope to bind their hands together for the handfasting ritual.

The twins' father would have overseen the marriage, and bells would have rung throughout the city to let the people know the heirs had been bonded. Music would flow out of the palace all night long.

The little cottage was quiet. There were no flowers, but Meg felt the weight of what she was doing all the same. She was binding her life to this man. It wasn't something she could walk away from, though. Liadan had advised her to run, but how could she? She could no more walk away from Cian than she would be able to watch a person drown and do nothing to save him.

It was more than that. She could never abandon half of Beck to fate. It didn't matter that he couldn't love her. She loved him. That was all she could control. She firmly intended to fall out of love, but she couldn't let his brother die.

Then she stopped thinking, or rather she ceased thinking her own thoughts.

Cian's brain assaulted her.

She was flooded with memory and thoughts, dreams and fancy, and everything that was Cian. Now she understood what the blonde had been trying to tell her. She was overwhelmed with him. Sights, sounds, even smells and emotions battered her system. She felt her body sag under the onslaught, but Cian's strong hands held her in place.

She saw a young girl. She was chasing her through a gleaming white palace. She was his sister. Bronwyn. The name was as clear in Meg's mind as the image was. In the vision, she was Cian, and she was a seven-year-old boy, full of mischief. Bronwyn had been a brat. She'd tossed a mud pie straight in his face, and he was going to get retribution. She could feel the cool marble under bare feet, hear the sound of laughter echoing. The palace was filled with light. Cian wasn't really mad. He was playing a game. In Cian's body, Meg ran past Beck. He was coming out of a room with his father. Beck looked so serious. He was somber, but she could feel him. She could feel how much he wanted to join his twin and their sister. Beck wanted to play, but he simply nodded at his twin and followed their father.

Math.

She was hit full force with a load of equations she grasped for a moment, and then they were gone. Cian's head was filled with math and science and theories on everything. He was so smart. His mind worked a thousand miles a minute. She couldn't process it all. Her brain hurt. Poems and stories and articles on anthropology and engineering written in several different languages flew in and out of her head.

She felt a pounding pressure begin.

And the women...so many women.

He loved sex. He craved it. He needed it to feel whole and complete. He got lost in his mind sometimes, but his body always insisted on having its fair share of time. There were blondes, brunettes, and girls with hair the color of the sunset. He was affectionate toward them all. He liked them one or two at a time, and he loved it when he shared a female with his other half. Cian liked to hold a lover in his arms while Beck fucked her. It had been so long since they shared a truly intimate experience. Beck had become so rigid in his sexuality. He hadn't stopped sharing women with his brother. He'd done something worse. He had stopped sharing himself with anyone. Beck had closed off entire sections of their being, and Cian felt the loss.

Meg's pulse pounded as she was flooded with memories of Cian's lovers. She had a brief vision of a beautiful blonde with her hand possessively on Beck's arm. They walked into a brilliantly lit ballroom and everyone cheered. Cian was left out. It was the night of his formal engagement, but he didn't want to be there. He couldn't stand the woman. Cian was sure she felt the same way about him. He was in the way, and he knew it. Beck was resplendent in his formal court attire, but his face was pinched with duty. Beck didn't love her, either. How were they going to get out of this? Meg was swamped with Cian's panic as he realized he was trapped.

She heard herself moan as the siege continued. Her hands tightened on Cian's arms as she held on for dear life. Tears squeezed out of her eyes as she became sure her skull was going to split. She hoped it did. It would relieve the overwhelming pressure.

No, she felt Cian protest deep in her soul as the scene in her brain changed. He didn't want to remember, but it was coming, anyway. It was far too strong to be denied.

Smoke was everywhere. She could barely breathe. She lifted her head and put a hand to her ears. The world was filled with cracks and booms that shook the ground beneath her. She was in the middle of a battle. There was fire, heat, and the sound of metal on metal. She looked down. A teenage girl was lying in her lap. She looked up with soft brown eyes. They were filled with tears.

"Mama?" the girl asked. She wasn't confused. She was asking a question.

She didn't remember what had happened? Didn't remember that she'd fought to save the last piece of their mother? That might be a good thing.

"She's gone, Bron." Meg heard Cian's voice speaking, saw through his eyes, was assailed with his memories. His voice was filled with sorrow. His mother was dead. He'd seen her die at the end of a soldier's blade. He hadn't been able to get to her. "Father's gone, too."

Bronwyn held her stomach. She was bleeding profusely. It was only a matter of time. They were trapped. There was fire at their back and an army behind the only doorway out. He held his sister close to his heart. Beck was still fighting, but he was shielding it from his brother. Cian would have known if his twin was dead. He wondered if Beck would die when he did. Would Beck feel it when the soldiers outside burst in and shoved cold iron through his gut?

Cian's hands shook, but he didn't let his sister see how scared he was. He needed to be strong for her. There was a knife at his side. He wasn't a warrior, but he would use it to defend her. He had killed a man with it already. The soldier who had stabbed Bronwyn hadn't been content with taking her life. He had to try to rape her as well. Now his corpse was cooling not ten feet away. Cian tried not to think of him. He focused his being on the sister he was losing.

"Love you, brother." Her smile reminded him of the five-year-old girl who had followed him around like a puppy.

"I love you, too." He choked the words out. Meg felt wetness on her face and realized Cian was crying.

Bronwyn's eyes went dull just as the door exploded inward. Cian looked up, clutching his sister. He was ready to join her.

Beck stood in the doorway, covered in blood. He held a bloody sword in his hand.

"We have to go," he said with dark eyes.

Then the images came rapidly. The gun that was Cian's brain suddenly went into machine gun mode. She couldn't keep up.

She was in a forest running from soldiers who had been sworn to hunt the twins down and execute them. She ran from plane to plane. Then she was building this cottage with Cian's hands. Refugees were everywhere. There was not enough food to feed them, and they looked to Cian and Beck.

A smoke-filled image invaded Meg's brain. Liadan stood by the bed, whispering to Cian. He tried to get up, but the smoke was too much. It was time to fade.

It was too much. It was too fast. Meg felt the moment her brain shorted out. She barely made a sound as she slipped into a blissful darkness.

* * * *

Cian Finn came to on the bed of the cottage he had built. It took him a moment to focus. It seemed to be morning, or maybe afternoon. He studied the shadows on the wall and decided it was definitely afternoon.

He felt magnificent. His head was clear. How long had he been like that? It had been a nightmare of chaos. The clarity in his brain was bliss after the long pandemonium he'd been living in.

Cian sat straight up in bed. Meg. She had bonded with him. It was difficult for him to sort through everything that had happened in the last few years. He was certain now it had been years since he began the long slide into chaos. He might never get those years back, but he remembered Meg. Meg was the clearest thought in his head.

She was his wife.

Cian felt a moment of pure panic when he saw her lying so still on the bed. Her legs were underneath her at an odd angle. For a moment, he was sure he had killed her, and he knew his life would be over, just as he had gotten it back. Then her chest rose slightly and he breathed a sigh of relief. She was alive. She'd survived the onslaught that bonding with him would have caused.

Gently, he opened the bond between them. It was new, but there was such strength to it. Her mind was tired but functioning. She was in a deep, dreamless sleep. Her brain needed respite.

He leaned down and pulled her legs into a more comfortable position. She sighed and rolled toward his warmth, as though she knew he would protect her. He felt a grin cross his face as she cuddled closer to him.

If he hadn't just put her through hell, he would consummate his marriage in the physical sense. Had she been conscious, he would roll her onto her back and get between those pretty thighs of hers. He would ride her until they both passed out from the exertion. She was his. He had seen down to her soul. He knew she was perfect for them.

As she had gone through many of the important events of his life, he'd gone through hers. He kissed the top of her head and inhaled her sweet smell. So many people had disappointed her. How could they not have seen how wonderful she was? Sure she was quiet, but her mind was quick, and she had the most delicious sense of humor. She was sassy and independent. Her sensuality had been completely untapped and unappreciated by the men in her life.

Cian wouldn't make the same mistake. He was considered to be the smartest man of his generation. He had no intention of proving dumb when it came to his wife. She was an amazing gift.

His hands clenched as he thought about the last little scene that had played out in his head. He was going to kick his brother's ass when he returned. He was an idiot, that other half of him. Beck had made Meg feel worse than that worthless ex-husband of hers.

She was exhausted. Her entire body relaxed as she slept so trustingly in his arms. He would make her see how beautiful she was. He would have to be careful, though. His brother had dug them a deep hole. Beck had taken her body but had refused to share his soul with her. It was selfish, and Cian intended to have a long talk with him about it. She was their responsibility. They had to fulfill all of her needs, and Beck would have to see that her needs were different than the women they had grown up with. Meg wouldn't want to be a perfect princess on a shiny throne. She needed to work. She needed to contribute. She needed to be valued for all the things that made her unique.

"*T à mo chroì istigh ionat,*" he whispered. *My heart is within you…*

He was about to kiss his sleeping princess on the forehead when he heard a knock at the door. Curious, he gently rolled away from his wife. He reached for a shirt and walked to the front of the house.

A small brown female was gingerly opening the door. She was dressed simply in a dark, threadbare skirt and linen shirt, with a colorful shawl around her thin shoulders. Her big feet were bare. Her head was a mass of scraggly, wiry hair and her own thick skin. Her eyes were huge in her small face and black as a moonless night. She was beautiful to him. Flanna was a brownie. The brownies had been domestic help on his home plane.

Here they were nothing short of family.

"Beckett." She squinted, turning her elderly eyes up at him. He immediately got to one knee so she could inspect him. She'd been his nanny throughout his childhood. It hadn't taken him long to get taller than the brownie who took care of him, but he always showed her proper respect. His throat closed up at the thought that he hadn't really seen her for years. She walked up to him with a smile that showed her gaping teeth. "I am glad you changed your mind, son. It's a mistake to leave your wife alone right now."

"She isn't alone, Flanna," Cian said, emotion welling in his heart. "She has me."

Flanna's jaw dropped, and she looked at him with wonder. "Cian?"

"Yes, little mother," Cian said. "I assure you, it's me. How long was I gone?"

Huge tears welled in her black eyes. "Years, Cian," she confirmed as she drew him into her motherly embrace. "I thought you would die soon."

"I did, too." He hugged her gently, taking great care with her fragile body. "I am so sorry, little mother. I got lost."

Tears coursed over her cheeks. "Where is she? Where is the queen?"

Cian smiled broadly and wondered if anyone had even mentioned that part to Meg yet. He doubted she knew she'd become the true Queen of the Seelie Fae. "She's asleep. The bonding was hard on her. From what I can tell, everything's been hard on my Meg, including Beck. You should know, I intend to thrash him soundly when he returns."

Her foot started tapping. "That will be the day. I think you've forgotten which twin you are if you think to fight your brother."

He let his face split into a slightly shady grin. "Well, I didn't intend to inform him of my plans to beat him. I assure you, I can have him unconscious and tied up in no time at all. He always underestimates me."

Flanna gave him "the stare." It was the one that let Cian know he was in trouble. "Now is not the time to be feuding with your brother."

Cian frowned. "You don't know how he treated her. He's been selfish and rude. He formed a bond with her, but from what I can tell, he didn't actually offer himself. He surely didn't open to her. She was shocked by the full bond. She hadn't felt it before."

Cian got to his feet, a new purpose humming through his brain. He'd hidden something, and now he hoped it had survived the years.

Flanna followed him into the kitchen. "Don't be so quick to judge your brother. He's only done what he had to do to survive. Your father was very hard on him."

"And he has a lot of responsibility, blah, blah, blah," Cian said with a frown. He studied the drawers in the hutch. He'd built it with his own hands, and he had put a hidey-hole in it. "You think I haven't heard this all my life? *Allowances must be made for the warrior king.* All I had to do was think and learn, but Beck had to fight. Father was particularly hard on Beck, so we should let him be a cold bastard? I won't let him ruin my relationship with our wife. She's everything I could want in a woman. If he's too stupid to see that, then he's welcome to keep to the Liadans of this plane."

There was something about Liadan. There was something about the blonde woman his brother had taken as his mistress that nagged at the back of his brain. He couldn't quite grasp it. It didn't matter. He needed to worry about Meg now. He pulled the left drawer out and carefully pushed his hand inside. He felt for the trap door at the back. It sprang free, and there was his treasure.

"You can't kick your brother out of your marital bed," Flanna was insisting. "You know that the three of you will never form a triad if you don't open yourselves to each other."

Cian pulled his hand free and opened the small bag he retrieved. "The triad is a myth. I'm not going to develop mystical powers from sleeping with my wife. I feel wonderful, I do, and I'm definitely looking forward to consummating my marriage. I promise I'll work my hardest to ensure you have some babies to take care of next year, but I won't become a Green Man, and Beck won't be a Storm Lord."

"Just because you don't have faith doesn't mean others don't," Flanna said with a superior look in her eyes. "Tell me something, Your Highness, what does this mean for the rest of us?"

He pulled out a small gold ring. There was a sun on the signet, the symbol of the queen. Bronwyn had pressed it into his hand as she lay dying. His sister had died trying to retrieve the ring from their mother's rooms. It was all he had left of their mother, and now it belonged to the rightful queen, his wife. "It means we have some decisions to make. I'm sure even now our aunt is trying to convince her daughter to start funneling money our way. We'll need it if we're going to bribe the Unseelie to back us."

Cian didn't want to talk politics. He had more important things to do. He turned the bag over. The rest of the contents tumbled to the table, making a delightful clinking sound. He did a quick count and was well-pleased. Flanna reached out and slapped his hands.

"You've been keeping money from your brother," she accused.

Cian shrugged. There was no point in denying it. "He would have spent it on something boring, like food. This was my drinking stash. Now, it's my get-my-wife-dressed-properly stash. Do you think you can come up with something nice for this?"

Flanna seemed placated that he was using the cash on Meg instead of at the tavern. "I happen to know that the dressmaker in the village is almost done with a beautiful gown for Liadan. I believe she was planning on wearing it to Beltain. It would have to be shortened from what I understand, but I'm sure she would alter it for her queen."

Cian smiled. If it pissed off Liadan, then so much the better. "Excellent. I'll take it. Tell the seamstress to let out the bodice as well. My Meg's got a lovely set of breasts on her. And Flanna, we should prepare the village for the influx of Fae coming to pay their respects to my queen."

"Beckett told me to keep her presence here quiet."

He understood what his brother was trying to do, but it wouldn't work. "Beck won't be able to contain the rumors. He either bought her or he fought for her."

"It was an open tourney," Flanna confirmed.

"Then the vampires know about it, too. They'll think there's something wrong with her. They'll think that the king is ashamed he had to take a human wife if he doesn't demand proper respect be paid."

"That isn't why he's keeping it quiet," Flanna corrected him. "Beck is worried about your uncle's agents. The pretender closed Tír na nÒg because he's worried Beck will steal onto the plane and assassinate him. He's been waiting for the two of you to fade. After you're gone, he'll be able to open the homelands and reestablish trade and contact. You can't think Torin wants the borders closed. He'll be furious when he discovers you've married. The queen is now a target."

Cian shook his head. "She'll be a target no matter what. I'm sure Torin knows about her even now. I have no illusions on that. He has his spies as we have ours. It doesn't change the fact that she will have a hard time being taken seriously if we don't treat her that way. The people will accept my queen, or I'll cease being their king. Well, I'll cease being half their king, anyway."

Flanna patted his hand, seemingly giving up the fight. "I will go and get things started. The village will feast tonight, my son."

"Yes." Cian looked at his mother's ring with satisfaction. "We will feast and dance and drink." And then he would set about seducing his lovely, brave bride.

# Chapter Twelve

Beck stood looking out the window on the hundred and second floor of the Dellacorp building. This was the penthouse his aunt lived in, and it always made him nervous to be so high in a non-natural structure. Below, the neon lights of the city gave the night an ethereal quality. It was an odd sight, and one he wished he could share with his wife. Meg would be fascinated by this world. He wondered if there was a Dallas on her plane. According to the vampire scientists who'd studied the planes, this one and the legendary Earth plane were oddly interconnected. He would have to ask her.

She would likely enjoy the ridiculous lights and soaring heights the vampires lived in. It made his stomach ache, but it might be worth it if Meg liked it.

He couldn't risk it. He couldn't risk the chance that she could run away here and probably find someone who would take her in and hide her away. Probably? He shook his head. She would have no end of handsome vampires willing to save her from her unwanted marriage. She was a beautiful bondmate, and they would consider her a perfect consort. She would have vampires fighting over the privilege of who got to save her from her husband.

"You are brooding, Beck." His aunt's voice cut through his thoughts and pulled him into the present. He turned and looked at his mother's sister. She was graceful and lovely, just as his mother had been. Her raven hair was in a neat knot at the nape of her neck. "I think sometimes you forget which half you are. You are a man of action. Leave the brooding to Cian." Alana Dellacorp's face fell as she remembered. "I'm so sorry. I shouldn't have said that."

He smiled at his aunt. The words didn't hurt at all since they no longer held truth to him. Now if his brother brooded, Beck could kick his ass because there was no reason for it. "It's all right. I wasn't brooding. Well, maybe I was. I was thinking about my wife."

He held himself still, watching for her reaction. He'd asked Dante to keep his mouth shut. He wanted to tell his aunt himself. He so rarely had good news to share.

Her face became a mask of well-bred horror. "Tell me you haven't married that Liadan person. Oh, Beckett. You can't give up hope. Annul the marriage. I will find a way to smuggle a bondmate out of Tír na nÒg. Your Uncle Don and Susie already have feelers out looking for the best way to do it. We have confirmation that Torin, the bastard, is making deals with other vampire families to sell them consorts. Obviously he would never make a deal with the Dellacourts, but we have plans."

He took his aunt's hand. She was a slave to fashion, as always, and her nails were painted an emerald green with small jewels on the tips. It was the fashion for consorts. "Tell them to stop. I'm not about to…what was the term Meg used…divorce my wife, though she might beat me when I return home. As for Cian, I spoke to him not thirty minutes ago on that contraption your son left. He's perfectly clear-headed and more like himself than he's been in years. He's just as pissed with me as Meg must be, though he's trying to hide it, the tricky bastard. I'll have to watch my step when I get home or he'll jump me."

Alana gasped as she understood the implications. Before she could say a thing, a bundle of feminine energy burst into the room and ran straight for Beck. Beck braced himself for impact and wasn't disappointed. Susan Dellacourt threw herself into his arms with a resounding thud.

"Beck! I can't believe it." His cousin looked up at him with joyful tears in her eyes. "You bonded! We all thought we were going to lose you. It's fate. I know it is."

"You'll have to excuse my wife, Your Highness," Colin O'Neill Dellacourt said with an indulgent smile. He bowed formally to his king. Beckett recognized the *sidhe*. He'd been one of the refugees to make it out of Tír na nÒg before the plane was closed. Unlike most of the Fae, Colin had settled on the Vampire plane and quickly found himself in the enviable position of consort. "She's been worried about you and Cian. She talks about you all the time. I've heard more stories about your childhood than you can imagine."

Colin was dressed in typical vampire attire. He was casual but elegant in slacks and a pearl-gray dress shirt. He'd come a long way from a farm in Tír na nÒg.

"Well, I remember when she was just a wee thing, and I used to pull her pigtails," Beck said, giving his cousin a squeeze. He often didn't understand his vampire relatives, but he loved them.

Susan shook her head and planted a kiss on his cheek as she noted her brother walking into the room. "That was Ci, dear. You were always too serious to play." She squeezed his hand. "Why didn't you bring your new wife and Ci with you? Everyone will be dying to meet her, and I would love to talk to Cian when I don't have to remind him who I am every five minutes."

"You aren't the only one, sis. He was completely loony when I left. Bonkers. It's funny now, of course, but at the time, I was concerned." Dante shrugged Beck's way. "Well, you told me to keep my mouth shut around Mother. You said nothing at all about Susan. Come on, man, she's my boss and my older sister. I gotta have something on her."

"How can you consider me your boss?" Susan asked with a roll of her emerald eyes. Beck heard Colin snort and realized this was a well-worn argument. Even Alana sighed as Susan continued her tirade. "You never show up for work. You're always out gallivanting around. Sometimes I wonder if the tabloids would have anything to do if Dante Dellacourt wasn't here to give them a headline every day."

Dante's eyes narrowed. "Well, we can't all be perfect CEOs and perfect spouses and perfect daughters. Some of us prefer to have a life."

"How can you call that a life?" Susan mocked her baby brother. "You drink and go out with a new model every night. That isn't a life. It's a blood disease waiting to happen. I don't even want to know where your fangs have been, brother."

"Susan!" Donald Dellacourt's voice boomed through the great room as he entered. Beck tried to hide his smile. His uncle was a bit larger than life. "Give your brother a break. He's a young man finding his blood. So what if he's a little wild? He'll fall in love and settle down one of these days. You have to be patient with him."

Dante's green eyes were suspiciously innocent as he poured himself a Scotch. Vampires might not eat the way the Fae did, but they could drink. "Father is right, Susie. I drown myself in booze and loose women to hide the pain in my heart from not finding true love. It could be that my tale ends tragically. I fell madly in love with a beautiful consort, and Beck stole her from me. I suppose I'll have to find something that will make me feel better. Perhaps a Ferrari. It won't fill the hole in my heart, but I have to make do."

His uncle rolled his eyes and readjusted his Stetson. "Don't push it, son. I'm not a fool. I started with next to nothing."

Dante's eyes glazed over. His mouth moved in time with his father's. He had obviously heard the tale about a million times, but then, so had Beck.

"All I had was a hundred head of cattle and a dream," Don was saying as he poured himself a Scotch, too. "A dream to refine their blood into an easy-to-swallow nutritional pill that made storage problems a thing of the past."

Susie was mouthing the familiar conversation as well. His uncle continued his story of building Dellacorp into a giant of the industry. Alana slid her arm around Beck's shoulders as her husband lectured their children about how easy they had it.

"Come along. He'll be at it for hours now." His aunt led him onto the balcony. The air was cool and the night calm, though in a city as large as Dallas, it was never quiet. "Tell me about your bride. How did she make it out of Tír na nÒg?"

"She didn't." Beck looked out over the city, feeling the distance between himself and his wife. It weighed heavily on him. Had he done the right thing? Should he have brought her with him? "She's from the Earth plane."

Alana stepped up to the railing. She didn't seem to have the same problem with heights that he had. "I'd heard rumors the Planeswalkers were taking advantage of Torin closing Tír na nÒg. Human are closely related to the Fae. Some historians believe we originated on their plane, after all. It follows that some would be suitable as bondmates, though I've heard that only human females have the ability to bond, and only a small percentage. She must have been terrified."

"To say the least." A vision of tears running down her pretty face when he'd left her at the cottage haunted him. She would never understand all the reasons he left. He could have put off this business trip for a few days until she settled in, but Beck feared what he would have done. The night before had been a close call. It was sad that the one woman he would ever love was the one he couldn't trust himself around. "Do you think she can ever be happy so far from her home?"

His aunt smiled brilliantly. "Of course she can. She'll settle in. I was overwhelmed when I first came to this plane. Still, I love your uncle. I wouldn't have it any other way. And your bride has two devoted men to make sure she's happy." A cloud passed over Alana's face. "You can love her? I know some bondings come without it, but if you can't love her, it would be better if you let Don and Susie try their plan."

"No." Beck's voice was harsh and his answer quick enough to put a smile on his aunt's face. "I don't want anyone else."

"Good," Alana said. "I'm glad you're happy with her."

He wished his mother were alive so he could talk to her. His aunt was the next best thing. "I wish she was happy with me."

"Give her time. She wasn't prepared for this life. You have to make allowances."

He felt his jaw firming as a part of himself tried to stop the conversation right here and now. It should have been easy. He should have simply kept everything inside as he always had. But since bonding with Meg, he was discovering nothing was simple anymore. "I can't control myself around her."

Alana put an affectionate hand on his. "Of course you can't. She's yours. When I said you had to make allowances, I was talking about you, too. You have to change your mindset. I've read about the humans. I find them intriguing. They're a passionate people. Sometimes not so smart, but passionate. You might discover she wants a different relationship than what you expect from a bondmate."

He shook his head. "She is trying to please me. I'm her husband, her king. She's saying what she thinks I want to hear. Women will say anything to placate their king."

With a short burst of laughter, his aunt put her hands on Beck's shoulders, turning him gently so he looked her in the eyes. "Perhaps some would, if the prize were big enough. But, Beckett Finn, you are the king of a refugee plane. You don't offer her enough to debase herself. Whatever she's offered you, she's offered because she wants it. I'm speaking to you plainly, as your own mother would have. Don't deny yourself and your wife. Your father treated my sister like a porcelain doll. It made her crazy."

"Mother was happy with Father," he argued.

"You saw what you wanted to see," his aunt insisted. "Your father trained you to be a great king. He didn't train you to be a good husband. Let your wife tell you what she wants. I assure you, if you don't, Cian will. If you aren't careful, you'll find yourself out in the cold." Alana patted him and moved back toward the doors. "Come inside. I'm sure dinner is almost ready. Go easy on Colin. He's nervous about dining with his king."

Beck nodded but continued to stare out into the night. He wished he was home getting ready to go to bed. It would be quiet there. Cian would have enjoyed his first day of peace in a long while. He imagined sitting in front of the fire with Meg on his lap. After a pleasant evening, he and Cian would lead her to the big bed and slowly undress her. They would make love to her together, bonding even further. Beck would be gentle and make sure she was satisfied before taking his pleasure. He would then, graciously, turn her over to his brother. He would sit back and enjoy watching Cian please their wife. Watching Cian fuck their lovely bride would get him hot and bothered again, but he would survive. Meg would be tired. She would sleep peacefully between them.

Instead, he would spend his evening dodging questions about when he would attempt to take back his throne. Beck turned to the penthouse doors and sighed. Politics. He hated politics, even when discussing them with family. At least Meg was safe from them. She was safe and protected on the little farm.

Beck took a deep breath and rejoined his family.

* * * *

Meg came awake to the sound of raucous music. It was cheery and a little bawdy. She couldn't understand the lyrics, but she knew bawdy music when she heard it. Her mouth felt dry, and she wondered if she'd gone on a bender the night before. She'd had the strangest dream.

151

"Head hurt, lover?"

She forced her eyes open, and, sure enough, her strange dream was staring her in the face. He was sitting back in an armchair, one ankle propped on his knee. He looked like she expected a pasha would look reclining in his harem. His face was exactly like Beck's, but this man was different. Beck Finn radiated authority and responsibility.

This man radiated sex.

"Cian?" Could that man sitting there looking at her like he was going to eat her up really be Cian? There was no cloudiness in his gray eyes now. They were filled with a sharp intelligence.

"In the flesh," he said with a crazy, sexy smile. His voice was deep, but there was a hint of humor in it. He was dressed in neatly pressed white pants, dark boots, and a tunic he hadn't bothered to tie. It left his perfect chest exposed. "And in my right mind, thanks to you."

Meg sat up and put a hand to her head. "It worked?"

Of course it worked. The evidence was sitting right in front of her like a piece of perfectly tempting chocolate cake she wanted to devour in one long bite. Memories of his life flooded her. She groaned as her head ached.

He was on the bed behind her in an instant. He pulled her between his long legs and cradled her back to his chest. His hands sank into her hair, strong fingers massaging her scalp. "Careful, Meggie mine. You took a whole lot of me. I'm sure you still feel the effects."

His hands felt good on her. So good. She relaxed into his warmth. "You're better now?"

"I am damn near perfect." Cian's voice was a slow seduction in her ear. He leaned close, and she felt his lips moving against her skin. "I don't know how to thank a woman for saving me. Can you think of any way I could please you?"

Even with her head throbbing, she could think of a way. Yep, she had a type and she knew exactly where that path would lead her. She shook his hands off her. She had to come to her senses. She wasn't about to get her heart broken by a second Finn brother.

"You don't have to thank me." She scrambled off the bed. She gathered her dignity around her like a shield. "I'm just glad you're all right."

His eyes darkened, but he relaxed after a moment. He leaned back against the pillows, not hiding his raging erection at all. It tented his pants admirably. He spared her not a single, delectable inch of his glorious body as he stretched out. "I am more than fine, wife. I'm perfectly healthy and prepared to serve you in any fashion you can think of."

She had to force herself to swallow because she was not having a problem with dry mouth now. This was what had gotten her heart in trouble in the first place, her inability to turn a Finn brother down when it came to sex. He was merely trying to show his gratitude. Besides, it had been a long time for him. He hadn't had sex since his illness had taken over. She hadn't forgotten their bonding. Cian was a carnal creature. He would want that pleasure as soon as possible. They needed to get a few things straight.

"Please don't call me wife," she said in a firm voice. Cian's brow arched quizzically, but he allowed her to continue. "I'm not from this plane."

"No," Cian interjected. "You're from the human plane. You were born in a place called Texas and lived in a city called Fort Worth. They have one of those on the Vampire plane, too. We'll go someday and you can tell me how different it is. I would find that fascinating. You lived in a small apartment, and you hated it. There was no beauty to it. The walls were beige. The carpet was beige. It wasn't a home. It was like purgatory, a place to wait. Explain this purgatory to me."

He sat up and crossed his legs. He switched from hot and bothered potential lover to curious student. She was struck dumb by how accurately he had described her postage stamp apartment. It had nothing of her in it. It was a place to eat and sleep. It wasn't a home. "How did you know?"

His expression was serene. It was disconcerting how quickly he could change. "We're bonded. I saw your soul, and you saw mine. It's the deepest bond two beings can form. You can try running from me, Meggie, but it won't work. I know you deep down. I know what you need."

She felt her whole body flush with embarrassment. She remembered things from Cian's life like they were her own memories. What had he pulled out of her head? She felt vulnerable in that moment, even more vulnerable than she had been with Beck. The bonding with Cian had been so different.

"Because Beck didn't offer you the full bond," Cian said as though he'd read her mind. He chuckled as she flashed a startled look his way. "It was a good bet that was what you were thinking, nothing more. I can't read your mind. I can see images at times, but I can't hear your thoughts. When we make love, though, I will be able to feel your pleasure and to give you mine."

She ignored the last bit. It was best not to even go there. "So Beck and I aren't bonded?"

"Not fully, from what I can tell," Cian stated as academically as possible. "Many choose not to form a full bond with their bondmates. You can help Beck bridge with me without seeing his soul. I, personally, think it's a cowardly thing to do. You're my wife, whether you accept it or not. I am your husband. I want you to know me, the good and the bad. I don't want to live my life without really knowing my wife. I want to know what she likes and doesn't like. I want to know what makes her laugh. I want to know that she feels like everyone will abandon her in the end because that's all anyone has ever done."

She turned away because he had seen way too much. Her hands were still shaking from the physical process of bonding.

He was suddenly behind her, winding his arms around her. His hair was loose and she could feel it on her skin, caressing her. "I won't ever leave you, wife. I know Beckett can be hard to understand, but he is loyal. He won't abandon you. We're here for you. We're bound together forever. You're safe with us."

She didn't believe that for a second. The door to the bedroom opened, and Meg was glad for the distraction. A small brown woman walked in. Woman? She obviously wasn't human so that likely wasn't the word she should use. Cian gave her shoulders a squeeze before shifting to stand at her side. He kept an arm around her. She could feel his affection for the strange-looking female.

"Meggie mine, this is Flanna," Cian said. "She's a brownie and a very valuable member of our court."

Flanna grinned, showing her gapped teeth. She was fascinated by another nonhuman creature. Despite her aching head, she kneeled down to get on the same level as the elderly woman. It seemed like the polite thing to do. She felt Cian's pleasure at her gesture. The bond made it easy to sense his moods.

"Hello, I'm Meg. It's very nice to meet you."

The woman bowed deeply. "And you, Your Highness. I cannot express my joy at this bonding. It has saved us all. Surely Danu herself sent you to us."

She looked up at Cian, hoping he would explain who this Danu was.

He merely grinned down at her. "I'll give you a full lecture on the religious beliefs of the Fae at another time, sweetheart. For now, our people await. They long to meet their queen."

She was up on her feet in an instant. "Queen?"

His smile was slow and sure as he leaned over and whispered in her ear. "What do you think they call the woman who fucks the king, my lover? I know you've been fucking big brother, and I mean to have some of that, too. I'll have you in my bed by the end of the week. I promise you won't want to leave." He dropped a light kiss on her cheek and walked to the door. "Get dressed, my queen. We have a party to attend."

With that, he winked at her and disappeared behind the door. Meg sank to the bed and took a deep breath. She'd thought Beckett was a lot to deal with. He hadn't actively tried to seduce her. Cian had just made a declaration of intent.

"He's a charmer, that one," Flanna was saying with a chuckle as she walked to the small wardrobe. She went on tiptoes to open the door and pulled down a sumptuous-looking gown. "I wouldn't bother trying to hold him off, Your Highness. He'll be in your bed before you know it. No woman can hold off Cian Finn when he wants her."

"What about Maris?" The name came straight into her head. She searched her new memories. The blonde Fae bondmate had been named Maris.

Flanna's eyes widened in obvious surprise. She handed the dress to Meg. "He performed a true bonding, then?"

"So he tells me." The dress was sapphire blue with flowing skirts. There was delicate embroidery around the bodice. It was like nothing she'd ever worn before. This was the dress of a faery princess. "She was his fiancée?"

The small woman nodded. "She was engaged to the princes at a very young age. Their father chose her. She came from impeccable bloodlines. She was very much the lady."

While the other woman's voice had been even, there was hostility there as well. "You didn't think she was right for Cian?"

"I didn't think she was right for either of them," Flanna corrected. "Come along, Your Highness. I will help you get dressed while we gossip. It's a sacred thing in a royal court, and I've missed having a queen to gossip with."

She allowed Flanna to pull and prod her into the dress while she spoke.

"Maris was a cold girl, and she would have become an even colder woman," the brownie explained. "Beck accepted the betrothal because Beck always obeyed his father. He convinced Cian to accept it as well, but I know Cian was worried about actually bonding with her. He would never have formed a full bond with her, I promise you that."

Flanna got on the bed to button Meg's dress up the back.

"He was pretty out of it. I don't know that he intended to go so far with me. Beck didn't." Meg watched in the mirror as Flanna put the finishing touches on the dress. She didn't recognize herself in the mirror.

She was a long way from Fort Worth.

"Don't let that worry you," Flanna said, getting off the bed. "Beck has his reasons. He's done things he's not proud of. Give him time. Let him come to trust you."

Shaking her head, she stood and smoothed the skirts one last time. Flanna gave her soft slippers for her feet. She had no intention of bonding with either brother any more than she already had. It wasn't fair, but she didn't intend to give Cian a chance to hurt her. She would get through the evening and then sit Cian down in the morning for a thorough discussion of how this "marriage" was going to work.

In the meantime, she would get used to her new home. From the sounds of the party going on in the front yard, it seemed as though she was about to meet the entire village. It was time to put her game face on and start that learning curve.

She allowed Flanna to escort her to the door. They walked into the living room. The music was louder out here. The door was open. She could see the night beyond was lit up with torches and a huge bonfire. All manner of Fae creatures danced around the bonfire. Some of them didn't look even vaguely human. Meg felt her jaw dropping and forced it to close.

A cheer went up when she walked into the yard.

"Welcome, Queen Meg," they said as she passed.

She plastered a stunned smile on her face as they welcomed her. Then there was only one person in the whole world as Cian Finn walked up to her. He was so beautiful that Meg felt her heart seize.

"My queen," he said, bowing. He held out his hand. "A dance for your poor husband?"

Meg let him lead her. When she was encircled by his arms, her head against his chest, she realized that Cian Finn might be even more dangerous than his brother.

# Chapter Thirteen

It was the horrible sound of the rooster crowing that woke Meg the next morning. It sounded like the damn thing was right outside her door. She tried to burrow under the pillow to escape the dreadful racket, but there was something attached to her little pillow, and it wouldn't move an inch. An arm wrapped itself more tightly around her waist and pulled her closer.

"Damn it," Meg cursed as she tried to get out of bed. She was tangled in a quilt and it was difficult to orient herself. Where the hell was she? Oh, yes. A bit of the evening before came back to her. She was on the little cot in the barn, but she quickly found herself on her ass in the middle of the cold, dirt floor.

"It's too early, lover." Cian's Irish brogue was even thicker when he was drowsy. His hand came out seeking her once more, but he didn't open his eyes. "Get back in bed. We'll eat the rooster for dinner tonight, I promise."

"You aren't supposed to be in my bed, damn it!"

She gave her clothes the once-over, grateful she appeared to be dressed. The princess gown she'd worn to the party was draped over the lone chair in the corner of the room. She had on the thin shift that went beneath it, and her undies were right where they were supposed to be.

All good signs that she hadn't done anything she shouldn't have.

Still, she wasn't sure how she'd ended up in bed with Cian when she'd promised herself she wouldn't. And there was a gold band on her hand that hadn't been there the day before.

Cian rubbed his eyes, yawned, and stretched his big body. He, on the other hand, didn't appear to be wearing anything. His glorious frame was on full display. "You told me you refused to sleep in the big bed. You told me you needed independence, and the only way you could have that was to live in abject poverty, with not a single comfort to your name."

"I doubt I put it quite like that," Meg complained.

She remembered last night, up to a point. There had been dancing and singing. She'd met Flanna's family and all the rest of the brownies. Meg had laughed and said that they ate brownies on the human plane. She then spent the better part of an hour explaining that she wouldn't be coming after Flanna's grandchildren. Sweets might not be a big part of Fae life, but ale was. It was the ale that did it. It had been slightly sweet and had a hell of a kick. Every time she finished a mug, someone put another in her hands.

Cian scratched his belly. It shouldn't have been sexy, but it was. His gray eyes opened fully for the first time. "No. You took a lot longer to explain it. It was quite the lecture. There was something about making your own way and roaring because you're a woman. I didn't understand it at all, and I consider myself a smart man. The only part I really got was when you told me we had to live here."

Cian showed no ill effects from the enormous amount of ale he had downed. He had to have doubled her intake. The boy could drink.

"No, I said *I* needed to live here," Meg corrected. Now she remembered that she had kissed Cian. She'd been slightly drunk, and everyone was urging them to kiss. She'd meant to placate them with a little peck, but Cian had dipped her back over his arm and overwhelmed her. His tongue had slipped into her mouth and had its way with hers. He'd rubbed his body against hers, and she'd felt every inch of his intent. He'd gotten her so hot she might have done him right there.

She needed to stay away from him. He was always touching her. The night before, he'd held her hand or had his arm around her waist all of the time. There hadn't been a single moment she wasn't aware of him.

Cian's face was sweet as he sat up and crossed his legs. He paid no mind to his nudity or to his morning friend. "I know. You think living here will prove something to Beck. I don't think so, but I'm willing to go along with what you want. Can we get a bigger bed, though? It was cramped last night. I have no idea how we're going to fuck on that."

He hadn't heard a word she'd said last night. "We're not. Cian, we need to talk."

"I can do that," he promised with a sober look on his face.

She couldn't take her eyes off his enormous erection. It lay almost flat against his belly. "How do you expect me to hold a serious conversation with you like that?"

He shrugged. "You're my wife. It's my permanent state around you. It would probably go away if you jumped on top of me and bounced around for a while. Well, it wouldn't go away for long."

Getting to her feet, she turned away from the too-tempting sight. Her second husband was proving even more troublesome than the first. She needed to get properly dressed and get her day started. Perhaps then she would be better equipped to handle Cian. Her day clothes were still in the cottage. She would take some time to collect herself and then see to the farm.

"I'm going to get dressed. You…I don't know. Just take care of that," she said, avoiding the delicious sight of him as she stumbled out of the room.

She expected to step out into the leftover destruction from the night before, but the yard was pristine once more, without a sign of what had gone on. The gathering had been huge, with everyone in the village showing up to dance and drink. She'd been introduced to *sidhe*, brownies, trolls, gnomes, and some dwarves down from the mountains. They had toasted Cian's health and the twins' marriage. Everyone spoke of Beck with great fondness, and Meg had learned a lot about her wayward husband. He'd saved many of the people of the village at great cost to himself. For years after the civil war, he'd worked hard to build a sanctuary for the refugees from his home plane.

It would have been easy for the king to settle on the Vampire plane. The Dellacourts were a wealthy family who would have taken in Beck and Cian. He could have lived in luxury, and no one would have blamed him. Instead, at seventeen, he decided to establish a village on a safe plane to give his people a home.

Beck was their protector. Without him, the Fae would have

dispersed and more than likely had trouble surviving on their own. Cian had given his brother all the credit for founding their own small kingdom. He'd explained to Meg that he'd simply followed his brother's lead. Beck had been the one to take charge in those dark years after losing their parents. Hearing the love and admiration for Beck did nothing to ease the ache in her heart that he couldn't love her.

She walked slowly, not minding the early morning's chill. It really was beautiful here. There was a gentle mist coming up from the pond. She saw the cows contentedly eating grass in the distance. The sky was a soft watercolor of blues, pinks, and oranges. It was similar to her plane, but it felt so different. Even the air here was gauzy and sweet. The whole world seemed quiet and still. A wistful thought stole over her.

She could be happy here.

Meg took a deep breath and continued on toward the cottage.

She *would* be happy here. Happiness was a state of being. It was something she could choose.

She opened the cottage door and decided to start by getting dressed and fixing breakfast. She would battle the judgmental chickens again, and this time she would try frying the eggs.

She stopped in the middle of the living room because an erotic warmth swamped her senses. It started in her pussy and pulsed outward.

"Oh, god."

She barely managed to close the door behind her as she felt the connection between her and Cian open. It was like someone flicked a switch on in her brain and the channel had changed. She was suddenly tuned to the Cian Channel, and it was playing porn.

He was stroking himself. She could feel it. His hand was gentle as he stroked from the base of his cock upward, all the way to the crown where he brushed his thumb firmly across the head. There was already wetness there. He used it to lubricate his palm and facilitate smoother strokes. He tightened his hold on the monster, and she felt him sigh as he spread his legs and upped the pace.

Drops of arousal wept from the slit of his dick. If she were with him, she would lean over and lick it off. Was that her thought or Cian's? The connection was so new that she had to wonder. A vision of exactly what Cian wanted her to do flowed over her brain, taking over

161

her thoughts. She would run the tip of her tongue just inside the slit and tease him lightly. His big body would shudder in response and urge her on. He would fist his cock while she sucked the head, begging him to feed her everything he had.

She felt Cian's chuckle as though it came from inside her own body.

"Bastard," she whispered.

He knew she could feel him. He was pushing the experience out toward her. It was like she was there with him, almost as though she *was* Cian. She could feel his pleasure and his intent. He wanted her. Oh, she could feel that. He wanted her so badly. She stumbled into the bedroom and threw her body on the bed. She wouldn't be able to ignore the vision. It felt too good to ignore.

His hand was firm now as he ran it up and down his cock. She writhed on the bed, her legs restless as he caressed himself. He was thinking about her. He'd moved on from thoughts of her mouth to other body parts. He was thinking how good it would feel to have her tight pussy all around him. The muscles of her pussy would clench around his cock, trying to tempt him to come. He wanted to give her his semen. It belonged to her. It was only right for her to take it.

He wanted her on top, her breasts bouncing as she rode him hard. He would love the view from that position. He would grasp her hips and help force her down so his dick could hit her sweet spot.

Her nipples were hard. Her pussy was already soft and wet. Every cell in her body had been taken over by Cian's assault. He was there with her although their bodies were apart. It was intimate, so intimate. It was a lot like the connection she'd felt with Beck in the arena, though this time she knew what was happening.

Cian pumped his cock. His hand slid from the head down, down, down to the place where the thick stalk met his balls. No wonder men did this an awful lot. It was completely different from touching herself. There was a harder edge to it that she found fascinating. It felt really good, and she suddenly knew Cian could do this all morning. He would be careful and prolong the experience. He wanted to keep her in this state. He wanted her writhing and begging. Eventually he would give it to her, but only after he was satisfied that he had the upper hand.

Maybe turnabout was fair play. Cian thought he had all the control. Could she break him? How would he like her pleasure? Would her softness feel as good to him as his rough lust felt to her?

She pulled down the bodice of the dress and let her hands find her breasts. She let every sensation flow over her and pushed it toward him. Cian's state of sexual arousal had her nipples peaked and sensitized. She moaned as she had the twin sensations of Cian's hand on his cock and her fingers pulling at her nipples.

How did this work? She closed her eyes and fantasized. She wanted Cian. He was different from his brother. He was so open with his sexuality it led her to be open with hers. In her fantasy, she saw Cian climb over her, his big body pressing hers down. She rolled her stiff nipples between her thumbs and her forefingers, tugging lightly. She imagined it was Cian's mouth there.

He would lick them at first. His tongue would curl around the nipple just before he let her feel the edge of his teeth there. He would bite down lightly, never crossing the line between pleasure and pain. He would bite just enough to make the nipple flare with arousal. He would pop the nipple in his mouth and lave it with affection. Then, because this was her fantasy, she brought Beck in to suck on the other one.

In her fantasy, Beck didn't deny her anything. He took her breasts because they belonged to him.

In her mind, she saw two dark heads bent over her breasts suckling. She would hold their heads to her breasts, her hand sinking into the silky darkness of their hair. Their hands were everywhere.

She felt Cian pick up the pace. His hand was pumping firmly around his cock. She couldn't stop the smile that spread across her face. He was definitely getting the picture. It was time to move on.

Fantasy Cian began to kiss down her belly. He licked and kissed his way south as Beck nuzzled her throat. In her fantasy, she was suddenly tied tightly to the bed. Beck's hand collared her throat. He told her everything he intended to do to her in a honey-dark voice that left no room for disobedience. He and Cian had plans for their wife. Cian was going to eat her pussy. Beck would play with her breasts, and after she had come, they would have their pleasure. Beck wanted her mouth. Cian would plunge that hard cock into her pussy. She would be helpless to do anything but feel them. They could do anything they wanted to her, and she would have no defense.

She didn't need one. They were her lovers, her husbands.

She felt Cian's deep approval at the image. Her fantasy had become his own. It was everything he wanted, both halves of his soul with one singular purpose between them—her pleasure.

He was getting close. His cock was pulsing as Meg thought about Cian's tongue fucking her pussy. Cian's would spear her as thoroughly and ruthlessly as any cock. Beck's tongue would play on her nipples. Beck would suck on her nipples while Cian would lavish his love on the tiny bead until she exploded.

Meg's fantasy and Cian's merged into one hot image. She couldn't tell what she was thinking and what was Cian's, but she didn't care anymore. His hand had tightened around his engorged cock. It was purple now as he raced to the finish line. She could feel his balls tightening. They were getting ready to shoot off. His control was blown.

It no longer mattered. She wanted the orgasm. She slipped a finger into her pussy, circling her clit with her thumb, her fingers playing out the images in her head. She closed her eyes and saw Cian and Beck working furiously over her. The two heads worked in perfect harmony, suckling her breast and her clit. They loved her taste. They couldn't get enough of it.

Cian firmly took hold of their connection. Her own fantasy fell away as she felt a tingle at the base of her spine. His hand was a fist now, pounding away at his cock.

An image of Cian between her legs was all she could see now. It was so real. It was almost as though he was right there with her, his weight pushing her into the bed. He'd parted her thighs and shoved his desperate cock deep inside her. He pushed himself in to the balls and still he wasn't satisfied. He wanted to merge with her. He wanted to be a part of her. God, he needed her so badly. He'd waited for her. The emotion swept over Meg, making her eyes water. She'd never felt so desired as she did when the connection was open and his heart was pouring into hers.

He was pumping into her, and he was close, so close, to giving her what she desired. She picked up the pace, plunging two and then three fingers inside her pussy and knew they didn't match what Cian could give her. She spread her legs as far as she could and curled her fingers up while she pushed the pad of her thumb forcefully at her clit and then…

Relief, blessed, sweet pleasure as Cian came. Semen spurted up onto his belly, but he didn't care. In his mind it was her pussy he was flooding. He pumped and pumped, the feeling all the more exquisite because it was shared. Just as she thought she couldn't take another moment of his orgasm, her own hit. It bloomed from her center, spreading out like a rushing wave across her body. She felt Cian's surprise as he came again.

It was like the best phone sex ever, and she giggled as she laid back and tried to catch her breath. A happy languor radiated across her body. That had been so much more than playful sex. Cian's emotions had invaded her as surely as his fantasies had. He'd been open and honest, and there would be no recriminations from this half of the man. She couldn't stop the smile that spread across her face. The happiness she felt was coming from Cian, too. He was happy. He was well-satisfied, and it wasn't all physical for him.

He was coming. And not in a sexual sense. She could sense him physically approaching.

He threw the door open and tossed himself on the bed next to her. He hadn't put on his clothes. She should be hurrying to get away. She needed to be smart about this. Just because he'd been open didn't mean this would end any better than it had with Beck. A million things could go wrong. She should be pushing him away and getting dressed. Instead, when he put his hand possessively over her stomach, she found herself moving her head to his shoulder, unable to force herself to break the connection.

"That was fun," he said with a wicked grin. He was so beautiful it made her heart ache.

"Is that the way you invite a woman to play?" It would be an effective seduction technique. Suddenly she felt so vulnerable. She'd seen his past. He'd had hundreds of women. They lined up for him. How could she ever compete?

His perfect face was suddenly very serious, looming over her. His gray eyes looked almost silver in the soft light of morning. He sank his hands into her hair and turned her face up to his. "I've never done that with any woman before. I've waited my whole life to connect with another soul the way we did, and we could have so much more, Meggie mine. You're my wife, my bondmate. It won't work with anyone else."

She looked up at him and finally realized he wasn't his brother.

Technically, he was half his brother, but they were so very different. How could she ever find happiness if she never asked for what she wanted? If she kept telling herself no, she never gave anyone a chance to say yes.

"I'm scared," she told Cian quietly.

"I know," he replied with soft eyes. He leaned down and pressed a soft kiss on her forehead, as tender as the pleasure before had been rough. "How about we do this? Let's take it slow. No more overwhelming you with my dirty self-pleasure. I want you, Meggie. I want you to come to me because you want me, not because I'm the only one available. Though I am, you understand. I know you are stubbornly telling yourself we're not truly married, but I wouldn't push that if I were you. I'm willing to be reasonable. I'm willing to be patient. I am not willing to watch you flirt with another man."

"I can't handle the two I have." It felt so good to sink into his strength. It helped her to find her own. "I want things, Ci. I have certain needs that Beckett found distasteful. I'm worried you will, too."

His laugh rumbled through his chest as he pulled her close. He tangled their legs together. "I don't find much distasteful sexually. Why don't you explain what you want? I saw flashes of it, but I don't completely understand. I liked how you looked tied up and spread out for me."

Meg took a deep breath and proceeded to explain Dominance and submission to Cian. He was patient and asked questions.

"You want me to make decisions for you?"

"No." Meg was sure of that. "That's the way it works for some couples, but I would rather we had a partnership in our daily lives."

"And at night, when we're alone, I'm your Master," Cian said, his voice hoarse. His hands tightened around her, and she could feel his cock starting to revive. "Your body is mine, and I do what I want with it."

She sat up and looked down at her husband who was, once again, sporting a huge erection. At least he seemed willing to hear her out. "I haven't tried this with anyone. I don't know what I'll like and what I won't. Hell, at this point I'm not even sure it was what I liked or if I was just overwhelmed by the bond. I have to admit I'm curious and a little scared by all of it."

"You liked what Beck did to you," he pointed out. He seemed to be carefully thinking through the problem. "Whether it was the bond or your own needs, you enjoyed yourself."

Meg nodded. "I loved it. It was the best sex I've ever had. I should warn you, though, I hadn't had great sex before that. It was mediocre at best. Beck was upset afterward. He doesn't think I should like it. It can't work if the Dom hates himself for dominating his submissive. It kind of defeats the point."

Cian propped himself up on one elbow and brushed the hair back from her face. "He's fighting himself. He's trying to be something we're not. Give him time. Meanwhile, I'm more than willing to explore this with you. I'll admit I'm not the dominant half. I'm very carnal, but I tend to be softer than Beck."

"If you don't..."

His finger came up to her lips. "Hush, I'm still male. I think I can handle it just fine. How about we make a vow? I'll fulfill your fantasies to the best of my ability, and you'll do the same for me?"

Meg grinned. "Deal."

He reached over and took her left hand in his. He brushed his thumb over the golden band that rested there. "This was my mother's. I told you about it last night, but I don't think you remember."

Should she offer it back to him until they were sure it would work? "I don't. It's beautiful though. Maybe you should take it back for now."

He gently squeezed her hand. "Please wear it. It would confuse our people if you didn't. But you should know that it's important. It's the queen's ring. My sister..."

Tears pierced her eyes because she remembered this part. "She died and the last thing she gave you was this ring. She wanted to save it because she'd watched your mother die. Ci, I'm so sorry about what happened."

She felt him sigh, his body cuddling hers.

"Is it odd that it doesn't feel as bad now that I've shared it with you? Now when I think of that terrible time, I'll remember that you were there with me."

Oh, how would she ever keep herself apart from this man? "I'll wear the ring, but if you ever want it back, I'll understand."

He sat up and kissed her firmly. "I won't. I promise you that. But, for now, we work on being friends. I want you to take this time I'm giving you. I'll back off, but the minute you say *yes*, everything changes. Do you understand?"

She nodded, seeing the trap he had laid. She would have to be careful with her words for a few days.

He laughed. "Smart girl. Now go get dressed. You're entirely too tempting like that. We have work to do."

"Thank you," she said softly. She leaned over and pressed her lips to his.

Cian's smile was rueful. "I'm glad I have your gratitude, wife, because my dick is cursing me."

Meg laughed, and they got up, dressed, and got ready to face the day.

* * * *

Liadan O'Neill watched as the idiot Cian ran from the barn toward the cottage. He was naked, and there was no doubt he was a man on a mission. She'd seen the human walk toward the cottage. She had no idea why they spent the night in the barn, but it looked like they were moving their lovefest inside.

She had to admit, he was a lovely man. He couldn't help it. He looked exactly like his better half. If Cian Finn had been anything like his brother, her job would have been infinitely easier. She could have seduced Cian and put a blade through his heart. She had one she'd made especially for him. It was cold iron and easy for her small hands to use. She'd cursed the blade herself and tested it on that moron she'd been forced to call her husband for years. A husband had been required to get her into the village. It had taken a long while to find the right plane, and once she was here, she needed to get close to the princes. Her husband had come in handy. When he'd discovered her true nature, she'd tested her weapon. It had proven thoroughly effective. Life as a widow had given her the freedom she needed.

She didn't dare try to use the knife on Beck. His instincts were too well-honed when it came to battle. His hands were quick, and he could disarm her in an instant. He was the warrior. There was no doubt about it. She shivered slightly when she thought about all the times she'd been forced to smile and welcome him to her bed. He was a predator. Even though he asked politely, she could feel what he wanted, and it disgusted her.

It had occurred to Liadan that the brothers were protected on many levels by their odd nature. Beck was protected by his fighting ability, but Cian had some strong defenses against her as well. He seemed to sense something was wrong whenever she was close. Liadan had caught Cian watching her as though trying to figure out what she was. At first, she'd worried Cian would give her away, but he'd never called her out. By the time she'd found them, Cian had started his descent into madness and likely hadn't trusted himself enough to accuse her.

He hadn't joined his brother in her bed. Liadan was glad that Beck hadn't figured out she'd attempted to seduce Cian first. She still hated him with a vengeance for turning her down.

Even without direct access to the intellectual half of the king, she'd almost managed it. Her magic was strong. Though Cian had been protected at night—by Beck when he was around and that nosy little brownie when he was not—she had managed to enter his dreams as a mist. It was a particular talent of hers. Her sisters had always been jealous of the ability. She simply poured her will into a spell and wrapped it in the mist that always surrounded the pond. It found its way to Cian. It whispered to him. It brought out all his fears.

In the end, it had been simple. Cian was weak. He'd chosen to fade rather than live in a world where he had no hope of bonding. He'd been close to complete chaos. She'd been mere days away from convincing the idiot to kill himself once and for all, and then Beckett Finn would be easy prey. He would have quickly dissolved into a death machine, and there would be no choice but to put the king out of his misery.

Then that bitch had shown up.

Liadan watched the cottage, trying to come up with a way to deal with the new problem she had. The *queen*—she couldn't believe these idiots were calling her that—presented a uniquely troublesome problem.

If the legend was correct, there was the possibility that the twins' power could be greatly increased by bonding with a strong mind. While she doubted the human was a truly strong mate, she didn't want to take the chance. Beck was powerful enough as it was, and Cian with a Green Man's abilities scared her. If word got back to Tír na nÒg that the twins were alive and had ascended into their power, another civil war would follow. She had to stop that because she wasn't at all sure her side would win.

She felt a warmth at her heels.

"Hello, Ain," she said with more affection for her black cat than she had ever felt for another being. She stooped over, and the cat gracefully leapt into her arms. The cat did more for her than any other being had.

"There she is," Liadan said, pointing out their enemy. The *queen* walked out of the cottage with a dumb smile on her face, holding Cian's hand as they moved toward the barn.

It would be simple if she could kill the bitch, but she was certain that yesterday Cian had destroyed that plan as well. According to the gossip from the party the night before, Cian had fully bonded with the human. If Liadan killed her, the queen would be able to send the image to her husband.

It was too risky. She couldn't change forms again, and she didn't intend to be revealed as the hag she was when a lynch mob came.

She watched the outcast king teach his second-rate mate how to milk a cow. She had played a very careful game. It would be stupid to risk it now. The game had changed with the insertion of the human. What she needed was a new plan.

Liadan smiled as she thought about all the vampires Beck had fought in the arena for the right to mate with that ridiculous human. He'd probably made them all angry. It was the one decent move Torin had managed on his own. Limiting the vampires' access to consorts had made them more amenable to certain negotiations. There were still vampire families that were loyal to the outcast king, but others were much more reasonable. Perhaps it was time get in touch with one or two.

"I didn't mean yes that way, Ci!" The human's squeal carried across the field as she playfully avoided Cian's hands.

Cian would be sad when the human was dead or gone. Liadan didn't care which. The vampires would probably rather take the girl. They had their uses for one with her unique talents. With Beck off the plane, she might find some vampires desperate or arrogant enough to think they could kidnap a consort. Or some might look for revenge and kill the bitch.

Either way would lead to Cian's fading and Beckett's death. Once they were gone, Torin could reopen Tír na nÒg, and she would march back into the homeland a conquering hero. She would take her place beside her sisters as the king's counselor. Their status would be assured.

Liadan turned toward home, her familiar nestled firmly in her arms. She could hear the newlywed couple playing. Let them have fun now. Theirs would be a short marriage if she had anything to say about it.

# Chapter Fourteen

"What is it?" Cian sat in the kitchen looking at the small, flat cake-thing his wife had been working on for days now. Meg had been working on other things as well, but this odd bit of food was her labor of love.

Cian had spent his days working in the fields that fed the village. He spent the day perfecting his irrigation system with the gnomes. At night, he entertained the Fae who came from all over the plane to welcome the new queen. Large tents had been set up around the village. It was as though a great fair had come to town. Cian was happy with the coin that was now flowing around the village as visitors spent money and traded goods with the locals. It had been a long time since his people had anything resembling prosperity.

His wife seemed to think she had something to trade, too—this odd-looking thing she was prepared to force on him. She looked so cute with an apron over her day clothes and flour in her hair. She looked good enough to eat, and the now familiar ache started in his groin.

He was going to die if she didn't say yes soon.

"It's a cookie," his wife proclaimed as though that meant something.

He was rapidly discovering that even with the bond, his mind still wandered. It was his wife's fault. She had a smile that tended to melt his insides. He forced himself to concentrate on her words and not how creamy her skin looked.

Meg continued, "I had to figure out how to substitute honey for sugar, but I think I have it. It's an oatmeal cookie. It's better with chocolate chips, but we don't have any. Try one."

That wasn't what he wanted to try. He wanted to get his mouth on her breasts and that sweet, soft pussy of hers, but he was playing a long game. Still, he couldn't disappoint her. He took the "cookie" and prayed it tasted better than the other meals she'd attempted to cook him. His bride was beautiful and possessed a sharp mind, but cooking was not a talent of hers. He'd had to choke down dinner all week and smile and tell her how edible it was. Flanna was attempting to teach her a few tricks to Fae cooking. So far, it wasn't working.

Her hand was on her hip, and there was an offended look on her pretty face. "It's not going to kill you, Ci."

He was pretty sure it wouldn't. He quickly calculated his odds of surviving Meg's cookie experiment. He was confident, when applying the laws of rational deduction, that his odds were in the 99.783% range. Her foot tapped impatiently on the floor. He had a 100% chance of pissing off his wife if he didn't eat the damn thing and manage to smile. Cian shoved the cookie in his mouth and gamely chewed.

It was not half bad. "It's good."

The smiled that quirked up her lips was wry. "You don't have to sound so surprised. I never was a very good cook, but I always could bake. I didn't get these hips from following a low carb diet."

He would have asked her what she meant, but he was eating a second cookie. It wasn't good. It was great. He'd never really liked oats. They tasted like paper, but Meggie's cookie was soft and sweet. He reached for a third.

She pulled the platter back. "Hey, I need those for the goblins. Flanna said they've set up camp on the other side of the village in the caves."

Cian shook his head. He knew all about the goblins. It was expected that they would show up. In a way, it was a good thing. They were good for the trade they brought. The goblins lived on the plane and had chosen to do business with the village, but they were not here to pay court to the kings and their queen. They were Unseelie. They were potentially very dangerous. "You aren't meeting the goblins, my lover."

"Why not? I've met everyone else," Meg pointed out with a breezy lack of concern.

It was a huge change from the worried girl he'd met a few days ago. Meg had settled in nicely. She was growing in confidence and proving herself a good partner. She was polite when she needed to be, and she had good instincts as to when a small show of temper was required. Patience and gentleness worked with the brownies and gnomes, but he'd been proud when Meg slapped one of the cave dwarves silly. The dwarf been downright rude about humans being a bit lacking in the brain department. She'd smacked his hard little head. *Sorry*, she had said with an innocent smile. *I'm not smart enough to control my impulses.*

The dwarves had all watched their tongues since. It was now being said that the queen could be viciously brutal when she wanted to be. It was a compliment coming from the dwarves.

He watched the cookies go into a basket. There were a whole lot of cookies. The goblins might not even like them. His wife certainly wouldn't be wandering into a goblin cave with her pretty smile and basket of treats. The goblins would just as likely eat her. "The goblins aren't here to meet you. They come because of all the trade that goes on at gatherings like this."

Meg looked thoughtful for a moment. "What would goblins trade?"

He loved her questions. She was the most curious woman he'd ever met. "All manner of things. They tend to scavenge, so you can bet they have items from other planes. If we had anything to trade, I'm sure we could find something to intrigue you. The only thing they make themselves is a strange form of liquor. It's a brown drink they brew from beans they find in the mountains. It gets goblins drunk, but it just makes me jittery."

"Because, of course, you have to try goblin moonshine," Meg said with an affectionate laugh.

He shrugged. "If someone tells me it's liquor, I'll try it. I didn't like this stuff, though. It smelled lovely, but tasted bitter."

Her hazel eyes flared and she was very serious all of the sudden. "Beans from the mountains? Makes you jittery? Would you say it's an acquired taste?"

"I don't know who would want to acquire it." Cian shook his head as he thought about that drink. It had been very bitter and acidic, and the goblins served it at a scalding temperature. "It makes you jittery if you drink too much, and then it's like you're addicted. If you don't get it, you have a headache."

"Like the one I've had for a freaking week and a half," Meg snarled. She took him by the shirt, fisting the fabric in her hands to draw him close. "You will take me to the coffee."

Cian's eyes widened, and for a moment he wondered if the dwarves hadn't hit it on the head. His queen did, indeed, look a bit vicious. "They don't call it coffee."

"I don't care what they call it," Meg swore. "I want it. I'm a pot-a-day coffee drinker who's been without it for weeks now. You will get me that coffee. Do you understand?"

"It's become my new quest, wife." He never argued with a woman when she got that look in her eyes.

Meg backed off and smiled. "Excellent. We can trade the cookies for the coffee."

She placed a cloth over the full basket and smoothed down her new skirts. Some of the women of the village had held a small sewing party to make the queen a functional wardrobe. Meg had been effusive in her praise of the three dresses, two pairs of pants, two shirts, and some nice undergarments. She'd made the women promise to teach her what they knew. Her gracious acceptance of their rather plain garments had endeared her to the women of the village. It was the kind of thing that Beck would have turned down, fearing he was taking advantage of his subjects.

What Beck didn't—wouldn't—understand was that people needed to be needed. Those women had enjoyed giving their queen a gift she appreciated. Beck held himself apart. While the people loved him for his loyal defense of their lives and property, they rarely spoke to him beyond saying hello. They rarely asked his counsel or wondered about his health. Meg was going to change some of that.

If she survived meeting the goblins.

"Are you ready?"

"No." He didn't particularly want to go meet the goblins without Beck at his back.

"Good," she replied as though he had cheerfully said *yes*.

She picked up her basket and walked straight out the door.

Where had his day gone wrong? He'd planned it all out. He had worked hard all week so he would be able to spend this afternoon seducing his wife, and now he had to follow her into a goblin cave where she intended to talk them into exchanging their precious liquor for sweetened oat cakes.

He'd gone down the wrong road.

Cian slid off his stool and ran to catch up with his wife. Her hips swayed invitingly in her pretty skirt. She turned and winked at him as she walked down the lane. He jogged the last of the distance between them and slipped his hand into hers. She was talking and moving with a sweet feminine energy that had him sighing.

He might be going down the wrong road, but it was the one she had picked. He would follow.

* * * *

Meg chattered happily with her husband as they walked through the village toward the caves where the goblins were based. She smiled up at Cian and realized she really thought of him as her husband. It wasn't merely a title someone had stamped on them. They were married. When had that happened?

The last week had been a revelation. She'd begun to fit into village life. She wasn't delusional. She realized she wasn't the best cook in the world. Her poor husband was suffering as she learned, but she wasn't about to give up. The cottage had rapidly become her domain. Cian had convinced her to stay there while Beck was gone. There had been many daily tasks that required a resident.

It had been a smart play on his part. She'd been unable to hold herself apart. She found herself rearranging the furniture to suit her. She found yards of gauzy fabric in a trunk in the closet and fashioned some pretty curtains with Flanna's aid. She weeded the front flowerbeds. The gnomes had been happy to give her bulbs to plant.

She was even becoming fond of the chickens. It would make it almost impossible to eat them. She'd become fond of all the animals. She'd learned to milk the cows and how to brush Sweeney's mane. She hadn't let Cian kill the rooster. The rooster only crowed about half the time. Cian's cock was a much better judge of when dawn was here. It pressed against her every morning as the sun rose, seeking relief.

It hadn't found any, yet.

176

That would change soon. She wouldn't be able to deny him much longer. She didn't want to. She dreamed about him at night, Cian and his brother. As wonderful as Cian was, she still was heartbroken over Beck. She missed him, but she needed to move on with Cian. He didn't know it yet, but she intended to do that tonight.

They both became quiet as they trudged through the forest toward the caves. She felt Cian's hand squeeze hers as he helped her over a puddle.

Beck had been sending letters. They'd begun arriving the day after he left. They popped up on the vampire computer, but each had been written in his own careful hand. Beck's writing was like everything else about him, carefully controlled and wholly masculine. There were two every day, one addressed to Cian and the other to her.

She'd refused to read the first one. Cian had read his aloud and then dictated his response. The brothers asked about each other's health and the status of their endeavors. Beck inquired about the farm and the village, while Cian asked about the job Beck was doing.

Meg remained silent.

She was going to have to deal with Beck eventually. She didn't understand him at all. Beck had left her behind, but then he wrote her every day. The day before, she'd broken down and read one of his letters. It had been full of him saying he missed her and wanted to make up for his treatment of her. He promised to come home soon with gifts. He promised her a life of comfort.

The trouble was she didn't want that life. She was enjoying the one she'd found. She felt a great sense of belonging and accomplishment when she thought about the changes she'd made to the cottage. She was bonding with the villagers and rapidly becoming important to them. Cian seemed to need her as well.

She had no intention of allowing Beck to hire a woman to do her work. Although, if he proved as insensitive as he had been before, he might have to pay someone to sleep with him.

"Are you sure you want to do this?" Cian's whole body was tense.

She smiled sweetly at him. She didn't have high hopes that Cian would be able to truly top her when it came to sex. He was far too indulgent. He was nothing like his brother. Beck would have ordered her to stay away from the goblins. If she disobeyed, he probably would have locked her away. Cian had followed even though she could tell he was reluctant.

"Yes." She didn't feel a bit of the trepidation Cian obviously was experiencing. She'd met vampires and faeries and trolls and those rude dwarves. How bad could goblins be?

"Aye," came a deep voice. "I thought I smelled something tasty coming this way."

*Holy crap. What the hell was that?*

She'd briefly seen goblins in the arena, but they were different up close. This one was as tall as she was, though it had to outweigh her by a hundred pounds. Like the little brownies who were so helpful, the goblin had a head of scraggly, wiry hair. This one's hair was black, and his leathery skin had a distinctly green cast to it. His eyes were large as though he spent most of his time in the darkness. They were pitch black and seemed a little dead, reminding her of a snake's eyes. His mouth was the largest feature on his triangular face. It was filled with razor-sharp teeth. He wore only a small animal skin around his waist, and she found herself very grateful for the attempt at modesty.

"I love to eat *sidhe*," the goblin grumbled, the words tangling around his teeth. He scented the air with the holes in the middle of his face that seemed to pass for nostrils. "And something else. You aren't *sidhe*, girl."

Cian tried to pull her behind him, but that seemed like running to her. She read an awful lot, and running was a good way to get oneself chased down and eaten by a predator. There were times when boldness was called for. If she was the queen, then she should start acting like one. And maybe Beck's name would come in handy. Everyone seemed to be afraid of him.

"I'm human, goblin," she said, keeping her voice steady. "And I'm Beckett and Cian Finn's wife."

The goblin did not look impressed. "So the boys finally found a mate, did they? I'm sure my king will be interested in that bit of news. Unfortunately for you, you brought the wrong brother to our camp, little girl. If you're going to greet the goblins, you should have brought the warrior with you. As it is, I'll tell my king all about the brothers getting married and then me eating one of them."

He looked ready to do it, too. His clawed hands twitched dangerously.

"I want you to run," Cian whispered into her ear. "Run and don't look back."

He was so dramatic. The goblin, on the other hand, was a big old bully. She gambled. She walked straight up to the goblin, and using her thumb and middle finger, she *thwacked* him on his sensitive-looking nostrils. According to many a nature documentary, it worked on sharks. The goblin howled and took two steps back.

"There. Now we're starting to understand each other." She looked at the small flask on his hip. "Is that what I think it is?"

The goblin pulled the flask out. He held it in one hand as he protected his nose with the other. He wasn't so scary now. "It is mine. You would not like it. *Sidhe* do not like our liquors."

She stalked the goblin. "I told you before, I'm not *sidhe*."

With a curious expression, he handed her the flask. "It is strong, I warn you."

Meg wiped the rim with the towel she'd placed on the basket of cookies. She wasn't sure, but she suspected goblins were probably not the most hygienic of creatures. It didn't matter once that smell hit her. Heavenly coffee. It was still warm. She tipped the flask and drank it down in one long gulp. It wasn't even as strong as an espresso.

"Strong, my ass," she said with genuine relief. "It isn't strong, goblin, but it will do. I'm going to need more. Take me to your leader or whoever the hell can negotiate a trade agreement."

The goblin's face approximated a version of friendly. He still looked like he wanted to eat her, but he was obviously impressed with her as well. He looked at Cian, who was openly gaping at his bride. "Have the Seelies finally found a decent queen?"

Cian walked forward and took her hand once more. "Remember that she is the queen."

The goblin scratched his belly and gestured around the forest. "I don't think she's the queen of much yet, *sidhe*."

"She is my wife and my brother's wife." Cian seemed much surer now. "That is all that matters. Beckett Finn might have lost his throne, but he did not lose his sword. Remember that, unless you want to feel it in your back when he avenges her."

Meg smiled fiercely. She walked up to the goblin. "Beck won't need to avenge me, Ci. Goblin Boy and I have an understanding. Don't we?"

The goblin bowed, but only slightly. "Yes, Your Highness. I have

179

come to realize you are insane and vicious, and you can handle your liquor. I respect that. Come, the chief will be interested in meeting you."

Cian's hand tightened around hers. He leaned over to whisper in her ear. "He's right about the insane part, my lover. I hope goblins like cookies or you might find yourself being eaten as a snack."

She grinned and leaned back to her nervous hubby. It was time to give him a reason to believe they would live. "Ci, I'm saying yes tonight."

He gave her a short, hard kiss and then pulled her along to follow the goblin. "Let's get this over with, then. Tonight starts early, my lover, and I promise I'm the only thing eating you this day." The goblin was looking back at them. Cian's face became gorgeously arrogant. "Lead on. I want to get this over with. I've got better things to do with my day."

\* \* \* \*

Three hours later, the chief of the goblin clan burped and slapped Cian on the shoulder. He was incredibly drunk. "Tell that brother of yours we're ready to negotiate." It came out in a low growl. The goblin's eyes were watery but serious. His hand reached out and tugged on Cian's shirt. "But I have to ask you to leave your queen at home. She is unreasonable."

Cian wanted to laugh but was diplomatic enough to keep his face straight. He looked into the goblin chief's eyes and tried to convey a kingly presence. "I can't promise you anything. The queen is formidable, as you have seen. I can only promise that you will get your ten dozen cookies tomorrow."

"I'll have them ready, damn it," Meg said irritably.

She clutched the two sacks of coffee grounds she'd gotten for her basket of cookies. She was jittery because she'd sat with the goblin chieftain, matching him shot for shot until the goblin had finally fallen out of his chair.

Cian had been amazed at how much she could drink. Somewhere in there, the goblin chief had asked for her hand in marriage. Cian had been forced to pull a knife to persuade the chief that he wasn't willing to give up his claim on his wife.

"Make sure you do." The goblin chief looked longingly at the empty basket.

The cookies had gone quickly. After the first had been tried, negotiations had begun at a swift pace. Meg had been hard-nosed. Cian had actually felt a little bad for the goblins. He could have told them that Meg had a backbone of pure steel.

She'd held out for two bags of coffee, a bolt of some sort of blue fabric she called satin, a six-pack of Dr Pepper which came from the Earth plane, and a pair of brown boots she said reminded her of Uggs. Cian didn't know what Uggs were, but the boots looked warm. Altogether, it had been a phenomenally good deal.

He would have been impressed if he hadn't been so damn sexually frustrated. His wife handled the goblins with pure diplomatic grace. She'd known when to be charming and when to beat the goblins over the head with her fists. She negotiated to give the goblins a second shipment of cookies in exchange for a set of sheets. She was very excited about the thread count. He didn't know what that meant. The other part of the deal was something she had designated as a player to be named later. Again, nothing he understood, but if it got him out of these caves and into her bed, he would support the deal all day long.

He was supposed to be the intellectual half. He should have been extremely interested in the negotiations. But today, he couldn't take his eyes off his wife's breasts. He was going to see them, touch them, get them in his mouth. His cock swelled again, and he'd had enough.

"I am very interested in chocolate," Meg was saying to the small goblin who served as a clerk. He was writing down the Seelie Queen's demands. "It's sweet and brown. You'll find it in bars. It's bitter in powder form. I'll take that, too. Surely, some other plane has to have discovered chocolate."

"I will ask around, Your Highness," the goblin promised.

Cian reached over and took his wife's hand. If he let her, she would stand here all day negotiating. She was drunk on her own power. It was wonderful for her to discover her power, but he didn't give a shit. He wanted to discover her pussy, and he'd been sitting in a dank goblin cave for hours wondering when his hard-on was going to get relief.

"I'll let my brother know you request our attendance when he returns." Cian managed a courtly nod of his head. "I expect him to return by the end of next week. I assume you'll be staying here for a while?"

The goblin chieftain staggered to his massive feet. His eyes were sleepy. "Yes, Your Highness. We will stay while there is trade to be had."

"Well, we need to discuss a deal for you to distribute my baked goods," Meg began with an entrepreneurial gleam in her eye. He knew that look. It would cost him another hour if he let her get started.

"And we can do that at a later date," Cian said, hauling her bodily out of the cave. "Good day to you."

Meg blinked in the light of day. "Hey, I wasn't through in there."

Cian strode forward, pulling her behind him. "Yes, you are, my lover."

It was far past time to make her his wife in every sense of the word.

* * * *

Meg looked back at the caves where the smaller goblin children were standing, looking at her longingly. They raised their little gnarled hands in sad good-byes.

At one point, while Cian had done some manly sort of thing with the chieftain, she'd found herself surrounded by the goblin children and their mothers. Meg had won them over with cookies and stories. She was rapidly discovering that all faery creatures loved stories.

The *sidhe* children liked heroic stories, so she'd been recounting the plot line from *Star Wars* by the village fire at night. The goblins were a bit more bloodthirsty. She told them *Nightmare on Elm Street*. They didn't get that Freddy Krueger wasn't the hero of the piece.

"I was having fun." She waved to the young goblins. She had to wave with the boots she was holding because Cian wouldn't let her free hand go.

He turned to her. "Now it's my turn. I heard a yes, Meggie. I told you, a yes changes everything."

Meg grinned at him. "I said I intended to say yes. I didn't actually say it."

He stopped in the middle of the forest, and when he turned to her, she almost took a step back. The playful, flirty man she'd gotten to know was gone. In his place was a man who didn't look like he would take no for an answer.

His eyes were dark as he stared at her. "What are you saying? Think carefully before you answer. I might not be my brother, but I assure you, right now, I'm feeling a bit of his rage. If you're telling me no, then I need to get away from you."

Everything in her softened. She'd pushed him hard over the last week. In some ways, she'd made him pay for her anger with his brother. She stepped into his arms and let her packages fall to the forest floor.

"Yes, Cian," she said, loving the feel of his body pressed to hers.

She slept beside him each night, taking his comfort and holding herself apart from him. Every single night she started out telling herself she would stay away from him, and every night she ended up wrapped in his arms.

She was done with pretending. She wanted to know Cian in every way possible.

Cian acted as though his leash had been thrown away. He pulled her against the hardness of his body, pressing his swollen cock to her belly as he kissed her roughly. He rubbed against her and seemed a bit out of control. The bond between them gave her his thoughts.

He needed her in a way he'd never needed anyone before. It made it easy for her to submit to what he wanted. When he thrust his fingers in her hair and held her still, she didn't fight him. She went passive beneath him and waited for his command. Her heart sped up as he stared at her like a starving man looking at a meal.

"Open for me," he growled as he took her mouth.

She didn't have to ask what he wanted. He wanted everything she had. She opened her mouth, and his tongue immediately invaded. She opened her mind and was swamped with his desire. It overwhelmed her. It made her groan in response. Her hand trailed down his chest, seeking that part of him that needed relief. She stroked him through the fabric of his pants.

"Harder," he commanded as his hands went straight for her nipples. He shoved the soft linen of her shirt aside, baring her breasts to the cool afternoon air. He looked down at her chest, his eyes eating her up. "You're gorgeous, wife of mine. Do you have any idea how long I've wanted you?"

"Well, you've only known me for a week."

He cupped a breast, his hand skimming her sensitive skin. He leaned in and spoke to her. "Don't joke now. I've waited my whole life for this. I might not have known your face, but I knew you. You were made for me. Everything I've suffered through, I did it to bring you to me."

Tears welled in her eyes. She reached up and cupped his face. He'd gone through hell, and yet she had the distinct feeling he meant every word he said. He would go through it again if it brought them together. She suddenly realized that she would do the same. She would make all the same choices, go through the same pain, if it meant standing here with this man.

"I want to be your wife, Cian Finn. I'm so proud to be your wife."

Her nipples were hard pebbles as he rolled them between his thumb and forefinger. He closed his eyes for a moment as he cupped her breasts. She felt his deep satisfaction at the contact and knew he could sense how much she enjoyed it, too. He molded her breasts with one hand as he pulled her close with the other. He kissed her, his tongue singing with his need.

She cupped her husband's erection. She pressed against his cock as his hips moved helplessly against her hand. He was huge, and she could already feel his arousal beginning to seep from the slit, wetting his trousers. "We need to get home."

"No time," he said. She found herself on her back looking up at the green canopy of trees. Cian towered over her. He started to work on the ties of his pants, his hands shaking slightly. His voice was perfectly clear, though. It was dark and rich and flowed over her with command. "Lift your skirts."

She struggled to sit up. He couldn't mean to do this here. They were on a well-used trail. "Ci, we're out in the open."

She tried to be reasonable, but it was hard. He wasn't guarding his thoughts. He was pushing them toward her. She could see an image of what he wanted to do to her, and it was dark and nasty and so tempting she wanted to cry. It made her wet and ready for him. He wanted to lie back in the grass and grip her hips. He wanted to skewer her with his cock. He wanted to pound into her so hard her breasts bounced. She could feel her pussy start to pulse, desperate to have him inside. His need had started an ache in her, but they weren't that far from the goblin cave. Anyone could come walking along.

"I said lift your skirts." His beautiful face was slightly savage. He'd gotten his cock free, and he was his brother's twin. Cian's cock was huge. He stroked it as though trying to placate the monster. "I want to see your pussy. Megan, I won't ask again. I won't accept anything less than what you're willing to give my brother. I'm in charge of this, and you're going to obey. Is that understood?"

He was trying to give her exactly what she'd said she wanted. He was trying to top her, and she responded. It felt good to chuck her inhibitions and concentrate on pleasing him. She spread her legs and pulled her skirt up. She wasn't wearing underwear. It was so much easier because she could feel how much she pleased him. It radiated off of him.

"You have a gorgeous pussy, Meggie mine. Now turn over and let me see that ass. I need to make a few things clear to you."

Meg had to force herself to breathe. She turned over, the grass soft under her knees.

"Higher, Meg. I want that ass in the air."

Meg leaned over, putting her face in the grass, forcing her backside high.

His hand came down in a stinging slap. "That's for keeping me waiting."

Meg had to smile. She'd disobeyed him all day, but she got that little slap for making him wait for sex. That was Cian.

"You won't make me wait again." Cian slapped her other cheek and then spread her wide. "Now, look at that, won't you? I'm going to fuck you here, Meg. Not today, but eventually. I'm going to rub oil all over my cock, and I'll fuck this pretty asshole. And you'll let me, won't you?"

Meg closed her eyes. He was staring at her asshole and it was doing something for her. "Yes, Cian. I'll let you."

"Damn straight." He slapped her ass again. "Now turn back over."

Meg rolled in the grass and immediately opened her legs so he could see his pussy.

He looked down, and she could feel something inside him relax. She could guess what had worried him. He had probably been worried she wouldn't respond to him as she had Beck.

"I love you, Ci," she said, and she meant it.

If he was worried that she wouldn't care about him the way she did his brother, then she needed to put that out of his mind. Cian had quickly become her anchor in this world.

She had seen deep into his soul. It was ridiculous to try to hold herself apart from him. Cian's soul was lovely and generous. He held back nothing. He'd shown her the dark parts of himself. She knew he was jealous of how seriously everyone took Beck while they viewed his contributions as unnecessary. Cian had longed for his father to give him half the attention he lavished on Beck.

"I love everything about you," Meg said, pushing her emotion outward so he would know it was true.

He fell upon her, done with any sort of play. "I love you, Meggie mine. Goddess, how I love you."

He was ferocious in his need, and she softened under him. His big body pushed her into the hard ground, but she didn't care. She loved his weight on her. His hands pressed her knees open. His mouth came down on hers. It was like he was trying to inhale her.

"Wrap your legs around me," Cian commanded. He reared up on his knees and lined up his dick to her pussy. He stared down at that place where the head teased her. "Goddess, that's a gorgeous sight. You're mine. I'll share you with my brother, but you should know you're mine, wife. Look at us. Look at how beautiful we are together."

Meg slid her legs around Cian's waist. She pulled her head up and looked down the length of her body. Cian was teasing at her pussy. His big cock glistened with her juices. It was a lovely picture. But she wanted more. She needed him inside her. "Please, Cian."

"Yes, wife, I want to please you." He pulled his hips back and thrust into her.

He spared her not an ounce of his weight. She was crushed beneath him, and he was everywhere. He was deep inside her, shoving his cock in until his balls hit her ass, only to pull out and thrust forward again. His mouth took hers, his tongue stroking, plundering. His hands clutched her tightly as though he was afraid to let go. And his mind, his mind was giving his pleasure to her.

It felt so good. She tightened around him, not wanting to lose an inch of him. His thoughts came quickly and threatened to overwhelm her. He wanted her so much. He loved the silky slide of her pussy sucking at his cock as he moved in and out. He adored the sounds she made as he hit her sweet spot. His entire being pounded with the desire to mark her. He wanted everyone to know that this woman was his.

Meg pushed back against him, rotating her hips to find that perfect place. She lost track of who was feeling what and simply let the experience fill her senses. Her hands found his well-muscled ass and prodded him on.

She moaned as she felt how close he was. Everything inside of Cian was tense, his body tightening as he approached release. He went up on his knees and fingered her clit with a firm swipe of his thumb as he thrust as far as he could go.

His head fell back as he came. Meg felt the pleasure he took in filling her with his essence. It flowed from his body to hers, and her womb clenched and released with waves of pleasure. Cian continued to thrust, making sure he gave her everything he had. Meg moaned at the little aftershocks she felt when Cian hit a sensitive place.

Her husband finally fell forward, completely exhausted. He pushed her deliciously into the ground as he buried his face in her throat.

"Love you, Meggie," he managed.

Meg smiled and held him to her.

# Chapter Fifteen

"That makes me sick." The vampire watched the couple as they made their way down the road toward the ramshackle cottage.

Liadan took in his measure. He seemed thin compared to a *sidhe*, but she knew that the vampire's lankiness probably hid a wealth of strength.

They were standing at the far edge of her property, hidden in a copse of trees. The tangled branches gave them a place to watch the road and not be noticed. They didn't need it though. Cian and his human whore couldn't see anything but each other.

"Well, it doesn't do anything for me, either," Liadan replied. She tried not to roll her eyes.

She was surprised at the depth of animosity she felt for the human. She hated the way the red-haired girl hugged her body to Cian's. She loathed him for smiling down and teasing her as lovers did. It was obvious that they were finally sleeping together, and that fact chafed.

"You told me she was at odds with the brothers." Kinsey Palgrave frowned, the expression marring his handsome face.

Liadan shrugged. She wasn't sure why it mattered. "I told you she wasn't sleeping with Beckett. He brought her home and left the very next day for your home plane. He didn't even spend that single night with her. He preferred to sleep in the barn. She wasn't pleasing to him."

Beck had never thought to sleep in the barn when he was seeing her. Then again, he had never actually spent the night. He had used her and then walked back to his own cottage. She was being forced to admit that her charms had not worked on either brother the way they should have. She'd been sure this form would work, but something had gone wrong.

"Well, Cian Finn doesn't seem to have the same problem." Palgrave's eyes darkened. "He's obviously fucking the consort."

"I don't understand why you care," Liadan said, studying the young vampire. He was a royal, like the twins' cousin, Dante. Unlike that imbecile they were related to, however, this vampire was serious. He was hungry for a mate and angry that the consort had been taken from him. He did not believe the competition had been fair.

Dante had told the whole tale at the tavern the same night Beckett had brought his bondmate home. Liadan had heard the name Kinsey Palgrave as one of the competitors Beck had brutally defeated. Kinsey had been easy to persuade to her side. He'd bought the story of how desperately the human wanted to leave this barbaric place. Now he was faltering. She needed to bring him back into the fold. She needed to convince him to kidnap or kill the human.

"Do you honestly believe she can be happy here?" Liadan asked. "She is used to a world with technology. She might enjoy sleeping with Cian, but living here? She's not used to the hardships. Beckett is still gone from this plane. His twin is vulnerable. All of his power is in his intellect. It will be easy for you to take the consort from him."

The vampire turned to Liadan, his fangs out. They had popped out the minute he saw that idiot human walking up the road. He had some form of visual aid device. Liadan didn't care to look through it. The vampires relied too much on their technology.

"It might be easy to take the consort," Palgrave agreed. "The trouble will be in keeping her. I came here because I believed she would go willingly with me. She doesn't look unhappy. I could kidnap her, but what's to stop her from running the first chance she gets?"

"You would." She was beginning to wonder if anyone had a brain. "Tie her up, for all I care. You would get the consort and your revenge. Beck will fade if he loses her."

It was the vampire's turn to sound disbelieving. "More likely he will simply go insane and attempt to track me. This is wrong. I only came because I thought the consort needed saving. I'm not about to get involved in carting off a screaming consort, and I'm certainly not about to hurt one. You know what they say, be kind to consorts or you will never find one yourself."

Liadan nearly screamed in frustration. Her plan was falling apart because of an old vampire proverb? The royals had rules about handling consorts, but she hadn't expected them to be vigorously upheld during a time when there were so few to be had.

The vampire turned away from the sight of the couple kissing. "Besides, it's a good thing in the long run. If the Finns can take back Tír na nÒg, our access to consorts will return. It is obvious that you are angry at the brothers. Did they break off relations with you? You have to be realistic, miss. They were always going to marry a bondmate. I have to be realistic, too." Palgrave pulled his hood up as he made to leave. "I came because I want a consort, and she's lovely. She isn't available, so the best I can do is make some money off the situation. I don't think anyone knows the Finns have bonded yet. I'm sure that Beck went to the Vampire plane to make a deal with his relatives. I might have time to buy up some Dellacorp stock before the price goes sky high. I'll make a bundle and look like a genius in the trades."

The vampire looked pleased with himself as he turned to go. He had come alone, and now she was grateful for that fact. It was easier to deal with a single vampire than a couple. The last thing she wanted was him telling his tale to all and sundry. The minute he mentioned her name, the brothers would be after her.

She pulled the silver knife from her sleeve. She said a quick spell to make her aim true and then plunged the knife into the vampire's back. She was much stronger than she looked. The form she presented made her look frail and weak, but her true body was solid. The vampire jerked once, and then he fell apart as his heart was torn asunder by the silver.

She shivered as she looked at her previously pristine clothing. She wished she hadn't worn her second-best dress. Killing vampires was a filthy business. They tended to explode when their hearts ripped apart. She was covered in blood.

If she moved quickly enough, she might be able to preserve some of it. Vampire blood was powerful. Perhaps the day wasn't a complete waste.

The sound of laughter filtered across the pond. She had to find a way to get that bitch alone. She had to get her off this plane and make it look like she had walked away. If the brothers thought she was taken, they would move mountains to find her. If they thought she'd been killed, it could get ugly. Liadan didn't like to think about what they would do to her. She had no plans to martyr herself.

As she made the long walk toward her cottage, an idea came to her.

\* \* \* \*

Beck strode out of the caves and handed his sword to Colin Dellacourt. The heat of the desert scorched everything it touched. He was filthy and covered in blood and he didn't like to think what else, but the job was finally over.

Colin took the king's sword and reverently wiped it clean. He motioned to the employees walking around camp. A young vampire walked up to answer the *sidhe's* call.

"His Highness is finished," Colin announced. "Take the telemetry unit and gather the data we need."

The young vampire looked to the mouth of the cave with anxiety. "He's sure?"

Colin's brown eyes narrowed. Beck hid his smile as the former farmer scared the shit out of a young executive with just a look. "Are you questioning His Highness?"

The young executive shook his head. "Not at all, Mr. Dellacourt. I'll get you those readings immediately."

Colin stared at the small group of Dellacorp employees as they scrambled to do his bidding. Beck pulled his filthy shirt over his head and reached for his robe. He needed a shower. The vampires had set up the camp with all the luxuries their technology had to offer. One of those luxuries was the portable shower that cleaned with something called sound waves.

Beck preferred a good soak, but that wasn't available out here in the desert. He thought about the gift he'd approved before he left for the Bad Lands, as they called this place. Susan had been insistent on getting them a wedding gift. It was probably being delivered this very day. He couldn't wait to lie in the soaking tub with Meg in front of him. He would hold her as they soaked in the hot water and talked about their days. He would tell her about the work he'd done in the fields, and she would talk about...

"What do you and Susan talk about?" Beck heard himself asking. He hadn't meant to. It just popped out. He wouldn't take it back, though. He was curious about the consort's relationship with his cousin.

Colin sat down beside him and pulled out a bottle of whiskey. He was quickly handed two glasses by an assistant who always seemed to anticipate his needs. Beck gratefully took the glass and tipped it back. He would be damn sore tomorrow.

Colin thoughtfully sipped at his well-aged whiskey. "We talk about everything, Your Highness. Mostly, it's business, of course. She is the CEO of one of the most powerful corporations on the plane. It helps that I have a fairly decent head for numbers and processes."

He did. It had surprised him when Colin announced he was accompanying his king on this job. Susan had nodded and told him to send detailed reports. She hadn't been his CEO when they parted, however. She'd been his wife. She'd asked Colin three times if he remembered everything and checked his bag. She'd kissed him good-bye and made him promise to call.

"I also have a very thick skin," Colin said cheerfully. "That helps a lot when your wife is also your boss. Damn woman can flay a man alive with that tongue of hers. I screwed up the quarterly reports a few months back, and she took a chunk out of my hide right there in the boardroom."

"She yelled at you?" He was surprised that his cousin would yell at a consort. Vampires were supposed to be as gentle with their consorts as the Fae were with bondmates.

"Yelled, screamed, threatened me with all manner of humiliation," Colin explained with a smile on his face. "That woman of mine is a righteous bitch when she wants to be. It's all right, though. I took my fair share out of her pretty ass later that night, if you know what I mean."

Beck thought he did. He'd spent a lot of time thinking about Colin and Susan while he was working in the caves. Colin didn't seem to want the type of life he'd expected a consort to require. He seemed to like to work, and he was tough. His wife didn't treat him like he would break, but she still loved him. "You were rough with her?"

The question came out with expectant curiosity rather than accusation.

"Vampires are rough, Your Highness," Colin explained without a hint of self-consciousness. "Relationships here, at least sexual relationships, involve a dominant partner and a submissive partner."

Now Beck sat up and poured himself another glass. Meg had used those words. "Are you the dominant?"

"Yes, I am. Susan prefers to give up control in the bedroom. It was strange at first. You have to understand, Your Highness, I was raised in an isolated part of the country. I didn't know I could bond until I came to the Vampire plane. I was a farmer. I'd been taught to treat females with great softness."

"We're bigger and stronger," Beck said, parroting the words he'd heard from his father. "They need our protection, not our abuse."

Colin's dark brows rose questioningly, and there was a distinct chill coming from him. "If you're worried about me abusing your cousin, Your Highness..."

"Say what you need to say, Colin." Beck encouraged the slightly younger man. "Forget I'm the bloody king. I'm your cousin. Talk to me that way. The goddess knows I need someone who'll be honest with me."

"Fine," Colin said, his eyes narrowing. "I'd tell you, cos, to get the stick out of your ass. My relationship with my wife isn't open for your judgment. I've heard that gentry marriages were cold exchanges of protection and money, for bloodlines and a proper bond. I don't want that. I want a real marriage. Maybe it's because I'm a commoner, but you can keep your perfect proper bondmate. I don't want to be treated like a bit of fluff to be taken off a shelf and fucked when my mate thinks about it. I certainly don't want to treat my wife like that. Life is hard, no matter your circumstances. You should have a partner, not a weight around your neck."

Beck felt his stomach drop. He thought about what he'd said to Meg. He'd told her she was a responsibility to be borne. She'd asked to be his partner, and he'd complained about having to feed and clothe her.

"I don't think of her that way," Beck said quietly. He didn't. He thought of her all the time, though. Now that he'd had her, he couldn't sleep without picturing her with him. He held a pillow close to his body at night and pretended it was Meg against his chest. Goddess, he missed her.

Colin poured another round. "It's hard in the beginning. Marriage ain't easy. You have to find your way. It's harder for you because there are three of you involved."

"Ci doesn't seem to be having a problem." He took a drink, shooting the warm liquor into his belly. Cian had been plain in his correspondence. He was pissed with the way Beck had treated their wife up to this point.

Everyone was mad at him.

"Then maybe you should listen to Ci," Colin said sagely. "He would listen to you when it came to killing gigantic bats."

That thought amused him and reminded him he did have a place where Cian didn't best him. "He wouldn't have time to listen. He would be running the other way." Cian had always been a baby when it came to things with fangs trying to kill him. "I want to go home, Colin. Can you get me home tonight?"

The big Fae smiled. "That I can do, Your Highness. I suspect I could get someone to drive you straight through to your village, if you like. If you go back to the city, you'll find yourself being debriefed for twelve hours."

Beck groaned. "Please, no more meetings."

Colin graciously inclined his head. "Go take a shower while I get a driver set up for you. I have to prep this site for mining operations, or I'd take you myself. As it is, I suspect I'll get in trouble with my boss. She's expecting you to report back like a good employee."

Beck grinned. "Then she shouldn't have paid me up front."

He rushed off to get changed. He was anxious to get back to his sleepy little village where his sweet wife waited to start their life together.

\* \* \* \*

Five hours later, Beck stared slack-jawed at the chaos around him. There were tents and campsites everywhere. His quiet village had turned into a raucous marketplace. There were people everywhere.

"Your Highness," a pretty *sidhe* said. "Welcome back. I hope your trip went well."

He thought her name was Bri. She was carrying a basket, and he could hear the coins jangling in her pockets. He searched his memory. Her father was the miller.

"It was fine," he replied, still dazed. "What is going on here?"

194

Bri's eyes were wide. "It's a celebration. It's the tradition. We're celebrating the kings' bonding with three weeks of festivities. Last night we had a great bonfire, and the priestess blessed King Cian and Queen Meg. It was a lovely ceremony. They're so in love." Her face was shining with remembrance. She frowned suddenly. "We've missed you, of course, but King Cian explained you had important business to attend to. Not that we forgot about you. Not at all. Your name was mentioned, Your Highness. Everyone cheered."

"I'm glad someone remembered me," Beck ground out. This was how Cian chose to protect their bride? He was supposed to hide her from prying eyes. Instead, he'd invited the whole damn plane to a party. The goddess only knew how many spies were reporting back to Torin. He caught sight of a big shape walking through the stalls and his jaw dropped. "Is that a bloody goblin?"

The young girl nodded. "Yes, they have brought so many strange wonders. Some of us worried they would not behave without Your Highness around to keep them in line, but they are terrified of the queen, so all has been well."

Beck felt his heart seize. His Meg had met the goblins? Cian had allowed a goblin to get close to their bride? Had he lost his mind? What had the girl said? "What do you mean the goblins are terrified of the queen?"

The girl smiled proudly. "Our queen beat them and threatened to never make another cookie for them if they ate her. She got the goblin chief to back down. Imagine that, a Seelie queen forcing an Unseelie lord to concede." She leaned in conspiratorially. "If you ask me, the force is strong with our queen."

Beck wondered if that damn vampire had taken him to the wrong plane. "Someone is forcing the queen to do something?"

"No," Bri said helpfully. "It's an old human legend. You see, the force represents…"

Beck saw someone who might be more helpful. Liadan was walking toward the shops at the center of the village. "Thank you, Bri. Tell your father I'd like to talk to him about the mill. We'll need more flour if this goes on for too long."

"Don't worry, Your Highness," Bri said as he started to walk away. "The queen has already taken care of it."

*Well, of course she had.*

He hurried along, pursuing Liadan across the square. Liadan wouldn't be under the new queen's spell as everyone else seemed to be. "Lia!"

The blonde turned and, when she saw it was him, made her bow. She was cool and polite. "Your Highness. You returned early. You weren't due back for another week."

That was why he'd thought he could get away with it. In another week, the three weeks of celebration would be over. His brother was a tricky bastard. Cian might not have been able to cover the fact that he'd called the festivities, but he would have been able to say they were small. He would have attempted to convince Beck that they were small but necessary to the villagers' acceptance of Meg. He was a sly one, his other half, and he was about to get that magnificent brain of his bashed in.

"Would you like to tell me what the bloody hell has been going on while I was away?"

Liadan smiled sweetly. "It is a celebration for your queen, Your Highness. I was surprised you authorized it. It is very expensive and seems a strange thing to do when so many are hungry. I wouldn't be surprised if our food stores are empty by the end of the festivities."

He hadn't thought of that. Cian always handled those things, but he seemed to be derelict in his duties lately. Beck had hoped that once he bonded he would go back to his responsibilities. "And what has my brother been doing?"

Liadan shrugged gracefully. "He rarely leaves the queen's side. He dotes on her when he should be working. She demands it. I thought she wasn't royal, Your Highness, but she certainly acts like it. She forced the women of the village to sew her a new wardrobe, and the miller to up his work all because she has to make some strange human food. She even took one of my dresses. The new queen thinks that anything to catch her eye should be hers, I suppose."

"Is that a fact?" Beck asked.

Liadan looked properly intimidated by his low growl.

"She's even forcing the villagers to work for her." Liadan pointed out a stall to her left. There was a long line, and two young *sidhe* were working hard to sell some sort of food product.

His queen had gotten out of hand while he was gone.

It was time she understood the king was back.

# Chapter Sixteen

Beck made sure he had a tight hold on his mental shields as he approached the cottage. Even as he looked around, he kept the walls up so he didn't alert his brother to his presence.

He was shocked at the state of his lands. He'd left a sad, rundown cottage and was returning to a home someone gave a shit about. Someone had weeded the gardens and planted flowers. The front walk was lined with orange and yellow marigolds. The walk had been swept, and someone had woven ivy up and down the front walls. The cottage looked lovely. There were pretty yellow linens hanging in the windows.

He stopped and looked out over the fields. Someone had been working there, too. It seemed that Cian hadn't been so derelict.

Liadan's words came back to him, making him worry about how so much had been accomplished in so little time. He hoped his twin hadn't been forcing the villagers to work while he paid court to their new wife. Cian could be lazy at times, but he wasn't cruel. He did sometimes take a different view of what was due to them than Beck did.

What if Meg sided with Cian? What if Meg thought it should be her right to take what she wanted simply because someone had put a title in front of her name? She was about to discover that it was his right to set her straight.

"You wanted to see me, Professor Finn?"

Meg's voice was soft but audible through the open windows. Beck paused before opening the door. He could see his brother and their wife through the open shades. She was so beautiful. She was wearing a pretty skirt and a shirt that dipped awfully low on her chest. She'd unbuttoned the top two buttons and her breasts swelled out of the white linen. It made his mouth water to remember how good those breasts felt in his hands and pressed against his chest. She wore her long hair in pigtails, tied with white ribbons.

"Yes, I did, Megan," Cian said in what Beck recognized as his teacher voice. It was stern and a little intimidating. Why was he using it on their wife? "You were a very naughty girl in class today."

Cian sat at the kitchen table, and Meg stood looking down at him. Beck couldn't see his brother's face, but he had an excellent view of Meg. She leaned over and her voice was slightly breathy as she spoke. "Please, Professor. I need to pass this class. I can't fail. My parents would be so angry with me. Is there anything I could do for extra credit?"

Beck let his pack fall to the ground. This was interesting, and he wanted to see exactly what they were doing. Cian often liked to play out scenes like the one he was performing with Meg.

Cian had a great imagination when it came to dirty fun. Beck felt his interest rising along with his cock. Meg seemed to be playing along willingly. The entire trip home, Beck had thought about what Colin had said. Meg didn't have the same expectations other bondmates had. What if she had been telling him the truth? What if she honestly wanted that submissive relationship-thing she'd talked about? Could he trust himself to give her what she wanted and not hurt her?

There was a deep chuckle. Cian sat back in his chair. "I don't know about that. I'd have to see what you have to offer me. Let's see, your Gaelic is horrible."

"I'm working on that," Meg promised with wide eyes. "*Tá grá agam duit.*"

She'd said *I love you* in passable Gaelic. It sounded pretty coming from her lips.

She'd said it to his brother.

"Nice, *a grhá*," Cian praised her. His long fingers tapped rhythmically against the table. "But I was thinking of something a bit more physical for this extra credit you need. You look like a strong young woman. Why don't you take off that shirt and show me your muscles? I've been looking for someone to help me carry my books."

Beck almost laughed out loud, but then Meg was dragging the shirt over her head. Her nipples came in view. They were a dusky pink and stood out, obviously aroused. She touched them. She rubbed her breasts brazenly. Her small hands caressed the mounds. They were round and gorgeous and perfectly made. They caused his mouth to water. He wanted to force her onto his cock and watch those breasts jiggle as she rode him hard.

Would she do it if he asked her? Would she do it faster if he ordered her?

"Do I look strong enough, Professor?" Meg's voice was husky, causing Beck's cock to react. He could only imagine what it was doing to Cian.

"I suppose so." Cian was playing the stern professor to the hilt. "You know, all that walking is going to require strength in your legs as well as your torso. I don't think I can give you this assignment until I've seen your legs."

Meg bit her lower lip and looked sweetly nervous. She was good at this. She seemed to enjoy the play.

He'd thought that once he and Cian settled down with a bondmate, their days of playing in such a manner would be done. Sexual relations with a bondmate were reverent, sacred acts. What if all that reverent sex bored his wife to tears because she was a dirty girl underneath? Maybe Colin was right. Maybe he should start thinking of Meg as Meg, rather than a bondmate. Maybe he should give Meg what Meg wanted rather than what he thought she should want.

She slid her right leg onto the top of the table, then carefully, slowly pulled her skirt up. Her fingers ran the length of her pretty leg, all the way to her hip.

"Now, Megan," Cian began authoritatively. "It is obvious to me that you're missing a very important piece of your school clothes. A good student doesn't come to class without her underwear."

Her mouth was a perfect *O* that would fit his cock when he shoved it in. He was so hard. He had to get a grip if he ever wanted to walk in that room. If he didn't, he would end up stroking his own meat in the flowerbeds.

"I must have forgotten, Professor Finn," Meg said as her finger started playing with her pussy. A wicked smile lit her face, and Beck felt left out. She looked at Cian like he was ten feet tall and had just slain a dragon for her. "Sometimes I forget. Are you angry?"

"The question isn't whether I'm angry, my lover," Cian said, slyly coming out of character. His head swung around, and he looked his brother straight in the eyes. "The question is whether our peeping Beck is enjoying the show."

Cian looked perfectly pleased with himself, and Beck knew his brother had been on to him for a while. Meg, on the other hand, looked horrified. She gasped and held the shirt in front of her like a shield. Beck sighed and picked up his pack. He stalked to the door of his home and stepped inside.

It looked like sexy playtime was over.

"How dare you," Meg said, going to stand behind Cian.

Beck went from being slightly upset at getting caught peeping to insanely jealous at the sight of his woman hiding behind another man. It didn't matter that the other man held half of his soul. It only mattered that Meg was seeking protection from him.

He forced himself to calmly put down the bag. He could be reasonable. In her mind, she had been treated poorly. Hell, in reality he'd treated her poorly, but he'd had his reasons. He would peacefully explain to her why he had treated her as he did and ask for another chance.

She had her back to him, shoving her arms through the sleeves of her shirt.

Cian grinned. "You were shielding, weren't you, brother? The minute your dick got hard, those walls came down. You can't hide from me when you're that aroused."

"You could have said something," Meg hissed at Cian. She sounded pissed, but her hands came down on his brother's shoulders as she turned her glare Beck's way. "I'm sure you're here to lecture me about how to behave."

"I was enjoying the show," Beck said evenly.

He wanted to go and rip her away from his brother, whose hand had come up to play with hers. It seemed to be an unconscious act between two people who were very comfortable touching each other.

"Well, I was acting like a whore, so you shouldn't be surprised," she said, bitterness evident in every aspect of her being.

"No, my lover," Cian corrected. "Tonight was schoolgirl night.

Last night was whore night." He leaned toward his brother. "She was brand new to her profession. I had to teach her everything she needed to know."

Beck ignored his brother, though he knew the scenario well. He focused on his wife. He had a lot of damage to undo. "You were a very sexy schoolgirl, Meg." He smiled as she flushed. "I like the pigtails."

He did. He thought about all the ways he could grip them while he fucked into her. He took a deep breath. Tossing her over his shoulder and forcing her to the bedroom wouldn't help his case right now.

There was an uncomfortable silence that Cian moved to fill. He stood and walked to his brother, giving him a manly hug. "It's good to see you, brother."

Beck softened. Cian was whole. It had been a long time since Cian had been complete. He enveloped his brother, the man who held half his soul, in a spine-cracking bear hug. He looked over to Meg. "Thank you," he mouthed.

Meg's eyes were suspiciously bright as she nodded.

"You feel fine?" Beck asked, looking over his younger brother.

"I feel fantastic," Cian replied seriously. "The bond, goddess, Beck, it's amazing. She's always with me. I can sense her moods when she's not hiding them. She's perfect."

Cian looked back at their wife, and she practically glowed under his praise. It made Beck remember the errand he'd gone on before leaving the Vampire plane. He reached down into his pack and pulled out the gift he'd bought for his wife.

"I got you a present, Meggie," he said, holding it out to her.

He felt like an idiot standing there hoping she liked what he'd bought for her. It took her a moment, but finally she accepted the small package from him and looked it over.

"This is *A Tale of Two Cities*," she said, looking at the old book with a growing smile. "Is it a vampire version? Does Sydney Carton eat the French Revolutionaries at the end? That would be cool."

He frowned and shook his head. "No. It's from the human plane. They promised me it was very rare. I thought you would like having something from your home. You said you liked books."

She touched the cover reverently. "This is one of my favorite books."

She stopped, some unnamed emotion choking her words. Cian

reached out and tangled his hand with hers. It annoyed Beck that Cian could calm her.

"Do you like it?" He'd searched for hours trying to find something to remind her of the world she'd come from. "I could get something else if it displeases you."

She shook her head. "No, Beck, I appreciate it very much. It's a lovely gift." She sighed as though making a decision. "Thank you."

She walked up and kissed him on the cheek.

It was a start. His hand went to her waist. He held her to him for a moment. He looked down at her uncertain eyes and chose to be bold. He cupped her face while he kissed her roughly. "I missed you, wife."

She was breathless when he let her go. Her hands shook slightly as she forced herself to back away. "I should go start dinner. I'll put this up before I begin."

She practically ran from the room. Something deep inside Beck eased. She still wanted him physically. Everything would be all right. He could ease them into the relationship they both wanted.

"Damn it," Cian said, slapping Beck on the back. "Why do you think I started the sex play early this evening, brother? I was trying to avoid Meggie's cooking. Don't get me wrong, the woman can make a damn fine cookie, but the rest of it is terrible. I'm dying here. I was going to exhaust her then slink off to Flanna's and beg her to feed me."

"It can't possibly be that bad," he said, shaking his head at his brother's dramatics.

"Oh, it can," Cian said.

Beck remembered that he had a bone to pick with his brother. "Why slink off to Flanna's when there's an entire festival going on in the village?"

"We should probably talk about that."

"Don't feed me some line of crap about wanting the villagers to accept Meg," Beck replied, cutting off that avenue of escape. "Did you think for one minute about how this affects things? Did you consider that Torin will know about her now?"

Cian waved him off. "Torin knew about her the minute you stepped into that arena. If I let you hide her, people would think we were ashamed of her."

"Why does it matter?" Beck shot back. "Who cares what people think as long as she's safe?"

Cian's gray eyes settled into a stubborn stare. "If you're so fired up about keeping her safe, then let me take her to the Vampire plane. She'll be perfectly safe with the Dellacourts. I'll get a job at the university. Problem solved. You'll never have to worry about either of us again."

"I'm not letting you take her anywhere," Beck said, feeling a bit savage. Did Cian think he could waltz off with their wife? "As far as I can tell, you've been a bad influence on her."

"What is that supposed to mean?" Cian was obviously feeling a bit of Beck's restless anger.

"It means she's getting quite the reputation in town," Beck said. "Have you been letting her run wild? She's met with goblins? She's forcing the young people to do her bidding? This isn't the way we run this village, Ci."

Cian's face twisted in confusion. "What are you talking about?"

"I'm talking about our wife taking whatever she wants," he said, trying to keep his voice low. "Those are new clothes. I can tell. As we didn't have a coin to our name when I left, I'm wondering where she got them."

Cian leaned against the wall as though he was completely unconcerned with his guilt in the matter. "I might have been hiding a bit of coin from you. I bought Meggie a dress, and the village women liked her so much they sewed her a few pieces. You couldn't expect her to wear the same thing every day. Where are you getting this from? She meets with those same women every other day for sewing lessons. They adore her. Everyone loves her. She's fitting in beautifully. Even the bloody goblins respect her. As for the stall she set up in the market, those kids are taking a cut. Meg does the baking, and the Shaw kids handle the selling. They take half the damn profits."

"What the hell is she doing selling stuff at market?" Beck asked. He was confused by the whole thing.

"Making money," Meg said quietly from the doorway.

Beck turned quickly, taking in her frown. She had straightened her clothes and put on an apron. Her auburn hair was pulled back in a neat bun. She looked every bit the proper Fae wife about to cook her husbands' dinner. He missed the naughty schoolgirl.

"I took care of it," Beck explained. "We should have enough coin to see us through the winter."

Meg's eyes dulled. She shrugged as though it didn't mean anything to her. "I'll keep it for myself if you don't want it." She moved toward the kitchen. "And I'll make sure to pay the women for their clothes. I'll do it tomorrow."

Beck ran frustrated fingers through his hair. "Meg…"

She held up a hand to stop him. "Just leave me a list of what I'm supposed to do and I'll get it done, Beck. I'll shut down the bakery stall, or I'll work it myself from now on."

"I didn't say that," Beck replied. *Damn it.* He didn't want to argue with her. "You're deliberately misunderstanding me."

"No, I'm being realistic," she said, her back stiffening with pride. "I'm not going to win with you. I could try to be this proper lady you want, but you'll always remember that you bought me in a marketplace. I'll always be a reminder that you didn't get to be with the bondmate you were promised."

Beck threw his brother a surprised glare. "Does she think we're pining for Maris? Where did she get that?"

"Not from me." Cian shuddered at the thought. "She knows how I felt about Maris. The best thing about having our kingdom ripped from us was not having to bed her. She damn near froze off my willy every time I stood next to her. I can't imagine having to put it in her."

"She wasn't your type, baby," Meg said with an intimate smile that didn't include Beck. "She was Beck's. Look, I've thought a lot about this while you were gone. I realize that you married me to save Ci. That doesn't mean you have to pay for it the rest of your life. I haven't talked about this with Ci yet, so I hope I'm not being too forward, but I think we get along well. I love him, I really do."

"I love you, too, darlin'," Cian replied sweetly with a wink.

"So I think that Ci and I should find our own place to live," Meg continued, sounding very sensible. She sounded like she was explaining her plans to redecorate, not ripping his heart out. "Cian built this house. He can build a new place for us, and I'll help him. We wouldn't ask anything of you. I'm making money now, and Cian knows how to farm. All we need is some land. I think it's best if we make it a clean break. I'll be close so I can still do the bridge thing, but you can find someone more suitable."

"Are you asking me for a divorce?" The question came out as a low growl.

Meg put her hands on her hips. Her eyes were suspiciously bright. "It hasn't been much of a marriage, has it? I embarrass you at every turn. You don't enjoy sleeping with me. It's for the best. I promise, though, that I will try to fix whatever I did wrong in the village. I thought they liked me. I thought I was fitting in. Do you mind telling me who said those things about me? Maybe if I talked to them, I could figure out how to fix it."

Beck's mind was still on the fact that his wife was trying to leave. He spoke without thinking. "It was Liadan."

"Oh, fuck," Cian muttered under his breath.

Meg's hazel eyes became dangerously narrow slits. "Liadan?"

"Yes," Beck said cautiously. "She's a well-respected woman in the village."

"I got every bit of brains between us," Cian said, shaking his head. "She knows about Lia, brother. Liadan made sure our wife knew she was your mistress."

"Are you telling me you come home and the first person you go to see is your girlfriend?" Meg asked as she stalked toward him.

"I haven't touched her since we got married." He had fallen into a trap and he needed to quickly find a way out. "It was mere chance that I talked to her."

He could plainly see that Meg was having none of that. She picked up the pack he'd set down. There was a righteous female fury in her eyes. She opened the door and tossed the luggage out toward the lawn. "I changed my mind. I'm staying here. You can go live with your precious, cold, perfect blonde. See if I care."

"I'm not going anywhere, wife." Beck promised, and there was steel in his voice. He hadn't done anything wrong when it came to Liadan. He'd broken it off with her. "I'm not getting thrown out of my home, and we're not getting a divorce."

"Meg, darlin'," Cian said, obviously trying to defuse the situation. "Why don't we all sit down and calmly discuss this. We're a family now."

"I'm not married to him," Meg swore between clenched teeth.

Those words and the bratty tone of her voice made his blood start to boil. His hands twitched as he attempted to gain control of the overwhelming desire to prove to her who she belonged to. "Are you challenging my claim to you, wife?"

"No, she's not," Cian tried.

"Like hell, I'm not," Meg snarled.

"Back down, wife." He forced himself to hold his ground when his every instinct told him to chase her down and bend her to his will.

"Meg," Cian said, looking into her eyes. "Don't do this. If you push him, he'll break."

She rolled her eyes. "No, he won't. He'll politely ask me if I might, at some point in the future, maybe want to have lame, boring sex. If I say no, he'll slink away and go ask his cold girlfriend if she'll have very vanilla sex. I was wrong about him. I thought he was a Dom, but he's just a bully. He wants utter control of my life without giving me anything back. Screw that." She turned the full force of her disgust on Beck. "I won't do it. I won't live with you. I've finally found what I want. I want Ci. Cian understands me. Cian gives me what I need."

"No, he doesn't, love," Beck returned, watching her move. He remained still, waiting for the perfect moment to pounce. All thought of doing this the easy way was gone now. This would go down hard, and damned if he wasn't looking forward to it. "He just plays at it. It's a game to him. I bet you have to tell him what to do."

Beck knew he was right when Meg looked slightly startled. She hid it quickly, but Beck caught that hint. All wasn't as perfect as she would have him believe.

"He just didn't understand what I wanted. I explained it to him."

"I think I did a damn fine job." Cian's gaze went from his wife to his brother. Beck knew he was awaiting the inevitable outcome of this skirmish.

"I know what you want," he growled.

She crossed her arms over her chest. The challenge in her pose made blood start to pound through his body. "You might know, but you aren't man enough to give it to me."

"Wrong answer, darling," Cian said, whistling a little.

Beck struck hard and fast. She was on the floor beneath him before she could scream. He held her easily, though she squirmed and looked to Cian for help. There would be none forthcoming. Cian wanted this as much as Beck did, and Beck knew it. Beck could feel the satisfaction coming off his brother in waves. It had been too long since Beck let his beast have its way. Beck knew Cian would enjoy the experience so much more because of the woman on the floor. She would bridge the two and allow them to share the feeling.

He smiled down at his wife, pure triumph running through his system. He gave her the smile of a predator about to enjoy a full meal after a lifetime of hunger. "As my vampire uncle might say, you wanted the bull, my Meggie. You're about to get the horns."

# Chapter Seventeen

Meg bucked beneath her husband. His weight held her efficiently as he sat on her midsection and calmly looked to his brother.

"Get me some rope," he said as though asking someone to pass the salt.

Cian walked off to do his bidding.

"Bastard," she grunted as she tried to force him off. His position was perfect. She couldn't quite get her hands on him, though she tried. "Get the fuck off me."

Beck looked entirely too pleased for her comfort. "Language, my love. Have you noticed, Ci, that our sweet wife has quite the mouth on her?"

Cian was smiling broadly as he returned with a length of material. She recognized it as a scarf she'd bought in the marketplace. "I did, indeed, notice the mouth on her. I've found when she gets that dirty mouth of hers going, it's best to shove something in it."

"Fuck you, too," Meg said. Cian was supposed to side with her, damn it. He was supposed to understand. He'd spent weeks listening to her and getting to know her. He'd understood how she felt about Beck. It had taken roughly three minutes for Cian to flip on her and take his brother's side. She should have known. She tried kicking her legs.

"I suspect there will be a lot of fucking," Cian promised. "This will chafe less than the rope."

Meg looked up at the faces staring down at her. They were twins, but she could tell them apart. Besides the slight differences living had brought to their faces, she could tell by their expressions. Cian was looking down on her with a sweetly lascivious grin. He was anticipating the sex he thought was coming. His hand had already begun to rub against the swell in his pants. Beck was an entirely different animal. He looked hungry. He caught her hands when she tried to hit him.

"No, Megan." He neatly wrapped the scarf around her wrists. "You will behave or I'll have you across my lap. I won't be nice about it either. You've pushed me too far, love. It's time we put this relationship of ours on a proper footing."

"It's time you let me up, asshole." Meg tried to kick again.

She hated the fact that even while she knew this would go badly, her pussy was starting to ache. She wasn't sure why Beck seemed to be willing to give her what she wanted. He would hate her afterward for this, but there was no question she wanted the change in Beck to be real. "I told you, I won't try to leave again. Let me go. I'll stay in the room in the barn. You two can fuck each other for all I care."

Beck hoisted her up by her bound hands. True to his word, she was pulled over his lap. She kicked, but he was far too strong. He held her down, placing one strong hand on her back. "I warned you."

He pulled her skirt up, tossing it over her back, and her naked ass felt the slight chill in the air. It wasn't cold for long as Beck's hand came down in a short arc.

She gasped as the pain hit her sharply. She didn't have a chance to breathe before he smacked her other cheek just as hard. These weren't the playful taps Cian had given her. Beck meant business. Tears formed in her eyes, but before she could shed them, the heat bloomed deep inside her, and she felt that smack deep in her pussy. Fuck him, but he was right. This was exactly what she wanted. She bit her bottom lip to keep from begging him to continue.

"That's a pretty sight, love," Beck drawled as he ran his hand across her cheeks. Meg heard him take a deep breath. "Open yourself to me. You're shielding. I don't like it. I can't tell if I'm really hurting you."

She stubbornly kept the mental walls in place as Cian had taught her. The mental walls stopped her from broadcasting her every emotion to the brothers.

Another sudden blow landed on her butt. Meg groaned, waiting for the pain to turn to arousal. She was glad they couldn't see her face.

209

"I can keep it up all night," Beck promised. "You'll give me what I want. I swear, by the time we're through, you'll surrender everything I ask for, and you'll do it with a smile on your face. Until then, I think there's another way to get the answer to my question."

She gasped as he spread her thighs and roughly shoved two fingers straight up her pussy. He wasn't shielding at all now, and she felt his deep satisfaction with what he found there.

"She's hot for it, isn't she?" Cian asked.

"Brother, she's on fire." Beck rotated his fingers inside her. Meg couldn't stay still. She squirmed, trying to get him to hit her sweet spot. He pulled out, and she wanted to cry at their loss. He slapped her ass again. "And she's not very attentive. Stay still. I'll tell you when you can move. I've thought an awful lot about what's gone wrong between us."

"You're an asshole." It just came out, and she closed her eyes before the blow landed. There was no hiding her low moan this time.

"You truly like this, don't you, wife?" Beck's voice was filled with gratified wonder as his hands caressed the spot he'd struck. She felt him lean over and place a kiss at the base of her spine.

"I told you," Cian said quietly. His hand joined Beck's. She turned enough to see that Cian had already tossed off his clothes. He liked to be naked as often as possible. Some days she had to force him into his clothes. If she didn't he would walk around in a constant, tempting state of undress. "She's perfect for us."

"Let's see if she is," Beck said with a laugh. He moved Meg off his lap and onto her knees. "You look so gorgeous with your hands bound. Your skin is flush with sexual arousal. Do you know what that does to me?" He calmly pulled at the fastening on his pants and freed his cock. Meg felt his eyes on her. She licked her lips as she took in the sight of him stroking that big, hard dick. "Are you going to obey me?"

That deep voice promised all manner of delight if she said yes. If she did as he asked, there was a chance he would reject her afterward. She'd pushed him to this. He'd been upset when she claimed she loved Cian, but not him. It wasn't true. She'd been crazy about Beck from the moment she'd seen him. She'd never believed in love at first sight, but that was pretty much what had happened with her and Beck. Somehow, she'd known she was made for him. She'd fought it, but the emotion she felt every time she even thought of him wouldn't go away. Her stomach was in knots of indecision before she finally realized she would take every chance he gave her.

"Yes, damn it," she said.

Beck sighed. "Ci, if you would."

She felt her skirt being raised just before Cian's hand came down on her ass. It wasn't as firm as Beck's, but it stung all the same. The skin of her ass hummed with heat.

"Language," Cian explained with a smile on his face. He winked at her before moving into position behind her. His hand went to the waist of her skirt. "It's time for this to come off, sweetheart. You're going to take care of Beck, and I'm going to have some playtime with that sweet pussy of yours."

"Not a word," Beck warned when she opened her mouth to ask a question. "The only word you need to use is *yes*. Now, lift up and let Ci take off that skirt."

She did as he asked, and Cian's hands smoothed the garment off her body. He pressed his pelvis against her backside, letting her feel how much he wanted her as his hand undid the ties on her shirt.

"I love these tits," he said, cupping them as he pushed his erection against the folds of her ripe pussy. She moaned as he teased her. He made sure he never hit her clitoris.

Beck looked down on her with approval in his gaze. "Ci can play with you all he likes as long as you do what you're told. Do you understand?"

"He's the carrot, and you're the stick," Meg said, trying to push back against the very large carrot in question. Cian laughed and smacked her ass again. "I mean, yes. I understand."

"Better, love," Beck said, standing up.

He pushed his pants off his hips and tossed them aside before doing the same with his shirt. Cian pulled her into position. Her hands stayed in front of her as Cian continued to torture her with his cock and his fingers. They slid through her soaking wet slit. She whimpered because he kept her perfectly aroused with no real hope of coming. She would have to please Beck before she had any chance at pleasure. She felt like a sweet toy between them.

It was her fantasy, everything she'd dreamed about since the moment she'd truly understood she had two husbands.

"Open." Beck held his cock in his hands and moved to her mouth.

She obediently parted her lips, and he thrust himself in. He groaned as the head of his cock entered her mouth. Behind her, Cian sighed. Beck was sharing the sensation with Ci.

"Lick it," Beck ordered. "Lick the head. I'm going to teach you how I like my cock sucked. I expect you to remember, love."

Meg pulled back and licked the engorged head of her husband's dick. She lapped up the cream of his arousal and whirled her tongue all around the ridge of his penis. Beck's hands petted her hair, letting her know he approved.

"Lick down to the base," he said as he closed his eyes. "I love the feel of your tongue all over my cock. That's right. Lick it."

Behind her, Cian was moving. He shoved her legs apart, but she made sure she didn't lose Beck. She gently licked down the shaft, making sure not to miss a centimeter of his erection.

Beck lifted his cock up, giving her access to his balls. "Lick the balls, wife, and then suck them, one at a time."

Just as Meg touched her tongue to his round, tight balls, she gasped as Cian slid under her and parted the cheeks of her ass. He sank his hands into the flesh of her bottom and held her still. He licked her from the edge of her pussy all the way to her clit as his fingers played with her asshole. The feeling was so forbidden that she shivered. One finger lightly rimmed her.

Beck growled. "I'll make him stop if it distracts you. You see to me first. I'm in charge here. Do you understand?"

She nodded silently, whimpering just a little as Cian grabbed her hips and shoved his strong tongue straight up her pussy. It felt so good, and she could feel his joy in pleasing her. Despite the walls she had put up, Cian's emotion was getting through. Cian's satisfaction with her taste and smell and touch swept over her mind. She tried to focus on the job at hand. She leaned forward and curled her tongue around his balls.

"Oh, fuck, that feels good, wife," Beck praised her. "Suck it into your mouth. Yes, hold it for a second. Oh, yeah."

She concentrated fiercely because Cian was doing his best to distract her. He tongue-fucked her pussy while trying to gently work his finger into the rosebud of her ass. It burned and tantalized at the same time. She had to force herself to keep still or she would be shoving her ass against that finger of Ci's. He pressed his finger in, and Meg felt her asshole clench around the invading digit.

"Stop," Beck commanded. She pulled back. "Open your mouth and relax. I'm going to fuck your mouth. You remember the arena? I liked that. It was the best sex of my life. You relax and let me use your mouth. Ci's going to let you come after I do, but only if you're a good girl."

"Yes," Meg said, wanting that orgasm with her whole being. She wanted to share it with them. Being surrounded by Beck and Cian, bombarded with their passion and emotion, was the most intimate experience of her life.

Between the pleasure Cian was giving her and the dominance Beck was showing, she was utterly breathless. Before she could inhale, though, Beck was shoving his dick forward, feeding his long, thick length into her mouth. She had to stop and remember to breathe through her nose. She went passive and allowed Beck to completely take the lead.

"That's right, love." Beck sighed. "Relax. I want your walls down. I want to feel you, all of you."

She let her walls drop away and the bond between the three of them opened fully.

"Yes, wife. That's what I want. Flood me with it."

"I told you she wants this," Cian said, pulling briefly away. "Can't you feel her joy?"

Once she opened the gates, she was flooded with them as well. She felt Beck's relief at finally letting his dominant side out. She felt Cian's peace at sharing her with his brother. Beck and Cian were complete. That was what sharing her meant to them. She completed them.

Beck's hands went to the knot at the back of her head. He released her hair. Beck wound his fingers in it and ruthlessly used it to control her movement.

Meg moaned. She was grateful for her bound hands as Beck began to fuck her mouth in earnest. It would have been hard not to touch him. Now it was simple to give up her will and concentrate on feeling.

Beck's thoughts assailed her. He loved the feel of her mouth. He loved how tight and warm she was and how her lips looked as they sucked on his cock. He was in full domination mode, and there was nothing more beautiful to him than the sight of her complying. He threw back his head and stopped thinking. This was what he'd always wanted, what he'd needed and not been able to get. A deep gratitude meshed with his desire, and it nearly brought tears to Meg's eyes. She felt the connection to Beck. It was what she had missed all of her life, too.

Suddenly Cian's feelings pushed at her. Beck's emotions receded to the background as Cian took over. Oh, she needed him, too. Cian loved the taste of her pussy. He could eat her all day. It was tangy and sweet in his mouth. He adored her. She was his to please, and that fulfilled something deep inside Cian. He needed someone to love and take care of. He needed someone who needed him. Cian's hand lightly caressed the cheeks of her ass as he devoured her pussy. He couldn't wait to fuck her there.

All the while, she sent out her own feelings. Their emotions meshed until she wasn't sure who was feeling what, and she didn't care.

Beck groaned, and Meg felt that he was close. She breathed deeply as he bumped the back of her throat.

"Swallow around me," he ordered roughly as he forced her to take the whole of him.

Meg complied, tightening around his pulsing cock. She swallowed and teased the sensitive underside of his dick with her tongue. He was so big he filled her, but she could move a bit.

Beck's voice was hoarse as he spoke. "Goddess, I'm coming. You swallow what I give you."

He pulled almost out of her mouth and then shoved his way back in. His hands pulled at her scalp as he held her still. He groaned low and then everything in him released. Meg felt the first hot jet hit the back of her throat. She worked furiously to swallow every drop of the salty cream he poured into her.

She sucked while his cock softened, and his hands gentled in her hair as he came down from the high. She licked his cock lovingly because she could feel his happiness. There was no abrupt break in their bond. He wasn't upset. A sense of peace flowed from Beck's mind. He wasn't about to reject her.

"*Mo shonuachar,*" he whispered with a happy sigh as he stroked her.

He was the passive one now, allowing her to lick his softening dick clean. She thoroughly cleaned him from the tiny slit of the head all the way to his balls. He loved having her play with his balls. She would remember that. She curled her tongue around one and then the other.

He chuckled before gently pulling away. He undid the ties on her hands. "Thank you, love. I believe it's Ci's turn. Do what he tells you to or I'll tie you up again, and I won't let you out the rest of the night."

Beck caught his breath as he sat back in the rocking chair. He looked satisfied and ready for a show. A lazily indulgent smile broke over Beck's face. Meg cried out as Cian pulled his face away from her pussy. He gripped her hips and shoved her down his body.

"Ride my cock, Meggie," he ordered. Her playful lover was gone. He used his hands to lower her slowly onto his throbbing dick. His face was turned up as he watched his flesh disappear into hers. "Do you know what he called you, *mo shonuachar?*"

She shook her head, concentrating on the exquisite feeling of Cian filling her. He moved with painstaking slowness. Cian had always been careful with her and enjoyed prolonging the pleasure.

Cian flexed his hips up and seated himself fully inside her tight pussy. "Soul mate. Our soul's mate. I love you, *mo shonuachar.*"

Tears welled in her eyes. She reached down and cupped the strong line of Cian's jaw. Her breasts pressed against his chest as she kissed him. "I love you, too." She sighed as she pulled her torso back up. She looked at Beck and opened her every emotion to him. "I love you."

Beck smiled. His face was open, and he looked younger than she could ever remember seeing him. Beck always had a heavy weight of responsibility clinging to him, but now all she could see was his satisfaction. "I love you, wife. Never doubt it. Now lean back and let Ci fuck that pussy. Put your hands on his thighs."

She leaned back. It pushed her breasts forward. They bounced with every thrust of Cian's cock. Beck was already getting hard again. Meg closed her eyes. Cian's hands gripped her hips. He slammed her down on his cock. He controlled the pace and swiveled his hips up, tunneling into her pussy and hitting that spot, making her moan.

"Does that feel good?" Cian laughed as he watched her jiggle on his cock. "I love watching you dance on my dick. I love hearing you scream for me even more."

His hand came forward, and he stroked her throbbing clitoris. Meg gasped as her womb clenched with pleasure.

"Send it out, Meg," Cian commanded.

She nodded as she started to come and pushed the sensation

outward. Waves of satisfaction rolled across her skin and out of her mind to her lovers. She cried out at her peak and watched Beck. He hissed as his cock started weeping again.

Cian growled as she started to go limp above him. He flipped her over and rearranged her limbs. She was languid with satisfaction as Cian propped her ankles on his shoulders and shoved his cock back inside.

"I want my own," he explained. "I shielded from you because I'm not done yet. You're not getting off that easy."

He drove into her soft body, bending her over to drive in all the way to his balls.

She would have complained that she was too sore for such rough use, but she felt Cian's joy in his possession.

"Fuck, Ci," Beck swore. He was stroking himself in short, tight strokes. "Finish her. I can't take much more."

Cian drove into her, pounding away at her pussy. She was helpless to do anything but feel his pleasure. Her hands sought something to hold on to and suddenly Beck was there. He lay down on the floor beside her and kissed her forehead, cheeks, and lips. His tongue tangled with hers as Cian thrust deeply into her. Beck's hands found her nipples, pinching them gently.

"These are ours," he said, his stormy gray eyes holding hers. "Say it."

"They're yours," she replied, because it was nothing less than the truth. She belonged to them. "Yours and Ci's."

Beck looked entirely pleased with her declaration. He got to his knees over her and spread her top so her breasts were completely open to him. He stroked his cock, and she could feel he was close to coming once more.

"You belong to us, wife," Beck claimed as his thumb rubbed across the engorged head of his cock. "Inside and out."

Cian cursed as his head fell forward, and he stiffened. He held himself inside her, pouring himself deep into her soft body. Beck came in the same instant as his brother in a long arc flowing straight on her chest, marking her in a primitive way. He came between her breasts as Cian filled her pussy. Meg wept as their dual pleasure flooded her senses.

Cian fell to her other side with a happy laugh. He kissed her thoroughly while Beck rubbed his seed on her skin.

"I knew you were a pervert." Meg practically purred under his hands.

He brought his cream-coated fingers to her lips. "You have no idea, wife. Open and taste."

Meg complied with a smile. She had created a monster, but he was her monster. And what a sexy monster he was.

\* \* \* \*

Twenty minutes later, Meg settled against Beck's chest in the soaking tub Susan Dellacourt had sent as a wedding gift. It was huge and had to be kept behind the barn. She'd had to explain to the brothers that it was called a hot tub on her plane, and they were usually kept outside.

Of course, hot tubs in her world didn't have small computers inside that automatically pulled and purified water from the nearest source and kept the water at a perfect temperature without the aid of electricity. It didn't matter, she thought happily as Beck's arms wound around her. It worked, and it was big enough for three. Cian sat across from her. His toes played with hers.

"I told you she was perfect," Cian said on a sigh as he let his head fall back.

"Not quite perfect," Beck replied. "She seems to think she gets to call the shots."

"What?" The question came out as a strangled shriek. She strained to turn her head around so she could see him, but he held her close. "Are you kidding me? I haven't called a single shot since some asshole demon kidnapped me and I woke up in chains."

"Is that true, love?" Beck nipped gently at her ear. "Poor Meg. We big strong men have held you down and forced you to do our will."

"Well, I liked that part," she admitted.

"I could tell." Beck chuckled. "But, my wife, you're going to have to explain your definition of submissive to me. I think we're speaking two different languages here. So far you've run from me and nearly gotten yourself and me killed. You've cursed me and my whole line at every given opportunity. You attempted to manipulate me into things I wasn't comfortable with."

"I did not." There wasn't a whole lot of enthusiasm in her defense. She'd pretty much done everything he'd accused her of. Cian snorted at the statement.

Beck ignored her. "The minute I leave, you decide to move out and start a life that doesn't involve me. I write to you. You refuse to reply. You use my own brother against me. These are not the acts of a submissive woman."

She flushed because he was right. "They were the acts of an impatient woman."

Beck turned her and forced her to look him in the eyes. "Megan, I'm sorry for the way we started. I'm clinging to a life that doesn't exist anymore." He sighed and tugged her close. "I love you. I haven't shown it because I didn't fully bond with you. I'm scared of it, to tell you the truth. I've done things I'm not proud of, and you'll see them. I won't be able to stop it. I'm scared that when you see me, the real me, you won't want me anymore."

She sat quietly, listening to Beck and trying not to wrap her arms around him. She wanted to press her lips against his and promise there wasn't a plane in existence where she wouldn't want him. Instead, she simply opened her mind. She let her feelings flow outward.

Beck sighed, and she knew he'd received the message. Cian came around the other side. He leaned over to kiss her hair.

"Beck is afraid of what I'll think, too, lover," Cian explained. "Once we bond properly, our connection will be complete. He doesn't want me to know what happened the night our parents died. I'm not stupid, brother. I know something happened. I also know whatever you did, I'll back you on it."

"I hope so. I hope, when the time comes, you'll understand. In the meantime, we need to discuss this marriage of ours." Beck's eyes were dark as he looked her over. "I don't know if you realize what you're getting into, love. I won't always look to your pleasure. You're mine. Sometimes, I'll just use you because I own you."

Cian's hands ran down her shoulders. "That's why I'm here, brother. I'll take care of her."

She leaned back and let Cian press his lips to hers. He was the soft touch. Though he'd been trying to be what she needed, he couldn't really work up the will to truly dominate her. He'd rather worship her and coddle her. He was the soft side of the man.

Beck pulled her attention back to him. He was the rough side. He was the dominant side that took what he wanted. It said something about the man that even his dominant half would never hurt her. He was hard and possessive, and they would all be so much happier now that he'd stopped fighting his true nature.

"I want a yes, Meg," Beck said quietly. "I want a yes, but before you say it, know that you can't take it back. Once you say yes, I won't ever let you go. You'll fight me every day for control. I'll try my damnedest to make decisions for you. I can't help what I am. Cian will balance me by being the biggest softie on the plane when it comes to you."

Cian grinned. "I have no shame about that."

Her heart swelled with love for them. It was hard because they were really one person in two bodies, their personalities stronger for it. Beck had to struggle with his own instincts because all the pieces that would balance him were in Cian. Cian felt weak and often unappreciated because the arrogance was mostly housed in Beck. She could help them once they bonded fully. They needed her.

"Yes," she said without hesitation. "Though I think you'll find me more difficult to deal with than you imagine. But I promise when we're intimate, I will be your perfect little submissive."

A happy smile curled around his mouth. "I'll try to take more, wife. I'm a bloody selfish bastard."

She leaned forward. "You're welcome to try, husband."

He kissed her roughly. "I promise I will. Now, you have a duty to us. You will wash your husbands' hair, and then we'll join the villagers. I assume there's a party. When I'm away, Ci always throws a party."

Cian was getting his hair wet. "The ale is already flowing freely, brother."

Beck shook his head. "We'll partake, then. I want the villagers to see how happy our bride has made us. Then, later tonight, we bond. All three of us."

She caught his strong jaw in her hands. "It's going to be fine, Beck. I love you. Ci loves you. Nothing is going to change that."

"Nothing," Cian promised.

Beck allowed Meg to start soaping his hair. She could see he hoped Cian's words would prove true.

# Chapter Eighteen

Liadan stood at the back of the crowd, watching the party going on in the middle of the village square. It wasn't lost on her that almost no one greeted her, but then they rarely did. She hadn't exactly made friends in her time here, but then that hadn't been the point.

She didn't make friends, didn't believe in the concept. Other beings were either allies or they were prey.

She was looking for prey tonight and that was why she was prowling the crowd. She'd stopped behind a duo of young ladies she knew had been spending time with the human queen. One of them might do.

"They look so perfect together." The miller's daughter sighed to her friend. She couldn't be more than sixteen, with soft skin and shiny hair. Her eyes were wide and clear, and her mouth was a perfect bow on her heart-shaped face.

Liadan hated her.

She hated her and all the little twits like her. They took their youth and beauty for granted. They wasted those perfect years. They didn't deserve their fine porcelain skin or firm bodies. If they understood an ounce of what she had to go through for a fraction of their youthful glow, they would be staggered by her strength.

"Bri, you're such a romantic. My mum feels sorry for the queen," the girl's equally young friend said.

The golden-haired girl named Bri looked offended. She was

obviously a fan of the twins. They sat at the edge of a crowd that gathered near a huge bonfire. There was much entertainment at this celebration, but Bri kept watching the kings and their queen. Beckett Finn had returned, and the villagers were effusive in welcoming their warrior king back.

It looked like he was finally taking his true place as their leader, as one of them. It was everything she'd feared would happen if he managed to find a bondmate. Beck was cool and held himself back. Cian was too soft. People loved him, but they didn't see him as a person who could truly lead. She'd always known if they could bridge their minds Torin would be in trouble.

If Torin was in trouble, she and her sisters were in trouble as well.

"How can anyone feel sorry for Queen Meg? She has two gorgeous, strong husbands," Bri argued.

The brown-haired friend shook her head. "My mum says that the queen must be sore all the time. I don't know why. Do you think they make her work the fields with them?"

Liadan stifled a laugh. She was pretty sure the girl's mum was right. Now that Beckett Finn had given in to his bride's charms, she was certain little Meg had her fill of men jumping on top of her. Beck had been polite and careful with Liadan physically, but he was a big man, and he could last forever. She'd felt his possession for days after that first time with him. She couldn't imagine having to sexually satisfy both of them.

Queen Meg sat in one of the brother's laps. Liadan thought it was Beck from the arrogant way he held himself. His arm was firmly, possessively around the woman's waist. He adjusted her, and she could see he was pulling her firmly into his groin to hide his erection. Cian leaned over with a knowing smile and whispered something to his wife. The queen laughed with far too much enthusiasm for a royal lady and kissed Cian full on the lips. The easy affection disgusted her. The human comported herself with all the subtlety of a tavern whore.

"The queen doesn't work the fields," Bri said smugly. "That is King Cian's duty. He's the Green Man."

Liadan felt her face lose its mask of cool indifference for a moment. They couldn't be taking the old myths seriously. She closed her eyes and called on her inner calm. She needed to be practically invisible tonight. She moved back into the shadows.

It was worse than she'd thought. If these idiots began to believe the twins had gained true triad powers, Torin's rule would come into question from more than mere Finn Loyalists. Even their alliances would be shaken if that rumor got out. The Fae had not seen a true triad for a thousand years. The last set of symbiotic twins to bond with a strong enough mate had taken over Tír na nÒg, and their line had ruled for hundreds of years.

She didn't believe for an instant that Cian was a Green Man or that Beck had incredible reserves of strength. They were mere *sidhe*, but the idea that they were something greater could cause as much trouble as it actually being true.

The political ramifications alone were awful. If the vampires became involved, Torin would have a fight on his hand. He was already forced to deal with a rebellion every few months. If word got back to the home plane that the twins were alive and had ascended to virtual godhood, there would be no stopping the citizens.

They would come for Torin, and his army of mercenaries wouldn't be able to stop them. To keep Torin on the throne, the twins must die. The first thing she needed to do was get rid of the bitch in Beck's arms. It was the simplest way. Cian would fade quickly if his beloved left him. Megan Finn needed to leave her husbands. Liadan had only found one way to make that happen.

She needed to place a call to a very specific deliveryman. Unfortunately, she couldn't send a note and ask him to call upon her. She needed something to tempt him. Little Bri would work perfectly well. There was no way that idiot wasn't a virgin. Demons highly prized virginity for some insane reason.

There was a purring sound at her feet, and Liadan sighed in delight. Ain always knew when she was needed. She reached down and picked up the black cat. She held the familiar to her breast, enjoying the purring sensation along her skin. Ain had been with her since she was a child. The familiar had always been a strong presence, reminding Liadan of her unique talents in a world of mundane idiots.

The cat's huge eyes glowed in the dim light.

"You know who I want?"

The cat licked her lips and purred contentedly. She knew what to do. Liadan winked at her familiar and placed her back on the ground.

"Bring her to me." She didn't need to add the admonition to be careful. Ain was always careful. She would work her magic and lead the miller's daughter to the proper place at the proper time. No one would suspect that Liadan had anything to do with it.

If asked later, a few of the villagers would remember that she'd been at the festivities all night long. She had been sweet and friendly, but a little sad. They would shake their heads and feel sorry for the woman who had lost her husband to an accident and her lover to the queen.

She hated their pity, but it was a useful thing.

Liadan withdrew to the woods as Ain curled herself around Bri's ankles. It wouldn't be long, and she had to be ready.

\* \* \* \*

Meg followed Beck into the bedroom. He moved slowly and deliberately, but she was well aware that carefulness had nothing to do with the ale he'd imbibed and everything to do with the act he was determined to perform.

"Beck," she said quietly, tugging on his hand. "We can wait, if you want. I'm happy with the relationship we have. I don't have to do a mental tour of your life if it makes you uncomfortable."

Beck's gray eyes were grave as he looked down at her. "I would be seeing into your soul, too, wife. Do you only want to share yourself with Cian?"

She rolled her eyes. "Now you're being deliberately obtuse. I wasn't trying to hold myself back because of my grand passion for Ci."

"Hey," Cian said, tossing his big body on the bed.

"Though I do love him passionately," Meg allowed.

"That's better," Cian said, patting the mattress beside him. "Stop worrying about Beck. He's nervous because he knows my half of our soul is prettier than his."

"I remember our teen years, brother," Beck snorted. "I'm sure our poor wife was assaulted by the sheer number of your sexual encounters."

"It was an education," she allowed with a grin.

Cian shrugged, obviously unaffected by anything as ridiculous as shame. "I was a curious lad."

"You were a pervert," Beck shot back, but Cian's mocking had done its job. Beck seemed more relaxed.

Cian sat up on the bed, crossing his legs as he'd done the day they'd bonded. Beck took the opposite position. They were near-perfect twins, and she was going to be in the middle. She started to climb onto the bed.

"What do you think you're doing?" Beck's eyebrows arched in arrogant surprise.

"What Cian told me to do," Meg replied. "He said I had to sit in the middle with my legs around your waist, since you're the one I'm bonding with. I'll be in the circle, touching you both so it flows from you to me to him."

Cian had explained how the formation of a permanent total bridge between the three would work. She would fully bond with Beck, and then Cian would open the connection between them. Once both brothers were connected to her, they would be able to tap into each other's strengths. She was the intersection that connected their roads.

"All that's fine, wife, but I wanted to know what you're doing wearing clothes when we're alone in our bedroom."

She'd definitely created a monster. He wasn't hiding from his nature anymore. He'd made that plain this evening. Beck was true to his word. He'd kept her close to him all night, kissing her, touching her whenever it suited him to do so.

When one of the village men had requested a dance with his queen, Beck had sent him such a dark look she was surprised the poor man hadn't peed himself. She'd been forced to content herself with dancing with Beck and Cian.

"You two are still dressed," Meg pointed out, knowing it wouldn't do her any good.

"That can change," Cian offered helpfully.

Beck simply stared and sent his will outward.

There was no fighting it. He would want her naked as often as possible. It was his nature. He liked her vulnerability and softness. He wanted her naked and draped across his lap. She was glad all her time with Cian had gotten her comfortable with her body. It made it simple to pull her clothes off without the added weight of self-consciousness. She draped them over the small chair to the side of their bed.

"That's better," Beck commented as Meg climbed onto the bed without a stitch of clothes.

Cian's hands "slipped" and teased her soft pink parts as she settled onto Beck's lap.

"Damn it, Ci," Beck admonished his twin. "This is a serious ceremony."

"I'm completely serious about fucking our wife again," Cian replied.

Beck pulled her onto his lap, and Cian leaned close, completely encircling her. "I swear, brother, I have no idea how they consider you to be the intellectual half of us. Your brain is constantly full of sex."

"I'm also calculating the approximate amount of rainfall we'll need in order to bring in the spinach crop within the month. If we don't get it, I have diagrams in my head for an even better irrigation system," Cian explained. "Another part of my brain is giving careful consideration to the argument I got into with Flanna about the monarchial system of government and its impact on the peasant class. I'm thinking about the fluctuations in the vampire stock market when they realize we've bonded. Sue and Dante are going to make a killing. But mostly, it's just sex."

"Are you sure you want to experience what it's like to be him?" Meg asked with a smile. "It's crowded in that head of his."

"I'll take my chances, wife," Beck replied and kissed her hard before resting his forehead to hers. "*Is tù mo ghrà.*"

She held his head in her hands and gave him back his words. "You are my love."

She pressed her forehead against his, thankful for the strength Cian was lending her. He held her shoulders and let her feel his devotion. She opened her mind and, in a second, became Beckett Finn.

*Such rage.* The emotion flooded her like it had the first moment they had connected. It was different this time because he wasn't pushing it through her. There was no madness to this. This was merely a piece of Beck. She heard Cian groan behind her and knew that he'd formed his connection. Cian pushed nothing outward but helped her to take in what Beck needed to give.

Need. The idea took over as she fell into Beck's mind. He needed so much. He was a lonely child. He missed his brother. They'd spent every second connected from the moment they were conceived until they turned five years old. That was when his father decided it was time for the warrior to learn to be a king. He discounted the importance of

225

Cian's input. In their father's mind, the warrior was all that mattered. Cian was an afterthought.

Beck often wished he could trade places with his brother.

She was suddenly staring out a palace window. In the background, there were men droning on about something or other. They usually complained about taxes or crop yield. Beck's seven-year-old self didn't care. He gazed out the window and watched Cian running after their cousin, Dante. He caught the young vampire and screamed something about him being "it." Beck wanted to run and play, but his father had explained that he was different. He was better. He could best his brother at running and fighting. He could best anyone at those things. He trained only with the greatest warriors. His physical skills were not things to toy with.

But Beck wanted to play.

He was only twelve the first time he killed a man. It was the first time someone tried to assassinate him. He could still remember the feel of the bright sun on his face as he followed after his father. There was an Unseelie ambassador in town, and it had almost caused a riot in the square. His father was trying to normalize relations with the Unseelie, but there was a faction of *sidhe* who would never accept it. They hated the Unseelie tribe. Many had lost relatives in the wars.

Beck shadowed his father through town. His father was arrogant and sure of his peoples' love for him. He only brought one guard with them. His name was Carlin, and he'd been the one to teach Beck how to play cards. Carlin had been sympathetic to Beck, sometimes slipping him a candied fig. He had two sons of his own, after all.

The arrow hit the guard squarely in the chest, knocking him back and off his feet. He was dead before he hit the ground. Meg felt the anger that suffused young Beck's being. His father tried to pull him to safety, but Beck had unsheathed his sword and opened his senses for the first time. It had been instinctive. His eye followed the logical track of the arrow. He rolled out of the way of the next one to come after him. She felt a charge of excitement as he shot to his feet and pursued the assassin and heard his father's anxious cries.

She felt the blood on his hands when he caught the assassin. He'd ignored the man's pleas for mercy. Beck's beast was loose, and he had no mercy. The large man had taken something Beck valued. He'd taken from Beck, and he would never do so again.

It was the first time Beck realized his father was afraid of him.

Meg groaned as the scene in his head changed. Sex, she sighed. This was Beck's outlet.

A woman named Sorcha, one of his mother's ladies, had taken it on herself to teach him. She gave him permission to do what he wanted, and he'd taken her at her word. He'd dominated her. He'd owned and possessed her. He fucked her when and where he wanted, and she obeyed. It took the edge off his rage knowing someone soft trusted him. Only Cian ever trusted him. Even Bronwyn looked at him with fear sometimes. Sorcha had begged him to fuck her. She cuddled in his arms afterward. That time was sweet, too. He enjoyed taking care of her after.

She felt the pain of his father hitting him with the flat of his sword. He'd done it in front of fifty of his strongest soldiers. He'd humiliated his son for his perversity.

Beck had sworn to never give in to those urges again. Shame had become a mantle to wear as he did armor.

Then all was blood and carnage.

Acrid smoke filled her nostrils and she felt Beck's heart pumping with rage as he realized his father was dead. There was a tiny part of him that reveled in the old man's death. He was king now. He was in his rightful place. No one would tell him what to do or how to act again. If they did, he would take care of it. He would be king not by right of ascension, but because he could kill anyone who questioned his place. Torin had given him this gift.

Meg felt his disgust at the thought. He was torn by his own nature. His father had abused and humiliated him, but Beck had loved him anyway.

The sword Beck held as he surveyed the decimation of Torin's guard was the sword of the rightful King of the Seelie Fae. He'd used it to kill a hundred of Torin's advance guard. He'd sliced through them with an easy efficiency. His body hummed with anticipation of more. He enjoyed it. He liked the blood and the feel of his sword penetrating flesh. He loved the dance of battle.

Through the smoke he saw Torin. His uncle was surrounded by guards. It was easy to kill them, too. More were coming. Beck could hear them. They were making their way through the chaos toward their leader. It wouldn't matter. Beck circled his uncle. Torin would be dead as they walked into the great hall, and then they would join their brethren.

Torin wasn't willing to go down easy. He held his sword, and his eyes were no longer arrogant. "Even now, my soldiers are hunting your brother. They will cut him down where he stands."

Beck's blood was up. "It will not kill me."

Torin looked disturbed by that statement. "It will, eventually. He is your brother."

Beck smiled. He knew it was a ghastly thing. He nodded to the throne where his father's body lay, still and cooling. "There lies your brother. Perhaps we are more alike than you think, Uncle."

Torin, who'd always been a pale imitation of Beck's father, twisted his unhandsome face into a mask of jealousy. "The crown should have been mine. My father always favored Seamus. It should have been mine."

Beck pointed to his father's crown. It lay on the palace floor, covered in his father's blood. "There it is, uncle. Take it if you can."

Torin looked between his nephew and the bloody crown he had slain his kin for.

Then Meg felt it. She felt Cian cry out in Beck's brain. She felt his panic and anguish. Cian reached out for the only person he had left, and Beck had felt the call in his soul.

It went against everything in Beck Finn's nature. His instincts cried out to kill the pretender. His prey stood before him, quaking in his boots. There was no question about the outcome of this fight, even as Torin's backup stormed through the doors. He could kill them all.

And lose Cian.

Deep in his heart, Beck knew that he wouldn't care once Cian was dead. It would free him in some ways. He could be the predator he'd always known himself to be. He could kill and kill and kill until someone was strong enough to take him out.

But Cian wasn't dead. He was alive, and he waited for his brother to save him.

Beck could avenge his father. He could save his kingdom and all of its people, or he could save the only person in the world to ever trust him, the person who carried all the good parts of his soul.

"I will return one day, Torin," Beck promised. "I will return, and I will kill you. Never doubt it."

The years sped by, each more desperate. Beck was alone. He was alone even as he took lovers. He was alone even as he and his brother tried to build a life. He was alone until he walked into a marketplace and found his heart waiting for him.

Meg sobbed as she came out of the bond. She threw her arms around Beck's neck and clutched him. "I love you. I love you so much." She looked into his deep gray eyes. They were still filled with uncertainty. "I would have no other."

\* \* \* \*

Beck squeezed her tight. "I hope you mean that because you won't have another. You're mine, and I won't ever let you go."

He pulled her hair back and took her mouth savagely. He needed to imprint himself on her. She'd been so open. He couldn't have imagined how good it would feel to truly bond with her. She had seen all of his bad parts, everything he loathed about his own nature, and she accepted him with a whole heart. He knew she had seen the very things he had been scared of her seeing, but instead of rejecting him, she told him she loved him.

"I love you, Megan," he rasped against her ear. He pulled her tight against his chest. He loved the warmth of her skin. He loved the trust she placed in him. It eased his soul. He looked behind her. Cian had gone pale. He sat back against the headboard. Meg might have accepted him wholeheartedly, but Cian seemed to be having trouble. "Ci? Whatever you want to say to me, just say it. It isn't anything I haven't thought about myself."

Meg looked back toward Cian and reached her hand out to bring him into the circle. Beck worried that he would refuse, but after a moment's hesitation he threaded his fingers through Meg's.

"You didn't kill Torin because you had to save me," Cian said quietly. "He was right there. It wouldn't have taken long."

"If I'd taken even a moment, the secondary front would have been on me," Beck tried to explain. He knew Cian would be upset that he'd let their parents' and sister's killer live when he could have slain him. "I would have been too late to save you. It was selfish."

"No, it wasn't," Meg disagreed.

"By saving Cian, I saved myself," he explained simply.

"No, brother," Cian said, emotion thick in his voice. "I don't believe it. I was there, just as Meg was. You didn't want to lose my part of our soul. You value the person I am. Goddess, Beck, I never knew how bloody hard it is to be you."

"You valued Ci over your father, revenge, and your own nature," Meg explained. "And don't think you missed out on saving the kingdom because you chose Cian. If you had lost him, the kingdom would have been in danger from you. I felt that, too. Don't expect us to turn away from you for making that choice."

"I always trusted you, Beck," Cian vowed. He pushed his chest against their wife's back. "Nothing I felt tonight changes that. It just makes me proud to be your brother." He grew very serious. "You don't want to go back, do you?"

Beck swallowed once, and then again. Of all the things it was hard to admit, this was the hardest. "I don't want to be king. I never wanted to be king. I want to be your brother and Meg's husband and father to our children, but I'm not sure that's possible. There's a whole plane out there that will pressure us to go back and fulfill our destiny."

"Then we'll have to make our own destiny, won't we, brother?" Cian returned. "Whatever comes, the three of us are in it together."

"We'll be beside you, no matter what." Meg's eyes were solemn and filled with promise as she made the vow.

"Yes, whatever happens, Meg will make cookies for the occasion," Cian swore with a long laugh.

It broke the tension, and Beck breathed easy for the first time in what felt like forever. He took a deep breath and found himself happy to be Beckett Finn for once in his life.

"I'll have to try one tomorrow, wife." He knew there was an incredibly foolish smile on his face, but he was enjoying playing her fool.

"And a potato," she announced with delight. It made her breasts jiggle, and Beck could feel Cian's interest surge. It was not unlike his own. Now that the bridge was open, Beck could feel Cian's emotions clearly.

"What is a potato?" Beck heard himself ask as he traced her pretty pink nipples with his fingertip. He'd bonded with her on a base level. He could feel her humming with happiness. It soothed and eased him. It also made him horny as hell. She was so close. Her skin was warm against his hand, and her emotions were open and flowing around him like a blanket, hugging him tight.

His wife loved him. His wife wanted and trusted him. She was his on every level.

"Do you have any idea how silly you sound with that accent asking me what a potato is?" She shook her head and was unconsciously moving against his body. She might not realize it, but she was responding to their interest. Cian cupped the cheeks of her ass and squeezed while Beck concentrated on her breasts. "Cian thought it was a weed."

"It is a weed," his brother said, kissing her shoulder. "It tasted terrible."

"Only because it wasn't cooked," Meg said with a gasp as Beck leaned down and licked her nipple. That bud stood at attention as he curled his tongue around it. "Oh, wow. You'll like it when I've baked it and put butter and salt on it. They're everywhere. We can feed the whole village."

"Later, wife," Beck commanded. He was done talking. His cock was hard and ready to fuck. "Play the queen later. Right now, you're our wife, and we have need of you."

"Oh, yes, we do," Cian whispered into her ear.

Beck palmed her breast and sucked the nipple deeply into his mouth. He opened the connection between them, and he could feel the way her body was responding. Her whole body began to sing with the triple arousal she felt. He felt it, too. He could sense her soft, warm arousal alongside his, and Cian's raging need. Cian gently bit her sensitive earlobe. She closed her eyes, and Beck felt the minute she gave over to them.

"I love that, wife," Beck growled as he sensed her complete surrender. Why had he waited so long to experience this? There was nothing perverse about her surrender or his own need to dominate her. Meg craved his dominance. She wanted Cian's worshipful love as well. She needed them both. "Cian, I'd like to taste our wife."

Cian pulled her back into his arms. His legs hooked under hers, spreading them wide for Beck's perusal. Beck got on his knees as he tugged his shirt off and tossed it aside. He stared at her for a moment, but that self-consciousness that had always seemed to hold her back had fallen away and he was left with a woman who was confident in

231

her own beauty. She was gorgeous, her pussy a ripe, pink jewel. Her clit pouted out of its hood, tempting him. Cian played with her breasts, and she moved restlessly beneath his hands.

Beck traced the outline of her pussy with his forefinger. She was getting wet. Her folds were getting slick with a pearly cream. She attempted to move against him, seemingly trying to get his fingers inside, but Cian held her tight. Beck let his fingers follow the seam of her pussy down to right above her asshole. *Oh, that was a pretty sight.* "Ci, have you fucked that little ass of hers yet?"

Cian chuckled behind her. He licked and nipped at her neck. "No, but I've played with it enough. I've stretched her. She's ready."

He saw Meg tense, but then she relaxed back against Cian's skin. It would be all right. She would trust them. She was theirs, and they would always take care of her.

Beck leaned over and settled himself onto the mattress, belly down. He shoved his nose in her pussy and breathed her in like he would smell a flower.

"I love your scent, wife," Beck growled before he swiped his tongue across the swollen folds of her pussy. They pouted and beckoned to him.

She cried out. Beck could feel the pleasure she took. It felt so good. Her flesh was engorged and throbbing. Cian's arms and legs were manacles holding her down for Beck's pleasure. It was everything she could have wanted, and Beck was happy to give it to her. Beck settled in to give his wife everything she desired.

\* \* \* \*

Meg sighed as Beck worked between her legs. She couldn't imagine anything hotter and cried out as he kissed her pussy.

"Hush," Cian ordered. "Look up."

She did as he asked, turning her head so she could see him. Cian took her mouth with his. His tongue delved deeply, tangling with hers. He thrust his tongue into her mouth in perfect rhythm with Beck's in her pussy. Beck licked and thrust his tongue into her as far as he could go. He pulled apart her labia so he left no piece of her untasted. Cian curled his tongue around hers as he palmed her breasts. She was utterly surrounded with them. Finally, when she thought she could take no more, he gently pulled back the hood of her clit.

"This little pearl is throbbing," Beck said with a satisfied chuckle. "It's begging for attention. Should I give it some, Ci?"

"You should make our little wife fly," Cian answered. "Make her come, so we can fuck her hard and she won't care."

Beck laughed and went back to his work. He sucked the bead into his mouth, and she came with a cry, every nerve in her body bursting to life. She pushed her orgasm out so the twins could share in it. She felt the swell of Ci's cock at her lower back. She struggled to breathe through the pleasure that rolled over her body, but finally let herself fall back against Cian.

Beck practically ripped off his pants as he shoved her knees even further apart. He pushed his enormous erection into her with one thrust. Cian hissed in discomfort and slid out from under her. Beck began thrusting away as Cian removed his clothes. He tossed them aside and stroked his cock as he watched.

She let her hands find Beck's backside as she came out of her languor, ready for more. Beck's need rode her every bit as hard as his body did. It was a shock when he pulled out and went onto his knees.

"Ci, you take her pussy," Beck ordered, pulling her up onto her own knees. Cian happily lay down on his back, and Meg managed to straddle him. He thrust up into her soaking slit before she could think to seat herself.

Meg groaned at the sensation. He went so deep in this position. It was Cian's favorite. He loved for her to ride him. She started to lose herself in Cian's passion when Beck pushed her forward gently. Cian put his hands on her hips to hold her still. Meg could feel the excitement vibrating off him. Cian wanted this.

"Don't tense up, Meggie," Beck said quietly, but with his eternal air of authority. "I'll be gentle."

She felt the coolness of the oil Cian kept by the bed. It was a clear color, and it warmed as Beck worked it into her flesh. He took his time massaging the oil into the rosebud of her ass.

"You're so fucking gorgeous, wife," he murmured while he rimmed her asshole and started to make forays inside.

He went slowly, methodically preparing her. She groaned at the sensation, but Cian distracted her by pulling her close for a long kiss. Cian flooded her with his desire. She felt the restraint he used to hold himself still inside her. It warred with his anticipation of the act. Cian wanted the three of them together, she knew. He wanted his other half sharing in the pleasure of their wife.

She could sense Beck's desire, too. The connection was stronger than ever. She might not know his every thought, but he couldn't hide from her when they were like this. For Beck, this act was his ultimate domination. His whole body hummed with anticipation. Making love in this manner was an act of complete submission, and she was giving it to him. Meg felt excited and overwhelmed with his emotion all at once. Then Beck wasn't thinking about anything except how tight she was.

"Relax, Meg," he said breathlessly. He pulled the cheeks of her ass apart. She moaned as she felt the broad head of his cock start to breach the rosette of her ass. He was so big, even with the oil to work as a lubricant, she knew this wasn't going to be easy. "Push back against me. Ci, help her."

Cian gently pushed against her hips as he held her on his cock. She took a deep breath and eased her backside toward Beck. It hurt, but not so much that she was willing to take this from him. She could endure it. She *would* endure it.

"I know it burns, love," he said. She could tell he was gritting his teeth. "I feel it, too. I'll stop if it gets to be too much."

"No." An idea suddenly hit her. "Overwhelm me. Let me feel what you feel."

In an instant, she gasped. It was so fucking tight. It was hot and ridiculously tight. It didn't feel like a pussy. Even the heat was different. No wonder they both wanted this. Beck was being careful as he tunneled his way into her ass, but he nearly came undone when he felt Cian deep inside her. It was so intimate. They were all so close. Both halves of the man were working together to bring her pleasure and take their own, to meld themselves into one.

"Oh, that's unbelievable." She had to force herself to breathe. They could feel each other. Beck worked his way in. She could feel the tightness of his balls as they bobbed against the cheeks of her ass. He slid all the way in. He rested his hardness against Cian's, only a tiny, soft bit of flesh between them.

"Oh, fuck," Cian laughed joyously. "You're so tight."

She was so full. She was full of them, and the connection came completely open. Feelings and emotions, sensations and moods, they were all open. They bridged through her, but the brothers could feel each other. It was so much more than simply sensing each other's moods.

They could access each other's strengths. Beck would always be the warrior, but through Meg, he could access the softer side of himself that was contained in Cian. Cian would always be the funny, sweet one, but Beck would give him strength and confidence. They were finally complete.

As they began to move, she found herself utterly caught between them. They set a rugged pace. Cian thrust in, and Beck retreated. Beck tunneled in, and Cian pulled out. Every second was a new sensation. All the way she was overcome with their pleasure. The hot, tight clasp of her body was a revelation for them. The dual sensations of constant thrust and retreat lit up every nerve of her body. She pushed and pulled, but there was no escaping the mounting pleasure. It assaulted her body and soul.

Beck came first. Her ass was too tight for him to last long. He groaned as he ground himself into her. Her ass was flooded with him. He bucked and fought to give her every ounce. The minute Beck came, Cian followed. His big hands pulled her tight against him. He swelled as he shot straight toward her womb. She cried and fought to prolong the feeling. It started in her pussy, but rapidly moved along her skin until her entire body hummed with red-hot sensation. She shook as she fell forward into Ci's arms.

Beck fell to her side and rolled her body between theirs. She breathed deeply as he pulled her close and covered them with a quilt. Even as her eyes closed, she knew something important had happened between the three of them.

"I love you, wife," Beck whispered in her ear.

Cian pressed his head to her heart. "Forever," he promised.

# Chapter Nineteen

$M$eg woke to Beck gently pushing his way into her body. Her eyes fluttered open, and she was on her back with Beck above her.

"Good morning, wife," Beck said as he moved his hips and worked his way into her.

"Good morning," Meg said with a smile.

She didn't protest his treatment of her. It was all a part of being Beckett Finn's woman. She hooked her legs around Beck's waist as he began to thrust in earnest. He buried his face in her neck. Meg was happy he hadn't gone back to being that polite lover this morning. A small part of her feared he would retreat again, and she wasn't sure she could handle it. The night before had been everything she could have hoped for. She could handle fighting him for control every inch of the way, but she would rather die than have Beck treat her as he had before. Now that she'd really tasted his passion and all that could exist between the three of them, she knew she could never go back.

Meg wasn't even warming up when Beck started to come. It didn't matter. Beck opened the bridge between them, and she nearly wept at the pleasure he took. It felt so good to experience what he felt. He loved to fuck her, and it was far more than simple sensation. He loved her. Everything about her. It came across in the emotion he pushed toward her. She was his, and he was a better man for it.

Beck's whole body tensed. His balls drew up almost painfully, but he welcomed the sensation.

She gave over and, for a few seconds, almost became Beck. His thoughts and emotions flowed over her as though she was the one having them. Beck loved that she was so warm and tight. He drew out only to shove his way back in. She was his, his to protect, to love, to fill. He was sure now that she wouldn't fight his claim on her. That fact gave him great peace. Beck was smiling as he pressed deep one last time and shared his orgasm with her.

She felt his deep contentment as he crushed her into the mattress. It took him a moment before he had the energy to roll off her, but even then, he gathered her close.

"How are you this morning, wife?" Beck asked.

Meg opened her eyes and smiled at him. Every cell in her body was sated and languid.

"I'm surprisingly rested after everything you and Ci put me through last night. Where is he?" She didn't see him.

Cian wasn't on her other side. When they'd finally settled down to sleep, Cian had been pressed to her. It was funny how she had gotten used to having him against her at night. She supposed she would quickly get used to sleeping in between her husbands.

"Love, we bonded fully last night," Beck said, gently brushing back her hair. His eyes were warm, but there was a tight set to his mouth. "You do know what that means? Cian and I are together now. We're one, thanks to you. I'm the dominant personality. I absorbed him, but he's here with us. He's always going to be with us." Beck put a hand to her heart. "He'll always love you, wife."

Tears began to well in her eyes. A feeling of panic threatened to overtake her. Cian was gone? How was that possible? She'd believed that by becoming the bridge between them, they would be stronger individuals. How could she have lost Cian? "I don't understand."

"Dominant personality, my ass," came a sarcastic voice from the doorway. "It looks like you've absorbed a great deal of my personality, brother, but I assure our wife that I am still here."

Meg sat straight up in bed. Cian leaned against the doorframe, his lips quirked up. Beck laughed at his own joke. Meg picked up a pillow and hit him in the head with it. "Jerk."

There were tears in Beck's eyes as she drew her gown over her head. "I'm sorry, love. I couldn't help it. He's right. I absorbed too much of his personality." Beck sat up and regarded his brother. "It feels good to laugh. Did you get any of mine?"

"I suppose I did," Cian allowed. "After all, I am up before the two of you. I decided I should go check on the fields. I put work before pleasure. It's horrible. I'll have to fight the instinct."

"Well, I woke up knowing full well I had a lot to do this morning," Beck said, pulling Meg back into bed. She couldn't help but laugh as he pressed his lips to her neck. "And still, I couldn't force myself away from our very warm, very sexy wife. I think I'm going to enjoy having a piece of you inside me, brother."

Cian rolled his eyes. "I'm glad for you. Unfortunately, I think the piece I took of you got stuck up my ass. If the two of you are finished fucking, I would like for you to join me outside. Something's happened."

Beck went still. "What is it?"

"You'll have to come outside to see," Cian said solemnly. "I really can't describe it to you."

Beck kissed her again and gently eased her off his lap. "Cover up, love."

He rolled out of bed and pulled on his trousers. He shoved his shirt over his head and lastly, made sure his sword was secure across his back. Meg simply grabbed her robe. Cian led them out of the bedroom, toward the door of the cottage.

"What on earth?" Meg asked as she was drawn into the living area. The ivy she'd woven around the doorway had invaded the house. She'd hoped one day it would cover much of the brick, but she'd known it would take years. Apparently not. Thick vines of green had come in through the door and the windows.

Cian grinned broadly. "You're not on the Earth plane anymore, lover. And here, things just got a little more complicated."

Her eyes grew round with wonder as she walked outside. The marigolds she had planted in the flowerbeds at the front of the house had multiplied overnight. The blooms were huge, and each petal brimmed with life. Even the grass around the cottage seemed greener and lusher than it had the previous day.

"What the hell happened here?" Beck asked.

Cian winked at Meg and let go of her hand. He pulled a large nut seed out of his pocket and held it up for their inspection. "Well, brother, I think I happened. You should probably stay back."

Cian knelt down and shoved the seed into the ground and held his hand there for a moment. It was a bare second before the dirt rumbled. Cian was forced to step back. The tree shot up, fully formed from the seed he'd planted.

"What does it mean?" Beck asked, his mouth hanging open. He walked slowly around the new tree, inspecting it from all angles.

She did the same, awed by the vitality of the thing. The tree that had been a mere seed moments before was lush and vibrant green, its branches reaching toward the sunny sky. It looked as though it had been growing for ten or fifteen years.

"You know what it means," Cian replied, looking more serious than she remembered him ever being. "Look at the fields, brother. Look at the fields and tell me the legends were wrong."

She turned with Beck and gasped as she took in the prosperous fields that had replaced the struggling ones. Crops that shouldn't be harvested for a month were ripe and ready to be picked.

Beck started walking toward the fields, stopping at the small garden close to the *brugh*. It had gone green and radiant, too.

"Someone needs to explain this to me," Meg said, since her husbands seemed to be speaking their own language.

"It's an old legend." Beck bent over as he inspected a particularly luscious strawberry plant. "Back in Tír na nÒg, the legend had it that when royal symbiotic twins were born, if they found the right bondmate, she would bring them into their true power."

"So now Ci is some sort of agricultural deity?" Meg asked.

It was hard to believe the question came out of her mouth, but she was starting to accept that things worked very differently in her new home. She'd negotiated a trade deal with goblins a few days ago. Why couldn't her new hubby become a god?

"I'm a Green Man." Cian spoke slowly, seeming to savor the words. "All things green and vital answer to me."

A wind suddenly whipped around the bottom hem of Meg's robe. It was an odd wind. It was strong and seemed happy to stay where it was. She turned around and had to catch her robe as the wind blew from underneath and exposed her legs.

"What the hell?" She moved to Cian, who was laughing at the wind's antics.

"And I'm a Storm Lord." Wonder filled Beck's voice as he lifted a finger and the wind calmed. It brushed gently against her cheeks, as though giving her a kiss. "My power comes from the winds and the rain. That's amazing. I could call the rains if I wanted. I know how to do it. It's like the information has always been in my brain, but now I can access it."

Cian's hand found hers. "That's how I felt this morning."

A thought occurred to her. "So you got the power to do cool stuff with plants, and Beck can make it rain."

"Beck can bring the power of a storm to our aid, and don't discount what I can do," Cian warned her. "I can trap an army in the vines and grass I can pull from the ground beneath us."

"I get that," she said with a frown on her face. "What I don't get is how this helps me. You two get superpowers, and I get what?"

Cian smiled broadly. "You have a power, Meggie. You have a magical pussy. It was sleeping with you together that brought us into our power. That vagina of yours is pure gold, lover."

She gave Cian a playful shove and rolled her eyes while he and his brother had a good laugh.

"Don't go expecting to use it on anyone else," Beck said as though the thought had suddenly occurred to him. "That only works on the two of us."

She walked up to him and gave him a saucy smile. "Yes, Beck, I was planning on opening up shop. I was going to hang a sign on the cottage door and charge for it."

Beck's eyes narrowed. He exchanged a glance with his brother. "This is that sarcasm thing she warned me about, right?"

Cian leaned in for a kiss from his wife. It was swift and sweet. "That it is, brother. Our Meg is very good at sarcasm. I don't think we have to worry about her with other men. Now that you've let yourself off the leash, I suspect you'll be between her legs three times a day. Try to remember I need her, too."

Beck stole a kiss as well, though his was neither quick nor sweet. His tongue plundered like the pirate he was. When he let her go, she held on to his arm to steady herself. "I promise nothing. And you seriously underestimate me if you think it's only going to be three times a day."

The downside to having two husbands suddenly became very obvious. "Let's talk about this."

Whatever else she had to say was lost as two of the villagers came riding up to the cottage. They rode swiftly, each man leaning forward in the saddle with great determination. The very air around her became tense. Beck reached for the sword on his back. It was in his hand as they made their way back to the cottage.

"Your Highnesses," one of the young men called out. Both of the men dismounted and made courtly bows.

"Niall, Eiric," Cian greeted the men. "What has happened?"

"'Tis the miller's daughter," the one Meg thought was Niall said. His eyes shone with unshed tears.

"Bri?" Meg asked, feeling her stomach clench. She was a sweet girl of barely sixteen years. Meg had spent an afternoon with the girl and her parents. What had happened to her?

"Yes, ma'am," Eiric confirmed. "There's been an accident. Her father begs Your Highnesses to come and figure out what has happened to his daughter."

"How bad is it?" Beck asked the men.

"'Tis bad, Your Highness," Niall replied. "Very bad. She's dead and I'll be honest, I am not sure this was an accident. The miller needs the wise counsel of his kings."

Cian and Beck shared a look between them.

"One of us should go and one should stay here with Meg until we determine if it's safe," Beck said.

"The women have gathered at the miller's house," Eiric offered. "Bri's mother is obviously distraught. The queen would be very welcome there."

"Assign a guard to the house," Cian ordered.

"At least three," Beck added.

Beck turned to her but she knew her duty. "Don't worry about it. I'll get dressed and go to Bri's mother. Niall can take me. You and Ci go and find out what's going on."

Beck sighed and leaned down for a kiss. "Stay safe, wife."

She held Beck's hand as she reached up to kiss Cian. It felt so right when the three of them were physically connected. "You two do the same. Come and get me when you're done."

Beck whistled, and Sweeney appeared from the fields where he tended to run free during the day. As her husbands followed Eiric, Meg raced into the cottage, promising Niall she would be swift.

Meg quickly changed into soft brown trousers and a linen shirt. She shoved her boots on and laced up the black vest that completed the outfit. She had a more formal dress, but she wanted to be prepared to work if she had to.

She grabbed her satchel and draped it across her shoulder so it hung over her torso and rested against the opposite hip. She made sure she had the small medicinal kit Flanna had taught her to use. Just as she was going back out the door, the vampire computer caught her eye. She picked it up and slipped it into the satchel. It couldn't hurt. If nothing else, it played movies from the Vampire plane. Perhaps a movie would entertain the children and keep their minds off the tragedy.

"I'm ready," she called out as she walked through the door. "Niall?"

He was on the ground, his head at the oddest angle. Meg tried to get to him, but before she could reach the young man, a hand grabbed her arm. Ice seemed to flow up her skin, causing her to shiver.

"Not so fast, Your Highness," a deep voice said.

Her stomach turned as she looked up into red eyes. They smoldered from a cadaverous face. She remembered that face. It haunted her dreams. The Planeswalker's skin was taut across his sharp bones, like a corset that had been pulled far past its wearer's comfort.

"What do you want?" Meg asked, forcing herself to breathe deeply.

There was no point in struggling. She could feel the strength in the demon's claws. The wicked talons the demon possessed were merely brushing against her skin. But she had no doubt they would sink into her flesh if she gave him the slightest provocation.

"What do I want? Oh, so many things, Your Highness," the demon said with a rueful sigh.

He towered over her at roughly seven feet. His body was long and thin to the point of emaciation. He stared down at her. Those eyes were pitiless pools regarding her with curiosity. She didn't know that she wanted a demon curious about her. "You really are their queen, you know. Even the hag has figured that out. Tell me something. Have the twins come into their magic yet? I rather think so. I can smell the power in this place now."

"Why don't you ask my husbands?" Meg tried. She knew it wouldn't work. Niall was dead not three feet away. The Planeswalker hadn't come to request an audience.

The demon chuckled. "I think not. I have a contract, you see. Someone is paying me to take you off the plane. Odd, isn't it? You're just a little cash cow, sweetheart. I made money stealing you from your plane, and now I make money taking you back. The village hag is paying me handsomely to get rid of you. She wanted me to kill you, but I told her she didn't have enough to pay for that. I'll have to stay away from this plane for a while as it is. If I killed you, I suspect the warrior half might never stop hunting me. I gave the hag a spell to take care of him, but I don't trust her to get it right. I can't have the warrior pursuing me."

"The intellectual half wouldn't be too happy, either," Meg commented. She was trying not to think about the hag the demon mentioned. It was impossible. Someone in the village wanted to hurt Beck and Ci. She started to panic. They were in the village right now. What if the incident with Bri had really been a trap? "I don't want to go back."

A sly smile split the demon's face. He showed jagged, sharp teeth. "Of course you don't, dear. You're a pathetic little nothing on your plane. Here, you're a queen." He shrugged. "It's kind of a crappy kingdom, though. At least on the Earth plane you'll have running water. Look at it that way."

"No," she said, pulling her courage around her. "I won't go."

"You're going to be trouble, aren't you?" the demon asked. "Oh, well. We can do it the hard way, then."

As the demon brought his fist down on Meg's head, she wished she'd been smart enough to lie.

\* \* \* \*

Beck had felt the moment the connection was cut. It was like someone had turned off part of his brain. No. His soul. Someone had cut a piece of it away and he couldn't reach for it anymore.

He'd been standing at the edge of the forest, talking to Cian and some of the villagers who'd found Bri's poor body. The young woman had been ripped to shreds. There was no accident there. There was murder, and a particularly vicious one. He and Cian had been discussing the possibility of an animal attack when his world had been torn asunder.

He pushed Sweeney to run faster, and the horse seemed to understand.

Behind him, Cian had his hands on his shoulders, holding on for dear life, but his brother wouldn't tell him to slow down.

Somehow, he could still feel his brother, though it was merely an echo of what they'd felt this morning. It was like a door had been closed between them and it muffled the sound.

She hadn't been where she'd told them she would be. The minute they'd felt something was wrong, they'd taken off for the miller's house only to be told the queen had never shown up. Neither had her guard.

They'd immediately made the run for home.

"I would feel it if she was dead," Cian said as Sweeney eased up and stopped at the back of their *brugh*.

"Yes, she's not dead." He couldn't even consider the possibility. "She's had an accident. She's unconscious." That had to be it.

"I don't know." Ci slid to the ground and started jogging toward the *brugh*. "We can feel her when she's sleeping. She's unconscious then, too. This is different. Something's gone wrong."

He knew that. He didn't need to tap into Ci's intellect to know something was wrong with their wife. He shoved down the bile that rose in his throat at the idea of something bad happening to their Meggie.

Nothing could happen. They'd just begun their lives after years of waiting for her. She had to be alive.

"I'll go around the right. You take the left," Beck commanded.

Cian ran. Beck pulled his sword and moved more cautiously. She'd cut the connection for some reason. That was all. Sometimes she cut it so they wouldn't feel what she was feeling. There were all kinds of reasons for that to happen. She might have thought they needed all their faculties to conduct the investigation.

Except he'd felt a jolt of fear before the connection had been cut. He'd felt it slam into him, seizing his heart and threatening to overwhelm him.

"Beckett!"

Cian's yell made him forego all caution. He ran toward the front of the *brugh* and what he saw when he got there stopped him in his tracks.

Niall's body was crumpled near the front porch, left there like a piece of trash someone had forgotten to sweep away.

"Meg!" He couldn't help the shout that came from his throat. It threatened to shake the ground.

No. That hadn't been his shout. That had been the thunder that accompanied it. Clouds, gray and ominous, were suddenly darkening the sky above, and it was all coming from him.

He didn't miss the way the trees shook all around him.

"Something took her," Cian said. "I felt her fear, but she knew what it was. Not who it was. What. She didn't know the name of the creature who scared her. I don't think it was a Fae."

A pit opened in Beck's gut. "Goblins?"

Ci shook his head. "They wouldn't dare. They're afraid of you and she made a good impression on them. She trades with them. They take that seriously."

"Then it's Torin." It was everything he'd feared. Torin would take her and offer to trade. Her life for theirs.

He would do it because his life didn't matter without Meg in it.

"We can't know that for sure," Cian said.

"Then who was it?" Beck felt his fear and frustration threatening to take over. They had no idea where she was. Someone could be torturing her right that moment. They had to find her. He took a deep breath and tried to quell his panic.

"We'll gather the villagers and start searching," Cian said. His face was drawn in tight lines. "She can't have gotten far."

They looked at each other and the words were left unspoken about exactly how far she might have gotten. There were whole other planes she could have been taken to.

"We should send word to Dante to have him search the Vampire plane." A few scenarios played out in his head. "There were a lot of vampires at the arena who felt like they'd been betrayed. Any one of them could have stolen her."

"They'll go into hiding then." Cian paced, his irritation obvious.

"Then we'll have to use our assets to find her." A plan played through his head. A stupid plan, but the only one he could think of. "Have you heard the rumors that Liadan has skill with magic?"

Cian went still. "I don't know that's such a good idea. I don't like that woman."

He never had, but he couldn't concern himself with Cian's picky nature. "She's the only one I know who can do a locator spell. I know Meggie won't like it, but I would make a deal with the devil if I thought it might get our wife back. Can't you say the same? If you won't, I will."

He started to run toward Liadan's cottage. His brother fell in step with him.

They would do whatever it took to get their wife back.

# Chapter Twenty

"Get moving, you bum," someone muttered as Meg stirred awake.

She held her head. It was pounding as she pushed at whatever was covering her body. Newspaper. Someone must have covered her with it. As her eyes came into focus, she stared up. It was night, but she could barely see the stars. There was too much smog and too much light. The stars were so bright outside the cottage. Where was she? Only a few nights before, she and Cian had lain out in the grass, watching the stars and talking. Cian had told her his people's stories for the constellations, and they'd made love on an old quilt beneath the nighttime sky.

She couldn't even see the stars now.

"Cian," Meg said, suddenly sitting straight up. It did nothing for her headache. "Beck."

His name came out as a whisper. She couldn't feel them. It was like someone had cut the connection and she was left with nothing.

"Miss, is there something we can help you with?" The question came from a middle-aged woman who stood at the end of an alley beside a well-dressed man. They stared down the short street where Meg had been lying against a huge metal dumpster. The smell was making her sick.

"Where am I?" She wasn't home anymore. That was one thing she knew for sure, but where had the demon left her?

"How much have you had to drink?" the man asked. The woman

elbowed him and sent him a dirty look. He sighed and answered Meg. "You're in Fort Worth, Texas. You're not far from Sundance Square. Did you get lost?"

Oh, boy, had she gotten lost. The trouble was she needed to get lost again.

"Did you see a big guy walk by? You couldn't miss him. He's really tall." Meg struggled to her feet, stretching her stiff limbs and wondering how long she'd been out.

"I haven't seen anyone really tall," the woman replied, shaking her head. "Do you need a homeless shelter? There's a very nice one on Cypress Street. It's not far."

"I don't need a homeless shelter," Meg said between clenched teeth, the full revelation of what that asshole had done to her hitting home. He'd brought her back here and she had no idea how to get to her husbands. "I need a Planeswalker demon."

The man took the woman by the hand and forced her away. Meg sighed. She would have to watch her mouth on this plane. She walked out of the alley and realized where she was. Down the block she could see the lights of a restaurant she'd been to a couple of times. Top. They had the best tortilla soup, and she often got it to go. It was one of the few things she missed about this place. Her tummy grumbled at the thought, but the freaking demon hadn't been nice enough to leave her with some cash.

Top was her touchstone in reorienting herself on the plane. It was half a block to Sundance Square. It felt like she was moving through a dream. It was all familiar, but no longer hers.

*Or was it?* She looked at herself in the window of a darkened storefront. She wore brown pants, a white shirt, and a black vest. She had on boots. It was what she'd put on to go see the miller's wife. She wasn't crazy. She had really gone to another plane and married two beautiful men. They needed her. Tears welled in her eyes.

What would happen to them? What happened when the bond was formed and then shut off? And the demon had said there was a hag after them.

How was she going to get home? Panic threatened because she had to get home. She couldn't stay here. They needed her and she needed them.

She was pulled from her panic as she was jostled by a passerby.

The sidewalks were crowded. She found herself pulled along with the throng. It was a mix of teens going to the movies, adults out on dates, families seeing the sights, and singles looking for the clubs and bars that dotted the square. They all had one thing in common. Not a one of them would believe she was the queen of another plane of existence with two husbands who'd just come into their legendary powers and were now at risk because a fucking demon had carted her off the plane—again.

She walked for what felt like an hour in a daze. She had nothing. She had no way to get home. She didn't even have a coat, and while she'd been gone, it had gotten cold on the Earth plane.

She walked until the crowds were gone. She walked through the quiet streets of downtown in abject misery. She would have to accept the fact that there was no way to get home. She couldn't find the door to the Faery plane. Even if she could, how would she open it? From what she understood the only creatures who knew where the doors were located were the Planeswalkers, and they required her eternal soul in exchange for passage.

Even if she was willing to sell it, how would she call one? It wasn't like the last demon had left a card.

Were there witches on this plane? Could they help her? How would she even go about finding one?

A great wave of sorrow rolled over her as she finally had to face the fact that Beck and Cian were gone. They were separated from her by that door as surely as death could ever force them apart.

Would they think she'd run? She couldn't stand the thought. She loved them.

Meg stopped in the middle of the sidewalk and leaned against the brick of a building. The tears would be held off no longer, and she sobbed into her hands. How could she be here, so far from them? She still felt them. Not the way she had before. They were in her heart. How could the distance be so great? The demon had been right. She was a nothing on this plane. She'd been someone on the Faery plane, and not because she'd been queen. It wasn't that Beck and Cian had loved her, either. Their love hadn't made her into the woman she had become. *Her* love had.

Loving them had made her a better person. Love had transformed her heart into a huge thing with the capacity to forgive even herself.

She would hold on to it. She would hold on to the love she had for them. If there was any way to get back to them, she would find it. There were vampires on this plane. Dante had talked about them. She'd read some interesting theories on them. Some believed they were the original vampires and that they had a whole hidden society here on the Earth plane, a mighty council that ruled the supernatural world. She would find them. That's what she would do. She was a queen and she could trade on that. The vampires would help her—if they didn't eat her first.

Meg felt better now that she had a plan. It was an insane plan, but it was a plan. She felt the satchel on her hip and sighed in relief. The vampire computer was still in it. Its shape and weight were a joy to her. She wouldn't be able to connect to the vampire version of the Internet, but there were thousands of DLs on every subject imaginable that she could read. Dante had shown her some anthropological articles from a scientist who had spent years on the Earth plane studying the vampires here before his contract with the demon had come up and he'd been dragged to hell.

Vampires were serious about science.

She stood. It was getting late. She had to deal with the fact that she didn't have a home anymore. She needed to find a place to stay. Where had the lady said the homeless shelter was?

Turning back to the sidewalk, a neon sign caught her eye. Her mouth dropped open as she realized that her salvation might not lie with a bunch of vamps. Fate. It was nothing less than fate. She suddenly knew beyond a shadow of a doubt that she would get home. She would see them again. The sign in front of her proved it.

She stood before a small store. The neon sign proudly proclaimed its name.

*Dellacourt Electronics*
*If it's broke, we'll fix it*

And it looked like someone was still home. There was a light on in back of the store, and someone was moving around.

The Vampire and Earth planes were mirror planes. She'd learned that, too, and that meant she might just have friends here. Oh, he didn't know they were friends, but he was about to find out.

Meg banged on the door with all her might. She pounded and pounded, not caring that she sounded completely insane.

"Dante!" she yelled with a mad sort of glee. "Open the door, Dante!"

After a long moment, she saw a familiar face peek out the window. His eyes were narrow with suspicion.

"We're closed, crazy lady." The human version of Dante pointed to the sign in the window that had been turned to *Closed*. He obviously thought she was insane, but he was still Dante. His eyes had moved straight to her chest, and he was boldly checking her out.

"I'm here for sex, Dante." She knew exactly how to manipulate him if he was anything like his other self.

Dante opened the door immediately.

"Really?" He was slightly thinner than his vampire counterpart and was dressed in worn jeans and a comic book T-shirt, but he was Dante all the same.

"No, idiot," she said with a tearful smile as she pushed her way in. She couldn't help it. She threw her arms around him. "But I am so glad to see you."

He hesitated only a second before letting his hands find her waist. "I'm glad to see you, too. How do we know each other? If I owe you money, I'm really sorry. I don't have any. Did my sister send you?"

"No, Susan didn't send me," Meg said. "You don't owe me money and get your hand off my ass. I'm a married lady. And you're going to help me get home."

Dante stepped back. "You want me to call you a cab?"

"If only it were that easy. I need a hell of a lot more from you, but I know you're up to the task. It's fate. Do you believe in fate?"

"Not for a minute," he said with a shrug. "Although, if it gets me something, I'll believe in fate, sweetheart. I can believe in anything you like."

Meg grinned as she reached into her satchel and pulled out the unassuming computer Vampire Dante had given her. It was all the proof she would need. "How about vampires?"

Human Dante made a couple of vomiting sounds. "Oh, god, no. Not one of those. Please go away, Twihard. Do you know how many comments I've gotten since *Twilight* came out? I know I look a little like him, but seriously, not even for tits like yours will I put in plastic

251

fangs and act like I can sparkle."

Meg snorted and rolled her eyes. "First, you do not look like him. Not even close. Second, I told you, I'm married. Third, please sparkle for me. It would be funny. Now, shut up and listen. I think you'll find this interesting." She handed the computer to him.

Dante took the tablet. "This is an iPad. I think it's nice that you have one. Can I go to bed now?"

"Let me turn it on." She flipped a switch and the menu came up. The menu in this case was a holographic female. As she'd been programmed by Dante, she was gorgeous and wore very little clothing.

"How may I help you, Dante love?" She also had a sexy voice.

"Holy shit," Human Dante swore. "Where the hell did you get this?"

Meg smiled. Now she had him.

\* \* \* \*

Dante Dellacourt shoved a hand through his red-gold hair. It was long, hanging past his earlobes. Normally it didn't bother him, but he was pretty sure it made him look grungy in front of the pretty woman sitting in his store. Not that perfectly combed hair would have helped. He smoothed his hands over his slightly wrinkled *Lex Luthor for President* T-shirt. Why couldn't he have done some laundry? And why did it matter? The chick hadn't come to try to date him.

He'd been listening to the craziest story he'd ever heard for the last hour and a half. The redhead was hot but completely insane.

She thought vampires were real. She also believed in faeries and demons and hags. She was sure she'd been to another plane of existence. According to her, there were many planes, some easily accessible, some not.

She was bonkers.

Except he'd been playing around with the computer she'd given him. It was far more advanced than anything he'd ever seen before. No one in the industry was even talking about a system that could do the things this one could. They were decades away from this kind of tech. What he held in his hand was a supercomputer. It stored so much information that Dante couldn't even think of a name for the capacity. It blew past terabytes. It had a connection to an Internet but claimed there was no connectivity here. Dante had played around and gotten the system to acknowledge his wireless connection. The superhot hostess had been unimpressed. She'd asked him why he'd connected her to such a primitive system and promptly downloaded the whole of the global Internet.

The whole fucking thing, and it hadn't slowed down for a second.

"Where did you get this?" Dante asked.

The woman named Meg rolled her eyes. "I told you. Your vampire counterpart gave it to me."

Yes, he remembered that part. There were many planes of existence and one of them was a Vampire plane. He was a royal there. He worked for Dellacorp, and it was a huge corporation that his family owned. His vampire counterpart obviously had it better than he did. He ran this shitty two-bit store he'd inherited from his father and was going nowhere fast.

The other Dante sounded like a guy who got an enormous amount of tail.

"As far as I can tell, this thing is nuclear powered," Dante said in amazement. "How can that be possible? And I think it took my blood a couple of minutes ago. It thinks I'm not edible. What's up with that?"

"Dante, well, the other Dante, he goes to a lot of different planes." Meg sipped the coffee he'd made and continued. "The computer is set to test potential food sources. I'm afraid it's decided you're toxic." She looked at the screen. "Too much pollution, and wow, apparently you have a lot of sugar in your system."

Dante unselfconsciously ate the second half of the Twinkie he'd been downing. It didn't bother him that vampires wouldn't consider him proper food. In his mind, it was a plus.

"The vamps here would probably love you, though," Meg said with a bright smile. "According to what I've read, they're not as picky."

"Good to know," Dante said, chugging a Dr Pepper. "So, let's say I buy this whole crazy story of yours." He looked around again for the hidden cameras. If he had any friends, he'd think they were punking him. "What exactly is it you want me to do?"

She chewed on her lower lip nervously. "I need you to help me get back."

"And how am I supposed to do that, sweetheart?" Dante asked.

"I'm not exactly a…Planeswalker demon." That was what she'd called them. Yes, she believed in demons, too. "How am I supposed to find this door you're looking for?"

Her hazel eyes filled with tears. She really believed the story. "I don't know. I only know that you're here, and you're going to help me. I believe it. It wasn't random coincidence that I found myself here. It was fate."

He wasn't so sure about that, but there was no denying that technology. He wanted it. If he had to do some Internet searches to placate the girl, he would do it. Besides, she was hot. Maybe when she realized there was nowhere else to go, she would turn to him. He could comfort her. It was a nice prospect. His brain started working overtime. He was going to look at it as a problem to solve, like he was taking the whole doorway to another plane seriously. After all, she'd dropped this piece of future tech into his lap. He kind of owed her.

"Okay, so no one knows where these doors are, right?"

Her pretty hair shook around her shoulders. "No, most of them are well-defined. People move easily through them. The door to this plane is hard to find, and I think there's more than one. I don't know why. And there's a whole supernatural world apparently. If we could find the vampire council here, that would be very helpful. Maybe they have a president or something we could talk to. Or a king."

"Nice. Yeah, I don't know where that is," Dante said. She was taking loony to a whole different place. "The door might be more helpful. So we have to suspect that this door is here in the city. Is it open all the time?"

"More than likely not," Meg explained. "The other doors aren't always open. I read that some people can open them at will, but others have to wait. The door from my village's plane to the Vampire plane opens twice a day. I think we can assume the door here is something like that. It's somewhere in the city. I don't think I was out very long."

"So there's a door to a different plane right here in Fort Worth," Dante mused. "It can't be in an office building. Someone would probably notice a door opening to a faery world a couple of times a day. I bet weird stuff happens around it. It's a long shot, but this baby is pretty cool." He pushed the button that brought up the menu. "I need to run a search."

"Of course, master," the computer said with an inviting smile.

"Which pornographic material should I seek out today?"

Dante grinned. "Really? You can do that?" He felt Meg's stare. He cleared his throat and got back to business. "Nothing like that. I want you to run a search on all strange happenings in the city of Fort Worth, Texas. Use the human Internet, the primitive, sucky one. Check things like police reports and news articles and even blogs. I need a list of locations around the city where strange things happen."

The hostess bowed her head and winked out of existence to start her search.

"There," Dante said to Meg. She was looking at a photograph he kept on his desk. "We'll have someplace to search soon."

Meg's face had gone soft as she looked at the picture of four men in tuxedoes. They were all smiling, with their arms around each other's shoulders. Dante knew the photograph well. He'd taken it himself. "The twins are my cousins. They're from Ireland."

She nodded and almost reverently touched the picture. "Their hair is short. It looks good, though. Why are they wearing tuxedoes? And who are the other men? Do they have other brothers on this plane?"

He was used to women drooling over his very attractive cousins. No one paid him a bit of attention when Beck and Ci were around. It gave him great pleasure to tell her where the picture had been taken. "Nope. Just a sister. They all live in Dublin. Those men are Beck and Cian's husbands. I took that picture at their commitment ceremony."

Meg's eyes widened, and she dragged him forward by the neck of his T-shirt. Her teeth were clenched and she shook him lightly. "You have to get me out of here. This isn't my home. I don't like it. Everything is wrong here."

"Jeez," he said, holding his hands up in submission. "I'm working on it, babe. Why don't you go upstairs? I have an apartment up there. You can take the bed. I'm going to stay up and play with this a little more. I don't sleep much at night, anyway. Never have."

Meg nodded. She looked exhausted. Crazy or not, she'd obviously had an emotional day. "Thank you, Dante. I really appreciate this. I know it will work. It has to."

She started up the stairs. He wasn't so sure it would work, but he was starting to believe her story. He knew one thing, though, as he stared at the magnificent machine in front of him—his life had just changed forever.

\* \* \* \*

Cian felt sick to his stomach. It had been hours since Meg had been taken from them. Hours when she'd had only the gods knew what done to her. He felt her loss like someone had carved his heart out of his chest and tossed it away.

"Where is she?" He thought they were wasting time, but Beck seemed so certain and he'd spent his life following his brother when things got dangerous.

"She said it would take her half an hour to gather the ingredients for the spell." Beck looked up from where he was inspecting the circle Liadan had explained she would need to attempt the locator spell.

Liadan had seemed concerned when they'd spoken to her. She'd seemed surprised to see them and then shocked at what had happened in their quiet village.

He couldn't stop thinking about the word *seemed*. It played through his head because something deep inside told him Liadan was acting.

"Why would she help us find Meg?" He was starting to ask the questions he should have been asking all along. Of all the people in the village, Liadan was the one who stood the most to gain if Meggie went missing. Or at least she was the only one who might think she had something to gain. If Meg was gone, Beck wouldn't go back to her, but this might not be about getting him back. It could be about revenge. The more he shoved his fear back and thought rationally, the more he was convinced this was a bad idea.

Beck seemed to think for a moment. "She's a part of our village. She wants to help."

Something about Liadan…

He hadn't liked her from the first. While Beck had seen a pleasant, lovely female, Ci had been put off. He'd never figured out why, but he didn't like being in the same room with Liadan. "Who would want Meggie gone? Lia. That's the only person in the village I can think of who would want to get rid of our wife."

Beck's hands went to his hips and he glared Cian's way. "Torin. Our uncle certainly would do anything he needed to in order to keep us weak."

"But we're not weak." The fact that Meggie wasn't dead and their powers weren't gone bugged him. It made no sense. Oh, he was fairly certain after a time that they would weaken due to the distance between the three of them, but it could take months for that to happen and the bond between himself and his brother would remain in place, weakened though it might be. "Torin would have killed Meg. If he'd sent someone to deal with her, it would have been to murder her, not to haul her off the plane."

"Or he kidnapped her and he's going to use her to force us to turn ourselves in," Beck pointed out.

A valid point, but there was still a problem with it. "I think I saw a Planeswalker before she passed out."

Right before he'd felt her terror, she'd managed to send a single image out to him. It had been foggy, but he was almost certain now that it had been the face of a demon—a Planeswalker. He'd never seen one in person but there were books with descriptions.

"Why would a Planeswalker come after Meggie?" Beck asked. "Do you think he's trying to sell her again? We would feel it if she was in the marketplace. Reeve would protect her."

Cian shook his head. "She's not on this plane and she's not on the Vampire plane. We would feel that. The doors are open too frequently. No, she's somewhere far away. Torin wouldn't have used a Planeswalker. Not even he's crazy enough to pay with his soul. And he wouldn't have to. He could send one of his men to do it. None of this makes sense."

Unless the plan had been initiated by someone who was desperate.

"It doesn't matter who took her," Beck insisted. "We're going to find her. Lia doesn't have a reason to hurt her. She understands. She told me so herself."

Something about Liadan...

"I think she had something to do with me fading the way I did." Over the course of the last weeks with Meg, the idea had been coalescing in his head. It had been a familiar voice that told him to fade, and it hadn't been his own. There had been smoke involved, a sickly sweet smell that always accompanied the loss of his will to get out of bed.

Beck sighed. "You were fading because we hadn't bonded. I was doing my own version of it, too. There's nothing more than a biological need at play in that."

"No, I was worse off than you." He was sure of it. Beck had been functional.

Beck turned and sighed. "Because you're the intellectual half…"

He stopped in the middle of his explanation because there was the sound of a thud and then Beck's right shoulder flew back as an arrow hit him.

Cian watched in horror as the arrow lodged in his brother's shoulder and blood began to bloom over his shirt.

"I think he was trying to say that you're the weak one, Cian." Liadan stepped out from behind a copse of trees, a crossbow in her hand. She'd changed clothes and wore a pair of pants and a black shirt, her cat slinking around her boots. "It took you long enough to figure out I was the one behind your need to fade. You weren't doing it fast enough. I had to help you along."

Beck had gone a pasty white. "Lia?"

She stood slightly away from them, the crossbow still in her hand. "Yes, Beckett. You're not the intellectual half. The idiot half who can't keep his dick in his pants, the one who didn't realize he was sleeping with a hag. His Majesty, King Torin sends his greetings. Your wife is gone and you won't find her again. I had to pay for it, but the Hell plane will be a lot like home for me. And I'll have all of Beckett's power."

Beck grimaced and pulled the arrow out. "I'm going to kill you."

Yes, no arrow could take the warrior king out. Cian had his sword in his hand, but he wouldn't need it. This was what Beck had been born to do.

Except when Beck started to reach for the sword on his back, he fell to his knees.

"Oh, feeling weak?" Lia asked. She started to nock another arrow into her bow. "That's because the arrow was spelled. It will remove all of your magic and shift it to me. I'm already quite powerful on my own, though I've had to hide it for years while I waited to destroy the two of you in my master's name. I'll return to Tír na nÒg a hero with vast powers."

Panic surged, but he had to tamp it down. He could feel Beck's weakness as his brother slumped to the ground. If he didn't work fast, Liadan would hit him with an arrow, too, and then she would have all of their power.

He needed help and the forest came to his aid. As though it heard him, the massive tree Liadan stood next to reached a branch down and caught the back of her shirt, hauling her up. She screamed but managed to hold on to the crossbow.

He had to get his brother out of here. He leaned over and was about to lift his brother when it hit him. Magic. The moment he touched Beck's skin, magic flowed into Cian, overwhelming him with all the powers of the storm. It surged through him, but he didn't know how to use it. He couldn't focus it, and it threatened to overwhelm him even as he heard thunder crack overhead.

Behind him he could hear Liadan struggling to get free. Her cat was climbing the tree in an attempt to get to her mistress.

"You have to run," Beck managed to say. His eyes were only half open, and it was easy to see he was fighting to stay conscious.

"Tell me how to kill her." If she was what she said she was, it wouldn't be easy.

"Run. Get us out of here, brother. Don't let her shoot you with one of those arrows." Beck was fading fast. "Find a place to hide. There's a hunting cabin not far from here. Hide us."

He knew the place Beck was talking about. He couldn't wait. If Beck didn't think he could defeat the hag, he had to take Beck's word. He had to hide them because he had no idea how to use his brother's power.

Rain had started to fall and thunder rumbled even as Beck passed out and became deadweight. Cian couldn't wait. He hefted his brother over his shoulder, securing him there with one arm.

Liadan grunted as she hit the forest floor.

Cian lifted his free hand and begged the earth to aid him.

Grass shot up all around Liadan, covering the hag with green tendrils. She screamed but Cian didn't waste another moment. He ran. He ran and ran, his feet pounding against the forest floor. His lungs ached as he kept the pace, his brother's weight slowing him down.

The forest around him shook with her laughter.

"You can run, Cian," the hag's voice said. It seemed to echo through the trees. "But you can't hide."

She was wrong. Up ahead he could hear the river rushing past the very place he needed to be. He *could* hide. The trees themselves would aid him. But he had to get deep enough into the forest. It was hard because he carried his brother's weight as well as his own. Only the traps he'd been able to set as he ran had saved him from suffering Beck's fate so far.

He felt something shoot past him. An arrow lodged itself in a tree not five feet in front of Cian and he stopped, turning and lifting a hand to bring up another wall of green between him and the hag.

It wouldn't hold her forever.

Eventually she would get close enough and if she hit him with one of those arrows, she would get what she wanted. She'd thought all of Beck's powers would go to the one who'd cast the spell. She hadn't counted on their unique nature. When his brother's magic needed a place to go, it had found a home in him. But if she got Cian, too…

Cian's brain felt like it was going to explode. He wasn't built to handle both his and Beck's magic. Every instinct in his body told him to hide and sleep. He needed to find safety and lay down so his body could rest. It was the only way they would survive.

Cian struggled because his brain was processing so much that it was difficult to concentrate on putting one foot in front of the other. He took a deep breath and pushed on. Liadan wouldn't stop to give him a break. She would follow him until she caught him.

The rain fell in sheets now and Cian realized he was doing it. Beck's magic was his to call upon. He willed the storm to become a hurricane. That would slow the hag down. His shoulder ached from Beck's weight, but he walked through the gale untouched as the world whipped around him.

He saw the small hunting cabin through the trees and immediately slowed the winds down. Beck was right. It was perfect, but it wouldn't be if it was destroyed because a storm tore it down. Cian made it into the small structure and gently laid his brother on the dirt floor. His hands were shaking as he did what he needed to do.

Within seconds, the cabin was engulfed in green. Inside, the cabin went pitch black as the world receded under a wall of vines and thorns. It was thick, and the trees themselves had orders to protect this place.

He could hear the storm he'd begun rattling the world outside. He fell to his knees and was grateful for the darkness. There was nothing but darkness now, and it would stay that way unless someone could find a way to bring Meg back to them.

As the hopelessness of his situation hit him, he lay down beside his brother. His body knew what to do. Beck had gone into a fugue state. He wouldn't wake unless their bridge returned. Only Meg could save them. Only Meg could give Beck back his strength and Cian back his mind.

"Come to us," Cian prayed as sleep overtook him.

Outside the small cabin, the storm roared on.

# Chapter Twenty-One

Meg took aim and slowly squeezed the trigger. She watched as the bullet tore through the target. Even at a distance, she knew it was a solid hit. She'd bought the Ruger .357 after trying out every handgun they let her rent at the range. Well, Dante had bought the .357 with his credit card. She didn't actually have much money of her own. She helped him around the store. She'd been doing his nightly books for the last three weeks, but she wasn't letting him pay her much. She wouldn't be here long enough to do the paperwork, so everything he gave her was under the table.

She checked her watch. It was almost time to meet him. He was picking her up to look at another spot that might be the doorway.

It had been the longest three weeks of her life. The computer had found an astonishing number of potential sites, and each one had been a bust. It was frustrating, but she had no other choice. She couldn't give up.

Dante had been a godsend. He'd quickly figured out how to use the computer from the Vampire plane to their best advantage. He'd learned through trial and error that the computer had settings to detect everything from atmospheric content to the pH of the soil. Dante had hypothesized that the door to the Faery plane could potentially be found by taking careful readings and comparing it to the rest of the area. Dante had been busy taking measurements and putting them into his program. So far, they'd had no luck.

"Hey, Meg." A familiar voice pulled her out of her thoughts.

She carefully put the weapon away as she greeted him. "I thought I was meeting you outside."

He shrugged and offered to carry her case. "It's no big deal. I wanted to get a chance to run by this one address I found. I think we have a shot there."

She studied the young man. It was odd how different he was from his vampire counterpart. They looked almost identical, but the differences in their lives had taken a toll on this Dante. He hadn't grown up with the privileges of the vampire version. He'd been raised middle class after his father sold his family's cattle ranch to a corporation. From what she'd learned, Dante's parents had split, with his mom returning to her Irish home with his sister Susan. Dante had remained behind and been forced to drop out of college to take care of his father.

This Dante lacked the confidence his doppelganger had. He was still funny and bright, but there was an aloofness to him that wasn't present in her Dante. She got the feeling this Dante would be loyal to very few people. He would keep his circle small.

He smiled. It was something she'd noted he rarely did. "Let's go check it out, and then we can get burgers."

"Okay." Meg pulled one of his old jackets over her T-shirt and jeans. Dante had tried to be generous, but she'd only allowed him to buy her a couple of pairs of jeans, some T-shirts, undies and two sweaters. It was all she would need because once she got home, she wouldn't wear them.

She glanced down and saw the ring on her finger, the one Cian had given to her. Her wedding ring. It reminded her always that she had a job to do and that was to get back to her husbands.

She climbed into his beat-up SUV and buckled her seat belt. Dante was going on about how his newest program had found this spot. He said something about a number of police reports and how often the property had been sold, but she was thinking about other things.

She'd been on the refugee plane for about a month, but three had passed here. Time moved differently on different planes. How long had Beck and Cian been wondering about her? Had they managed to stop the hag's plans? Her hands clenched with anger when she thought about someone in the village pretending to be their friend. All the while, this hag had been waiting to pounce the instant the twins showed vulnerability. The hag would seem like a normal villager because she could take different forms.

She'd been reading up on hags and knew it could be any of the females of the village. She had her suspicions, hence the .357 she intended to take back with her. If Liadan gave her even a hint that she wasn't what she said she was, Meg intended to put a couple of rounds in her. She felt a wicked smile crease her face. She really hoped it was Liadan.

"That's a scary look," Dante said with a grimace.

"Sorry," Meg apologized and schooled her face into something less bloodthirsty.

It had been hard to readjust to this plane. She'd thought she would immediately fall back into patterns of working and watching TV, but something intrinsic had changed within her. When she finished with work around the store, she prepared for the day she would go back to her men. She'd spent hours and hours making lists and gathering items she wanted to take with her.

She had a large duffel bag filled with items that would be helpful. She'd bought her ten favorite books at a half-priced store, along with five DVDs she loved. She was sure Vampire Dante could make them work on the computer. She had a thumb drive filled with music she'd downloaded. She'd bought a couple of first aid kits and essentials. Her bags were packed. Now she just needed that ticket home.

She hadn't completely ignored this plane. Meg found herself looking her own name up on the Internet. There had only been a single article on her as a missing person. Her mother had commented that she believed her daughter had run off with some man and would get in touch when the relationship soured. It was odd, given that Meg had never exactly run off before, but if it gave her mother comfort, she would go along with it. Besides her mother wouldn't recognize her anymore.

She wore her hair down now all the time. She moved with an ease and grace that came with being comfortable in one's skin. The awkward, shy girl was gone. In her place was a wife who had one job to do—get back to her husbands.

"That's it," Dante said as he pulled into the small parking lot.

They were on the outer edges of downtown and parking spaces

were more plentiful. She stared at the warehouse. It was dilapidated and hadn't seen better days in years. The door hung haphazardly from its frame and the staircase was missing some steps.

Dante opened his door and slid out. "The last two owners sold it at a loss. It's had ten owners since it was built twenty years ago. It was supposed to be a warehouse for one of the big department store chains. They had so many accidents the company closed it down. I came out here yesterday morning and installed a couple of cameras. I thought I would cover some of the big spaces and see if anything came up."

There was something about that building that pulled at her. "I think you may be on to something," she said with the first real enthusiasm she'd felt in weeks. "Let's get those cameras."

Four hours and a half-eaten burger later, Meg thought her eyes were going to burst out of her head if she had to watch one more minute of nothing.

It was like watching paint peel. She wasn't going through frame by frame, but she couldn't speed it up much either for fear of missing something. Dante had covered as much of the space as he could with four cameras. So far, there had been nothing but the eerie green glow of the night vision.

"Anything?" Dante walked into the office from the store. He strode past the long table cluttered with laptops and desktops, their inner workings open to the air.

"The place has rats. Other than that, nothing except a few pigeons that flew by the camera. This is the second camera I've sat through."

"Whoa, what the fuck was that?" There was real alarm in Dante's eyes. He had gone a little pale.

"What?" Meg queried as she moved the mouse to back up the feed. Her heart seized with joy at the sight of a long, thin man gliding past the camera. His body was swathed in a hooded cape, but there was the briefest glimpse of his eyes. She wanted to jump and shout her happiness to the world but settled for announcing triumphantly, "That's a Planeswalker demon."

Dante slumped into the seat behind her. "You aren't crazy."

She slid him a bemused glance. "I thought we'd settled that a few weeks back."

"Nope," he said, shaking his head. "I was still certain you were loony."

"Then why have you been helping me?"

"I don't know if you've noticed, sweetheart, but you have fabulous tits," Dante said with a sigh. "I figured once you gave up on the whole idea of being queen of the faery world, you might consider sleeping with me. Now I see that demons are real. I'm going to church tomorrow."

She didn't think she wanted to get into how to save his soul. She chose to concentrate on the question at hand. "What was the time? Did you see which way he came from?"

Dante backed up the tape and checked the time log. "It was three minutes after midnight last night."

"That makes sense. It's an in-between time. I read about it. The veil between worlds is thinnest then. That's when the door opens." She looked at the clock. It wasn't even ten yet. There was still time. "We can make it."

Dante took a moment and shoved his hair back, running his long fingers over his scalp. "You're really leaving."

She turned to him. She'd noticed that he didn't have a lot of friends. He seemed content to spend his free time working on computers or helping her. "I have to go back. On my plane, I'm married to your cousins. I love them very much, and they need me. I hope you understand."

He smiled slightly. "And I'm a vampire? What am I like there, Meggie? Am I lonely?"

She laughed at the thought. "As if. Dante Dellacourt doesn't lack for anything except tact."

"Tact is overrated," Dante pointed out.

"Spoken like your vampire self." Meg let her hand drift over his. "The Dante Dellacourt I know doesn't let anything stop him. He once told me that if he was going to do something, he would do it big. There was no point in anything less. Of course, he was discussing lying through his fangs at the time."

"I sound like a character there."

"You could come with me, you know," Meg offered. He reminded her a little of herself before fate had changed her life completely.

Dante shook his head. "I don't think that's a good idea. One of me is probably more than any plane should have to handle. I think I'll have to try to make a go of it here. Besides, I have my shop, you know."

He was scared, and she didn't blame him. She might have spent more time trying to convince him, but she only had two hours before that door opened. "If you change your mind, you know where the gate is."

As she turned toward the stairs that led to the apartment, she saw Dante sitting very still, obviously deep in thought.

* * * *

Meg hefted the duffel bag in one hand. It was heavy but nothing she couldn't handle. Her heart raced as Dante slammed his door shut and turned on his halogen flashlight. Her boots crunched the gravel beneath her feet as they made their way to the door of the warehouse. The air was cool around her, and she pulled her sweater closer.

Dante went first, pushing the heavy door aside and holding it open for her. He held his free hand out. "Let me carry that for you. Come on. It's my last chance to be a gentleman."

Holding the bag out, she allowed Dante to take it. She took the flashlight. He slung the bag over his shoulder and followed her into the darkened recesses of the warehouse. It was different from when they visited earlier in the afternoon. There was a gloom over the whole place that seemed very foreboding. She took a deep breath and had to force herself to continue moving forward.

"Wow, I really don't like this place," Dante said. "I want to leave."

She looked back at him. His face was pinched and tight with fear. She sympathized. If she didn't have to be here, she would probably be running right now. "It's the doorway. I'm sure there are wards to protect it. Don't worry. I'll be fine. You don't have to come in with me. I can make it on my own."

His eyes narrowed, and even in the shadows, she could see she'd pissed him off. "Just lead the way, sister. I might not be a vampire, but I can handle it."

"Of course you can, Mr. Dellacourt," a silky voice said from the shadows. Meg nearly jumped out of her skin as the light revealed that they were not alone. A Planeswalker stood on the steps leading to the second floor. He turned his head away from the brightness she held. "If

267

you please, Your Highness, that is intrusive."

She directed the flashlight away from his face. Her hands were shaking as she faced the demon. Was this the same demon who had taken her here? She thought she recognized the voice. "Are you here to stop me from going home?"

The demon's laugh filled the space. "No, Your Highness. I'm here to use the door. I walk these planes on a daily basis. I gain strength from crossing through the veil. My body requires that energy to function. I also take contracts and receive payment to access the doors from those less intelligent than yourself and the great Mr. Dellacourt."

Dante snorted. "Yeah, I'm great. I almost peed myself when you started talking. Is he going to kill us?"

The last bit had been whispered Meg's direction.

"As I haven't been paid to do so, I will forego any murders this evening," the demon promised, proving his hearing was excellent. "I was looking forward to a very dull passage. Now I have a bit of excitement. It was clever of you to find the door, Your Highness. The hag is going to be somewhat upset to discover you've found the way back to your kingdom. I believe her employer will be upset as well."

"Torin," Meg surmised.

The demon smiled, showing his jagged teeth. "Yes, the pretender is terrified of the warrior king. He should be even more frightened now. The philosopher king has a bit of the warrior's rage since the bonding. He could prove even more formidable than his twin."

"Beck isn't sure he even wants the throne anymore," she said, remembering the bond they shared. Her warrior husband was tired of fighting.

The demon studied her shrewdly. "I doubt he'll have a choice when the time comes. As for you, Mr. Dellacourt, your choices are just beginning. There's a whole world open and ripe for the plucking. I think you've made the first choice that will take you on the road to greatness."

"I don't know what you're talking about." There was an odd look on Dante's face. If Meg hadn't known better, she would have sworn he looked guilty.

"Don't listen to him," she said, grasping his hand in her own. He was shaking slightly. "He's a demon. I don't think they're known for their honesty."

"On the contrary, Your Highness," the Planeswalker said with an offended air. "I never lie when the truth is so deliciously awful. But Mr. Dellacourt's future is neither here nor there. It is your future that is at risk. I'm looking forward to seeing if you can save those boys of yours."

"They're in danger?" Meg asked the question, but she knew the answer. They would have been weakened without her to bridge their minds. They'd been in danger the minute she was taken from them.

"Oh, yes," the demon said smoothly, as though he were discussing some juicy gossip. "The hag managed to catch one of them with her spell, but the intellectual half evaded her. I'm afraid she didn't ask the right questions. She asked for a spell that would shift the warrior's magic. She assumed it would shift into her. That was a mistake."

"Cian absorbed it," Meg realized. "Then he was strong enough to run with Beck?"

"Oh, yes, Your Highness. King Cian was able to flee with his brother on his back. His own poor body, however, could not handle the strain of both their powers. He had to find safe haven. Both he and the warrior are currently in a fugue state. They sleep, waiting for the one who can set them to rights."

Tears pooled in her eyes. "I have to get to them."

The demon nodded sagely. "Yes, I suspect you do. The hag was getting close to breaking through the barriers to their haven when I moved through yesterday. If you could kill her, Your Highness, I would be grateful. She signed her soul over to me, you see. As she should live a very long time, I doubt she was worried she would have to pay up. I could use her skills on the Hell plane. There's much going on here on the Earth plane. A new power is rising and I could use the hag's skills."

Meg wouldn't do it to help the demon. She had her own reasons for killing the hag. And she wouldn't feel an ounce of regret when the demon dragged the bitch to hell. "I promise I'll kill her the minute I get the chance. I have a plan, you see."

Her plan was currently in a shoulder holster under the sweater she wore.

"Excellent," the demon said.

There was the slightest feeling of air moving through the warehouse, followed by a quiet pop. The demon's eyes widened. His body seemed to swell. "Ah, the veil is open. It's time to go, Your

Highness. Now, now, I see the suspicion in your eyes. You found this place yourself. I'm merely offering to travel with you. The door is in an unusual space. It might take you a moment to find it, and then it would be closed again. You would have to come back tomorrow night."

"I'm not signing a contract," she stated firmly.

"And I'm not asking for one," the demon replied. "I believe you will kill the hag. I'm helping you entirely for my own selfish purposes, dear."

Meg turned to Dante, who handed her the duffel bag. She settled it on her back and hugged him. "Good luck, Dante."

"You, too, Meggie." His hands tightened around her waist, and then he backed away. "I hope everything works out for you. Look me up if you ever come back this way."

She leaned over and kissed him on the cheek. She would miss this version of Dante, but it was time to go home. She followed the demon up the stairs, aware that Dante watched her the entire way. The stairs creaked and shook under her weight.

"Hurry, dear," the demon called from the darkness above. "You don't want to miss it."

She braced herself and took the final step. The demon looked out over the railing. He pointed to a spot just below them. "There it is."

No wonder it was so hard to find. It was in the middle of the air. She would have to jump. If she missed, she would break her legs at best and her neck at worst.

The demon gracefully leapt onto the railing. "Follow me."

He jumped from the railing, feet first, and disappeared completely.

"It'll be all right, Meg," Dante said from below her. "It's fate, right?"

"Yes." She climbed on the railing. It shook and rattled under her weight. There was nothing stable about it. Moonlight filtered in from a window above, illuminating the ragged warehouse. Her hands were shaking as she made the mistake of looking down.

There was another popping sound, and she knew her time was running out. The door would close, and she would have to wait another full day before it opened again. She couldn't risk it.

Meg closed her eyes and took a leap of faith.

\* \* \* \*

Dante watched Meg disappear through the veil. A piece of him was sorry to see her go. She'd been lovely, and he'd liked her spirit. If she had stayed, he might have been able to love her.

Still, as he pulled the vampire computer from his jacket, she hadn't left him with nothing to show for his efforts. He stared down at the computer. He'd slipped it out of the duffel bag when he'd gallantly taken it from Meg. He hadn't been able to let her take it with her. It was his because he'd been smart enough to steal it. And she would find another one. He had plans for this one.

When Meg had suggested he go with her, Dante hadn't told her no because he was afraid of going to another plane. He wasn't afraid of visiting other places. It just seemed silly to waste time when this plane was so ripe for the conquering.

Why should he settle for being a little fish on a bunch of planes when he could be a shark on this one?

The computer in his hands was his ticket to the big time.

Dante Dellacourt left the building, his mind racing with plans.

# Chapter Twenty-Two

Meg hit the ground with a great thud and promptly landed on her ass in the mud. It had been a clear night back on Earth, but here it was day and it seemed to be storming.

The demon shrugged over her. "Not the most graceful of landings, Your Highness, but it will do." He walked on without offering to lend a hand. "Good luck."

She scrambled up and looked around her. She was in the forest. The door closed roughly six feet above her. No wonder it was hard to find. It would be even harder on this side of the door since there was no handy set of stairs to climb up. She tried to shield her eyes from the rain as she looked up the path. It looked like the storm got even worse up ahead.

The demon seemed to have disappeared again, and she was alone in the forest with no sense of direction. She ran for the shelter of a thick tree. It was less wet beneath the tree's wide canopy, and she tried to pull out her computer. She went through the bag three times before admitting the truth.

"Bastard." It was obvious that the human version of Dante had helped himself to a souvenir of her visit. That damn computer would have been helpful.

She heard rushing water to her left and knew she was in luck. The village had been built to take advantage of the river. She could follow it, and she would be able to see houses and docks when she got close.

She repacked her duffel bag and prepared herself for a potentially long walk. There was nothing else to do. She couldn't sit here, and Human Dante had taken away her ability to call his vampire counterpart.

She trudged to the river and realized she had another decision to make. She had no idea where she was in relation to the village. It could be north or south of where she was. She could walk for days, only to discover she'd gone the wrong way. What was she supposed to do? Any wasted time could cost her husbands. She stared through the rain, trying to see if there was anything familiar. The only times she'd come into the forest, she had been either righteously pissed off at Beck or sleeping peacefully in his arms. She hadn't been memorizing landmarks.

Ahead in the distance, she spotted a beautiful horse standing in the water, and her decision was made.

"Screw you, you cannibal horse," she shouted at the kelpie and turned the opposite direction. It was enough of a sign for her. Decision made, she began to jog.

Half an hour later, she was still cursing that damn horse because she seemed to be walking toward the intensifying storm. The rain pelted her. There wasn't an inch of her that wasn't soaked. She shivered as she hiked on.

After a few minutes, she heard a magnificent sound. It started like a slight whir, and there was no mistaking its man-made nature even over the sounds of the storm. Well, there was no mistaking its vampire-made nature.

She stopped and turned toward that sound. It wasn't more than thirty seconds before she could see the bike in the distance, getting closer and closer. It moved fast, hovering over the soaked ground. The rider was outfitted for the storm in head-to-toe water-repellant gear. Even his eyes were covered with goggles. He steered the bike right toward her.

Even before he lifted the mask on his helmet, she knew who he was.

"Get on." Dante had to shout over the noise of the storm. "We need to talk."

Twenty minutes later, she gratefully accepted the towel Dante handed her. Like everything else about Dante's little camp, the towel was high-tech. She rubbed her hair, and suddenly, it was dry. She didn't question it. She was simply happy to be warm. The tent was toasty and dry, with soft lanterns giving the room a nice glow. It was everything she could ask for.

"Where the hell have you been?" Dante asked, pouring himself a Scotch. "Do you have any idea how bad things have gotten while you were doing whatever it was you were doing?"

"Well, I didn't go willingly." She rubbed her hands together before shrugging out of her sweater. "Someone paid the Planeswalker to take me home."

Dante's mouth hung open slightly as he stared at her. "You went to the Earth plane?"

"And then found my way home. I didn't even need a demon to help me, though I did my return trip with one."

Dante sighed. "You came back."

"Of course I came back," Meg replied. The vampire had really believed she'd abandoned them. "I love my husbands. I never wanted to leave them. Now, tell me everything. Are they alive? Has the hag been able to hurt them? How did you find me?"

Dante looked slightly amused as she pelted him with questions. "As far as I know, they're still protected. I can't get close. The storm is horrible. It's kept the hag away, though she's closing in. Once that blonde bitch gets into their hidey-hole, she'll be able to slit their throats and there's nothing they can do about it. As for how I found you, I planted a locator device on your back that first day we met. Remember, I gave you a big hug and slapped you on the back? The locator device is small and burrows into the skin. I had a feeling you would be trouble."

"You LoJacked me?"

Dante shook his head, seemingly unconcerned. "I don't know what that is. However, I did make sure I could keep tabs on you. Don't mention it to Ci, but I *LoJacked* him a long time ago. I was too scared to try it with Beck. I do it to the people I care about. I like to know where they are."

"So where are Beck and Ci?" She chose to set aside Dante's questionable actions for now. Those locators had proven fortuitous any way she looked at it.

"About a half a mile north. I don't know what happened, but the twins took refuge in a small cabin in the middle of the forest. It's covered with vines, and let me tell you, those vines have thorns. I tried to hack my way in while the hag was sleeping. The plants took exception."

She pulled off her wet jeans and shirt and ran the towel across her skin, marveling at the way it instantly dried her. "That's Cian's doing. He came into his power shortly before that asshole demon hauled my butt back to Earth."

"Cian's a Green Man?" Dante lisped a little around his fangs. She threw him a dirty look. "What do you expect? You're half-naked. It would be rude not to get horny. Now tell me about Ci."

She rolled her eyes and accepted that Dante was just Dante. She moved to her duffel bag and was pleased to find that everything she owned was not soaking wet. "All that legendary stuff about royal symbiotic twins is true." She put on the soft, suede-like pants the village women had sewn for her, and her shirt and vest. "Cian is a Green Man. Beck can control storms."

"Well, he's not doing a good job of it, is he?" Dante asked, referencing the raging storm outside. "It's been like this since I got here a week ago. I came when your locator signal went off-line and I couldn't get the computer I gave you to answer me."

"About that, I'm going to need another one of those. Your human self stole mine, the little weasel. I have no doubt he is, even now, plotting something ruthless. He had that look about him."

"Nice," Dante said, showing off his fangs. "So you met the human version of me. How hot was I? I was really rich, but, like, on my own, right? I see myself as a self-made man."

"You were sad and sweet and potentially very selfish." She strapped her shoulder holster on. "Your life wasn't as good there as you have it here. I'm actually worried about what you, the other you, is going to do with that computer."

Dante looked vaguely pleased. "Probably something incredibly evil. I always thought I'd make a good super villain."

She checked the .357. The weight felt good in her hands. "Speaking of villains, tell me the blonde bitch who's trying to kill my husbands is Liadan."

"Is that the chick Beck's been banging?" He quickly corrected himself. "I mean was banging before he met his one true love and started being completely faithful?"

She should have expected that Dante would back his cousin up. "You're a good wingman. And yes, I'm talking about Beck's ex-honey. Please tell me I get to kill her."

Dante took a long gulp of Scotch. When he looked back, she saw the fear in his clear eyes. "If she doesn't kill you first. She's quite horrible. I saw her face, her real face. I wish I didn't have to see it again."

She looked back at Dante as she placed the .357 Magnum in the holster and reached for the jacket the vampire had offered her. It was too big, but it would keep her dry. "You don't have to. You point me in the right direction, and I'll take care of her. It's my responsibility, not yours. You've done your job."

Those clear green eyes rolled back. "Stuff it, sweetheart. Don't give me the lone warrior routine. I'm still a freaking vampire, and I have my pride. Besides, my cousins would kick my ass if they found out I sent their wife in to face a hag and her nasty cat while I stayed safe and dry in my tent. I'm going with you, and that's that. Now, since we've gone ahead and acknowledged that we're about to die, how about some end-of-the-world sex? If we're going out, we should go out with a bang and a really good orgasm."

She pointedly zipped up the jacket Dante had given her. "You're worried Beck and Ci will be upset if you send me in alone, but you think they'll be okay with a little infidelity?"

"It's for a good cause," Dante explained innocently. "Besides, if they don't understand and we happen to survive and they happen to survive, then the ass-kicking I get will be totally worth it. And if you do anal, that would make my impending death so much more meaningful."

"I might shoot you myself," she promised as she pulled the hood over her head.

"What are you going to shoot me with?" Dante zipped up his own jacket. "And what was that cool-looking toy you hid in your jacket?"

She stopped and stared at the vampire, trying to figure out if he was joking. "You don't know what a gun is?"

"No." Dante pulled the hood of his jacket over his red-gold hair. "What does it do?"

If the vampires didn't have guns, then there was no way Liadan would know what was coming.

"They kill people, my friend." A deep satisfaction settled inside her soul. Finally, she had the upper hand. "And here's something even better. I'll make you a deal. If you manage to survive, I've got a present for you. I brought back three bottles of the strongest sunscreen from the Earth plane. I'm sure that one of those brilliant vampire scientists will be able to reverse engineer something from them."

Dante's eyes lit up. "Oh, yeah, they can, and I'll be the one who brought it to them. This is going to get me out of refurb hell. Nice. I'm totally going to live. Profits are on the line. No vampire goes down when profit is on the line."

"I thought you might say something like that," she replied, heading for the door to the tent. "But, Dante, I'm going to need a cut."

She let the flap close behind her as she heard the vampire curse.

\* \* \* \*

Meg looked through Dante's binoculars. The enhanced glasses gave her an up-close view of Beck and Cian's small fortress, even through the rain. Dante eased down next to her and nudged her. He pointed to a figure standing mere feet from the green sanctuary. A black cat twitched anxiously around the woman's ankles. Kitty didn't like the storm, it seemed.

It was Liadan, all right, but she didn't look the way she had before. She stood on the ground with her hands at her sides. Her previously pristine dress was soaked and caked with mud. There was a deer walking toward her as though she had called it. In an instant, Liadan was attacking the gentle creature, slitting its throat from ear to ear.

"She uses the blood to strengthen her spells." Dante leaned close. "I wish she would use a spell to make her not look like that."

*Damn, girlfriend was ugly.* Liadan had shed the vestiges of her public persona. Gone was the lovely Fae woman, and in her place was the hag. Her face was withered and cracked. Her hair, though still blonde, was gnarled, as though rats had nested in it. She had long fingernails, and she used them to extract the blood she needed.

The hag began chanting something in a language Meg didn't understand. After a long moment, some of the vines protecting the sanctuary retreated. Now she could begin to see the walls of the structure. The minute Liadan managed to unveil the door, she would be on her husbands.

"She's been doing it for days," Dante explained. "She's getting close."

If only she could stop the driving rain. It poured down in sheets, making visibility a real problem. While she could see Liadan's body, the downpour made it a hazy thing. She wasn't sure she could properly aim. Weeks of practice had sharpened her skills, but she didn't want to risk it in this drenching downpour. She might only get one real shot.

She couldn't stop the storm, but she knew someone who could. She had to hope her husbands weren't so far gone that they couldn't respond. Silently, she put the binoculars down and opened the connection she had with her husbands. She closed her eyes and sought them with her mind. A tendril of psychic energy brushed against her brain. Cian. It was a soft touch so she knew it was her intellectual husband. That wave of psychic energy reached out toward her. He was weak, so weak, but she sent the message anyway. She let her mind wrap around his energy for a moment, almost pleading with him to be okay.

After a long moment, the rain receded.

Dante tensed beside her. He looked up as though he could figure out why the rain had stopped. "Is that a bad sign? Does that mean something's wrong with Beck?"

She reached up and tugged on Dante's jacket until he knelt back down. She didn't want to give up their position because now the hag was trying to figure out what had happened, too. Liadan was paying attention to the forest around her. The hag turned, those black eyes of hers flashing back and forth, taking in everything.

"Beck is fine. I made contact with Cian and asked him to shut off the waterworks," she whispered. The jacket Dante had provided her with was set to camouflage mode. So far, the hag hadn't seen them. It wouldn't take her long, though. Already the black cat was staring in their general direction, her triangular head tilted in a curious manner.

"I'll take the hag. You get the cat." She never took her eyes off Liadan. She stared in almost helpless fascination. The hag appeared bigger than she had before, her body stronger. There was no question that Liadan was a predator.

Dante's voice cracked a bit. "I don't like cats. They're creepy. I'm more of a dog person."

"I'm not asking you to take it as a pet," she practically snarled back. "I'm asking you to kill it. I'm taking on the big, scary hag. You can handle one kitty."

"We need to talk about this new trend toward emasculating me at every given opportunity," Dante muttered. She stared at him, her eyes narrowed. "I can handle the cat."

"Do that."

She pulled the gun from the holster and shrugged out of the confines of the jacket. She no longer felt the chill in the air. Her skin was hot with the anticipation of the next few kill-or-be-killed moments. Her heart was pounding as she faced down her enemy. Liadan was looking the other way. There wouldn't be a better time. Meg stood up.

"That's not a good idea." Dante tried to pull at her hand.

"Just take care of the kitty," Meg shot back at him.

She looked out across the forest that separated them and took aim. The cat hissed, the sound so much louder than it should have been. It echoed through the forest. As the hag turned, Meg let out the breath she'd been holding and pulled the trigger.

The hag was quick, but not fast enough. She moved to the left. Meg had been aiming at her heart. Blood bloomed across the hag's shoulder, and she shrieked as the hollow-point lodged itself in her flesh. It wasn't enough. Meg cursed when Liadan staggered but did not fall. She remained on her feet despite the blood that was beginning to soak her dress.

Liadan snarled as her eyes found Meg. Meg pulled the trigger again, but Liadan was ready this time, jumping across the space. One moment, the hag was there and the next she was ten feet away, the bullet flying useless through the forest. Liadan held her good hand up and spoke some words Meg didn't recognize.

It was as though a giant rush of pure energy struck Meg squarely in the chest. It knocked her off her feet, but she didn't hit the ground. She flew back, the air sucked from her lungs. The hag grew smaller as Meg raced backward through the forest. The world around her seemed to spin out of control. The weight of the gun in her hand was the only thing that seemed real. She clutched it tightly and didn't try to fight her flight. Her back hit the rough bark of the tree, but Meg let her head fall limply forward.

*Breathe.* Beck's voice spoke inside her mind. He was calm and patient, and suddenly she didn't feel so alone. Beck was with her, and he was lending her his experience.

She dragged in a breath as her body slid to the muddy forest floor.

*Stay down and take cover. Don't panic. You can do this. Take out her heart and she'll die.*

"Easier said than done," she complained quietly as she shoved the gun in her holster and forced her aching body to crawl through the mud toward a downed log. Every inch she moved made her bones ache, but she'd managed to hold on to the gun.

"So, the little bitch made it back." The hag's voice boomed through the forest. "I wonder how much that cost you. What did you have to pay the demon for the trip? And he gave you some form of magic as well. You must have given him a lot."

She made it to the relative safety of the large downed log. It was time to set up her next shot. She eased the gun back into her hand and peeked over the curve of the log. Dante was still in his hiding place. He was crouched down, his eyes seeking something. The cat prowled not far away. Her feline nose scented the air with predatory grace. The hag paced back and forth as though the pain from her arm was bugging her. Her black eyes scanned the area up and down, seeking any sign of where Meg had landed.

"I had to sacrifice a virgin to that damn demon. Then I had to sign a contract offering him my soul," the hag admitted. "And look what it got me."

Meg clenched her fist. The hag was trying to force her out. She'd been the one who killed Bri, and she knew that would make Meg angry.

But the voice inside her head was urging patience. Beck whispered to her that she had to stay calm. Calm won battles.

"I slit that stupid girl's throat, and you're back anyway," Liadan said with a sigh. "Do you have any idea how messy that can be? She had a lot of blood in her. It should have gotten me something better than this. Ah, Ain found your friend."

There was a loud hiss and then something that sounded like a five-year-old girl's scream. Apparently, Dante hadn't lied about not liking cats.

Dante landed on his back as the cat pounced. Ain, as Liadan had called her, was a hissing mass of claws and sharp teeth. Blood streaked across Dante's face as the cat's claws found purchase in his flesh. Dante wrapped a hand around the cat's throat and squeezed.

"I changed my mind," Dante yelled. "I'll take the hag. You take the cat."

"Too late," said a voice right beside Meg's ear. Meg turned and the hag was at her side, so close Meg could smell her fetid breath.

She twisted her body and rolled up into a crouch, every muscle screaming in pain. The hag's fist came out, lancing from her body. It crossed Meg's jaw and the impact snapped her head back. The gun slipped from her hand.

She groped for the gun, getting it back in her hand, but Liadan was too close. Forcing herself to keep moving, Meg kicked out as Liadan tried to jump on her. She heard a satisfying groan from the hag as her foot made contact with Liadan's gut. Meg got to her feet, and Beck was whispering to her.

*Take the advantage.*

She kicked Liadan again with all the force she could muster. She planted her boot in Liadan's chest as the hag got up. Liadan hit the muddy forest floor. She jumped on the downed woman, planting her knees on Liadan's torso. She was taking no chances this time.

Meg placed the barrel of the gun against the hag's chest. She steadied herself to pull the trigger when a terrible pain lashed across her back.

Ain leapt on her, scratching and clawing through tender flesh. Pain screamed through her system. She tried to get a hold of the blasted thing, but it sank its teeth into the back of her neck and wouldn't let go.

"Oh, no, kitty cat," Dante growled.

Meg looked up and saw Dante in full claw and fang mode. He was covered in blood and looked like he'd had just about enough of cats for the day.

"We weren't done," Dante said.

Relief flooded through her as Dante hefted the cat off. She pulled the trigger to finish off the hag, but Ain had bought Liadan just enough time. Liadan grinned up and thrust her hand forward.

Meg flew back, and this time her head cracked against the log where she had previously found safety. She saw stars and the world started to go dark around her.

*You stay awake.* The voice was ferocious now. It slapped at her mind and forced her eyes open. It wouldn't let her go under.

Liadan fell on her. She sat on Meg's waist, holding her down with the bulk of her body, and wrapped her good hand around Meg's throat. She tried to struggle but she couldn't get her legs to move under the heavy weight of the witch.

"I need more blood to get through that fucking wall the king erected," Liadan explained with a ghoulish grin.

Meg felt for the cool metal of the .357 Magnum. She'd dropped it when she hit her head. She clawed through the mud, desperately trying to find it. Liadan's hands were choking the life out of her. Meg fought for breath, but the hag tightened her hold.

"Do you know what I'm going to do to those boys when I get to them?" Liadan moved close enough she could smell the blood on her breath. It turned her stomach. "I'm going to gut them. I'm going to pull their insides out. Why don't I give you a demonstration?"

The witch cackled and pulled back, showing off the way her fingers changed into thick, dirty-looking claws.

Meg dragged in air the instant she could. Liadan pulled her clawed hand back just as Meg's fingers met metal. Pulling the gun up, she brought it between her chest and the hag's.

Meg pulled the trigger right before those knives on the hag's fingers met her flesh. The report boomed through the forest.

Liadan looked down at the hole in her chest dumbly before falling over dead.

Meg was shaking and trying to drag air into her lungs as she forced herself up.

Dante walked over, holding a limp body in one clawed hand. His handsome face was a map of scratches, but his clothes had already mended themselves. The nanites were fast suckers. She kind of wished they worked on throats. Hers was going to be sore for a while.

"You okay?" Dante growled down at the cat's corpse before hurling it through the forest.

"I'll live." But just barely. She stared down at Liadan's body. The flesh of the hag's face was wrinkled and desiccated, as though the body before her had lain dead much longer than a few moments.

"If I never see another fucking cat, it will be too soon." Dante offered her a steadying hand. "It didn't even taste good. It tasted evil."

Meg managed a laugh. Adrenaline was still coursing through her system, making her feel jittery even as a fierce joy curled in her heart. She was alive. They were alive. Her husbands were still breathing. "What does evil taste like?"

"A little mangy," Dante replied. "I've decided I'm a lover, not a fighter. I'm rich, damn it. I'm the only son of one of the most powerful families on my plane. From now on, I'm paying poor people to fight my battles. Better yet, next time tell Beck to handle his own shit."

Meg's hands shook, but that didn't matter now. "I'll tell him." She turned to the cabin overrun with vines. "Better yet, tell him yourself."

She managed a smile as she looked toward the sanctuary where her husbands lay in safety. They were still weak, but she felt them deep in her mind. She felt Beck's love deep in her soul, and then Cian's joy washed over her.

They knew she was coming for them.

Dante sighed. "I'll go get the chainsaw, but I warn you, those damn trees are dangerous. It's like they have a mind of their own."

"I won't need it," she said with utter certainty as she walked toward the small cabin.

The trees weren't afraid of her. They knew her. They had been waiting for her. As she approached the cabin, the vines receded quickly, unveiling the small, dilapidated hut Cian had sought to hide. The sun came brilliantly out from the clouds, flooding the whole forest with bright light.

"You know, you might have a career ahead of you as a landscaper if you can do that on a regular basis."

"I can shoot you, too, you know." This was serious business.

Dante smiled and wisely closed his mouth.

She pushed open the door and immediately saw her husbands. They lay side-by-side in complete stillness. Light from one small window filtered in, illuminating her men. Had she not been able to feel them in her body and her soul, she would have thought they were dead. She would have wept over their lifeless bodies.

Instead, she knew exactly what to do.

She placed herself in between them and put a hand on each. Their flesh was cool, and not a breath seemed to come from their bodies. She wasn't sure how they were alive, only that they were, and she was the key to wake them.

She opened herself wholly and let them invade every inch of her soul. She sighed as the connection opened and flooded through her. Everything the hag had taken from Beck had been safely stored in Cian. Now that magic flowed through her, seeking its true home. Beck received his magic with great satisfaction, and Cian let her feel his relief as he released all he could not handle.

When it was over, Meg let her head fall forward in exhaustion. She wanted to sleep, but she had one final task.

"Come back to me," she said as she pressed her lips to Beck's. His eyes fluttered open.

"Come home, Ci," she requested before doing the same to Cian. His lips tugged up. She was rewarded with loving, gray eyes.

It was enough, she thought as the world went dark around her.

As she fell into a deep and restful sleep, their arms were there to hold her.

\* \* \* \*

Meg awoke to bright sunlight and the wonderful smell of breakfast cooking. Her body still ached, but it didn't matter. She was home, and she was never leaving again. Tears pricked at her eyes.

This was home. She'd searched for it all her life. She just hadn't realized home wasn't a place. Home was a person—two in fact. Home was Beck and Cian.

She forced herself to sit up. Voices filtered in from the living room.

"What do you think she does with this?" Beck asked.

"It's underwear, idiot," Dante cracked.

Cian's voice sounded sweet to her ears. "It's pretty, but I can see through it."

"That's the point," Dante replied. "Seriously, you two should have spent more time on my plane. If you would have come with me on my tours of the better brothels, you would know all this stuff. Don't put that on your head. It's a bra."

Meg got to her feet. Though she was unsteady, she wasn't staying apart from them one moment more than she had to. She pulled her robe around her and walked out of the bedroom. Sure enough, Beck was holding her super-sexy demi-cup Victoria's Secret bra.

"What are you boys doing pawing through my undies?"

"Megan." Beck tossed the bra aside.

He crossed the room in two strides. He pulled her into his arms and immediately covered her mouth with his. His tongue invaded, and his mind reached out to hers. She opened herself and exchanged her love for his.

Cian's arms went around her waist. "Don't ever leave us again, wife."

Meg smiled and turned to look at him. "I won't. You get into trouble when I'm gone."

She pressed her lips to Ci's and found herself pleasantly squished between their big bodies. She never felt safer than when she was surrounded by them.

"It was awesome, Meg," Dante said, laughing. "You should have seen them when we walked by Liadan's corpse. She was all shriveled and shit. Beck went green."

"Well, she didn't look that way when..." Beck's mouth became a stubborn line.

Cian grinned brilliantly. "I never slept with her. I'm the smart one."

"Yes, you are, baby." She rewarded him with a kiss. It seemed impossible that she was here. If this was a dream, she never wanted to wake. She turned back to Beck. "We don't have to worry about Beck's bad taste in women anymore. He's taken, you see."

"I am," Beck said, kissing her forehead. "Forever, wife."

"*Le chéile go deo*," Cian whispered.

"Together forever, I promise," Meg vowed.

Flanna walked in, her small face glowing with happiness. "Your breakfast is ready, Your Highness, but I fear you have no time to eat. The village has been informed you're awake at last."

"They camped outside the cottage, waiting for word on your health," Dante explained with a grin.

"Really?" She'd left one plane where no one noticed she'd been alive, only to find this one where a whole village waited to find out if she was all right.

"They love you, wife. They want to see their queen." Beck held his hand out.

Meg brushed away the happy tears that sprang to her eyes.

"How could they not love you?" Cian asked, taking her other hand. "You're their queen, their brave, kind, and beautiful queen."

Flanna opened the door. The brownie hadn't lied. The entire village was standing outside. A cheer went up as she joined her people.

This small piece of heaven was her kingdom. These were her people, not because someone put a crown on her head. They were hers because she loved them.

She looked out across the crowd and realized that there were many decisions to be made in the coming years. Torin would try to kill her husbands again. Beck and Cian would be under pressure to take back their homeland. There were hundreds of things that could go wrong. But in that moment, as she walked among her people, the sun shone down and she was surrounded with love. The future could come with all its uncertainties and danger. It wouldn't matter.

She would fight for it if she had to, but she would have her happy ending.

\* \* \* \*

Dante and the royals will continue the faery tale with *Beast*, coming October 15, 2019.

# Author's Note

I'm often asked by generous readers how they can help get the word out about a book they enjoyed. There are so many ways to help an author you like. Leave a review. If your e-reader allows you to lend a book to a friend, please share it. Go to Goodreads and connect with others. Recommend the books you love because stories are meant to be shared. Thank you so much for reading this book and for supporting all the authors you love!

# Beast

A Faery Story, Book 2
By Lexi Blake writing as Sophie Oak
Coming October 15, 2019

*Re-released in a second edition. Re-edited but no substantial changes.*

*A playboy who needs to grow up*

Fresh from his latest tabloid scandal, vampire playboy Dante Dellacourt has been given an ultimatum. Either he takes a consort and settles down, or his family will disown him. Unwilling to lose everything he has, he reluctantly agrees to find a wife. Marriage is just another kind of contract, after all. No one said anything about love being a part of the bargain.

*An outcast who has only known hardship*

Exiled by her pack, Kaja is a werewolf without a home. Her life was never easy in the frozen tundra she grew up in, but it was familiar. Waking up in a foreign landscape, surrounded by bright lights, loud noises, and far too many people has left her overwhelmed. Frightened and with no one to trust, she savagely fights to get free of this strange new world.

*A passion strong enough to change them both*

Called to defend the gnomes of the marketplace, Dante is almost blinded by the radiant light coming off the fierce werewolf. Kaja glows like no consort he has ever seen. Gorgeous and wild, she calls to him in ways he had not dreamed possible. For Kaja, she finds in Dante a man unlike any she has ever known. They could not be more different, but she finds him irresistible.

In order to claim his werewolf bride, Dante must first discover how to overcome their differences. Will he tame his ferocious beauty, or will she unleash his inner beast?

# About Lexi Blake

Lexi Blake is the author of contemporary and urban fantasy romance. She started publishing in 2011 and has gone on to sell over two million copies of her books. Her books have appeared thirty-three times on the *USA Today*, *New York Times*, and *Wall Street Journal* bestseller lists. She lives in North Texas with her husband, kids, and two rescue dogs.

Connect with Lexi online:

Facebook: Lexi Blake
Twitter: authorlexiblake
Website: www.LexiBlake.net
Instagram: www.instagram.com/lexi4714

# Other Books By Lexi Blake

ROMANTIC SUSPENSE

## Masters and Mercenaries
The Dom Who Loved Me
The Men With The Golden Cuffs
A Dom is Forever
On Her Master's Secret Service
Sanctum: A Masters and Mercenaries Novella
Love and Let Die
Unconditional: A Masters and Mercenaries Novella
Dungeon Royale
Dungeon Games: A Masters and Mercenaries Novella
A View to a Thrill
Cherished: A Masters and Mercenaries Novella
You Only Love Twice
Luscious: Masters and Mercenaries~Topped
Adored: A Masters and Mercenaries Novella
Master No
Just One Taste: Masters and Mercenaries~Topped 2
From Sanctum with Love
Devoted: A Masters and Mercenaries Novella
Dominance Never Dies
Submission is Not Enough
Master Bits and Mercenary Bites~The Secret Recipes of Topped
Perfectly Paired: Masters and Mercenaries~Topped 3
For His Eyes Only
Arranged: A Masters and Mercenaries Novella
Love Another Day
At Your Service: Masters and Mercenaries~Topped 4
Master Bits and Mercenary Bites~Girls Night
Nobody Does It Better
Close Cover
Protected: A Masters and Mercenaries Novella
Enchanted: A Masters and Mercenaries Novella

**Masters and Mercenaries: The Forgotten**
Lost Hearts (Memento Mori)
Lost and Found
Lost in You
Long Lost, Coming February 4, 2020

**Butterfly Bayou**
Butterfly Bayou, Coming April 7, 2020

**Lawless**
Ruthless
Satisfaction
Revenge

**Courting Justice**
Order of Protection
Evidence of Desire

**Masters Of Ménage** (by Shayla Black and Lexi Blake)
Their Virgin Captive
Their Virgin's Secret
Their Virgin Concubine
Their Virgin Princess
Their Virgin Hostage
Their Virgin Secretary
Their Virgin Mistress

**The Perfect Gentlemen** (by Shayla Black and Lexi Blake)
Scandal Never Sleeps
Seduction in Session
Big Easy Temptation
Smoke and Sin
At the Pleasure of the President

URBAN FANTASY
**Thieves**
Steal the Light

Steal the Day
Steal the Moon
Steal the Sun
Steal the Night
Ripper
Addict
Sleeper
Outcast
Stealing Summer, Coming soon!

LEXI BLAKE WRITING AS SOPHIE OAK

Small Town Siren
Siren in the City
Away From Me
Three to Ride
Siren Enslaved
Two to Love
Siren Beloved
One to Keep
Siren in Waiting
Lost in Bliss
Found in Bliss
Siren in Bloom
Pure Bliss
Chasing Bliss
Siren Unleashed
Once Upon a Time in Bliss
Back in Bliss
Sirens in Bliss, Coming November 12, 2019

**A Faery Story**
Bound
Beast, Coming October 15, 2019
Beauty, Coming October 29, 2019